DON'T
BLINK

L.G. DAVIS

Don't Blink
L.G. Davis
Copyright © 2019
All Rights Reserved.

Cover design: The Cover Collection
Editing: Mitzi Carroll and Michelle Storrusten

For my darling husband.

PROLOGUE

The man on the other side of the door resembles a stranger. With greasy, disheveled chestnut hair and an unkempt beard, he could be older than his twenty-two years. But the unusual gunmetal gray eyes are the same as my late mother's.

My brother, Ryan, is back in Corlake, Florida, bringing with him feelings of disappointment and hurt, but also relief.

He never stays in one place for long. When he disappears, it's often out of the blue. One minute he'll be heading out to buy eggs for breakfast at Simple Joe's down the road; the next, he calls me from a pay phone in some unknown town in Mexico. When he returns, it's usually because he needs more money than what I wire to his account every month.

Shortly before he left town six months ago, we had a major blowout when I discovered he stole money from me, minutes after I'd given him most of what I had left for the month.

But he's my brother, my responsibility. I'd rather give him the money than have him get it elsewhere illegally and ending up in prison like our father.

I'm five years older than Ryan, and I'd just turned nineteen when Mom died. The day of the funeral, I promised Ryan I would take care of him, and do a better job than our parents ever did.

The first years were tough as I worked multiple part-time jobs to care for my depressed brother while pursuing a distance, scholarship-financed degree in education and mathematics, determined to build a solid future for us.

I never once wavered on my promises to him. But it hurts when Ryan now uses those very promises to take advantage of me.

I force air into my lungs, my hand tight around the door handle. Then I allow a smile to curl my lips.

Six months is a long time. Maybe he's changed. If he hasn't, he's in for a great surprise. Things are no longer the way he left them.

In the time he was away, I did a lot of thinking that led me to decide I no longer want to be his personal cash cow.

I swing open the door.

Ryan's dilated eyes sparkle as he opens his arms wide. I fight the urge to gag when the stench of stale alcohol and cigarettes plugs my nostrils. "Long time no see, Sis. Did you miss me?" He draws me into a tight hug, pressing my cheek to the hardware attached to his rough leather jacket.

I squeeze him back. As much as I dread having him around, he's the only family I've got, and I love him so much it hurts sometimes. Beneath the layers of disappointment at the direction he's chosen to go with his life, relief washes over me that he's alive and not rotting in a ditch or a prison somewhere.

He pulls back and grins down at me from his towering height that he inherited from our father.

When I look into his eyes, I see my mother—images of a wasted life. In the depths of his gaze, I detect broken shards of glass floating in pools of gray.

My mother never tired of telling me that I inherited my grandmother's plain looks, including her china-blue eyes. It disappointed her that I didn't inherit her supermodel good looks that earned her the title of Miss Florida, before everything came crashing down. Her words never bothered me. I decided then that I'd rather be plain than fall into a bottle of booze to drown my sorrows brought on by the fear of aging and fading looks.

I wish I could reach into Ryan's eyes and

pick up the shards of glass and piece them back together.

"Ryan, of course I missed you. I …" I glance past his left shoulder at the white Toyota parked on the curb outside the gate of our small townhouse that our mother had won years ago, along with the Miss Florida title. A man with a full beard and a mohawk hairstyle leans out of the driver's side, plumes of cigarette smoke distorting his features. The end of the cigarette glows as he drags on it. In the passenger's seat is another guy. Both are staring in our direction. They make me feel uneasy somehow.

"Who are those people?" My eyebrows draw together. "And where have you been for six months?"

"Where have I been? Here and there."

"Who are those men, Ryan? They look … They look dangerous."

Ryan glances over his shoulder at the car. When he returns his gaze to me, the smile has melted from his face. He shrugs. "Just people I hang out with." He jams his hands into his jeans pockets. "They gave me a ride here."

"Why are they still here?" I whisper.

"I owe them a little money, that's all. As soon as I give it to them, they'll be gone."

I cross my arms in front of my chest. "Ryan, when will you stop owing people money?"

"Don't be like that, Sis." He leans against the

doorframe. "I've had a long day, and I'm not in the mood for a lecture."

"I'm sorry if it makes you uncomfortable to hear some truths," I say between clenched teeth. "But you're here because you want money, aren't you?"

"Are you saying you won't give it to me?"

"Not if you're going to give it to those guys." I'm talking to him, but my eyes are on the Mohawk Guy. "When I give you money, it's for you, not for anyone else. And not for spending on booze." My shoulders sag. "I can't do it anymore, Ryan. What about all the money I send you every month?"

"Look, I know we parted on bad terms last time. I'm sorry, okay? You have to forgive me. We're family. Each other is all we've got." His mouth stretches into a thin line. "Help me out one last time. I really need your help, Sis."

Unable to stand the creepy stares from the Toyota, I wrap my hand around one of Ryan's firm biceps and pull him into the house. The door slams behind us as I turn on him. "How much do you owe them?"

"Don't look at me that way." He touches my cheek with the tip of a callused finger. "You know I wouldn't ask if it weren't important."

"Every time you ask me for money you claim it's important. It's my money. I deserve answers. How much, Ryan?"

He throws his hands into the air and drops them at his sides. "Way to go, Sis. Rub it in my face. You just have to make me feel bad, don't you? How many times have I thanked you for everything you do for me?"

"Let me think." I tap my lips with a forefinger. "That would be never."

"I may not have said it in words, but you know I'm thankful. You know that, don't you?" He scratches one side of his face. "Will you give me the money or not?"

"This has to stop. You're twenty-two years old." I form a steeple with my hands, my fingertips touching the place under my chin. "You're old enough to get a job and look after yourself. I don't mind financing a better future for you. If you tell me you want money to go back to school, I'd do everything in my power to help you. I'd take on extra jobs if I have to. But I can't finance this dangerous lifestyle you're leading. I barely make enough on my salary to pay the bills and the debts Mom left behind."

"You know what?" His upper lip curls as the words shoot out of his mouth. "Forget it. I'll get the money from someplace else." He grabs the door handle, but instead of opening the door, he leans forward, pressing his forehead against the slab of wood.

I blink away tears and place a hand on his

shoulder.

He shrugs me off. "Get your hands off me."

"Ryan, I'm just trying to help you. I'm doing this because I love you."

"To hell with your love and money." With that, he yanks the door open and stomps out, his boots thudding against the cobblestone path all the way to the rusty gate.

I remain in the doorway, watching as he kicks the gate open and bends down to exchange words with Mohawk Guy. The guy tosses out his cigarette and bares his teeth at Ryan.

In response, Ryan slams a hand on the hood of the car, then turns his back to him. He walks back through the gate and glances back at Mohawk Guy in time to see him draw a finger across his throat.

A shudder ripples through me as I watch my brother walk toward me.

Thank God, Ryan won't be leaving with them.

When Ryan makes it to the middle of the path, a sharp crack splits the night air.

Ryan sinks to the ground as if in slow motion. I never even saw Mohawk Guy pull out the gun.

My scream is drowned out by the grunt of the car engine as the Toyota peels away from the curb and shoots out of sight in a screech of tires. As it disappears into the night, I run to Ryan. The pit of my stomach falls at the same time I drop to his side, small stones digging through the thin fabric of my satin pajamas and into my knees.

A pool of blood spreads around him. Its surface glints in the moonlight like that of a stunning Burmese ruby's. But nothing could be uglier than this moment.

CHAPTER 1

At 2:00 p.m. my students gather their belongings and jump to their feet. Backpacks are zipped shut, chairs scrape the floor, and sneakers squeak in the rush to escape the classroom. In the hallway, their murmurs merge with the sounds of lockers slamming shut.

Swept away by a wave of excitement that accompanies the end of a school day, they don't wait for me to wish them a good day. All that stays behind as a sign of their earlier presence are the fading scents of smelly shoes, sweet lip gloss, and hairspray.

As usual, I stroll down the desk aisles, picking up crumpled papers and abandoned stationery, pushing in chairs and straightening desks. I pick up an abandoned algebra textbook and stare at it for a moment. My mind drifts to the past.

My love for math started in childhood. On rare occasions when my father was not high or drunk, we'd spent hours doing sums and completing Sudoku puzzles.

Who would have thought my love for numbers would keep me going when things got tough, that it would be a shield I'd use to protect myself from pain, disappointment, rejection, and loss? Math is the only constant in my life—the one thing I can count on to remain the same.

The thrill of taking on complicated equations always leaves me excited. I try to instill that same excitement into my students. I want them to embrace math instead of letting it intimidate them.

Back at my desk, I drop into my cushioned chair and cradle my head in my hands, my loose locks falling to the table in waves.

Most of the teaching staff will leave the school grounds by 4:00 p.m. Not me. I'm often the last one to leave, no earlier than 6:00 on most days.

At the mere thought of going home to face Ryan, a suffocating sensation tightens my throat. Work is my escape, my chance to breathe again when the air at home is just too thick.

My head snaps up when the door to my classroom swings open and Thalia Norman walks in, her long, shiny braids swinging from side to side as she approaches my desk. As usual, she carries with her the scent of ripe peaches and bergamot.

She's two years older than me—a history teacher—and my friend since my first day of work at Baxter Junior High School or BJHS, as most call it.

It never ceases to surprise me how she continues to be my friend, even during times when I'm incapable of being the friend she deserves, which is most of the time. But she's always there, always ready to listen, even when I don't say a word.

She perches on the edge of my desk, crosses her long, jean-clad legs, and observes me for a moment, eyes narrowed. "You look like hell."

"Thank you." I don't feel the smile I give her.

"I mean it, Paige. You're in need of a little pampering."

Thalia is the true definition of a girly girl. She treats herself to manicures, pedicures, massages, and a facial at least once a month.

It's not that I don't like those things; it's just that I don't have the money for it, and even if I did, I can't stand the stab of guilt that accompanies my indulgence.

On the other hand, Thalia doesn't have the kinds of responsibilities I do. She can afford to treat herself, to enjoy the money she makes, to do what feels good to her. Unmarried, and without kids or mounting debts, what she earns is hers to splurge on what she wants.

"You're right. Getting pampered would probably do me good, but I can't afford it." I occupy myself with tidying my desk, picking up the pens and dropping them into my black mug, emptying the plastic homework tray.

The topic of money makes me uncomfortable. It's the one thing that tortures me on a daily basis.

"Who said you have to pay for it?" Thalia jumps off the desk and removes a cream envelope from her back pocket. She waves it in the space between us. "Look what I've got here."

"What's that?"

The palm of her hand meets her smooth, chocolate forehead. "Don't tell me you forgot your birthday again."

"Oh, that." I shrug. "Actually, I didn't forget. I just don't think it's a big deal."

"Stop that." She throws me a stern look. "You have to quit putting your needs on the back burner. I get that Ryan needs you, but it's okay and healthy to think about yourself once in a while."

"You know I don't make a big deal about my birthday," I say. "What's the point of celebrating it when the life I'm given sucks?" I throw my hands in the air. "Look, I'm sorry. I didn't mean to vent." I take the envelope from her, one of many she'd given me in the last five years. "Thank you for this. I mean it."

"I hope things get better for you, sweetie." Thalia lays a hand on my shoulder. "If it's too overwhelming to care for Ryan, maybe you should consider getting him help."

"I can't do that." I square my tense shoulders. "He's my brother. I can't discard him just like that."

"It won't be just like that." Thalia crosses her arms, wrinkling her violet silk shirt. "The truth is, I don't think he'd be so reliant on you if he didn't drink so much."

"He drinks because he's miserable, and I'm responsible for making him that way."

"But he drank even before he got into that wheelchair."

I lower the envelope she just gave me into one of my desk drawers before locking it. I lean back in my chair. "He'll feel as though I'm pushing him out of my life, and I don't want him to ever feel abandoned. This is the life I signed up for, Thalia."

"But there are so many wheelchair-bound people living normal, happy lives. Ryan can have that if he wants. But does he really?"

"I just don't want to lose him. I almost did when that bullet hit his head." It's been two years, and in my moments of stillness, I still hear the crack in the air as the bullet that changed our lives sliced through it to get to Ryan. I still see my brother sinking to the ground like a rag doll. For a few terrifying seconds at the hospital that night, his heart had stopped beating. The doctors said he's lucky to be alive. He doesn't feel that way.

I didn't care whether he survived with a spinal cord injury. I was just glad to have him back. And I promised myself I would do everything to take care of him, to make it all better. I'd never have forgiven myself if he'd died.

"I know that was scary as hell." Thalia pauses. "You're one of the strongest people I know."

"If only I believed that."

"Seriously, Paige. I don't think I would've been able to do what you do for Ryan. He's not only paralyzed, but he drinks and disrespects you every chance he gets. He takes you for granted."

An ache spreads through my chest. "He's going through a hard time. I don't know what kind of person I would be if I were in his shoes." I push out of my chair. "So," I say, changing the subject, "what are you doing this evening?"

"Some of us will be meeting up later to hit the Simmering Grill for juicy steaks." Thalia's eyes brighten. "I wish you would come. It's your birthday. Take an evening off, for goodness' sake."

"You know how he gets when I don't make it home on time."

"It shouldn't be like that. Don't you see? It's completely unfair." Thalia purses her lips. "You have the right to your freedom. Instead, he treats you like his prisoner."

"He doesn't make me do anything. I make my own choices."

"Out of obligation."

"That's beside the point. It only matters that I'm there for him. That's not about to change anytime soon—"

"Or ever," Thalia adds.

Pain grips my chest as her words sink in. What if Ryan never recovers? The doctors said at the start that with an incomplete spinal cord injury, there might be a possibility for him to walk again, but the chances would become slimmer as more time passes. I refuse to give up hoping for a miracle. But he needs to want it, too.

What if ten years from now, I'm still in this place, still stuck in this same moment? Can I really do it for that long or longer? Whatever the case may be, I'll be there for Ryan for as long as he needs me.

"Maybe next time," I say. "Have fun at the

Grill." I lift my floral fabric tote from the back of my chair and heave it onto my shoulder. "Thanks for the gift."

"Thank me when you actually use it." She pauses. "I mean it, Paige. Don't just push it in some place and forget about it." She glances at my desk drawer.

"You know what?" I jam a hand into my bag and dig out the key to the drawers. "You should take it back. Why don't you spoil yourself instead?" I wink. "On me."

"What in the world are you talking about?"

"I might never use it. I don't want it to go to waste."

"Like all the other presents I gave you before?" Thalia lifts a perfectly shaped eyebrow.

I run a hand through my hair. "I'm sorry." I open the drawer and pull out the envelope. When I hand it to her, she takes a step back.

"I won't take it back. It's a gift. Whether you decide to use it or not, is up to you. But I want you to try and take advantage of it sometime within the next six months."

"I promise to try." I no longer return it to the drawer together with all the other gift cards she's given me, but push it into my bag.

"I guess that's more than I can ask for." She gives me a tight hug. "Happy birthday, sweetheart. If you need anything, you know I'm here always." She pulls back and gives me a bright smile. "At least take a break from worrying tonight."

"Easier said than done."

"Oh, I know." She steps toward the door and blows me an air kiss before walking out. The door clicks shut behind her.

After she leaves, I spend the next hours preparing for tomorrow's lessons and killing time. At 6:00 p.m. I count to a hundred, then leave the classroom to face the consequences of my past decisions.

CHAPTER 2

I ring the doorbell of our apartment and wait for Ryan to come to the door.

After the shooting, we had to sell the townhouse because I couldn't live in the house again knowing what happened on its doorstep.

I was lucky to find a wheelchair-accessible apartment with two bathrooms. The bathroom Ryan uses has a slide-in bathtub, a wall-mounted sink with no cabinet underneath, and grab bars. I prefer to use the tiny shower in my bedroom.

Despite the high monthly rent, which I'm still struggling to pay, it brings me peace to know Ryan is able to live in a safe environment.

The reason I ring the bell has nothing to do with the fact that I forgot my key, but because I want Ryan to move. He spends most of the day in the living room, stuffing his mouth with junk food, watching violent movies or playing equally violent video games.

I like for him to change his environment even for a few seconds every now and then. I'm well aware he hates it, but I do it anyway. I count to sixty but Ryan still doesn't come to the door.

I press my finger on the little white button again, keeping it there. Hopefully he'll get annoyed to the point he opens the door just to get rid of the noise.

Sometimes it doesn't work. He either increases the volume on the television or plugs in his earbuds.

But this time, the door is flung open within three minutes. Suddenly, my brother is in his wheelchair in front of me, several pounds larger than he had been before he was shot.

"Are you mad?" A thunderstorm rages in his gray eyes. The whites of his eyes as usual are bloodshot from too much alcohol.

"Good evening to you, too." I give him a smile with nothing behind it but teeth. "You okay?" It's a question I ask every day to show I care.

"What's it to do with you?" He starts to wheel himself away.

As I watch the back of his head, a wave of loneliness sweeps through me.

We live side-by-side like strangers sharing an apartment. It kills me to watch him slip away one day at a time. I live in constant fear that one day he could end up dying the way my mother did, that I'll walk into the apartment to find him choked on his own vomit or worse.

That's one horror scene I'll never be able to get out of my head no matter how many years pass between my mother's death and the present. If history ever repeats itself, I don't think I'll be able to handle it a second time.

When I enter the kitchen, dropping my bag on the counter, I hear the squeaking sound of his wheelchair at the door.

I turn with a small smile. "Did you have something to eat?"

"I was waiting for you." His voice is flat. "I sent you a text to bring me pizza. Didn't you read it?" The ever-present slur in his voice distorts his words.

"I *did* read your text." I pull a pan from a cabinet. "But I wanted to make spaghetti with pesto sauce."

"Stop treating me like a freaking child. I said I want pizza."

The bite in his voice makes me turn, fire burning in my eyes. "No, Ryan. You are a twenty-four-year-old grown man, who has chosen to let his life rot. You stay here all day doing nothing but playing games and eating unhealthy food that messes with your health. Don't you care about your life at all?"

A sneer stretches across his face. "What's the

point?"

"You're my brother. I love you." I lean against the counter. "If you don't want to do it for yourself, do it for me."

"What have you done for me lately?"

I reel inwardly as though slapped hard across the face.

"That's right, Paige. All you do is whine about this and that. 'Ryan, you eat too much junk food.' 'Ryan, you watch too much TV.' 'Ryan, stop playing games all day and get some sleep.' All you do is whine in my face. Frankly, I don't get why you even care."

"I'm not in the mood to go through this with you tonight." I ignore the lump blocking my throat. "I'll cook dinner and you will eat it."

He watches me for a moment, then swivels himself around, returning to the living room without another word to me.

Seconds later I hear the sounds of gunshots as he plays one of his favorite games. For someone who's been shot, it surprises me that he chooses to surround himself with violence.

Once the food is ready, the aroma of herbs and spices swirl in the air. I fill his plate with food and take it to him in the living room, the steam curling upward to warm my face. I wish he could join me at the kitchen table, but we never eat together.

I pull the coffee table close to his wheelchair

and lower the food on top of it. Ryan glances at the meal and looks up at me with disgust.

"Take it away," he demands.

"I won't do that. I made an effort to cook for you. At least taste it." I straighten up, a hand pressed on my aching lower back.

"Fine. If you won't get rid of your damn food, I will." He swings back his hand and then brings it forward. It collides with the plate and sends it crashing to the wooden floor next to my feet. The ceramic plate snaps in half and the sauce flies through the air. Some of it lands on my bare legs. The strands of spaghetti crawl across the floor like worms.

I jump back, but rage courses through my veins as I glare at him. "You can't always have everything you want. I work hard to look after you, but the only thing you do is throw it all in my face. It's time you start showing some appreciation."

"Are you actually surprised about the way I'm acting?" He tightens his grip around the armrests of his chair. "I don't see why you should be. Isn't it your fault that I'm in this damn chair?"

He wheels himself from the living room. Moments later, his bedroom door slams against the doorframe.

I won't see him again for the rest of the evening. He'll stay in there until I go to bed.

Then he'll return to the living room to continue drinking until he passes out.

Tomorrow, it'll start all over again—the insults, the pain, the regrets.

With tears sliding down my cheeks, I clean up the mess he made. The mess *I* made.

CHAPTER 3

My eyes are sore and heavy when I force them open to face a day I'd rather not be a part of.

I sink deeper into the pillows. If only I could stay buried under the warm, comforting bedspread. The cold fingers of fear wrap themselves around my heart, clawing, tearing, digging into my already tender flesh.

Ryan doesn't have to be in the room for me to feel his presence. I'm completely surrounded by him, consumed by his anger and pain, the hatred in his eyes.

As hard as today will be, I have no choice but to get through it one labored breath at a time. No choice but to live the life I am given.

I pull myself up in bed and lean against the headboard. Eyes squeezed shut, I send up a little prayer that ends with me whispering words of encouragement to myself.

"You've got this, Paige Wilson. You don't have to feel strength to be strong. What's one more day?"

I open my eyes and watch the slivers of sunlight slice through the place where the heavy drapes meet in the middle.

Maybe today will be different. It could be one of Ryan's good days, even if those are few and far between.

I can't remember the last time I saw him smile. The sound of his happy laughter is a distant memory.

I drag myself out of bed, placing first one foot onto the worn-out carpeted floor and then the other, holding onto the edge of the bed for support as I continue to force air into my lungs. Then I push myself to a standing position and launch into the life I've been handed.

One thing that gets me through every single day is doing without thinking too much about it. Today will be no different.

I take a long shower, longer than I'd planned. I have two hours to spare before I leave for work. Getting up early helps me feel more in control of my life.

After the hot shower, I brush my teeth, and rinse out the sour taste of bile lingering at the back of my throat.

Back inside the bedroom, I throw open the window and stick my head out into the clean, early June air. The air is thinner outside, scented with freshly-mowed grass, damp earth, and traces of sea air. It flows into my lungs without hindrance, diluting the stagnant air inside me.

Ned Porter, the landlord's teenage son, is out in the yard, mowing the lawn for the third time this week.

As usual, he's wearing his black knitted hat, pulled low over his big forehead. His upper body is shirtless; his skin scorched by the sun as he spends so much time gardening.

I smile at him. No harm in pretending to be happy. In fact, my mind might actually be fooled into believing it.

I step away from the window, still determined to remain positive, choosing happiness instead of misery.

As I slip into one of my black dresses, I scramble inside my head for happy memories to hang on to. Nothing comes to mind.

With my bag on my shoulder, I head to the kitchen to make breakfast. I'll make Ryan's favorite—eggs Benedict. It's been a while since I did that for him. Hopefully a little treat will make the day go by smoother.

Just as I'm done preparing the meal, Ryan wheels himself into the kitchen. My stomach recoils from the stink of alcohol that detaches itself from his body and mingles with the warm aroma of eggs and bacon hanging in the air around me.

"Morning, Ryan." I pretend last night didn't

happen.

He glares at me, but no words leave his lips.

My stomach clenches at his non-response, my earlier confidence and hope crashing at my feet, splintering into a thousand broken moments.

I turn back to the stove—fake smile still frozen on my face—and silently count to ten, steel myself, and turn to him again.

He's now pushed himself closer to the oak kitchen table. Like my heart, it has also been the object of his abuse over the past two years. On his worst days, he had slammed his fist against the wood, driven knives into it, or scratched the surface with forks to let out his frustrations.

He's still glaring at me, but his eyes are flat, as though he doesn't see me at all.

"I made your favorite breakfast today." My voice sounds unnatural to my ears. I'm pretty sure Ryan can see right through me.

He knows me better than anyone else. He knows my fears and which buttons to press.

I lower his plate of food in front of him and pour him a glass of fresh orange juice. Then I switch on the small radio by the window. Pop music floods the kitchen, but it fails to flush the tension out of the room.

When I look back at Ryan, I find his plate empty, the food I'd served him on the table next to it.

Something inside me snaps. There's a pounding in my ears as I cross the room in a flash and slam my fist on the table. The plate and glass rattle on the wood in reaction to my rage. "Why are you doing this?"

A sneer curls a corner of his lips as I meet his gaze. His eyes remind me of those of a snake. In them I don't see my brother at all— just an angry, bitter stranger.

Gritting my teeth, I start to clean the table, but then I stop, throw my hands in the air, and let them drop again. "No," I say. "I won't do this again. I'm not your maid. Clean up your own mess." My hands clench and unclench at my sides. "All I do is try to make you happy and comfortable. And what do you do? You do the exact opposite for me. It's so unfair, Ryan."

"You think that's unfair?" His laughter makes the air between us vibrate. "You brought this upon yourself. Don't forget it was you who put me in this damn chair." His nostrils flare with each word. "I'm chained to you, Sis. Whether you like it or not, I'm the noose around your neck. If I'm miserable, I'll make damn sure you're miserable, too. Want to know what's fair? When you hurt as much as I do."

His words are chilled around the edge, cold as ice, sharp as knives. He means every one of them. He's determined to inflict more pain. I'm not sure how long I can handle it before I break.

"Enough!" I point a shaking finger at him. "That's enough. I've had it with being blamed for what happened to you." I yank his wheelchair away from the table, spin it around to face me, my hand planted on the armrest, my head so close that his warm, booze-tainted breath hits my face. "You are responsible for this. It was you who made friends with the wrong people, you who took money from them to buy God knows what. It was you who messed up your own life." I catch my breath. "Yes, I refused to give you money that night and it was well within my rights. All you did was take and you flushed all the money I worked so hard for down the toilet every single time. That night was the last straw." My teeth are clenched so tight my jaw aches. "I'm done tiptoeing around you. You got to this place because of your own bad decisions. It's time for you to face the consequences. I'm no longer carrying them for you. Being in a wheelchair is not an excuse for you to throw away your life or to be disrespectful. I—"

Before I can say the next word, Ryan rounds his mouth, and spits into my face. "Go to hell where you belong."

The palm of my hand itches to meet the skin of his cheek, but I count to five and stumble away from him as if burned, my hand wiping away the slimy saliva now making its way down the side of my face, catching it before it drips off.

Fear and regret harden in the center of my chest. I can't take this. I need to get away from him before I forget myself.

Removing myself from the toxic environment, I stomp out of the kitchen and burst into the living room. For a moment I stand there, catching my breath, pulling myself together.

I hear the squeak of his wheelchair entering the room. Our eyes lock. He gives me that smile again—the one that eats away at my soul.

Still not ready to be in the same room as him, I push past him toward the door. Before I exit the room, I make the mistake of glancing back.

His smile is wider, more spine-chilling.

"You can't get rid of me," he says. "You'll pay for what you did. I'll make your life a living hell."

I slam the front door shut, but his words and toxic laughter grip my entire body as I escape from the apartment to my car. Since I'm in no position to drive, I sit in my personal space, eyes closed, until I'm calm enough.

Breathe, Paige. All you have to do is breathe.

When I open my eyes again, still rattled, I glance up at the living room window on the fourth floor, and there he is, watching me.

I ignore the shiver down my spine and start the car. But we both know I'll be back for more torture.

CHAPTER 4

The moment I enter the classroom, my back hits the closed door. The room is still dim. My breath comes in short gasps as I pull up the blinds and throw open the windows to release the stale air.

Aside from some of the cleaning staff, I'm the only person at BJHS so far. I'm grateful for the moment alone to catch my breath before the day starts, to wipe the pain from my face before the students arrive, to pick up some of the pieces of my shattered heart.

With my head in my hands, I crash into my chair, Ryan's last words still going around and around inside my mind like a broken record. Desperate to block them out, I move my hands to my ears, as if that would shut them off. No chance. His voice only gets louder, fighting through my resistance.

I'll make your life a living hell.

Goose pimples brought on by my undiluted

fear push through my skin, scattering across the surface. Where is my brother? Where is the little boy who used to adore me as a child? The one who climbed into my bed when my mother came home drunk, and he needed my protection? What if I never find him beneath all the pain and anger?

What if he never learns to live again? Tears come, but I blink them away. I will not cry at work.

Thirty minutes later, my phone rings. Thinking it's Ryan, I ignore it. But the sound of chirping birds seems to get louder so I reach into my bag. The caller is Lin Hu, Ryan's physical therapist.

Massaging my temple, I answer.

"Sorry, Paige, did I wake you?" She pauses. "I wanted to catch you before your classes."

"No, Lin. It's fine." I place a hand on my forehead, trying but failing not to pay attention to the approaching headache. "Are you calling to confirm today's appointment?"

"No, Paige." She pauses. "I ... actually, I'm calling because I can no longer work with your brother. I'm really sorry. I didn't want to tell you this, but last time I went to your place he refused to open the door. When I came back later, he let me in, but he was too drunk to do anything."

"Lin, please ... please give him another

chance. I'll talk to him tonight."

I can't afford to lose Lin after only three months. She's one of the few affordable physical therapists in town. And I can't allow Ryan to quit physical therapy. It's important not only to him but also to me. I desperately want him to walk again.

"You're a nice person, and I'm sorry to do this to you, but I can't work with him. He's too rude and disrespectful, and drunk half the time. It doesn't feel right for me to take your money when I'm unable to help your brother. I want to help people who actually want to improve."

I bite down on my bottom lip. I can't find any words to talk her out of her decision. She's gotten a taste of Ryan's dark side. How could I force anyone to look into the eyes I saw this morning and subject them to the kind of abuse Ryan puts me through every day? Lin's words are hard to swallow. It shatters me to think Ryan wants to remain in the dark hole of depression, to stay stagnant.

"I ... I understand." My voice is barely a whisper. "Thank you for trying. Lin, if you change your mind, call me, please."

"I'm sorry. I wish there was more I could do."

After ending the call, fury rushes through me. The desire to call Ryan and give him a piece of my mind burns through my veins, but I resist the temptation. I'm still not ready to talk to him, to take more insults. After a fight, I'm often the one who reaches out and begs for forgiveness, even when I'm not in the wrong. Not today.

Today, I won't call him at all, even though I normally check up on him every few hours. Today, I'll focus on my job. I'll put myself first.

Blocking all kinds of negative thoughts from my mind, I push myself out of the chair and move to the window. From my classroom, I can see the sparkle of the ocean in the distance. I watch it for a few heartbeats, wishing I were out there in the water. I love to swim, but I never get the time to do it.

Finally, I unlock the door to give the students permission to enter, then I spend the time preparing for my lesson with a confidence I haven't felt in a while. When the students finally trickle in, some of them bringing in the smell of unwashed bodies, I greet them with a fake smile. Some respond, but others are too distracted by conversations with their fellow classmates to pay attention to me.

Behind my desk, I watch them in silence as they take their seats, scraping the wooden floor.

Once everyone has settled down, I rise.

The hairs at the nape of my neck bristle when the breeze, from the window closest to my desk, touches my skin, drying my sweat.

I greet the students again. This time they all turn to face me. In a few words, I remind them of my classroom rules. No chewing gum, no phones, no talking when I'm talking.

The rules have to be repeated every day because they seem to expire after a couple of hours.

Sinking into my chair again, I flip open the textbook in front of me. Before I can start the lesson, Margaret Harris—the principal—walks in with a somber expression on her face.

"Paige, could I have a word?" she whispers into my ear. Her breath is laced with the mint chewing gum she always has in her mouth.

My chest tightens immediately. Whatever she has to say to me must be important for her to walk in during a class.

Most times when Margaret asks to speak to me, my immediate reaction is panic that I've done something wrong, something that puts my job on the line. My worst nightmare is losing my job and not having enough money to care for Ryan.

"Sure." I follow her outside, the door closing softly behind us, blocking out the whispers inside the classroom.

Margaret leans a shoulder against the wall closest to the door, lays a hand on her chest. "I have some bad news."

"Oh." I try to say more, but the words die on

the tip of my parched tongue.

"I got a call a few minutes ago, that Isaac Baxter passed away from a heart attack last night, while on vacation in Greece."

Every person in Corlake knows Isaac Baxter. He was not only the town's only billionaire and owned half the businesses and buildings in town—including where we live—but he was the founder of Baxter Junior High, the largest private school in town.

"Oh, God." A cloud of worry settles on my mind again. How will his death impact my job? "What, what ...?"

"His loss will definitely be felt throughout town. And I'm sure every student or teacher at this school will be impacted in some way directly or indirectly. Isaac was a friend of mine. We went to school together." Margaret brushes away a tear.

"I'm sorry. I'm sorry for your loss," I say.

"Thank you." She runs a hand through her bleached blonde hair. "I'm calling for an urgent assembly in an hour. It's best you don't mention anything to the students just yet. I'll break it down to everyone during the assembly."

As planned, an hour later, the entire school is congregated in the assembly hall. I'm in the row assigned to teachers, facing the podium, Thalia next to me.

"Let's hope his heirs don't move too many jobs out of town. The man owned the whole bloody town." Like everyone in the room, Thalia is shaken by Isaac Baxter's death.

"Yeah." Thalia just voiced my worst fears. The entire time Margaret addresses us and the students from the wooden podium, my mind is drifting. My job is the only stable thing in my life. What would I do without it?

Teaching jobs are scarce in Corlake. If BJHS closes down, we might have to move to another town, and Ryan is not one to embrace change.

My thoughts move to my worries about the rent that's due. Any day now, Mike Porter will show up at my door for the second time this month, and I'll beg him again to give me more time.

Most of the money I earn goes toward Ryan's medical bills and the debts my mother left behind. The disability payments he receives don't come close to being enough to support both of us.

What if Isaac Baxter's heirs decide to sell our apartment building? We might never find another like it.

In the moment of silence for Isaac Baxter, I clutch my hands in my lap, drop my head and pray not only for Isaac Baxter's soul, but also for Ryan and myself.

After the assembly, I manage to get through

the rest of the school day in a daze.

Once the students have left the classroom at the end of the day, I pull out my desk drawer and reach for my phone.

Twenty missed calls—all from Ryan. He left several voice messages and one text. I read the text message first.

Your worst nightmare will be right here waiting for you.

CHAPTER 5

Six o'clock strikes, and I'm still at my desk, alternating between staring into space, tidying up, and preparing for two days' worth of lessons. The only time I move from my chair is when Daisy, the cleaning lady, enters my classroom with a mop. She asks if she should come back, but I shake my head.

"It's fine. I was just about to go home." The last place I want to be is home, to face *my worst nightmare*.

I leave the school grounds, but instead of going home to Ryan, I pick up a few groceries and drive for an hour around town with no destination in mind.

I pretend to be a tourist in my own town, forcing myself to be swept away by the beauty of whitewashed houses framed by pastel-colored picket fences and the lavender blooms of the jacaranda trees lining the streets. The round, mother-of-pearl clock on the St. Peter's

Catholic Church is already lit up for the evening.

I slow down when I approach The Cake Palace, admiring the colorful display of sweet treats in the window. I stick my head a little out the window and inhale deeply, imagining breathing in the aromas of baking bread, melted butter, sugar, and the tang of lemon icing.

As a child, I never walked past The Cake Palace without stopping to stare through the window at the gourmet cupcakes. I used to see myself biting into the cushion soft icing, my mouth watering in response.

Lucy-Anne Taylor knows the value of her baked goods and makes sure to charge what they're worth. In spite of steep prices, her baked goods are always a hit at the annual Sweets & Blooms Festival that takes place a week before Christmas, a way to end the year on a sweet note.

I drive past the newly-renovated post office, the firehouse, and the library, and turn into a street that affords me a direct view of the sugar white sandy beach, turned golden at sunset.

It's ironic that despite being surrounded by the breathtaking beauty and calm of Corlake, happiness eludes me.

I drive to the beachfront, where I park the car across from a closed ice cream shop with a pink plastic cone at the entrance.

I close my eyes and take a calming breath before switching my phone back on. I'd switched it off after reading Ryan's text.

I ignore more missed calls and messages. One message has done enough harm to last me a couple of hours, days, weeks even.

What I need now is a break from him. In spite of my love for water, it's been a while since I went for a swim or a walk on the beach.

Even if we're apart, Ryan refuses to let me go. He continues to whisper venomous words into my ear. I can still feel the trickle of his saliva on my cheek, the area it hit pulsing like a heartbeat. The heat of his gaze still burns into my flesh.

He controls me even from a distance.

But I still have the power to choose. Today, I choose not to go home until I'm ready.

Though a part of me feels guilty, the other is rebelling. The thought of walking through the apartment door makes me feel sick to my stomach.

It's impossible to breathe inside my own home when Ryan sucks the air out of every room before I step into it. He follows me around the place, making sure I get a good look of his broken state, that I see the anger etched into every corner of his face. That I breathe in his pain.

Before I lose my nerve, I swing my legs out

of the car, remove my shoes, and cross the road to get to the promenade.

The sea breeze sweeps across my face, brushing my hair back, refreshing my skin, drying the sheen of sweat on my forehead.

My hunger for freedom pushes me to run, stopping only when my feet sink into the warm evening sand. There are barely any people on the beach at this time of day, only an occasional jogger or dog walker.

While listening to seagulls squawking, I draw in the scent of sea air mixed with traces of suntan lotion left behind by the afternoon sunbathers. I tip my head upward as a seagull flies by, exercising the kind of freedom I wish I had. I'd give anything to be that bird, to fly high above my troubles, to flee from my dark place.

The sun is setting now, a ball of fire in the horizon—magical, warm, and soothing.

I should come here more often instead of rushing home every day. Maybe if I do it a couple more times, Ryan will get used to it. If he doesn't, he'll have no choice but to deal with it.

Since he doesn't appreciate me, it could be time I put myself first for a change. I could come to the beach on the weekends, prepare for lessons while sitting on a lounger, gazing at the water. The soothing energy of the sea would help me cope better with his dark moods and unpredictable behavior.

An old woman with a stooped back and a golden retriever trotting ahead of her, mumbles a greeting to me in passing. I nod and return her smile.

As she walks off, I can't help wondering what kind of challenges she'd had to overcome in her life. Are her struggles as hard and heavy as mine? Could they be responsible for the hunched back she now carries? She disappears into the distance before I can figure her out. Her life is none of my business anyway.

Instead of wasting time wondering about other people, I better make the most of this time alone before the guilt rushes in to torment me.

On my way to the edge of the water, I step on whole and broken seashells.

Instead of coming to a halt where the water ends, I walk straight in. Clenching my teeth from the shock of cold, I keep moving into the waves until they engulf me, invigorate me.

I don't care that I'm fully dressed. If someone sees me from the beach, they might think I have suicide on my mind. I don't care. For the first time in months, I'm doing what I please.

Once I get to a deeper part of the ocean, I throw myself headfirst into the water, tasting the salt on my tongue. And then I start to swim.

I swing my arms from back to front, slice through the thick liquid until my lungs scream with exhaustion, until my muscles burn with pain.

The pain is good. It reminds me I'm still alive. It distracts me from my scattered emotions.

When I emerge from the water, I feel different, my heart lighter than it had felt earlier.

Nothing calms me quite the way water does.

My love of water started in childhood. It drove my mother nuts when I ran into the rain every time it poured, gazing up at the sky, giggling as drops of water tap-danced on my face and sluiced down my petite frame. On one particular day, we had just come home from a birthday party and I was wearing a new princess dress grandma had given me weeks before her death—a fancy dress with butterflies scattered across the hem. When we stepped out of the car, it started to rain. My mother shouted for us to run into the house before we got wet. Ignoring her, I twirled in the rain, jumping in puddles, laughing with rare happiness as liquid diamond drops fell around me. It was a high price to pay.

When I recall that day now, what stands out the most is pain. My mother had pulled me into the house by the hair, threw me onto the floor of the entrance hall, and attacked me with one of dad's thick belts. The buckle sliced into my skin, cut through the flesh, drew blood. My screams ricocheted off the walls as I covered my face to protect it. When I cried for her to stop, the only responses I got from her were insults and more beating. The only time she stopped was when she was exhausted and I was broken.

When I think of my mom, that's one of the memories that comes to me, vivid even in the dark recesses of my mind.

The more she wanted me to stay out of water, the more I craved it. I couldn't help myself. Another vivid memory is of her throwing a glass of wine at my head. It shattered on my skull and a piece of glass left a gash at the tip of my eyebrow. Still, I could not allow her to take away the only thing that brought joy into my life. When trying to survive a terrible childhood, some children turn to imaginary friends, some overeat, and others cut themselves. I turned to water and math. Without those two things, I'd have gone insane.

I have no idea how long the relief I found in the ocean will last, but I hang on to it until I get back to the car, dripping wet, ignoring the curious glances from passersby.

From the trunk, I remove a towel I keep in there for moments like this, moments when it starts to rain and I feel the urge to dance, moments where I rush into the ocean on a whim.

I dry myself off and squeeze the water from my hair, then cover the driver's seat with the damp towel.

Cold now, I climb into the car, slam the door shut, and close my eyes, trying to hang on to that good feeling that's already starting to dissipate.

My phone rings from the passenger's seat.

I don't need to see his name on the screen to know he's the one calling. He wants to know where I am and when I'll be home.

Instead of answering his incessant calls or returning them, I step out of the car again. I don't care that it's close to 8:00 p.m.

Outside the car, my dress still damp and sticking to my skin, I go for a walk along the promenade. I shiver when a breeze wraps itself around me.

I spot a newspaper on one of the wooden benches.

Isaac Baxter's face is plastered on the front, his salt-and-pepper hair thick on his head, his face swathed in a smile. I lower myself onto the bench to read.

Margaret must have received the wrong information. In the paper, it says Isaac Baxter died three days ago. It also goes on to say his billion-dollar estate will probably be passed on to his only son, Dylan Baxter, who takes care of his businesses in New York.

Unfortunately, it doesn't shed light on what will happen to his many businesses in Corlake.

After reading the paper, I remain on the bench for a little longer. Let Ryan take care of himself tonight. He's perfectly capable of doing that.

I won't apologize for taking a huge step toward getting my life back. Even as I try to be brave, I get an inkling deep inside my heart that I'll be paying a high price for this moment of freedom.

CHAPTER 6

∽

Something is wrong. I know it as soon as I turn onto our street. My plan when I left the beach was to go home, jump into the shower, and head straight to bed. But I'm now getting the feeling that that's not going to happen.

Alarm bells go off the closer I get to our apartment. The moment I see the building, it hits me that the alarm bells are not inside my head.

A plume of smoke is curling out of our kitchen window into the night sky. The sound I had been hearing is that of the fire alarm.

An invisible hand tightens itself around my stomach and wrings my intestines so hard I double over.

The pain is soon pushed out of the way by a surge of panic. Panting, I jump out of the car.

Within a few minutes, I burst out of the elevator onto the fourth floor. By the time I reach our front door, my lungs are screaming with pain, my body tense as I jam the key into the lock.

The moment I step into the apartment, a cloud of smoke plugs my nostrils and rushes into my lungs, which reject it, causing me to cough uncontrollably.

My eyes stinging, I grab a handful of my still damp dress and hold it to my mouth.

The smoke inside is so thick I can almost touch it.

The fire alarm is still shrieking, making my head ache, but the first thing I have to do is get to the source of the smoke.

On the stove, all the burners are glowing hot. On top of one of them is a pot with smoke pouring from it.

With tears brought on by the smoke trickling down my cheeks, I turn off the stove and reach for the burning pot. I jump back when I hear something pop. I watch in horror as the bottom of the cheap pot melts off and forms a silver river down one side of the stove.

Before the entire pot can melt away and cause damage to the stove's surface, I grab it and toss it into the sink. I turn on the water, and the moment it hits the pot, more smoke is released into the air. I can barely breathe as I grab a broom from behind the cupboard and send it crashing into the fire alarm on the ceiling until the sound dies only to be replaced by sirens outside the building.

Unable to breathe, my hands clench around the edge of the sink, my eyes closed tight. My fear is immediately overtaken by a rush of burning rage.

My nails bite into my palms when I stomp out of the kitchen and crash into the living room, where I know he'll be waiting for me.

Through the curtain of smoke that managed to get into the room, I watch him sitting at his usual place in front of the TV, watching a movie where people are shooting each other.

I slam the door shut and lunge for him, spinning him around. My palm meets his stubbled cheek so hard it hurts even me.

"What the hell is wrong with you?" I yell in between bouts of coughing. "Are you out of your mind?"

His smirk chills me under the skin.

"Please ... Please tell me you didn't do it on purpose." The words feel painful inside my throat as I push them out.

"Nope. And I could do worse," he says, his tone unapologetic.

My head snaps back as if he, too, has just struck me across the cheek.

"Next time you don't come home on time, something worse could happen."

My hand lands on his cheek again, harder this time. "How dare you say that? This is my life. I can come and go as I please."

My attack doesn't even make him flinch. "Your life, huh?" First, he laughs and then he coughs, not bothering to cover his mouth. "You actually think you have a life?" His words come out like sharp darts striking me one by one, digging into my skin, headed for my heart. "What happened tonight is nothing. I promise you that."

"You are such a—"

"Call me what you want. But from now on, when I call you, you answer or return my calls within an hour. If I don't hear from you, I won't be responsible for my actions." He pauses to cough. "As long as I don't have a life, you won't have one either."

"Is that a threat?" How dare he say that when I break my back every single day to support him?

A chilled, black silence falls between us as I wait for him to respond.

When he does, his voice drips of poison. "Does it sound like one?" He cocks his head to the side. "In that case, that's what it is. Take what I said as a serious threat."

His words hit me so hard I'm lost for words. I'm almost relieved when the doorbell rings and I can get away from Ryan.

I wipe the tears from my face first and then open the door.

Two firefighters in uniform stand before me, ready to get to work.

"I'm so sorry," I say, placing a hand on my heaving chest. "It was a false alarm. A pot burned. There was no fire, just smoke."

"Are you sure you're all right, ma'am?" One of the men searches my face in a way that makes me feel as though he can see right through me, as though he can see the oozing wounds etched in the fabric of my heart.

"I'm fine." I press my hands to my burning cheeks. "Everything is fine. I left the pot on for too long. I'm sorry for your trouble."

"Are you sure you don't want us to take a look?" the other man asks.

"There's nothing to see. There's no fire in here."

I finally get them to leave. When I return to the living room, the door is closed. For the first time, I regret choosing an apartment that does not have an open floor plan, like most in the building. But the rent had been lower.

I stumble into the kitchen and barge onto the attached tiny balcony. My hands grab the cool railing. My head hits my chest.

After counting to fifty, I hear a commotion from behind me. At first, I think he has come to join me on the balcony, but when I turn around, I notice him on the other side of the glass sliding door, his eyes cold as they move to mine.

He winks, then turns away and leaves the kitchen.

This is the first time I can truly admit my brother terrifies me.

I pull in a few deeper breaths, and when I decide to return into the apartment, to confront him yet again, I'm unable to.

He has locked me outside.

All I can do is laugh so hard tears fill my eyes and my stomach hurts. And then panic overcomes me and I slam my fist against the glass, yelling for him to let me in.

Someone—from somewhere in the building—shouts for me to shut up.

I continue to hit the glass, this time with the palms of my hands until my skin screams. My knees give way and I crumple to the floor. My back leans against the glass.

Once I run out of breath calling for Ryan, I hear a soft click. When I turn to look, I watch him wheel himself toward the kitchen door.

I crash into the kitchen, but this time I'm too drained and frightened to walk into another fight with the monster that was once my brother.

I grab my bag from the kitchen counter and head to my bedroom.

My breaths burst in and out of my lungs. I wait for something to happen, something worse, for him to do something else to scare me. Sometimes I fear I might wake up one night to find him next to my bed, weapon in hand, ready to end it all.

I wish I could kick him out for what he did tonight, but I can't. I'm partly responsible for the man he has become.

I have no choice but to lie in the bed I've made.

CHAPTER 7

When the lunchtime bell chimes and the kids flee from the classroom, I lean against the door to catch my breath.

It's been hard to keep it together, to go on as though my life is in one piece. It was exhausting running out of the classroom every hour to call Ryan. At times, I forced myself to remain seated, to continue doing my job without feeling intimidated by my brother, but the thought of what he might do next pulls me out of my chair each time.

My heart hasn't settled since discovering another side to Ryan, an even darker version of himself.

But I have to breathe. That's all I have the power to do right now.

"You'll get through this day one breath at the time," I whisper to myself, but the words taste like a lie on my tongue.

On shaky legs, I cross the classroom and sink

into my desk chair, yank out the drawer and pick up my phone. The fourth text message from him is the same as the three before it. Three little words on a small screen that carry so much power.

Be on time.

He called me thirty minutes ago, but since I was in the middle of a lesson, I couldn't return his call. Now I have thirty minutes left to touch base before he goes nuts.

My thumb trembles to the call button. "Hi," I say, the heel of my hand pressed hard against the place between my eyebrows.

"Just on time." He pauses. "I'm glad you're taking my threats seriously."

"I have to get back to work, Ryan," I lie. No need for him to know I'm on a break.

"Of course. I don't want to keep you. As long as you call every hour, we're all good."

I cut him off before he can say more.

Making it through the rest of the day without a scratch sounds almost impossible. The scratches I carry are so many, I might as well be a living, breathing, oozing, aching wound.

Before I can pull myself together, Thalia pokes her head around the door. The sounds of yelling kids in the hallway spill into the room before she closes it.

"Ready for lunch?"

Our eyes meet from across the room.

"Hey, Paige, are you okay?" As usual, she comes to perch on the edge of my desk. "You look like you've just seen a ghost."

I consider not telling her anything for fear of what she'll say, but my tears break through my resistance and trickle down my cheeks before I come up with a convincing lie.

Her brows are knitted when she slides of the desk and slings an arm around my shaking shoulders. "What happened?" Her hand moves to my hair, smoothing it down. "Did something happen with Ryan?"

"Everything in my life always has something to do with Ryan."

"Is he okay?"

"Yeah." A sarcastic laugh bursts from my lips. "He's doing great, actually. Having the time of his life making my life hell."

"What did he do this time?" Thalia goes to the door and locks it. Before she returns to my side, she grabs a chair from one of the desks and comes to sit next to me.

"So, tell me. I'm your friend, remember? You don't have to go through all this alone."

"I don't know how to do it anymore." Tears plop onto the papers on my desk. I shove them to the side before they get drenched. In a few words, I tell her what happened yesterday and watch as her chocolate eyes darken.

"That's unacceptable," she breathes, her jaw

tight. "You can't let him get away with this."

"Every time I stand up to him, he tells me I'm responsible for his injury. He reminds me every chance he gets that I put his life on pause."

"But he's the one who hung around with the wrong crowd. He was hurt by the people he chose to be friends with."

"That's what I keep telling him. But he doesn't see it that way. All he cares about is that I made a decision that landed him in a wheelchair."

"So he's going to spend the rest of his life punishing you?" Thalia blows out a loud breath. "Paige, if you don't do something about it now, it will never change."

"Every morning when I wake up, I tell myself this is the day things will be different. Then he goes and does something that shakes me." I lift my hands from my lap and drop them again. "What if he harms himself ... again?" Six months after Ryan was dismissed from hospital, he attempted suicide with the help of his pain meds. Fortunately, I found him in time to rush him to the emergency room.

"Do you really think he'll try to take his own life again just to prove a point?"

I press my fingertips into my temples. "I honestly don't know what to think anymore. I already feel guilty as it is. If he harms himself again, I won't be able to forgive myself."

"You'll just give up your whole life for him?"

"I already have." A sad smile taints my lips. "He has me in the palm of his hand, and I have no idea how to crawl out of it."

"You need to have a serious talk with him. Tell him if he doesn't stop terrorizing you, you'll send him to rehab. Frankly, I don't think that would be such a bad idea."

"He's my brother." I swipe a hand across my cheek. "Inside the monster I see every day is still my little brother. He's scared … crying out for help." I yank a tissue from the box on my desk and blow my nose. "And he's right. I made the decision that led to the shooting. If only I had given him the money."

Thalia shoots out of her chair and plants both hands on my shoulders. "But you've paid for that decision so many times over. He should be grateful that you've stuck by him this long."

I turn to face Thalia, her hands falling off my shoulders. "Trying to reason with Ryan is like pouring gasoline into a raging fire."

"And doing what he wants is setting *your* life on fire. One day you could wake up to find your life in ashes." She pauses. "How long do you think you can go on like this? You don't go out, don't date anyone, and all because of him. I'm sorry you don't want to hear this, but I think you should try harder to make him see sense."

"Easy for you to say. If you were in my shoes, you'd think differently." I peel my gaze from hers. "You don't understand. No one does."

Before our conversation can continue, someone knocks at the door. I wipe away the tears as Thalia goes to open it.

Holly Webber, one of my students, walks in. Her heavily made-up eyes glance at each of us in turn as she walks toward her desk in the back and picks up a cellphone. I avoid her gaze as she leaves the room.

Not long after Holly walks out, Thalia plants a kiss on my cheek and leaves as well.

Even though I'm doing my best to keep her words of advice from sinking in, they do. Maybe she's right, and I should try one more time. Something definitely needs to change or the stress will break me.

Determined to face Ryan again tonight, I leave work immediately after the staff meeting, but thanks to traffic, I make it home by six-thirty. The moment I step through the door, the hairs on the back of my neck bristle.

The air feels different on my skin, inside my lungs. Ryan has kept his promise. He must have.

He's not in the living room or the kitchen. Screaming out his name, I search the entire apartment and come to a screeching halt in the doorway of the bathroom.

He's lying under a tub full of water, in black shorts and a red t-shirt. His eyes are closed, arms floating at his sides.

Fear claws through me as I lunge for him, grabbing him by the shoulders out of the water. I consider opening the tub door, but that would flood the bathroom.

With surprising strength—the kind I never knew I possessed—I transfer him from the bath onto the tiled floor, next to his wheelchair.

I'm drenched and breathless as I call out his name and drop my head to his chest to listen for a heartbeat. I can barely hear anything through the sound of my own pounding heart. I feel for a pulse, but I'm not sure I detect one.

"Come on, Ryan. Can you hear me?" The palms of my hands push down on his chest. No reaction. My tears are dropping onto his face now, my jagged screams cutting through my throat.

I consider calling for help but my bag is in the other room. What if the seconds it would take for me to get it are all it takes for death to snatch him, if it hasn't already? Instead, I close his nose with my thumb and forefinger and lower my mouth to his, sharing my breath with him, praying I can bring him back.

"Don't you dare leave me, you hear?" I cry

harder. I glance behind me, still contemplating calling someone for help. When I turn back to him, my body goes cold.

His eyes are open wide, the twisted smirk I've come to know so well pasted on his face.

"Scared the hell out of you, didn't I?" He draws in a breath. "That's what happens when you don't listen to simple instructions. If you disobey me again next time, things could get much uglier than this little game."

CHAPTER 8

I'm just about done arranging some of the freshly-baked cupcakes in large containers when Ryan fills the kitchen doorway.

No sound comes from him as his gaze searches my face. Is he trying to read my mind?

Two weeks have crawled by and we've barely said a word to each other. The wall between us has hardened so much that it's almost impossible to reach him.

I never know what to say to him anymore, so I communicate with him only when it's absolutely necessary. Each morning before work, I greet him. If it's my lucky day, I receive a grunt in response. Then I remind him of his appointments and leave for work, breathing out in relief the moment I cross the threshold.

I've finally found and hired another physical therapist for him. Sandy Meiers was recommended by Margaret.

I was honest with Sandy from the start,

telling her that Ryan is depressed and can be difficult at times. I was relieved when Sandy assured me she'd dealt with many clients like Ryan.

Unlike Lin, however, she would only come to our place for the first session. Ryan has to drive himself to her practice after that. It might actually be a good idea for him to get out of the house more.

Seven months ago, I bought Ryan a secondhand, wheelchair-accessible minivan—a present for his birthday. My intention had been to give him a slice of his freedom back while freeing me from having to take time off work to drive him to his medical appointments.

Dan Summers, a seventy-year-old retired cop, renting an apartment on the second floor of our apartment building, sold the vehicle to me after his wife died of a heart attack. She had spent most of her life in a wheelchair after being involved in a car accident as a child.

Even though I had to take out a loan to buy the van from Dan, he sold it to me for less than he was asking for it. He received many requests from tenants interested in the van, but he chose me. Maybe it's because I water his plants and feed his cats when he's out of town, or because he was feeling sorry for me. Either way, I was ecstatic when he handed me the keys. Even more so when he spent a few days showing

Ryan how to drive the vehicle.

The day I presented the van to Ryan, I saw something resembling joy in his eyes, but the emotion was so fleeting, I decided I must have imagined it. He never once thanked me, not that it bothered me. What bothers me is that he hardly uses the van.

I had hoped he'd go out to meet people, to visit places he had enjoyed going to before the shooting. The only person he's interested in being around is me. His idea of fun is tormenting me.

I cover up the containers and put them in the fridge.

"Do you want one?" I ask when he won't stop staring. "I baked them for school but you can have some if you like."

He shakes his head, but barely.

I reach for a dishcloth and wipe my hands. "We have a fundraiser tomorrow afternoon to raise money for an orphanage in town. Family and friends are welcome. Want to come?"

The silence between us is broken only by the ticking of the clock above the door while Ryan works his mouth with no words coming out. "What time?" he finally asks.

A flicker of hope warms me from the inside. "It starts at one and ends around six. It would really be nice if you can come. Since your physical therapy is at eleven tomorrow—Sandy is coming over for your first session—you'll be able to make it to the fundraiser in time."

"What makes you think I'd want to come to your crappy fundraiser?" His pupils are like boiling pools of lava. "Your groveling sickens me." He wheels himself back out of the kitchen.

As I stand with feet glued to the floor, he returns. The darkness has returned to his features.

"You said I make you sick. So, what do you want from me?" I can't stifle the bite in my tone.

"Be home by six thirty tomorrow," he says in a commanding voice.

"No." The word exits my lips like a dart. "No, Ryan. You have no right to tell me what to do. I'm seriously tired of your mind games."

"Is that so? That's too bad because I'm just getting started." He runs a hand down one side of his face. "And by the way, tormenting you is much more fun than some boring fundraiser." He leaves again before I can respond.

I charge out of the kitchen, determined to continue the conversation, but he has locked the living room and the TV is blaring. Even if I shout, there's no way he'll hear me. Left with no option but to walk away, I squeeze my eyes shut, count to ten and switch the lights off as I head to my bedroom, barely glancing at the wall where a single photo of my broken family hangs.

A father who died in prison, a mother who, like her husband, found comfort at the bottom of a bottle and eventually death. And then there are my brother and me, the kids who carried the scars of their parents' decisions.

The picture was taken a week before Dad received a one-way ticket to prison for bank robbery and other felonies. Six months into his seven-year sentence, he was involved in a brawl that drove him to the grave.

I lock the door behind me and stand in the middle of my room, between the door and my bed, chest rising and falling as I take and release painful breaths.

What the hell can I do with Ryan? I'm seriously tempted to threaten him with throwing him out if he refuses to change his behavior. But the guilt would eat me alive.

But how can I just stand here watching my life crumbling before my eyes?

In the stillness between one beat of my heart and the next, the little voice inside my head gives me an answer that both gives me hope and terrifies me in equal measure.

If you really want things to change, only *you* can change them.

§

In the morning, as soon as Sandy arrives for

Ryan's physical therapy session, I exchange a few words with her and usher her to the living room.

She's a tall, middle-aged woman with a shock of ginger hair in a pixie cut, clad in gray and white yoga pants and a tank top that shows off her small, but athletic frame.

As we enter, my nose wrinkles at the smells of rotting food, dirty socks, alcohol, and body odor. I'd opened the windows and was about to clean up, but Sandy came half an hour earlier than planned. I would have cleaned up last night, but Ryan had not opened the door until I fell asleep.

"Sorry about the mess." I pick an empty plastic bottle of Coke from the floor.

The only area of the living room that's tidy is the path Ryan cut through the mess for his wheelchair to move, the path leading to the TV screen.

"That's all right." I'm both touched and horrified as she helps me clean up.

"You don't have to—"

"Don't worry. I'm used to it." She gives me a sympathetic smile that makes me feel worse. "I have a son whose hobby is to trash the living room."

"Thanks." I hide my shame with a smile.

"Anything I should know that you haven't already told me over the phone?" Sandy fishes a sock from underneath the couch and hands it to me.

"Yeah." I release a deep sigh. "He's not been in a great mood lately."

"Don't worry." She strides over to her bag, glancing at me over her shoulder. "I've handled worse."

Before we can finish our conversation, Ryan appears at the door. His dark gaze travels between Sandy and me and takes in the somewhat tidy living room. It returns to Sandy.

"Hey," he says to her and enters the room.

"Good morning, Ryan. It's nice to meet you." Sandy extends a hand toward him, which he ignores.

Wishing the ground could swallow me up, I move to the door. I clear my throat. "I'm afraid I can't stay. I have a fundraiser to attend at school."

"That's fine. Go ahead." Sandy gives me an assuring smile. "Ryan and I will be just fine."

I give a small nod and ignore the snorting sound coming from Ryan.

To calm my nerves, I take a long shower. As warm water bounces off my skin, I try not to think of Ryan floating in the bathtub only days ago—the fear I'd felt.

Today, I choose a different color from my usual shades of black. I often reach for black clothes automatically. Black makes me feel safe, hidden. But today I want to be seen, so I opt for a cornflower blue cocktail dress and complete the look with a pair of tan espadrilles.

For the first time in a long time, I put on some makeup—a pale pink lip gloss and mascara. I'm determined to feel good about myself.

Maybe if I look good on the outside, it'll reflect on the inside. It doesn't hurt to try. After the sleepless night I've had, I now realize that I've reached my breaking point. I'm tired of feeling bad every day, tired of feeling guilty, exhausted of walking on eggshells every time I'm around Ryan.

I step out of my bedroom, planning to slip out of the apartment before Ryan is done with his session. My blood runs cold when I find him in the dim hallway, a few inches from my door, a smirk on his face.

"What are you doing?" My eyebrows draw together in a frown. "Aren't you supposed to be—"

"I needed a break." He watches me through his hooded gaze. "Why are you all made up? Are you meeting someone? I thought you were going to a work thing."

Scraping up the courage to stand up to him, I plant my hands on my hips. "That's right. I'm going to the fundraiser event. And as a staff member, I have to look presentable." My gaze doesn't waver. "Do you have a problem with that?"

"I don't have a problem with you going to the stupid fundraiser. But I *will* have a problem with you meeting up with anyone." He sucks in air through his teeth. "You better not be lying to me."

There's no point in discussing anything with Ryan, so I walk past him, ignoring his presence as I get the cupcakes from the kitchen and leave the apartment, feigning a confidence I don't feel.

Inside my car, I pull in a few deep breaths. I force myself to remember the earlier feeling of excitement and the hope that had filled me minutes before I saw Ryan. Through the windshield, I look up at our apartment in time to see the curtain twitch. I don't need to see his face to know he's watching.

CHAPTER 9

Inside the staff bathroom, I hang up the phone and drop it into my bag. Then I meet my eyes in the mirror, gazing into them, forcing myself to look past the searing pain, in search of the brave woman I long to become.

"You're doing well, Paige. You're having fun." I allow a smile to sweep across my pink lips. It doesn't matter that I don't feel it inside.

The fundraiser has been in full swing for two hours now. The entire time I'd done my best not to think about Ryan, not to allow thoughts of this morning and last night to poison my mind.

The only times I thought about him was when I had to call him once an hour. I still wrestle with myself before giving him a call, the stubborn part of me daring me to ignore the impulse, only for the little voice inside to remind me of one of the things he did when I didn't obey his rules. This can't go on. I have to think of a solution to this quandary before it escalates to greater proportions. For now, the image of him inside the bathtub makes me pick up the phone.

I have another hour to banish him from my mind, to try and enjoy my time away from home.

The compliments I received for my new look from both my colleagues and the students have been overwhelming, and my cupcakes keep people coming back for more. To some extent, this has given me a boost of confidence in myself. The confidence Ryan does his best to crush every day.

When I exit the bathroom, my phone rings, the sound bouncing off the walls.

What does he want now?

I don't have time for this. I need to get to the assembly hall.

Isaac Baxter's son, Dylan, who has apparently been in town since his father's funeral, will be giving a speech in ten minutes.

Still walking, I scramble inside my large tote for the phone.

Before I can locate it, I crash into something. No, someone. My head snaps up.

My eyes lock with an intense emerald gaze. A warm, unfamiliar sensation spreads through my cheeks.

The stranger in front of me must be

somewhere in his mid-thirties. He has dark curly hair that tapers to the collar of his crisp white shirt. His jaw is strong and slightly square under the neatly-trimmed beard. He has the kind of looks that belong on a movie screen.

I can't help wondering if he's the father of one of the newer students. I don't recall seeing him around. By now, I've met most parents at least once.

"I'm so sorry, are you okay?" He places a warm hand on my shoulder, then seems to think twice about it. It falls back to his side. But the movement has released the scent of soap and warm woodsy cologne.

"No." I shake my head. "I'm sorry. I wasn't watching where I was going."

"No problem. You might want to get that." He glances at my bag with a slow smile that awakens dimples in his cheeks and makes his eyes crinkle at the corners.

"Yeah ... I ... I should. Bye."

As I walk away, still searching for my phone, the back of my neck tingles. He's watching me.

I keep walking.

Before I exit the hallway, I finally locate the phone. "We just talked," I say to Ryan. "What is it now?"

"I'm aware of that." He pauses. "Bring me Chinese food when you come home."

"Absolutely not." I shove open the wooden

door to the assembly hall. "There's frozen lasagna in the fridge. Pop it into the oven. You know how it works." I hang up before he can say anything else.

Inside the hall, I take my place next to Thalia as usual. Margaret is on the stage, informing the audience that Mr. Dylan Baxter will be a few minutes late. The shuffling of feet, an occasional cough, and whispers fill the hall along with the ticking of the large clock on the front wall above a large painting of Isaac Baxter.

Five minutes later, Dylan Baxter arrives, smiling as he appears next to her, shaking her hand. The way she's beaming up at him, he could have been the president.

My heart jolts at the sight of Dylan Baxter. He's the man from the hallway. No wonder I haven't seen him before. This is a small town. There's no way somebody that handsome would walk around without causing a wave of gossip to sweep through town.

"Gorgeous, isn't he?" Thalia says with a sigh.

I respond with only a nod then return to staring at Dylan who, if I'm not mistaken, is also staring at me from across the room.

He finally clears his throat and peels his gaze from mine. "Good afternoon, students, staff members, and parents of Baxter Junior High. It's an honor to be among you today and to witness the dedication you have toward making a difference in this town. When I heard about this fundraiser, I knew I had to be present. I felt it would be the perfect opportunity for me to introduce myself to you." His smile falters. "My father loved this school. He often said it was one of his greatest accomplishments." Dylan's eyes flicker in my direction again before returning to the room as a whole. "If it's any comfort, I would like to assure all of you that even though he is no longer with us, nothing will change. My hope is that BJHS will remain a cornerstone of this town." He moves on to praise Margaret as well as the teaching staff, then finally, he presents a check with many zeros, a gift from the Baxter Foundation, to be added to the money raised today.

Once he walks off the stage, I release a breath I didn't know I was holding. The relief of hearing that my job is safe rushes through me.

After the applause dies down, we're asked to return to our stands and continue to sell our products. With only ten of my cupcakes left, it won't be long before they're all gone.

I'm arranging them on the tray to make them more visibly appealing when the air around me shifts. I look up, and there Dylan is. This time as well, my body reacts.

"Hey there, nice to see you again." He

glances at the cupcakes. "Those look delicious. Did you bake them yourself?"

"I ... Yes, yes, I did." I glance at the cupcakes. "Would you like to have one?"

A smile curls the corners of his lips, causing a dimple to flutter in one of his cheeks. "I'd love one." He rolls up the sleeves of his shirt and loosens his midnight blue tie. "May I?" His hand hovers over the cupcakes.

"Of course." Being in the presence of someone who has the power to impact our livelihoods makes it hard to breathe. "Have two ... if you like."

"How much?" He bites into the cupcake he picked.

"Hmmm ... nothing." I run the palms of my hands over my dress, wiping away the sweat. "I mean, they're free for you."

He doesn't say anything for a long time. As he finishes up the cupcake, his eyes are on my face. Behind him, two people are lining up for their turn, and others are walking by, staring at us.

"These are fantastic," he says finally, and my shoulders sag with relief. He picks up a napkin next to my pitcher of lemonade. "They're too delicious to be free." He reaches into his back pocket and pulls out his wallet. He removes a hundred-dollar bill and hands it to me.

My mouth drops open. "I can't take that. A

cupcake costs two dollars. That's way too much."

"They're worth more than that. I'm paying for their true worth." He flashes his very straight, very white teeth at me. "Go ahead, take it. It's for the kids."

"For the kids." I stifle a giggle. "Thank you, I guess. Do you want another? On the house, this time?"

"No, I'm good." He leans slightly forward and on reflex I lean back. "I'd like your number, though. I wanted to ask for it in the hallway, but you went away too fast."

"My number?" Heat floods my cheeks.

"Yes." He narrows his eyes. "You *do* have one, don't you?"

"No." I twirl a strand of hair around my finger. "I mean, yes, I have one. But you can't have it."

"That's rather honest." A quiet smile plays on his lips. "I have to say it's refreshing." The people behind him melt away to move on to other stands. I can only imagine what they're saying to each other about me and the billionaire heir.

"Why? Are you not used to women saying no to you?" I place a hand on my lips, the heat in my cheeks exploding into flames. "I'm sorry. I shouldn't have said that." What's wrong with me?

"I like it. People are way too careful around me." He pushes his hands into his pockets. "I'd really love to continue this conversation over coffee."

"I don't drink coffee." It's amazing how this man manages to pull me right out of my comfort zone. He's a billionaire and I'm talking to him like someone I've known for a long time.

"I'm sure we can find something you enjoy the taste of."

"Maybe." I looked to my side and notice Thalia staring at us, her hands clasped in front of her, face beaming. "But I don't go out for drinks with the boss."

He leans forward again and says in a loud whisper so I can catch the words over the sound of country music that just started playing. "I'm not your boss. Margaret is. Just think of me as any ordinary guy. That's what I am."

"That's not true. You're no ordinary guy. You're Isaac Baxter's son."

He straightens up again. A fleeting shadow crosses his handsome features.

"I guess I am. But I prefer to be called Dylan."

"Dylan, thank you for the invitation. But I can't go out for drinks with you."

"I'll be around here for a few more minutes. I'll come back to see if you've changed your mind." He gives me another dimpled grin and walks away, hands still in pockets as he moves on to a flower stand. The man oozes confidence.

As soon as he's swallowed by the throng of people, Thalia hurries to me.

"What did he say to you?" Her breath is coming in such quick gasps. She looks about to burst with curiosity. "You guys spoke for a while."

"He asked for my number." I shrug as though it's no big deal. "I actually saw him in the hallway earlier, before his speech."

"Your number?" Thalia places a hand on her heaving chest. "I hope you gave it to him. You did, right?"

"Of course, I didn't give it to him, Thalia. And you know why."

"No, actually I don't know why." She places a hand on one hip. "Stop using Ryan as an excuse not to live your life. You were just asked out by a drop dead gorgeous billionaire and you said no. Are you out of your mind?"

"Maybe I am." The moment I say the words, the hairs at the nape of my neck bristle.

My gaze drifts past Thalia to the entrance of the hall, and blood drains from my cheeks, leaving them cold.

Ryan is wheeling himself through the entrance, people making way to let him pass. As soon as he enters the hall, he wheels himself to one side and just stares at me. I would've been happy he came after all, but the look on his face tells me something is wrong.

When his gaze shifts from me to Dylan, I get it. Ryan must have been here for a while. He must have seen me talking to Dylan.

Thalia touches my shoulder. "Hey, what's up? You've gone all quiet. Are you okay?"

"I have no idea what okay means anymore."

CHAPTER 10

❦

A storm rages in Ryan's eyes when I approach him.

"Hey, you came."

He turns his face away and won't say a word to me.

The caring sister that I am, I leave to get him something to eat—a ham and tomato sandwich and a cold Coke. To my horror, he swings back his hand and brings it crashing against mine, the one that holds the Coke. The can drops to the floor with a bang and explodes, sending foam and dark liquid flying in all directions.

If we weren't in public, I would've smacked him.

Tears clogging my throat, I avoid the looks of both pity and disdain coming from all directions as Thalia helps me clean up the sticky liquid.

My gaze sweeps the hall for Dylan Baxter. I hope he didn't see what happened.

Thalia leans into me and whispers that she saw him and Margaret exit the hall a few seconds before Ryan lashed out.

After the cleanup, I leave Ryan sitting there and get back to my stand to finish selling the cupcakes. My shoulders are stiff with tension, pain flaring between my shoulder blades, but I'm determined to do my job.

It hurts like hell that he made the effort to come all this way only to embarrass me in front of everyone. My instinct urges me to pack up my things, to get out of here. Since it's exactly what Ryan wants, I do the opposite. He doesn't leave, just sits there by the door, eyes on me.

Thankfully, Dylan doesn't show up again at my stand as he had said he would. Maybe he figured I might not be worth the effort. I'm sure he has enough ladies vying for his attention—women with no baggage.

Once the event is over, Margaret thanks us for coming, announces the amount collected, and wishes us a nice evening.

Ignoring Ryan, I walk past him to take my things to my car. His presence is suffocating as he follows me outside. Saying nothing to me, he wheels himself to his van and enters with the help of the automatic ramp. He drives off without a backward glance.

When I arrive at the apartment, his van is already parked outside. As I enter our home, every bone in my body warns me this evening will not be pretty, that we've reached the point of no return.

Even though I dread the ugly conversation we'll have, I remember the words my inner voice whispered to me yesterday, that I have the power to change things. Continuing to show Ryan my weakness only strengthens him to the point he might do worse things.

What if he becomes a danger both to me and himself? It has to end. I need to breathe again, and he doesn't let me do that. He's determined to suffocate me under the blanket of guilt that hovers over me. If I choose to look the other way today, I don't think I'll ever find the strength to try again.

I find him in the entrance area next to the coat rack. He doesn't give me a moment to breathe before turning on me. "Who was the man you were talking to?" His sharp voice stabs the air in the room.

"I talk to a lot of men, Ryan." I walk past him to the kitchen to pack away the groceries I picked up on the way home. I need to think about what to say to him, but he follows me. Instead of lifting the milk, dishwashing liquid, and sugar from the grocery bag, I stand with my back to him and jump right into the conversation that I know will change everything. "It's none of your business who I talk to. But if you really must know, the man I was talking to was Isaac Baxter's son."

"Why did he talk to you as though he knows you?"

"Why he was kind to me, you mean?" When I find the courage to face him, I'm numb with rage, my breath hot inside my throat. "It must have been a shock for you to see that not everyone treats me like crap the way you do!"

His gaze doesn't flicker. "I wish they would. You deserve to be treated like the piece of crap you are."

I take a few steps closer to him and lower myself to his level. Someone has shown me kindness today and all my brother can say is I deserve to be treated badly? Instead of making me feel small, his statement only fuels the fire inside me. "You no longer scare me," I whisper. "I'm no longer going to put my life on hold just so you can feel good about yourself. I don't care if you hate me. I refuse to hate myself. Whether you like it or not, there *are* people out there who care about me. If I want to talk to any man, I will. If I want to date someone, you can't stop me. I'm no longer your prisoner."

"Are you sure about that?" A greasy lock of hair sweeps his forehead when he dips his head to the side. "Have you forgotten what happens when you betray me?"

"Of course not." I wrap my fear in a blanket

of fury. "How could I, when you went above and beyond to scare me?"

"As I said before, that was nothing." He runs the palms of his hands on his thighs. "I warned you before and I'm warning you now. Betray me again and you'll find out what I'm capable of." The spittle foaming at the corners of his mouth makes my stomach roll.

"Well, looks like you better get started on coming up with something even worse. Give it your best shot." I move back to the kitchen counter. "Do whatever you want, Ryan. I don't give a damn anymore." My ears pound as fireworks go off inside my head. "I've done everything I could for you. If you don't want to live your own life, that's your business. But I'll no longer let you put mine on hold." I pause for effect. "I'm done apologizing for that night, even when I'm not the only one responsible for what happened. What happened to you was just a ripple effect of your poor decisions. I won't play your games anymore." I pull the carton of milk from the grocery bag and yank the fridge open. "What you did today, embarrassing me at my place of work, was the last straw. That's the job that puts food on the table, the job that pays the bills ... your medical bills. The fact that you don't see that is disturbing. So, I'm done trying with you. I did enough, don't you think?"

"That sounds like a threat," he croaks. "Are you threatening to throw me out?"

"No." I turn on him. "I'm not that cruel. You're still my brother even when you don't act like it. You can stay here, but from today, your stupid rules no longer apply. From this moment on, I make the rules. I will go to work in the morning and I will return home at a time that pleases me. If I come home late, you will not ask me who I was with because it's frankly none of your business. If I cook something, you either eat it or you starve. It's your stomach and you can treat it any way you like. And if you're not interested in physical therapy, please tell me so. I'd be happy to have something less to pay for."

I walk over to the sink and start washing the containers that had carried the cupcakes. The moment I turn on the water, something crashes against the back of my legs. I grab the edge of the counter so I don't lose my balance.

I whirl around in time to see Ryan backing up. Before I can digest what he's doing, he barrels into me again.

Pain explodes in my shin when the bone connects with the metal of his wheelchair. I jump away before he can hurt me again, limp out of the kitchen and out the front door.

As the front door crashes against the frame, my brother's guttural roar of anger and frustration breaks through the walls and echoes in the hallway. Despite the throb of pain in my leg, a heady rush of victory spurts through my entire body. It's done. I've finally touched a nerve. Every fiber of my being tells me I'm free. I feel so good I don't even feel the pain in my leg.

CHAPTER 11

∽

My hands tighten around the steering wheel. I'm both excited and terrified about what just happened.

There's a high possibility it could all blow up in my face, that I could end up regretting yet another decision I've made concerning Ryan.

The urge to get out of the car and go back into the apartment to apologize to him burns through my body, but I can't do that. I've done everything I could for him. It's time he starts treating me with respect. It's time I treat myself with respect, as well.

I rest my head on the steering wheel, feeling the sweat between the leather and my skin. Then I take a deep breath, raise my head, and lean it against the headrest. Time to move forward, to be strong for both Ryan and me. The longer I baby him, the longer we both remain stuck and unhappy.

I turn the key in the ignition, and the car

grunts to life, its energy vibrating right through my body, giving me the strength I need to move forward. As the car moves, so do I, pulling away from my troubles.

I drive back to the grocery store. For a few minutes, I sit and stare at the large building with its floor-to-ceiling windows. I watch people going in and coming out, some accompanied by friends and family, others alone. Happy people laughing and talking, living their lives.

I get out of the car and a gust of wind whips my hair from one side of my shoulders to my back. I face in the direction it's coming from and close my eyes, allow it to soothe me, to dry the sheen of sweat on my skin.

Inside the air-conditioned store, I limp down the aisles, headed for the snacks aisle. I grab two bags of salt and vinegar potato chips and a box of chocolate chip cookies.

Before leaving the aisle, I grab more snacks and head to the cash register.

An old lady with only one item—a bottle of sparkling water—taps my shoulder and asks if she can go first. I let her. I'm in no hurry to get anywhere.

Five minutes later, I'm in my car with the radio blasting, on my way to the edge of town where Thalia lives in a quaint little cottage she inherited from her grandfather six years ago.

My phone rings. The number is

unrecognizable.

Conditioned to react with fear each time the phone rings, anxiety spurts through me.

What if it's someone calling to tell me something happened to Ryan? What if it's the hospital or the police? What if he burned down the apartment building? All kinds of thoughts scramble for space inside my brain. Should I ignore the call or pick up? What if he's testing me?

I decide to answer, but I'm ready to put him in his place if he resorts to his manipulation tactics again. I turn on the speaker.

"Hello?"

"Is this Paige Wilson?"

The voice sounds both familiar and foreign at the same time.

"Yes, this is Paige." My breath quickens. "Can I help you?"

"Paige, hi. This is Dylan Baxter. We met at—"

"Dylan." My shoulders slump with relief. "Hi." I shake my head. "How did you get my number? And how do you know my name?"

"In a town of barely eleven thousand residents, it's pretty easy to get information."

"And you're a powerful man who gets what he wants, am I right?" Without meaning to, I find myself laughing. "So, Dylan, why are you calling?" My heart flutters inside my chest like a bird trapped inside a cage.

"I still want to take you out for that drink … or dinner. Whatever you'd like."

The fact that he has gone to the trouble to get in touch with me must mean he really likes me, but I have no idea how to feel about that. It's been a while since I dated anyone. In fact, I haven't dated since Ryan's accident. Ryan made sure of it.

I nibble on a corner of my lip. "Look, Dylan. Right now, my answer is no. I can't tell you if it will be different tomorrow, but at the moment I can't have a drink with you. I'm sorry."

"Then it helps that I happen to be a very patient man." He pauses. "And you were right. I usually get what I want. Believe me, Paige Wilson, sooner or later, I'll have that coffee with you."

I stifle a smile. "I told you I don't drink coffee."

"Dinner, then."

"I guess we'll have to see about that." I turn onto another street, into a more affluent part of town with expensive, pastel-colored cottages on one side and the beach on the other. Some of the cottage owners are walking their dogs under the trees lining the road, soaking up the last of the day's sun.

"I'll give you a call again tomorrow," he says. "Let's hope you've changed your mind by then."

"I can't guarantee it." My smile widens as I enter Thalia's street.

"We'll see. Goodbye for now, Paige Wilson."

By the time we hang up, I'm in front of Thalia's cottage. A cute, whitewashed house with powder blue shutters and a small well-tended garden. Thalia loves gardening and it's evident in the health and beauty of the lush leaves and blooms around her home.

A pebble mosaic garden path—created by Thalia herself—cuts through it to a front door the same color as the shutters.

The door flies open before I get to it.

She stands at the top of her front steps, hands on her hips. "What a wonderful surprise. Please tell I'm not dreaming. Is that really Paige Wilson?" She runs down the path to meet me, engulfing me in a hug of soothing coconut.

The contact with someone who cares for me brings me to tears. I clamp my lips to control the tortured sobs, but they tear right through me.

Thalia pulls back and searches my face. "Did something happen?"

I smile behind my tears. My hands grip hers. "Yes. Something huge. I—"

"Come on, tell me everything inside. We don't want to give the neighbors something to talk about." She links her arm with mine.

When I enter the cottage, I notice she'd done a little renovating since the last time I was at her place. The walls are painted in a soft peach, and her grandfather's old furniture has been replaced by vintage pieces. Thalia loves all things vintage. Still holding my arm, she takes me out onto the terrace that overlooks the sea.

"I'll get you a drink." She disappears back into the house and I lower myself into one of the white porch swings, listening to the sounds of crashing waves. The sea breeze is still warm and I love the way it strokes my face, drying the tears.

"You have no idea how happy I am to see you," Thalia says when she returns, a silver tray in her hands. "I don't remember the last time you came over."

"And it's all my fault. I'm sorry." I accept the iced tea she hands me, my fingers curling around the cold glass. I raise it to my lips and take a sip. The thin lemon slice taps my upper lip.

Thalia prides herself on making the best homemade iced tea in Corlake, and I agree. I take my time to savor the gentle sweetness on my tongue.

She sits next to me with her own glass, twisting her body to face me. "Okay, talk to me."

"I did it. I stood up to Ryan once and for

all." I lower my glass to my thigh. "I just snapped."

"What did you say to him?" A frown touches her brow. "I hope you gave him a piece of your mind. What he did to you today is unforgivable."

"I did. He went too far this time. I couldn't overlook it." I take another sip. "I didn't have any more space to move under his thumb. So I squirmed out."

"About time. How did he take it?" Thalia turns to face the ocean while twirling one of her thin braids around her finger.

"I told him I've had enough. This time I meant it. I have a feeling he felt it, too." While I finish my iced tea, I replay to Thalia exactly what happened, ending with how he crashed into me with his wheelchair.

"Oh my God." She glances at my legs in horror.

"Don't worry, it's not that bad. It was painful in the moment, but not anymore."

"Do you think he's dangerous, Paige?"

"I don't know. I don't think so. What can I say? He's my brother."

"Paige, are you sure about that? That he's not dangerous? He did some pretty disturbing things over the past two years."

"I know." I lift my shoulders in a half shrug. "But there's no way I'm going to throw him out. If it weren't for his drinking, he'd be perfectly capable of living on his own. But I can't turn my back on him ... not in that way."

"You're a better person than I could ever be." Thalia pulls her feet up onto the swing. "You know I admire you for your loyalty to your brother, but please keep your eyes open. You have no idea how he'll react to you standing up for yourself. Crashing into you is pretty bad to me."

I nod and decide to change the subject. "Guess who called me on the way here."

"Ryan?"

"Nope." I can't help smiling. "Dylan Baxter."

"Nooo." Thalia turns to me with wide, brown eyes. "How did he get your number?"

"He said this is a small town. My guess is he got it from Margaret."

"Well," Thalia puts down her glass and leans toward me. "What did he say?"

"He called to ask me out again."

"Please, please, tell me you said yes." She drums her feet against the floor. "Tell me you didn't turn the billionaire down a second time."

"It doesn't matter to me that he's a billionaire. I'm just—I don't think I'm in the right place to let a man—any man—into my life now."

"I don't get why not. Don't you want to find

someone to spend the rest of your life with?"

"I already have someone to spend the rest of my life with." My fingers tighten around my glass. "When I think of the future, I see only Ryan and me."

"Ryan is a grown man. Maybe one day he'll pull himself together and decide to live his own life, to be more independent. Who knows, today could be the start of that."

"Maybe I'll change my mind tomorrow. I've made enough decisions for the day."

"I guess that's fair." Thalia reaches for my grocery bag, which I completely forgot about. "What have we here?" She brings out the box of cookies and rips it open. "I hope these are for me. If not, too late." She laughs and bites into a cookie. Crumbs fall onto her lap.

"Of course." I'm laughing as I reach into the bag for my chips. "You know what? I feel good. I'm a little scared, but the feeling of being free trumps everything else. I can finally breathe."

"I can't tell you how proud I am of you." She squeezes my hand. "Please, promise me not to go back."

"Back home?"

"No, back to the person I knew a couple of hours ago. I like this stronger version of you. Fight for yourself and your life. It might end up being good for both of you."

"Ryan made it clear he doesn't want me

dating anyone. I'm a little terrified of what he'd do if I go out with Dylan."

"Don't let him stand in your way. If you *do* decide to go out with Dylan, I'll help you." She shrugs. "I could drop by your apartment a few minutes after you leave, pretending to be looking for you."

I raise an eyebrow. "I don't see how that's supposed to help."

"He'll probably tell me you're not home, but instead of leaving, I'll insist on waiting for you to come home. While I'm there, I'll keep an eye on him and let you know if he does something scary."

"What did I do to deserve you? You're the best friend ever."

"I know I am." She beams at me. "No need to remind me of that."

Once the sun has set, we disappear into the cottage. She cooks us garlic roasted potatoes that are both crispy and tender. We enjoy them with sausages and green salad.

After dinner, we settle in front of the TV to watch a few episodes of *Friends*.

I leave her place shortly before midnight, wishing I didn't have to go.

I find Ryan outside our front door, gazing down the hallway at me. I'm about to fall right back into his trap, to show him my fear, but I hang on to Thalia's words.

Promise me not to go back.

I pull myself together and keep walking until I reach the door. He follows me into the apartment but says nothing. He's trying to intimidate me.

I'd be damned if I give him what he wants. As I get ready for bed, I hear a scratching sound outside my locked door.

He's out there, doing his best to frighten me, but I don't care. I'm done bending to his will.

CHAPTER 12

I'm up early on Sunday morning. I'm going to church today. It's been a while. My relationship with God is a complicated one. I could never understand why he didn't stop the bad things happening in my life.

Now I realize, he might have needed a little help from me. Attending church would also give me another chance to get out into the world, to prove to Ryan that things are not going back to the way they were.

I'm still excited by the changes I made yesterday, still strong. Even though at the back of my mind I'm praying Ryan hasn't done something stupid during the night, something to prove he still has power over me.

After my shower, I dry myself off, and gaze at my reflection in the mirror. A small smile dips a corner of my mouth. "You're doing great, Paige," I whisper. "Just keep going."

I'm worth it. My life is worth it. I can't let

anyone get in the way of me and my freedom ever again.

I rummage through my wardrobe for something that isn't black and find a pink floral vintage dress in the back, bought a year ago along with several other pieces that never had a chance to be worn.

Today, like yesterday, I put on a little makeup, brush my hair to a sheen, then step out of the room.

I expect to find Ryan at my door, but he isn't sitting in wait for me.

I'm surprised to find him in the kitchen, at the table, eating scrambled eggs and toast, a glass of orange juice close to one of his hands.

"Hi." I open the fridge and take out the orange juice. I don't care that no response comes my way. I pour myself a glass. The yellow stream of liquid hits the bottom of the glass. I follow its journey as it swirls upwards, racing toward the rim.

I drink it while watching him.

Something certainly changed. I can't remember the last time Ryan prepared food for himself.

Maybe I really *did* reach him this time.

His food gone, he drinks up the juice then leaves the kitchen, slamming the door behind him. I eat a quick bowl of cereal and leave the kitchen.

Before I leave the house, I stop by the living room door and shout over the sounds of gunshots.

"I'm going to church. See you later." From the surprised look on his face, one would think I told him I'm going to climb Mount Everest. But he says nothing.

I leave the apartment, more alive than ever before. In the car, I call Thalia to tell her that I'm okay. She had called several times while I was in the shower.

"Nothing has changed today, I hope."

"No way. The new Paige is here to stay." I start the car. "And guess what, Ryan made himself breakfast. Can you believe that?"

"That's a first."

"You can say that again."

"Do you think you got through to him, then?"

"I don't know. With him, I never know anything. There's no harm in hoping, though."

"What are you doing today? If you're free, we could spend the day on the beach to celebrate your freedom."

"A day on the beach sounds fantastic, but later. I'm actually going to church right now."

"Church? Since when do you attend church?"

"There are many things I've neglected over the past year. It's time to get them back."

"I like the sound of that."

"We could hit the beach later in the afternoon, if you're still free. How about we have a picnic on the sand?" I ask.

"Yeah, that would be great. Come to the beach near my place. It's less crowded. Call me when you're on your way."

"Sure."

§

Inside the cool interior of St. Peter's Catholic Church, I slide into the last pew.

My body is present, but my mind is scattered. I'd woken feeling confident and determined to live my life, but sudden thoughts of Ryan now cloud my mind. I tuck them into a dark corner and listen to the sermon. I sing and pray with the congregation, my earlier nervous energy melting away.

At the end of the service, I greet everyone who greets me on their way to the door, and stand so the lady next to me can get out, then I sit back down.

Once most of the people have trickled out, Father William, a stocky man with a shock of white hair and matching beard, notices me from the pulpit and approaches me. He welcomes me to the church, then leaves me to have my moment alone with God.

In the space between the beats of my heart, I utter a single prayer.

"God, if you're listening, please save Ryan from himself."

I remain in my seat for another fifteen minutes, enjoying the peace, listening to myself breathing. When I finally get up to leave, I feel ready to deal with any side of Ryan.

I return home to find him where I'd left him, in front of the TV, a pizza box on his lap, a bottle of gin between his knees. It's almost as if nothing had changed since I left, except for the pizza and the bottle of booze, of course. He doesn't acknowledge my presence and I don't strike up a conversation.

I head to my room, where I flop back onto the pillows, my high spirits still intact. It feels incredible to be inside my home, free from the fear of what Ryan might say or do.

I'm about to drift off to sleep when my phone vibrates. I forgot to crank up the volume after the church service.

"How was church?" Thalia asks.

"Amazing ... freeing in a way. I think I'll go more often."

"Great. Maybe I'll join you next time. When can we paint the beach red?"

"How about in an hour?"

"Wonderful. We still have some snacks left over from yesterday. I'll bring them along."

"And a good book. Bring me something from your library."

"Wait, you mean you won't be doing Sudoku puzzles?" She laughs.

"I'm choosing to take a break today."

"What genre are you interested in? Gritty or something sweet?"

"Something light." I've had enough darkness in my life. It's time to shine a light into my soul.

"I have to say, I'm really liking this new Paige."

"So. Am. I." A smile stretches across my lips. "See you later."

After the call, I save the number Dylan Baxter called me from yesterday and drop the phone next to me on the bed, link my hands behind my head and close my eyes.

When I reopen them, Ryan is in my doorway. I shudder at the thought that he opened my door without me even hearing him.

"What are you doing here?" I pull myself to a seated position.

"What does it look like? Watching you." He plants his hands on his knees.

"Don't do that," I say through gritted teeth. "Next time, knock."

"Quit telling me what to do." His voice is edged with steel. "You think you've got it all worked out, don't you?" He cracks a knuckle. "You think you're free of me?"

"I don't think. I *know* I'm free of you." My drowsy eyes don't waver as they meet his. "You have no control over me."

"You can't get rid of me that easily."

"That's never been my intention. You're my brother and I don't want to get rid of you. I just want to live my life."

"I'm sorry I'm such a burden." It's not an apology, it's a sarcastic statement, a weapon meant to inflict pain.

"You said that, not me."

"You don't need to say the words. It's written all over your ugly face."

I let out a stream of air. "Ryan, I'm not in the mood for a fight."

"Whatever." He moves his hands from his lap to the armrests of his wheelchair. "I just came to tell you that nothing around here has changed."

My hand grips the bedspread, forming a fist around the cotton fabric. "I ..."

"What's that? Something you'd like to tell me, Sis?"

"Yes. Get the hell out of my room."

"I'm not inside your room. I'm in the doorway, or have you suddenly gone blind?"

Heat flushes through my body and I slide off the bed and charge toward him.

I plant my hands over his large ones and push him into the hallway, then slam the door, lock it, and lean my back against it before sliding to the floor.

Tears burn the backs of my eyes, but I refuse to cry. That was a test. He wanted to see if I'm still as fragile as I used to be. The moment he detects my weakness, he'll strike.

I pull myself off the floor, grab my striped beach bag and toss everything I need into it: swim suit, towel, sunscreen lotion, my phone, tests that need grading, a Sudoku puzzle booklet, and pens. When I leave the room, Ryan is no longer in the hallway.

I walk out of the apartment without bothering to tell him where I'm going.

He may think things are still the same, but he's wrong. I've changed. There's no going back to yesterday, not for me.

The day on the beach with Thalia is invigorating. In between my dip in the ocean, I read half a chick-lit novel, do some puzzles, and take naps.

By the time I return home, exhausted but happy, the sun is just about to set. After a quick shower, I prepare two potato and sausage casseroles. One for dinner and one for freezing.

I eat alone in the kitchen. When Ryan is hungry, he knows where to find the food.

Halfway through my meal, he shows up. He says nothing. After a few minutes of glaring at me, he turns and leaves.

I go to bed early, but I'm jolted awake by water pouring over my body. I'm inside the shower in my pajamas with no idea how I got in. The water is fast changing from warm to hot by the second.

Panic courses through my body as I step out of the shower and grab a towel. I look into the steamy mirror at my face.

I *do* know how I got into the shower. It can only mean one thing. I'm sleepwalking again.

My sleepwalking episodes started in childhood. When things were hardest at home, I woke up in strange places around the house or garden.

The last episode was right after Ryan's accident.

Why now, when I've finally come to a place where I'm experiencing the kind of peace I've never felt before?

A shudder races through me as I peel off my wet clothes and wrap the towel around my body. I open the bathroom door and freeze. My room looks as though it was hit by a tornado.

Clothes are everywhere, bed covers on the floor, bedside lamps lying on their sides, torn papers scattered on the floor. A total mess.

I'm holding my breath as I take cautious steps into the room, turn to the door. It's wide open. How's that possible? I swear I locked it last night.

As I continue to stare through the doorway, I hear a squeaking sound and then Ryan wheels himself past, a creepy smile on his face.

Does he have a spare key to my room?

CHAPTER 13

I wake up an hour earlier than planned and spend the time straightening out my room. I'd been too weakened by shock last night to do anything but lie on my bed, staring up at the ceiling in a daze.

My temples throb with rage as I gather the torn papers, and piece some of them back together as best I can.

Ryan reminded me last night that he's out to ruin me, but the fear of being stuck in a life I don't want is greater than the fear of him.

Still blinded by fury, I move from one corner of the room to another, gathering shoes, bags, and other belongings, returning everything to its usual place.

Today is a new day, another day for me to prove to him that he doesn't get me back, that he doesn't get to win.

When everything that's not broken is back in its place, I get ready for work, and leave the apartment without confronting him. I get to school a few minutes before six.

Instead of dwelling on what happened last night or what Ryan will do next, I throw the windows open and settle at my desk.

I pull out my phone. I find Dylan Baxter's number and give him a call. He called while I was in church yesterday, but I didn't hear the call as the phone was on silent.

"What a great way to start the week," he says.

"Dylan, I'm sorry I missed your call yesterday. Do you still want to have that drink?"

"Sure. I take it your answer has changed."

"I think ... yes." I smile. "Yes, it has."

"How soon? The sooner, the better for me. We've already wasted a couple of hours, don't you think?"

"You're really pushy, aren't you?" I shake my head.

"I'm a businessman." His laughter fills my ear, deep, warm, and smooth like honey. "This kind of skill gets me far in business and in my personal life."

I glance at the calendar standing at one corner of my desk. "I can do tomorrow evening."

"I'd very much prefer tonight." He pauses. "Unless you're extremely busy, of course."

I lift my shoulders and allow them to fall.

"Fine, you win. Let's meet tonight."

"Lacey's Place at eight? That work for you?"

"Yes, that's fine." Lacey's Place is one of the more exclusive restaurants in town. I can't afford anything expensive, but I have to get myself something fancy to wear. I'm short on cash, but I deserve a gift to celebrate the new me.

We end the call and I pull the gift card from my bag, the one Thalia gave me for my birthday. It's time to use it.

The school day goes by in a blur. By the end of it, I'm exhausted but also excited about the evening.

Thalia walks into my classroom just as the last kid leaves, and eyes me suspiciously. "I hope you haven't changed your mind." She looks great in a canary yellow linen dress suit that makes her rich skin glow.

"Not a chance." I gather up some papers from my desk and slide them into a folder. "I'm ready if you are."

"Perfect. Where do you feel like going first?"

"Let's go shopping." I push back my chair and grab my bag.

We end up spending too much time shopping for the perfect dress because Thalia rejects all my choices, pushing me to get something a little sexier. In the end, we both agree on a brown and cream chiffon peplum dress in a length that makes my legs look longer than they actually are. Since it's on sale, I spend way less than I thought I would.

The next stop is The Goddess Parlor, where thanks to Thalia's gift, I'm treated to a facial, a manicure and pedicure as well as a hairdo.

"Wow," Thalia breathes, putting aside the gardening magazine that she had been reading while she waited for me. "I can hardly recognize you. Those highlights sure do bring your hair to life."

"I agree." A smile spreads across my face as I do a little twirl, my new vibrant hair sweeping in soft curls across the tips of my shoulders. The pearl blonde highlights make my hair look rich and striking.

Thalia gets to her feet and approaches me, making a circle around me. "How do you feel inside?"

"Renewed. I can't believe I never took advantage of your gifts before."

"There's always a first time. Let's get out of here; you've got a date to prepare for." She had proposed that I get dressed at her place so as not to get attacked by Ryan, but even though he tried to scare me last night, I'm not going to tiptoe around him.

Outside The Goddess Parlor, I open my car door and turn to Thalia. "Are you really sure you want to come over after I leave? You don't have to."

I didn't tell Thalia what Ryan did last night, because I don't want her to be too worried about me. But it makes me uncomfortable to think of her in Ryan's presence. What if he's really more dangerous than I think?

"I don't mind. I don't have anything important to do tonight anyway. And if keeping an eye on Ryan helps you focus on your date, I'm happy to do it. Don't worry about me. Concentrate on having fun tonight. Dylan seems to really like you. Give him a fair chance."

"I'll do my best." I give her a quick hug and get into the car. "I'll call you when I leave the apartment."

§

Before coming to Lacey's Place, I did a little research. Turns out, it's one of the many businesses the Baxters own, and it's named after Dylan's mother.

There were quite a few times I'd walked past the restaurant, pretending not to peer through the floor-to-ceiling windows at the glittering chandeliers inside, the tables draped in mint green, scalloped-edge linen cloths topped with floral centerpieces.

Never in my wildest dreams would I have thought I'd dine in a place like this.

My stomach rolls with nerves as I step

through the glass doors, but I refuse to let my discomfort show. I push my shoulders back and hold my chin up.

Of all the girls in this town, Dylan Baxter chose me to have dinner with.

"Do you have a reservation, Miss?" Even though she's trying to be discreet, I can feel the eyes of the waitress giving me a once-over, judging without even knowing me.

My skin tingles from her penetrating gaze, but I force myself to remember my confidence.

"I'm meeting Mr. Dylan Baxter for dinner. Is he already here?"

The woman's hard demeanor softens. "Yes, yes, of course, you must be Miss Wilson." She moves out of my way. "He's already here waiting for you. Let me take you to your table."

Eyes are on me as we weave our way through the elegant round tables, and I do my best not to look tense.

Even though my dress had looked extravagant in the boutique, a quick look at what the other diners are wearing makes me feel underdressed. But I have something they don't. I have a date with the boss.

We finally arrive at a secluded table in a closed-off room at the back of the restaurant, where we find Dylan on the phone. As soon as he sees me, he hangs up and rises from the table.

"Here you are, Miss. May I bring you something to drink?" She hands me a leather-bound menu with Lacey's Place embossed into the skin in gold lettering.

"Not yet." I breathe in and glance at Dylan. The scents of burning candles, fresh flowers, and his cologne are calming.

"We'll let you know once we decide," Dylan says.

"Yes, sir." The waitress gives a small nod and leaves.

"You look beautiful, Paige. Your hair is lovely." He kisses me on both cheeks, his lips hot on my skin. "Thank you for meeting me tonight." He pulls out a cushioned chair for me, then takes a seat, studying my face through the dancing flames of the candlelight. "I wanted to see you before I go back to New York tomorrow."

I smooth my napkin over my lap and lean forward. "I thought you planned to stay for a couple more weeks."

"Where did you hear that from?" He leans back in his chair, an amused expression on his face.

"You happen to be a superstar in Corlake, Mr. Baxter. And this is a small town, as we both know."

"What else do you know about me, Miss Wilson?" The light from the candles reflects in

121

his green eyes.

"Not much." I avert my gaze, focus instead on an abstract painting on the wall behind him. Even though I agreed to have dinner with him, I'm still not sure whether I'm interested in taking things further than tonight. My life is still a mess.

"In that case, is there anything else you want to know about me?"

"I can't think of anything off the top of my head." Our eyes lock again and my senses leap to life.

There's no denying the fact that he fascinates me, but asking questions about him would give him the impression I care more than I want to. It could lead to him asking me out on more dates.

"All right, then. Let's order something to drink. How about champagne to celebrate this wonderful evening?"

My chest tightens. "Sorry, I don't drink alcohol."

He gives me a crooked smile. "You don't drink coffee and you don't drink alcohol; what do you drink?"

"Everything else." Since it's our first dinner, there's no need for me to explain why I don't drink alcohol. It would open up a can of worms I'd rather keep shut for one evening.

Asking no further questions, he calls for the

waitress, and since I'm unable to decide which of the non-alcoholic expensive drinks to choose, he orders me a glass of pomegranate juice and a white wine for himself.

While the waitress gets our drinks, I'm relieved when Dylan moves our conversation to the town of Corlake and BJHS. I find myself starting to relax, but once the drinks arrive and the waitress disappears, he leans forward.

"Tell me more about yourself."

I take a gulp of my juice and avert my gaze. "I hate to disappoint you, but I'm not as interesting as you might think."

"There's something interesting about every person." He reaches out and his fingers curve under my chin, raising my face to meet his intense gaze. His touch is cool and smooth against my skin. "Tell me what's hiding behind that gorgeous face?"

My pulse skitters as I move my head back a fraction. He gets the message and lowers his hand to the table.

"Sorry about that. I got carried away." He tilts his head to the side. "I just feel so comfortable around you."

I don't tell him that I feel the same way and that it scares the hell out of me.

"Did you spend most of your life in Corlake?" He takes a drink of wine.

"Yes," I say. "I've never lived anywhere

else." Before he digs deeper into my life, I change lanes. "I'm sorry about your father."

"Thank you." He pauses. "Was that your brother? The one who came to the fundraiser?" His voice is low, cautious.

A heavy feeling settles in my stomach like a brick. He was in the hall during Ryan's visit? Did he stay long enough to see the scene Ryan made? I swallow hard. "He ... yes. My brother, Ryan."

Dylan nods, but his eyes are still filled with too many questions—questions I'm not sure I want to answer. "You care for him all on your own?"

I nod.

This man is asking questions, but I get the feeling he has most of the answers already. To ask me that, he must know that my parents are dead and that I have no other family members aside from Ryan.

He rakes a hand through his wavy hair. "That's incredible."

"Incredible?"

"Not many people would be willing to take on the job of caring for a paralyzed sibling."

"You sound like you know quite a bit about me?" I drain my glass.

"People talk a lot around here." He finishes his wine. "I think you're amazing for what you do for your brother."

I fold and unfold my napkin, then smooth it on my lap. "It's hard sometimes."

"I can only imagine. I saw what he did at the fundraising event. And still you don't turn your back on him."

Guilt gnaws at my insides. "Of course not. He's my family." I raise my eyes to his face. "And you? How are you coping after your father's death?"

"You're changing the subject again, aren't you?" A dimple flutters in his cheek as he smiles. "But that's fine. I understand how uncomfortable talking about your brother must be."

"I'm curious about you; that's all." I came here to forget about my life for a while. Discussing Ryan would only taint the evening.

"I'm managing fine." His voice is lower, a few shades darker than before. "My dad and I weren't particularly close."

"Why not?" I frown, curiosity swirling in my belly.

"My father loved this town. You may not believe this, but that trip to Greece was the only time he left Corlake. Ironic, isn't it?"

"Yes." Dylan's father was a wealthy man but when you walked past him on the street, you'd never know it. He lived in a villa, but he never deliberately flaunted his wealth in any way, never drove cars or wore clothes that made him stand out.

"He wanted me to share the same love, to move here and work by his side, but I'm a big city kind of guy. Even as a child, Corlake was too small for me." He releases a sharp breath. "When my parents divorced—I was ten—I followed my mom to New York without hesitation. My mother shared my love for traveling. Unlike my father, I wanted to see the world, to spread my wings. You know what I mean?"

"I do." The idea of flying around the world, seeing new, exciting places sends adrenaline coursing through me in spurts. But because of Ryan, leaving town had never been an option.

"I know you're renting one of the Baxter apartments," he says, causing me to tense up again. "Are you happy there?" He glances past my shoulders. "Hold that thought. Let's order some food first, then we can talk some more."

This time, too, I allow him to order for both of us. He chooses filet mignon with balsamic glaze and creamy Caesar salad with torn croutons. The food is mouthwatering and my tongue agrees. My stomach, on the other hand, refuses to settle during the meal. I know he'll soon get back to talking about me living in his apartment building.

If he knows that I'm one of his tenants, does he know that I'm behind on my rent?

"Back to my question." He slices into his meat. "Are you happy in the building?"

"I am." My gaze drops to my food. "Very much so. It's very wheelchair friendly."

"I'm glad to hear that." He's quiet for a long time as he chews. Then he puts down his knife and fork and dabs his lips with his napkin. "I haven't known you for long, Paige Wilson, but I think you're a good person. If you ever need anything, just ask."

"I appreciate that, but I can't ..." My voice drifts off. How could I ask someone I've only known for a couple of days to share my burdens? Why would he help a woman he's just met anyway?

"Why not?"

My phone vibrates inside my bag before I can respond. As I pull it out, dread locks me in a vice.

My eyes flutter to Dylan's face and then back to the phone. "Sorry, I have to take this."

"Sure. Go ahead." He picks up his fork again.

I rise and step away from the table, headed for the ladies' room. The vibrating has stopped so I call Thalia back. "Tell me everything is all right." I enter one of the cubicles, close the door and sit on the closed toilet seat.

"No." She sighs. "I'm sorry, honey. I really wanted to help you, but—"

"What happened, Thalia?" I pinch the bridge of my nose.

"Your brother, he's deeply troubled."

"Did he do something to you?"

"He threw a bottle of alcohol at me and threatened me with a knife when I refused to leave." She pauses. "I think he knows why I came over."

"He threatened you with a knife?" I feel the blood drain from my face.

"I know he's your brother, but he's dangerous, Paige. You should have seen the look in his eyes."

"I'm so sorry, Thalia. Please ... please go home."

When I return to Dylan, tears are coating my eyes. I blink them away before he sees them.

"Everything okay?" A frown appears between Dylan's brows.

I glance at my unfinished food, but don't sit back in my chair. "Dylan, this was nice, but I need to get home."

"Is it your brother?"

"Yes." I reach for my handbag and meet his gaze head-on. "I'm sorry to leave you hanging, but I have to be honest with you. I'm not at a place where I can date." Better to put all the cards on the table. I wouldn't want him to think he has a chance with me. "My life is a bit of a mess right now."

"Anything I can do to help?"

"No." I raise a hand when he starts to get up. "It's nothing I can't handle alone. But thanks."

He sits back down. "I'd really love to see you again. I love talking to you." He pauses. "I'll be leaving for New York tomorrow, but I'll be back in a week. You have my number. Let me know if you need anything. While I'm away, think about whether you'd like to have dinner with me again so we can finish what we started."

"At the moment, I can't promise you anything," I say and walk out of the restaurant.

CHAPTER 14

When I get home, I stand at the front door, hands clenched tight at my sides. I'm afraid of what I might find on the other side. When I climbed out of the car a few minutes ago, I'd peered up at the living room window but saw no light on. I doubt Ryan is sleeping though.

I force my hand to be still as I insert the key into the lock and turn it. My heart jolts when I hear the familiar click. Teeth clenched, I push the door open, ready for war.

I'm surprised not to find him in the living room. It looks the way it always does, a complete mess, but the TV is off tonight. What's he up to?

My next stop is his bedroom. I take a breath before pushing his door open. Seeing inside his bedroom chills me every time.

Last year, he decided to repaint the walls black. But he didn't stop at that. He also replaced the old furniture with black pieces. Till this day I have no idea where he got the money to pay for everything, and to hire people to do the work. All I know is that one night he shared his plans with me, and I refused to give him the money. A few days later, there was a knock on the door. Two men stood there with buckets of black paint and other material needed for painting. The same day, a furniture truck pulled up in front of the apartment building. By the end of the day, the old furniture was gone and the light inside Ryan's room had been turned off. No splash of color in sight.

I didn't ask where he got the money for everything. There's no way the allowance I give him weekly would afford him the expensive leather furniture he purchased. The only explanation is that he found a way to make money on the Internet without my knowledge. The first thing my mind went to was gambling. The thought terrified me so much I brought it up with him, only to have the door slammed in my face as usual.

Tonight, the onyx silk bedsheets hang from one side of the bed, and pool onto the black tiled floor like ink water. The matching curtains are drawn.

Ryan's not in here, either.

My head swimming, I back out and close the door. I check his bathroom, the kitchen, everywhere I can think of. No Ryan.

I come to a halt in the hallway, bracing myself. If he's inside the apartment, there's only one room he can be in. My skin prickles with each step I take toward my bedroom door.

I push open the door, flick on the light, and jump back.

Ryan is on one side of my bed, his hooded gaze on me, eyes like frozen marbles.

"Hi, Sis." A sadistic smile taints his face, darkening his slurred words. "Looks like you're a little late coming home tonight."

He lowers his gaze to his lap. I follow it.

My hand wraps around my neck as I force myself to breathe, to remain calm.

"What is it? Is something the matter?" He wheels himself in my direction. "Don't say you're afraid of your little brother." He tuts as he nears me.

I take two steps back into the hallway. He picks up the butcher knife from his lap and runs a fingertip along the sharp blade. Even from where I'm standing, I notice the smear of red on his finger. He doesn't react to the cut.

My muscles tighten, ready for flight, but I don't move. I keep my feet firmly planted on the floor. My eyes are hard as they meet his from across the room.

"What are you planning to do, Ryan? Will you kill me? Is that what you have planned for me tonight?" I swallow the rock wedged inside my throat. "You think murdering me will solve all your problems?" I harden my voice. "What do you think will happen to you when I'm gone, huh?"

"You've got it all wrong," he barks. "Killing you would be way too easy. The suffering involved is too fleeting. I want you to stay alive, to live each day regretting ever being born." He slices his finger on the blade again, his eyes never leaving mine. "If you send anyone to babysit me again, I might just change my mind." He clears his throat. "But if I *do* choose to snuff out your useless life, I'll do it very slowly and very painfully."

Our eyes lock for a few beats more, then he breaks the connection and wheels himself out of the room.

Before he leaves me alone, he turns around. "One more thing." He rubs the side of his face with the bloody hand, smearing blood from his temple to his jaw. "Your new look disgusts me. It will never be able to hide your ugliness from the world. You can change yourself on the outside, but the guilt will continue to eat you alive every day." He narrows his eyes to slits. "And whoever you're seeing, end it today."

CHAPTER 15

At 6:00 a.m., the ringing of the phone drags me from the clutches of troubled sleep. My head feels like it's filled with bricks as I raise it from the pillow and fumble for my cell on the nightstand.

"You okay?" Thalia asks from the other end of the line. I don't know how many times she's asked me that question.

"No, I'm not." No point in sugarcoating anything. "Things got out of hand when I got home last night." I roll my head to release the tension in my neck. "Hey, I'm so sorry again for putting you in that situation."

"It wasn't your fault. I offered, remember?"

"I should have rejected your offer right away." I rub the sleep from my eyes. "For so long I fooled myself into thinking he's harmless. But last night ... Last night he showed me an even darker side to him."

Thalia gasps. "Did he threaten you with a

knife as well?"

"He threatened me with more than the knife." I drop my head back on the pillow, the palm of my hand over my glowing forehead. "He said it would be too easy to kill me, that he'd rather I suffer in life."

Momentary silence plugs the line until Thalia breaks it. "Paige, listen to me. I think you have to do something more than just ignoring him." She pauses. "He needs professional help."

"I'm starting to think you're right. I'm not just afraid for myself. I'm afraid for him. The way he had looked at me, Thalia ... He really hates me."

"What will you do? Something drastic needs to be done."

"I think I need to make some calls. I'll tell you later what I decide."

As I hang up the phone, I dread getting out of bed. I hate myself for feeling like the old me. Terrified to go back there, I fight through the fog in my mind and push myself to the edge of the bed, my head in my hands. One more movement, just one more and I'd be out of this bed and on my feet again, standing up for my life, for my freedom.

I squeeze my eyes shut and get to my feet.

After splashing my face with warm water, I call Margaret and ask for the day off. Since I hardly ever ask for a day off, she grants my wish without hesitation.

"Jane will step in for you. Focus on getting well," she says. "Do you want tomorrow off as well?"

"No. One day is enough."

After the call, I force myself to walk out of my room.

I find Ryan in the living room, staring at the blank TV screen. When he looks at me, his face is as crumpled as his clothes.

He glances at one wall of the living room.

My fingertips touch my lips as my eyes take in the pages of paper plastered across the bottom half of the wall. Each of the six pages has three words written on it in black marker.

I am sorry.

I yank one of the papers from the wall, stare at it for a moment, then look at Ryan. "Sorry is not enough." My voice is cracked around the edges. "After what you did yesterday, sorry is not enough."

His chin hits his chest. "I'm hurting, Sis. You know I haven't been myself since the shooting. Sometimes it feels as though there's something inside me, a force that takes over and makes me do things I don't want to do."

"You can fight that force if you want to." My fingers let go of the page and it flutters in slow motion to the messy floor. "Being hurtful is a choice you make every day." I ease myself into the couch, crushing a pizza box. I'm too tired and frustrated to care. "What you did yesterday … the things you said …" I swallow a sob. "You threatened my friend with a knife, and you threatened me."

"It wasn't me, the real me." His head is still bowed. "You have to understand that this monster inside me scares me just as much as it scares you. I can't do it alone, Sis."

"And yet you resist any help I offer you." I wipe a sheen of sweat from my forehead. "I'm starting to think maybe I'm not the right person to help you."

"Please." His head snaps up; his bloodshot eyes meet mine. "Don't … don't send me away. It will destroy me. The only thing that keeps me sane is knowing I have you."

"I don't get it. How can you say that, when you hate me so much? You've made that clear way too many times. All you do is hurt me, and you enjoy it."

"I'm sorry. I'm so sorry, Paige." He drops his head into his hands. "It's just that … I often get the feeling you're pushing me away."

"*You* are the one pushing me away. I've tried so many times to reach out to you, to help you, to share your burden, but you shrink away from me every time."

"I don't mean to." The eyes that look at me now are those of the little brother I used to know and love, the one I swore to protect. What if this is his way of manipulating me?

"I love you." I tear my gaze from his and gaze out the window at the bright morning sky. "I don't know if you believe it, but I love you so much. If I didn't, I would have walked away long ago."

"I know. I've made life hell for you, but I'm willing to change." He pauses. "I've decided to make changes in my life." He waits for me to respond. When I don't, he continues. "I'll stop drinking. I'll no longer be a burden. You don't even have to support me financially anymore."

"Will you get a job?" My gaze returns to him. Many times over the past months I'd come home with printouts of job ads only to have him crumple them up and throw them in my face. It wasn't so much that I wanted him to earn money. Most importantly, I wanted him to get out of the house, to be surrounded by other people.

"I started an online business."

"What kind?"

He peels his gaze from mine. "That's not important. What matters is that I make enough money to help with the expenses. Thousands of dollars."

"You make thousands of dollars and you watch me struggling to pay our bills and Mom's debts and say nothing?" I push down the sob rising up my throat.

"I wanted to punish you. It was cruel. Please don't throw us away." His bottom lip quivers. "You're all I have."

"I never wanted to turn my back on you, and you know that. But you attacked my friend with a knife. You cut yourself." My gaze moves to his left hand. He's wearing a Band-Aid around the finger he'd sliced with the knife.

"I wanted it to be just us," he says. "We don't need anyone else in our lives."

"*I* do." My voice is firm. "I love you, but I need other people in my life. I need a life outside these walls."

"Are you saying I'm not enough for you?" The angry thunderclouds return to his eyes.

"I'd be lying if I said you were." I refuse to let him intimidate or manipulate me. "Just because I need friends in my life doesn't mean I love you any less."

"And a boyfriend?" he asks. "You'd like one, too?"

"Why not? What's wrong with me wanting to be in a relationship, with having someone love me?" I rake a hand through my hair. "I want to get married one day, to have children. I want a life."

His mouth takes on an ugly twist as if he tasted something bad. "You know as well as I do that marriage sucks. You've seen what happened to Mom and Dad, the kind of marriage they had. They hated each other." He turns to face the TV again. "Why would you want something like that?"

My heart shrinks a little, but I breathe new life into it. "I want to do things differently. I've seen what they did to each other, and it just inspires me to have a different kind of marriage."

"You're living in a dream, Paige. It's time to face reality." He shakes his head. "Don't you see? Reality is dark, painful, and filled with nightmares. There is no heaven on earth."

"I never said there was. But I want to be happy. I won't apologize for it."

"You don't get it, do you? Happiness is for other people. Our family is cursed." When he looks at me again, his features are cold. "Accept it."

"I'm sorry, Ryan, but no. I won't accept a life where I have to push my way through nightmares. I want more than this."

"A life that doesn't include me, right?" He turns his wheelchair to face me. The monster in his eyes is back.

"You know that's not what I mean." I shut my eyes and open them again. "I just know we can't live together without hurting each other. I remind you too much of what happened to you that night. And you can't resist punishing me." I bury my hands in my hair. "The only solution is for you to move out. We can find you a place close by, maybe even in this building. Someone from the first floor moved out last week. Maybe they haven't found a new tenant yet. But before you stay alone, it might be best for you to go to—"

"Rehab?" His voice is like a sharpened sword, ready for war. "That's not going to happen. I'm not going anywhere. If you force me, I'll kill myself and leave you with more guilt to live with. Are you sure you can handle that?"

"I'm tired of your threats." I push myself to my feet. "If you want to kill yourself, go ahead." I cross my arms in front of my chest to keep my hands from shaking. "I'm giving you one month to decide what you want to do with your life. And if you threaten me again or do anything to harm me or anyone close to me, I'll call the cops or have you committed to a place where people can make sure you don't hurt yourself or others again. The choice is yours."

As I step toward the door I turn, fire still blazing in my eyes. "Just so you know, this is my life and I can choose who to spend it with. If I want to date, that's my business. If I want to get married one day, that's my business." My hand hovers over the door handle. "And if I want to be happy, that's also my choice." With that, I leave him to think about what I said.

Inside my room, I grab my phone. Dylan had called and left a message.

"Paige, how are you? You were pretty upset when you left yesterday. Please let me know if I can help in any way."

The phone rings before I put it down. It's him.

"Hi, Dylan." I lower myself to the edge of the bed, my free hand clutching one of my trembling knees. "How are you?"

"The more important question is, how are *you*? Are things okay with your brother?"

"Not really. But I'll get through it." I meant every word I said to Ryan. If he doesn't pull himself together within a month, I'm kicking him out.

"Is there anything at all I can do for you?"

"I don't think so. I really appreciate your offer, but there's nothing anyone can do."

"How about lunch? I can bring it to your place. I was at the school and Margaret said you're not coming in today. She mentioned you're not feeling well."

"She's right." I pick up a pillow and hug it to my body. "I'm sorry, but I ... I prefer to be alone today, if that's okay."

"Of course, it's okay."

"Thanks for calling, Dylan. Will you still be flying to New York today?"

"No," he says. "As it turns out, there are

quite a few issues related to my father's estate that I need to deal with first. If you decide you want to see me, I'll be in town for a while longer."

"Why me?" I fall back onto the pillows, and the headache piercing my temples makes me regret the sudden movement. "There are so many other beautiful women in town, women without problems."

"They don't fascinate me the way you do."

He just doesn't quit, does he?

"I don't want to waste your time," I say honestly. "The truth is, I'm not in the place to date anyone right now."

"Maybe I can change your mind. Meet up with me again one more time. We can just talk. Allow me to help you. Like I said, I haven't known you for long, but it feels that way."

"I like you, but there's too much going on in my life at the moment."

"I understand." He pauses. "If you *do* change your mind about lunch or dinner, I'm a phone call away."

"I'll remember that," I say with a smile.

I spend the early hours of the day in my room, sleeping, completing Sudoku puzzles, and listening to classical music, trying to get rid of the empty feeling inside me.

At midday, when thoughts of guilt threaten to break down my resistance, I grab my swimsuit and the novel Thalia had given me and head out the door.

On the apartment doorstep, I find a bag filled with takeout cartons of Indian food. The aromas of meat and spices rise to my nose. My mouth waters.

A white handwritten note is pushed between the cartons.

Paige, since you're unable to come to lunch, I brought lunch to you. Enjoy. Dylan.

CHAPTER 16

∞

I change my mind about going to the beach and take the Indian food into the house. Too exhausted for another conversation with Ryan, I eat my Tandoori chicken and chapati on the windowsill of my bedroom window while breathing in the fresh air.

I left the rest of the food for Ryan on the kitchen counter as there were two portions of each meal.

I haven't seen Ryan since our conversation in the morning. When I walk past the living room, I don't spot him inside. He's inside his room with heavy metal music making the walls shake.

I wave at Ned Porter when he takes a break from planting something in one of the flowerbeds and sees me at the window.

The food is so delicious that I find myself returning to the kitchen for more. On my way back, I stop by Ryan's room and knock on the door. I doubt he'll be able to hear me over the jarring sound of the music so I let myself in. Maybe he really *is* thinking about what I said to him earlier.

He's in his wheelchair, facing one of his black walls. When he senses me at the door, he spins around.

"Can't you just leave me the hell alone?" His eyes are as hard as they had been hours earlier.

"There's food in the kitchen, if you're hungry." I close the door before he has a chance to respond.

Back inside my room, I call Dylan to thank him for the food. "That was awfully kind of you."

"I'm glad you enjoyed it."

"Did you bring it by yourself or have it delivered?" For a moment I wonder how he knows where I live, then I remember he owns the building.

"I may be many things, but I'm not a stalker." He laughs. "Even though I was tempted for a minute to drop it off myself, you need your space, and I respect that."

"Thank you for being thoughtful."

"I kind of have an ulterior motive."

"I'm sure you do." I chew a corner of my nail, nervous about what I'm about to do, what it means. "Dylan, I've changed my mind. I'd like to see you again."

"Looks like my plan worked. And all it took

was some delicious Indian food." He chuckles. "I'm joking. I'm thrilled you changed your mind. Propose a day and time and I'll be there."

"Not today, unfortunately," I say quickly. "I'm still not feeling well." Even though I feel better than I did in the morning, I wouldn't want Margaret to hear from someone that I was seen out with Dylan Baxter while on sick leave.

"How about tomorrow? If you're well by then. We can also meet on the weekend, if you prefer."

"That would be better for me. Saturday?" I need a few days to recover from what has transpired between Ryan and me and to prepare myself for questions Dylan might have.

"That's perfect." He pauses. "I look forward to seeing you again."

"I look forward to seeing you, too, Dylan." I find myself smiling as I speak the words.

§

On my way to meet up with Dylan, I stop by the living room.

Four days have passed since I gave Ryan an ultimatum, and it splinters my heart to see that he has returned to his old self.

He's watching TV while holding a bottle of vodka in his left hand. He glares at me, his gaze drilling through me, questioning my intentions, daring me to speak to him.

"I'm going out. I might be back late. Dinner

is in the oven."

"Who are you meeting?" His mouth is set in a hard line.

I hoist the strap of my handbag onto my shoulder. "That's my business. I'll see you later."

The moment I walk through the door, I release a breath.

As I step into my car, I pray that I won't come home to a nasty surprise, another one of his warnings.

On my way to Lacey's Place, I give Thalia a call.

"How did Ryan react when you told him you're going on a date?"

"I didn't tell him where I'm going. I don't owe him any explanation." I pause. "My fear of him is gone. I just woke up this morning and didn't feel terrified when I thought of facing him. The past few days were hard, but I think I've reached the point where I can be me and allow him to be himself."

"I'm happy to hear that. Let's hope life gets better for you. You really deserve to be happy."

"So do you, Thalia." I slow down at a red traffic light. "By the way, how's Mr. Nice Guy?" Thalia has been seeing someone for the past two months and she keeps complaining that he's too nice.

"Still busy being nice. It drives me nuts."

I shake my head in confusion. "I don't see why that's a problem."

"I also don't. Kevin is perfect. He's the kind of guy many girls would love to introduce to their mothers." She sighs. "But I don't know. It just doesn't feel right for me."

"I know what your problem is," I say when the traffic light turns to green. "Your heart is addicted to heartbreak."

"You could be right." She laughs. "Last year, when Xavier broke up with me, I swore to myself I'd never date a bad boy again. But what if my heart only responds to bad boys?"

"I see only one solution here. If you don't feel it's right, maybe you should go your separate ways."

"But he really likes me. You should have seen how he took care of me when I had bronchitis. He would make the perfect husband."

"And your heart wants an imperfect man, I assume. You do know how weird that is, right?"

"Stop teasing." she laughs. "I didn't tell you this, but I almost broke up with him two days ago. I couldn't go through with it. I know how it feels to have a broken heart. I don't know how I could do that to someone else."

"So what will you do? Will you just continue to pretend you feel the same way about him?"

"Not exactly. I'll give him another two

months … A chance to see where things go. If anything, I'll have eight weeks to come up with a gentle way to break his heart."

"But you do have to give him a real chance." I pause. "When you introduced me to him, I saw in his eyes that he really likes you."

Unlike Thalia, I would like a man like Mr. Nice Guy for myself. Could Dylan be that kind of guy? As much as I'm drawn to him, I'm finding it hard to believe I could enter into a relationship with a man like him. We are from two completely different worlds.

"I will. I promise. Enough about me. Go and have fun with Dylan. Let me know how it goes."

Even though I arrive at Lacey's Place fifteen minutes early this time, I still find Dylan there, at the same table we occupied last time.

"Are you always so punctual when meeting up with someone?" I ask after we order drinks.

He gives me a gaze that makes my skin feel both hot and cold.

"Only if that someone is special." He places his hands on the table, one on each side of the centerpiece, palms facing up.

I have no idea what gets into me, but I find myself placing my palms on top of his, soaking up his warmth. As quickly as we touch, I come to my senses and withdraw my hands.

"I apologize." He leans back. "I don't know

what gets into me when I'm around you. I tend to do things I don't normally do."

"That's fine." I smile up at the waitress when she places my sparkling water in front of me and a cappuccino in front of Dylan.

When the waitress walks away, Dylan watches me over the rim of his cup before taking a swig. His eyes are still on me when he lowers it to the table. "Paige, before we eat, I should be upfront with you."

I lower my glass to the table, stomach clenched tight. "Okay?"

"There's another reason why I wanted to see you tonight." He lays his hands flat on the table, fingers splayed. "I did something without your permission and I hope you won't take it the wrong way."

"What ... What did you do?" It's hard to get the words through my dry throat.

"A couple of days ago, I found out that you're behind on your rent." He raises a hand before I can protest. "You have to believe that it wasn't my intention. I was merely doing paperwork related to some of my father's rental properties when I came across your records."

My mouth parts but no words come out. I have no right to be upset as the apartment building *does* belong to him. "I—"

"Hey, don't look so frightened." He takes another swig of coffee. "I just want to tell you that you're in the clear. I've arranged for you to stay in the apartment rent-free for six months, if you like."

"What?" Embarrassment stirs in my belly and heat creeps into my cheeks. I drink my water to moisten my tongue before I speak. "Dylan, that was very kind of you, but you shouldn't have done that. I don't want you to think I'm meeting up with you because—"

"That's not what I think. I wanted to help; that's all. We never have to talk about it again."

I drop my head into my hands to collect myself, then look back up at him. "I don't know what to say."

"No need to say anything." He dips his head to the side. "And don't feel like you owe me anything."

"This is rather embarrassing."

"It doesn't have to be. Sometimes people need help, and there's nothing wrong with it."

"Thank you," I say. "Thank you for putting me in the clear, but I'd still like to pay my rent for the next six months." The fact that I no longer have to pay the overdue rent is already help enough.

Ryan hasn't brought up the topic of his online business again and never offered me any money, but I plan on asking him to help out with some of the bills. But I have the feeling he'll dangle the carrot in front of my nose and then snatch it away.

"You don't have to. I'm offering you a break, and it's okay to take it."

"How can I be sure you don't want anything in return?"

"If you are referring to my feelings for you, be assured that my helping you has nothing whatsoever to do with what happens or doesn't happen between us. I'd love to see you again, but if you decide this is our last date, that's okay. I'll walk away knowing I made at least a little difference in your life. Does that make you feel better?"

"Yes, yes, it does. Thank you." As the words leave my lips, something inside me shifts. I hate to admit it to myself, but it does feel good to be taken care of for a change. This time I'm the one who places my hands on the table. He lays his warm, comforting hands over them and squeezes.

The rest of the evening, our conversation is focused on him, which is a relief. He tells me about his childhood in New York after his parents' divorce, and about his trips around the world.

"I've always wanted to travel abroad. I'd like to see Africa one day." I raise a crispy Baja fish taco to my mouth, careful not to spill the delicious goodies.

"Maybe one day you will." He chews his

toasted sesame and ginger salmon. "Where in Africa would you go?"

"I never really thought about it."

"What's the first country that comes to mind when you think of visiting the African continent?"

"Namibia. I'd love to see the Namibian desert." I smile at him, swept up in the moment. What do I have to lose by dreaming?

"Namibia is a beautiful country. I was there three years ago. It's an amazing safari destination." He dabs his lips with a napkin. "Who knows, maybe I'll take you there one day."

Conflicted about how to respond to what sounds like an offer, I continue to eat my food in silence while I think of the appropriate thing to say.

"I'm getting ahead of myself a little, aren't I?"

"A little." I nibble my lip.

"I guess I can't help myself." He pauses. "The thing is, I'm not the kind of person who beats around the bush. I like you. I really like you. I feel a connection between us that's kind of hard to ignore. Tell me you don't feel it."

"I do ..." I drop my head.

He tips my chin up. We gaze into each other's eyes again. The moment stretches until it's broken by the waitress appearing with our dessert.

Heat radiates through my chest as I enjoy my white chocolate mousse.

As if nothing intoxicating has transpired between us, he tells me more about his adventures in Namibia.

After we leave the restaurant, he takes my elbow and walks me to my car.

Before I get behind the wheel, he lowers his head to mine, and I find myself dipping my head back.

Our lips meet at the same time an explosion goes off inside my head.

CHAPTER 17

It took one kiss to change my life. The moment my lips touched Dylan's on our second date, something inside me shifted. The resistance I'd had toward dating him melted away before my eyes, and I allowed him to sweep me off my feet.

It's been three weeks, and I never regretted my decision. At first, I thought it would be awkward to date a billionaire, but Dylan is surprisingly normal. Although occasionally he takes me out to fancy restaurants and buys me expensive gifts, most of what we do when we're together is normal.

With him, a quick dinner at the hot dog stand before we go to the movies is just as thrilling as dining under chandelier lights. I appreciate that he tries very hard not to make me feel uncomfortable, and when I refused to allow him to pay my bills, he respected my decision. I don't want him to think I'm dating him for the money, because all I'm interested in is his heart, something I didn't even know I wanted.

On our third date, he opened up that he had just come out of a serious relationship that ended due to them wanting different things in life.

"Did you break up with her or did she end the relationship?" I asked, scared to be his rebound girl.

"It was me who ended things," he said, then he assured me he had never felt for any woman the way he feels about me, and that he was giving me a real chance.

I believed him. Even though the little voice at the back of my mind often insists that it will not last, that there's an expiration date to my happiness and I should catch my fall before I hit the ground, I turn a deaf ear.

For the first time in my life, I'm truly happy. I'm determined to hold on to the good feelings for as long as I possibly can. It tells me that this is just a dream and it's only a matter of time before I wake up to face the nightmare that is my life.

After three weeks, my feet still haven't touched the ground. But tonight, they just might.

Over the past few weeks I've wrestled with whether or not to introduce Dylan to Ryan.

Initially, I didn't want to introduce them because I feared it might not last, but now that I know I want Dylan to stay in my life for as long as he wants to be in it, it might be time for him to meet Ryan.

Many times when we were together, Dylan had shown interest in meeting Ryan, but I've always found an excuse to delay the inevitable.

Tonight, we just finished eating dinner at a fast food restaurant three blocks from my apartment. When he brings me back to my place, I don't kiss him and say goodnight. Instead, I invite him into the apartment to meet Ryan.

"Only if you're sure, babe." He lays a hand on my cheek. "I wouldn't want to push you into anything. I only want to meet him because he's such a big part of your life."

"You're right, he's a large part of my life. And so are you." I clasp my hands in my lap. "But before ... There's something you should know. Something I haven't told you."

"About Ryan?"

"Yes. About how he got into the wheelchair."

I tip my head back and close my eyes. The reason I haven't had the courage to tell him about that night is because I was terrified he'd look at me differently, decide I'm not the woman he thinks I am.

"What is it? You know you can tell me anything."

Without looking at him, I tell him the dark side of my story. He already knows about my mother and how she died, how I decided to take care of Ryan. So, I tell him about that night, how Ryan showed up on my doorstep asking for money, how I refused. And how my decision led to the shooting.

"He was shot with a little help from me. If I had only given him the money, things could be different now. He could be walking … living—"

"You don't know that for certain. I think you're wrong to blame yourself for what happened."

He places a hand on top of mine, the heat of his touch reaching into my skin, soothing my nerves. "What if you had given him the money and the guys decided they wanted more and shot him anyway? For all you know, he might still have ended up in a wheelchair."

"Ryan disagrees." I glance up at the apartment building and a knot starts to form in the pit of my stomach. "Anyway, don't expect him to be nice to you. He's a very angry and bitter person. He lives in the past."

"I'm not afraid of meeting him." Dylan twists his body to face me. "Maybe it would help him to see you living your life. You might inspire him to do the same."

"I doubt it." I haven't told Dylan about how evil Ryan can be sometimes, the dangerous threats he makes. The last thing I need is for Dylan to think I'm in danger and feel the need to take steps to protect me, maybe even call the cops. "Are you sure you're ready to meet him? It won't be a big deal if you change your mind."

Dylan lays a hand between my shoulder blades. "I won't change my mind. This is your life, and I want to be a part of it."

"Okay." I open the door and step out of the car. A gust of wind blows my hair into my face and I sweep the strands back, tucking them behind my ears. I glance up at the apartment. My skin crawls when I spy Ryan sitting by the window, the living room light creating a halo around him.

Even from a distance, his cold stare makes me shudder. No way. I can't do this to Dylan or to myself.

I turn to Dylan, who has come to stand next to me. "I'm sorry, sweetheart. I thought I was ready." I push a hand through my hair. "I don't think I am. Can we please do it another time?"

He gathers me into his arms, his cologne wrapping around me like a warm cloak. "Absolutely. If you need more time, that's fine. I'm not going anywhere."

"What did I do to deserve you?"

"What did *I* do to deserve you?" He kisses me hard on the lips. He tastes of the mint and chocolate candies he keeps in his car.

Ryan's stare scalds the back of my head, but I don't care that he's watching. I sink into Dylan's arms anyway.

I'm the one who breaks the kiss. "Thanks for understanding. I'll call you tomorrow after work."

"Good. Don't forget that I'll be cooking you dinner." Dylan has already cooked me a few delicious gourmet meals in the kitchen of the villa his father left him, and he's an amazing cook.

He kisses my forehead and gets into his Mercedes. Before he drives away, he sticks his head out of the window. "And don't worry about tonight."

"All right." I wrap my arms around my body as I watch his car drive down the street.

My feet are heavy as I enter the apartment. I find Ryan still by the window, his features distorted by fury.

A week left before we reach the deadline I gave him, and he hasn't changed one bit. Once or twice I thought he was starting to live his life. He's on the phone more often now and for longer periods of time—and not just to order food.

Two weeks ago, I came home to find two

glasses of wine on the kitchen counter. One had lipstick stains on it. Four days ago, I saw a red Pashmina scarf on his bed. The color had stood out drastically against the inky black sheets.

The idea of him possibly seeing someone excited me. I thought it would put him in a better mood, that he would be open to me dating Dylan. I was wrong.

The day I told him I was dating, he threw a bottle of wine at me. I ducked at the last second and it hit the wall behind me instead. I still shudder when I remember the dangerous look in his eyes when he told me to break things off with Dylan. Of course, I refused and ignored his tantrums whenever I went out to meet up with him.

Why does he feel he can date while I'm not allowed to? Last week I found the courage to ask him whether he was seeing someone. He told me to back off. So I did. I continued to date Dylan, to focus on my own happiness. But I reminded Ryan of the decision he had to make.

"You were with him again," he says now, his voice a grainy rumble in his throat.

"Yes, Ryan." I slump against the doorframe. "He's a part of my life, and I wanted you to meet him. I told you that before I went out tonight."

"Why isn't he here then? Is he some kind of

coward?"

"Shut up." I form a fist with my right hand, my nails digging into the flesh of my palm. "I won't let you talk about him that way. Dylan is a good man, and he's been kind to me."

"What does he do when you're together, huh? Does he listen when you whine about me? Does he offer you a shoulder to cry on?" He moves to the center of the living room, runs his tongue across his bottom lip. "What do you tell him about me, Sis? Do you tell him how terrible I am, how I make your life hell?"

"No," I push away from the doorframe. "I try not to think about you when I'm with him. When I'm with Dylan, I choose to be happy. Whether you like it or not, he makes me happy." I straighten my shoulders. "I'd also be happy for you if you find someone you care about, someone who cares about you. I'd love to meet the girl you're dating."

"Leave her out of this." He clenches his jaw tight.

It's confirmed then. He really *is* dating someone.

I shrug. "Fine, you don't have to introduce me to her, but I'd still like you to meet Dylan. He really wants to meet you. And he offered to buy you one of those high-tech wheelchairs."

Ryan is quiet, but the veins on his neck push against his skin. "I can't be bought," he says in a low voice. "He and his high-tech wheelchair can go to hell."

"He's not trying to buy you. He's just being kind. There's nothing wrong with accepting kindness from people." I grab the door handle, ready to end the conversation as it's not getting anywhere.

His hand slams the armrest of his wheelchair. "Not from him." The words come out of his mouth like a roar. As soon as he says them, his wheelchair starts to shake, and then in a flash of a moment, it topples to its side seconds before it hits the floor hard with him in it.

"Ryan!" He's squirms out of the wheelchair as I rush to him, my knees hitting the floor.

With a bellow, he swats my hands away. Like someone possessed, he lifts his head and crashes it into the wooden floor, over and over.

"Please, Ryan, stop it!" Tears choke my voice.

Watching my brother hurt sends a bolt of pain hitting my chest. I want to erase his pain, to hold him and make it all go away.

Tears flowing, I gather him into my arms and hold him tight as he struggles, then finally stops rejecting my touch. He's crying now, as well. I can't remember the last time I saw him cry. His whole body is shaking and breaking apart in my arms. My little brother is back.

"Tell him to go away," he begs between

sobs. "I want it to be just us."

How can it be just us when he's also seeing someone?

I don't respond, just hold him for a while longer, rocking him, stroking his greasy hair. It feels good to finally connect with him. I don't remember the last time we touched without hurting each other. The last hug I gave him was on the day that changed our lives forever. I have missed him so much. Even with him in my arms, I still miss him.

As I embrace the moment, he suddenly yanks his head away from me and sinks his teeth into my hand. I yell and let go.

To my horror, he continues to hurt himself, his head hitting the floor harder. I weep with my hands covering my mouth, cry harder when I see his blood taint the wood. He needs help, the kind I can't offer. Tears plop onto my hands as I grab my purse and I pull out my phone.

"Don't you dare call anyone," he says through clenched teeth, taking a break from hurting himself. "Do it and you'll regret it."

"Then stop it, Ryan. Stop doing that." I drop the phone. "You're scaring me." I swipe a hand across my cheek.

"Then promise to stop seeing him."

"You can't ask me to do that." A sudden coldness hits my core. "You can't ask for me to give up being happy just because you want to have me all to yourself."

"Promise. To. Leave. Him." He repeats the words slowly this time.

"Promise to stop hurting me." I pull my legs to myself and hug them, rocking back and forth.

He rests his head on the floor and just lies there, eyes blank, exhausted, staring at me with no life in them whatsoever.

"You have to let me help you. Let me take you to a place where you can be helped. The longer you stay here, the more you hurt yourself. The more you hurt us. We're not good for each other. You hurt me just as much as I hurt you."

"This is my home." His voice is broken around the edges but firm at the core.

It's true, this is his home, not just mine. And it kills me to know I have to send him away. But what choice do I have? We've reached the end of the road. He needs to go somewhere else where he can heal, then maybe we can start again.

"I'm not sending you away for good, Ryan. Once you're better, you can come back home. I just want you to get help." I wipe my cheek with the back of my hand. "I want you to be happy."

"What if being like this is what makes me

happy?"

"I doubt that. I don't for a second believe this is what you want."

I crawl across the floor toward him, ignoring the dull ache at the place he bit. My brother needs me.

He doesn't fight me as I help him back into his wheelchair. And then I lower myself to his level, grab his hands, and meet his eyes. "Please, let me help you."

After a long silence, he nods.

I glance at the bleeding gash on the side of his head. "You need stitches. Let me take you to the hospital, then we can talk."

"No hospital." He drops his head.

"Okay. Will you let me clean it up?"

"Yeah." I barely hear the word.

He no longer speaks as I clean the wound and cover it up. When I'm done, I hesitate, then hug him. He lets me. "I love you, Ryan. Never ever doubt that. Whatever I do, whatever decisions I make, are because I love you." I pull away. "Say you believe that."

"Yeah." He still doesn't look at me. He has reached a broken state. I'm tempted to give it another try with him at home, but I know that tomorrow could be different. The dark monster in his eyes could return any moment with revenge on his mind. I have to act before I change my mind.

"Then allow me to make some calls. We can do it together; we can choose a nice place for you. Remember, it will only be for a while."

He nods.

He has so many issues I don't even know which kind of facility would be good for him.

While he sits by the window, I call several residential rehab facilities I discovered on the internet, not only in Corlake, but surrounding towns. The third place is cheaper than the others, and when I tell the woman about Ryan, she assures me that they can help him. They offer to give him a place for a month and then he can return home—as a better person, hopefully. I tell Ryan about it, and he nods again. The only request he has is that I should send him there after two days. He wants to spend a little time at home. I agree hesitantly.

I cook him dinner but he refuses to eat so I wish him a goodnight and go to bed feeling drained and hollow.

Dylan calls twice but I don't pick up. I have no idea what to say to him, what to say to anyone. The way I feel is hard to put into words.

Since I'm just as broken as Ryan, I'm not even sure anymore if Dylan will be able to heal me.

CHAPTER 18

My body and mind feel rejuvenated as I move my car out of my assigned parking spot at school.

Today's the day I'm sending Ryan to rehab. It still hurts to let go. As much as I hate to admit it, I've become attached to him just as much as he's attached to me. But deep down, I'm relieved for both of us. We need time to work on ourselves before we can start over as a family.

The last two days, I'd been on pins and needles the entire time, waiting for Ryan to change his mind about going to rehab. I held my breath when we went through the material the facility had sent me. But nothing happened.

I can't say he's changed completely. He still drinks, stuffs himself with junk food, and spends the entire day in front of the TV. But he hasn't been violent toward me. No threats, no harsh words, no evil looks.

This morning before I left for work, I stopped by his room to find him curled up underneath his black sheets, his mop of brown hair spilling onto the pillows. Next to the bed was his wheelchair and a packed bag, ready to go.

For a moment I'd stood at the door, watching his chest rising and falling as he slept. He's a grown man, but every time I look at him, I see a little boy stuck inside a man's body.

Before I could walk away, his eyes opened, and he smiled at me for the first time in two years. "Is it time?"

"Not yet. I'll drop you off in the evening." I caught his smile with my heart and gave him one in return. "We could have lunch together first. I asked for a short work day today. I'll be home before twelve."

"I'd like that," he says and pulled the bed sheets up to his neck.

As I near our apartment now, I'm both excited and nervous about seeing him. This morning he was ready to go, but what if he was playing me? What if, now that I believe in him, he suddenly pulls the rug from under my feet?

As usual, before entering the apartment, I draw in a few breaths. I never know what will be waiting for me on the other side of the door.

I finally get the courage to take a look.

The entire place smells different, the air fresh

as though it had been scrubbed clean.

I come to an abrupt halt in the doorway to the living room. I almost don't recognize it. The blinds have been pulled up, the windows wide open to let in fresh air. But what shocks me the most is that the room is clean. No takeout boxes, no discarded socks, no speck of dust. The floor has been vacuumed and the couch is free of papers, candy wrappers, and video game covers.

Everything is neat and in its place. It feels as though I'm seeing the living room for the first time.

Tears prick my eyes as I glance at the blank but gleaming TV screen. My phone rings as I'm leaving the living room. It's Dylan.

"Afternoon, beautiful lady. Are you at work?"

"Hey, babe. No, I left early today."

"How are things with your brother? When are you dropping him off?"

"In the evening." I stop by my bedroom and toss my bag onto the bed.

"Call me when you get back home. I have meetings all day, but we could grab dinner tonight."

"Sounds good. I'll see you later." I'm still smiling when I leave my bedroom and go to Ryan's.

Like the living room, it's spotless. The bed is

made for the first time in God knows how long. The clothes he's not taking to rehab have been put away instead of left to hang out on the floor. His bag is on the foot of the bed. Looks like he's ready to go, but where is he?

I search for him everywhere in the house but don't find him. He's also not in the garden, and his van is still parked outside. I call his number but it goes straight to the mailbox.

Confused, I enter my room and sink down onto the bed, staring into space. Just as I'm about to stand up, my hand touches a piece of paper that sticks out from underneath one of my pillows. I pull it out, wondering if it's one of my students' homework pages I'd forgotten somehow. I unfold it at the creases and start to read.

A cold shower of dread trickles down my back as I allow each word to drop into my mind.

Looks like you got what you want. I'm gone and you can have your life back. I hope you're happy now. Have fun living with the guilt.

Ryan

My fingers part involuntarily. The note falls from them and onto my lap in slow motion. I stare at it but no longer see it. The words are blurred before my eyes.

This has to be a joke. It has to be.

I'm not even sure how to react to this new

change of events.

I know I should do something, get up and go looking for him, but I'm frozen in place, rooted to the spot. My heart gallops while my body has forgotten how to move.

He's only trying to scare me. Maybe he's back to playing some of his sick games.

But what if it's true? What if the note means what I think it actually says?

The fear of that last question being true causes my adrenaline to spike, bringing my body back to life.

Gulping down breaths to calm myself, I scramble through the house, searching every corner, shouting Ryan's name until my throat feels raw. No answer. No wheelchair. No Ryan. Not even the smell of him.

In a moment of desperation, and unsure of what else to do, I call the police, but they tell me I cannot file a missing person's report until twenty-four hours have passed since Ryan has disappeared.

"Please, help me. Something is wrong. I feel it. He left a note." I tell the officer what the note says.

"Ms. Wilson, calm down," the husky-voiced police officer says. "His note tells me he left willingly. Unfortunately, there's nothing we would be able to do in that case."

"What if he's hurt? What if he did something

to himself? He … he tried it before." I swallow hard. "Ryan hardly leaves the house." I move to the window of the living room and glance outside. "His van is still here. Where would he go without his van?"

"Maybe he didn't go somewhere far." The cop's voice carries traces of boredom. "Call us again after twenty-four hours. For now, contact people he knows. Go to places he frequents. Or just wait. He might come back home."

"I don't think he will. Don't you get it? For all I know, my brother could be in a ditch somewhere." My voice rises as I clench and unclench my hands. "What if all it takes are those twenty-four hours for it to be too late? Isn't it your job to protect people from getting hurt?"

"I'm sorry, ma'am. There's nothing I can do for you at this point. Call again in twenty-four hours."

Since I won't be getting anywhere with him, I hang up the phone. I'd rather use the time to search for my brother instead of trying to reason with a police officer who is unwilling to help me.

The next person I call is Thalia. Of course, she doesn't pick up. She should be in class right now. I hang up and wander from one room to the next, even though I've already searched through them.

"Where did you go, Ryan?" I can barely breathe as I call his name. I hold on to walls and doors for support because my knees are so weak they threaten to give way.

I can't do this alone. I call Dylan.

"I need your help," I say.

"I'm in a meeting. Give me ten minutes. I'll call you right back."

He calls back sooner. "Paige, are you okay? Why do you sound like that?"

"He's gone. He left a note." I crumple to the floor. My hand clutches my chest.

"What do you mean? Who's gone?"

"Ryan. My brother. He's gone."

"He went to rehab by himself?"

"No." Tears scatter everywhere with a shake of my head. "He left a note. It sounds like ... a suicide note. I found it under my pillow." It's painful to repeat the words written on the piece of paper, but Dylan needs to know how serious this is.

"Are you home?" His voice sounds rushed, as though he's walking fast or even running.

"Yes. I can't find him." I grapple for air but can't get enough. "I need to find him, Dylan."

"Stay where you are. I'm coming over."

"The police won't help. They want me to wait twenty-four hours before filing a missing person's report. They think he'll come back."

"That's ridiculous. I'll give them a call."

After we end the phone call, even though Dylan told me to stay home, I can't. I run out of the apartment and burst out onto the street, asking people on the sidewalk if they've seen him. I knock on the neighbors' doors.

Not one person I talk to has seen him.

Where are you, Ryan?

§

Dylan arrives twenty minutes after we talked, but it feels like an hour has passed.

Next to him is a police officer with a widow's peak. From the husky sound of his voice, I know he's the man I talked to on the phone.

"Ms. Wilson, I'm Officer Bruce Sawyer." He stretches out his hand to shake mine, but I don't take it. "I'm sorry about your brother's disappearance." He clears his throat and looks away. "We will do everything we can to find him."

I'm tempted to give him a piece of my mind for refusing to help me earlier, but there's no time to waste. What matters is that Dylan got him to come here.

Dylan pulls me into a hug and I hold onto him, tears flooding my eyes. "We need to find him. I want him back."

"And we will. We'll do whatever it takes." Officer Sawyer pulls out a notepad from his breast pocket as I escort both him and Dylan into the living room.

Dylan whispers that he's going to get me a glass of water. I'm about to tell him where the kitchen is, since he's never been inside my apartment before, but he tells me he already knows. He must have seen it when we walked past on our way to the living room.

He leaves me with the cop, who takes a seat and starts asking questions. I settle on one end of the couch.

"Does your brother have any friends?"

"None that I know of." I bite my bottom lip. "But for a few weeks now, I kind of got the feeling he was seeing someone, but he never admitted it."

I stand up from the couch and move to the window, staring out, but seeing nothing.

"So you don't know this supposed friend's name or what she looks like?"

I shake my head and wrap my arms around myself.

Sounds of glasses clinking and water rushing out of the faucet drift in from the kitchen.

Officer Sawyer writes something on his notepad then looks back up. "And you're sure there's no one else he sees often."

"No. He kept to himself most of the time. And he didn't leave the apartment often unless he had doctors' appointments."

Officer Sawyer leans back and crosses his

arms. "Tell me a little more about your brother, anything I should know that might help us find him."

Before I get started, Dylan walks through the door and hands me my water. I take a sip and hold the glass a little too tight. Then I launch into my story, telling the cop everything. The more he knows, the better he'll be able to help.

After I finish the story, he whistles and swipes a hand across his forehead.

"Why didn't you tell me any of this before?" Dylan comes to sling an arm around my shoulders.

"I didn't want you to think he was dangerous."

"He sounds pretty dangerous to me." The officer scribbles for a long time in his notepad.

"He's my brother." I return to the couch and twist my body to face the officer. "Please, find him."

"We'll do our best, Ms. Wilson." Officer Sawyer rises. "If you think of anything else, please call." He hands me a card with his name on it. "Every piece of information is important. We'll call you if we find anything."

"If you find him, you mean?"

He clears his throat. "Yes, if we find him … or anything that might point to his whereabouts." He pushes his notepad into his pocket. "Tell me one thing, when was the last time you saw him?"

"This morning. He seemed fine. He was kind to me. I told him I'd be home by twelve so we could have lunch together before he goes to rehab."

"Did you try to call him?"

I run my hands up and down my arms. "Yes, several times. His phone was switched off. He never switches his phone off. Ever."

"Okay." Officer Sawyer moves to the door. "We'll try to find him."

When the officer leaves, I fall into Dylan's arms. "I don't want to lose him, Dylan."

He places a hand on my head, sweeps his palm over my hair. But he doesn't say anything, and I know why. He's probably thinking of the things I said about Ryan tormenting me, but he doesn't want to share his thoughts with me in case he hurts my feelings.

CHAPTER 19

Twenty-four hours after Ryan's disappearance, I'm sitting in the kitchen in front of a plate with cold scrambled eggs and toast. I decide to call the police station.

I'm immediately transferred to Officer Sawyer.

"I'm afraid we still don't have any good news for you, Ms. Wilson. But I can assure you we're doing everything we can to find him. I'll give you a call as soon as I know something."

"Thank you." I hang up and drop my aching head into my hands. I've barely slept all night, missing the sound of the loud TV and the squeak of Ryan's wheelchair when he moved around the house. But the night was quiet, disturbed only by the sounds of my sobbing.

I push away the food and get to my feet. A wave of dizziness washes over me and I grab the edge of the table. I close my eyes for a moment, squeezing out the remaining tears from the corners.

Once strength returns to my legs, I barge out of the kitchen and throw open the door to Ryan's room—the fifth time this morning.

Murmuring his name, I turn his belongings upside down, yanking out drawers only to slam them shut again.

I need closure, something to help my heart settle. I hate to believe he took his own life, but if he did, I'd still like for a chance to be able to say goodbye. It kills me to think I wanted him out of my life, that I wanted him gone. Now he is.

There were times I hated him for what he did to me, for putting me through hell, but right now I'd do anything to have it all back—the good *and* bad.

After searching the closet and dresser and finding nothing, I flip over his mattress, expecting to find nothing, as well. But between the bars that support the mattress, I spot a dark blue shoebox. It's not unusual for a person to keep a shoebox under the bed, but the way it's tucked into a far corner looks deliberate.

Holding my breath, I push the mattress support aside and pick up the box. My knees next to the bed, I lift the lid. My eyes widen.

I'm not sure what I expected to see, but I didn't expect to see money. Not just money, but stacks of hundred-dollar bills, lined up next to each other, filling the box completely. Thousands of dollars.

I trace the money with my fingertips.

I can't believe he's had all this money lying around and never once offered to help me with the bills, only because he wanted to make me suffer. But being angry with him right now won't get me anywhere. In spite of his imperfections, I want him back in my life. And this time, we'll make it work. I'll never turn my back on him again. I'll let him heal at home.

With my hand still on the cash, I think of his expression when I saw him yesterday morning. He had looked so defeated, as though he had given up the fight. Had he given up life as a whole?

If anything happens to him, I'd be the person responsible yet again. For the second time in his life, I made the wrong decision.

Unsure what to do with the money, I close the lid and push the box back under the bed. As soon as I put the mattress back in place, the sound of the front door closing vibrates through the walls.

Maybe it's him. My heart leaps, but crashes again when I hear Thalia's voice coming down the hall. Within seconds, she fills Ryan's doorway.

"Sweetheart, how are you?" She drops a bag filled with folders to the floor and rushes to my side, puts her arms around me. "I couldn't go to work without finding out how you're doing."

"I told you on the phone." I pull away.

"I could hear in your voice that you're not fine. You don't have to pretend in front of me." She tucks a strand of hair behind my ear and goes to sit on the bed. I'm glad I've hidden the box of cash since I don't have answers to questions she might ask about the money.

I sit next to her, my hands wedged between my knees. "I'm so worried, Thalia. I don't know what to do. I searched everywhere. I even called the rehab facility." I catch my breath. "No one has seen him."

"What are the cops saying?"

"Nothing yet." I rub my sore eyes. "I can't believe he just disappeared into thin air like that. How's it even possible? This is a small town."

"I know," Thalia says in a quiet tone. "Yesterday evening, I also drove around, looking for him, but nothing."

"You think he could have left town?" I search Thalia's face for answers she doesn't have. "But where would he go? Why would he leave without saying goodbye?" A tear rolls down my cheek. "I thought we were at a good place, finally."

"What about the note?" Thalia asks cautiously.

"I don't know how to explain it, but I don't think he's dead. He might be in trouble." My mind wanders to the money under the bed. What if it belongs to someone else, someone dangerous, someone who hurt Ryan?

I want to discuss the money with Thalia, but something inside stops me. I wouldn't want to put Ryan in any more trouble than he might already be in. If the cash is stolen, and he returns home, he could end up in jail. The cops would question anyone who knows him. Telling Thalia about the money would put her in a difficult position.

"How did you get into the apartment, anyway?" I ask.

"You gave me an emergency key last year, remember? I thought it might be time to use it."

"Yeah, I forgot." My voice sounds strange to my own ears.

"Did you even get any sleep?"

"How could I? When I close my eyes, I see Ryan, the way he had looked the last time I saw him."

"You really don't believe there's a possibility he could have—"

"Killed himself?" I shake my head. "I ... I just don't feel it."

Thalia watches me for a long time, but before she can respond, the doorbell rings.

§

"Did you find him?" I ask before the police officer and his partner—a burly man with a handlebar mustache and bushy eyebrows—have a chance to step through the door.

"You may want to have a seat, Ms. Wilson."

"Why? What did you find out?" I wrap my arms around my body as my pulse skyrockets.

"Can we come in?"

I don't respond, just stare at him, waiting for answers.

"Please, come in." Thalia appears at my side and opens the door wider. I don't say anything as she takes my hand and leads me to the living room where she helps me sit on the couch. She offers the cops a place to sit as well, then excuses herself to go and prepare coffee.

"Tell me," I say in a whisper. I need to know the truth, however much it hurts.

Officer Sawyer runs the palm of his hand down his thigh, then lift his eyes to meet mine. "I'm afraid we don't have good news."

"Is he ...?" The words die on my tongue.

"We found his wheelchair on a deserted area of the beach. He was nowhere near it."

I swallow hard and lift my chin. "How do you know ... How do you know it's his wheelchair?"

He reaches into his breast pocket and pulls out a photo, the one I had given him yesterday of Ryan in his wheelchair. "It's this exact one.

Only without him in it. But we also found this at the edge of the water." He pulls out another photo and hands it to me. I clutch on to it with trembling hands.

"His shoes?" I stare at the picture, blinking away the moisture in my eyes. I don't look up when Thalia returns to the living room and places the tray on the coffee table.

"One of them." Officer Sawyer accepts his coffee from Thalia and thanks her, then continues, "We were unable to find the other shoe."

Bile rises up in my throat when the coffee smell makes its way to me.

I want to tell the cops it's not his shoe but I would be lying. Ryan always wore the same red sneakers, a pair I bought him last Christmas.

"Ms. Wilson, can you confirm that that's one of your brother's shoes?"

I bite my lip and nod. "But, where is he?" In my mind's eye, the horror image of Ryan pushing his wheelchair through beach sand and then throwing himself out of it to crawl into the sea, makes me sick to my stomach.

"Unfortunately, that's a question we can't answer ... yet." Officer Sawyer takes a swig of coffee. "But our team is looking into it as we speak. I'm sorry to say this, but I think you should prepare yourself for the worst."

"He's not dead." I look from Officer Sawyer

to his partner, desperate for one of them to believe me. "I know my brother is alive."

Officer Sawyer drinks more coffee, and when he lowers the cup, I notice the sweat on the tip of his nose. "Ms. Wilson, what if your brother lied to you?"

I swipe a hand across my cheek. "What do you mean?"

"I'm just saying that the wheelchair was found a distance from the water. Could it be he was able to walk himself into the sea?"

My mouth drops. "I don't know what you are implying, officer, but no. My brother couldn't walk."

Thalia lowers herself beside me and takes my hand. I don't like what I see in her eyes. "Paige, think about it. Maybe that's why you sometimes felt watched when you were out with Dylan. He could have followed you around."

I don't answer because I don't want anything they're implying to be true.

After everyone leaves and I'm left alone, I get a call from Dylan. He asks to come and see me, but I tell him I need to be alone to process the information I received.

I spend the night in Ryan's room, staring at the black ceiling, thinking about what the officer said.

No. Ryan wouldn't do that to me. He was cruel, but surely not that cruel.

CHAPTER 20

Thalia places a hand on my shoulder. "Ready?"

"Will I ever be?" Her features are distorted by the tears filling my eyes.

"I'm so sorry, Paige."

"So am I." I bite back tears. "I can't believe he's not coming back."

"Yeah, me too." Thalia zips up the back of my plain, black cotton dress.

It's no secret she didn't care much for Ryan, but I can see in her eyes that she shares my pain. As a true friend, she was desperate for him to be found for my sake.

Hand in hand, we step out of Ryan's room and I close the door behind us. I've been sleeping there for three weeks now, surrounded by darkness. But I don't think I'll be able to sleep in there again after today, after what I'm about to do.

The police say they did everything they could to find Ryan, combing the coast and even searching in nearby towns. They only managed to find his second shoe, not far away from where they'd found the first.

Every day, I'd held on to the hope that every time I called them, they'd have some good news for me. They never did. Each time I hung up the phone, my heart broke a little more.

Last week, Officer Sawyer urged me to face the possibility that Ryan might not be coming back home. I'm sure what he really wanted to say was that I should come to terms with the fact that he might be dead. I lashed out at him and hung up the phone, but after a night spent drenching my pillow with tears, I woke up feeling more distant from Ryan than ever before.

Two days later, I forced myself to say goodbye even if it was the last thing I wanted to do.

I'll never stop hoping he will one day show up at my doorstep as he used to do before the accident, but if I want to keep myself from going insane, I'll have to find some kind of peace.

Before leaving the house, I release Thalia's hand and enter the living room. My gaze lands on the space between the couch and the TV, the spot where Ryan's wheelchair used to be parked.

My hand covers my chest as pain blooms in

my heart. I'm desperate to hear the sounds and noises I used to hate, desperate to smell the scents that used to disgust me. But nothing is left of Ryan except the bad memories that I hold on to as though they are good. They're all I have of him.

I don't care how many times they tell me it's not my fault he's gone. I don't believe them.

My decision to send him to rehab was not only for him but also for my own selfish reasons. I'd wanted my life back. Even with all the pain he'd caused me, I can't imagine a life without him. My world had revolved around trying everything I could to make his life comfortable. With his departure, all that's left is a black, empty hole inside my heart.

"Paige," Thalia whispers and I turned to follow her out of the living room. In the entrance hall, I catch sight of my face in the small round mirror hanging on the wall. I hardly recognize myself. My hair, in a limp ponytail, looks lifeless. My skin is pale like it hasn't been touched by the sun in months, and the bags underneath my eyes are proof of the sleepless nights behind me.

"Let's go, sweetie," Thalia says, brushing my arm. "Dylan is waiting."

I nod and pick up a basket filled with white rose petals I'd left by the door.

As kids, Ryan and I had neighbors with a

white rose garden. We used to love watching them bloom. Sometimes, Ryan would steal a few blooms to bring home to me. It didn't matter how often he was punished by my mother for doing so. He did it anyway because he delighted in the way they cheered me up.

It takes us less than twenty minutes to get from the apartment to the dock closest to where Ryan's shoes were found.

Dylan is on the deck of his boat, khaki linen trousers and white shirt flapping in the early morning breeze, hair teased by the wind.

The boat is pearly white, with the name *Baxter* in gold and black letters on one side. It's the same boat I'd been on a couple of times in the past days as Dylan helped me sweep the ocean for my brother, the same boat that always brought us back to land empty-handed.

"Come here, my love," Dylan says when we step onto the boat.

Thalia takes the basket from me and I walk into the arms of the man who has stood by me every day since Ryan disappeared.

I tighten my arms around him, breathe in his masculine scent before it's stolen by the wind, and bury my face into his shoulders while blinking back tears.

After we break our embrace, he kisses me softly and goes to man the boat.

I'm grateful for the fact that both Thalia and

Dylan don't try to involve me in a conversation. They leave me to stand on the side of the boat, holding on to the railing, my ponytail being swung by the wind from side to side, water spraying onto my face.

They understand that I need to be alone to grieve in the only way I can. Dylan keeps going, waiting for me to tell him to stop. I have no idea where we're going, but if the police were unable to find Ryan, he must be somewhere deep in the ocean.

Finally, I hear a cough behind me and turn around.

"Let's stop here," I call over the rush of the wind. Dylan doesn't seem to have heard me, so Thalia taps him on the shoulder. He glances back at me for confirmation.

I nod and he slows down until the boat is bobbing back and forth on the water.

Thalia hands me the basket of rose petals. I grip the handle with one hand and reach into it with the other, curling my fingers around a handful of blooms. Swallowing the sob inside my throat, I lean over the railing and open my fingers one by one. The fragile petals fall into the water like snowflakes and drift away to nowhere.

"Goodbye, Ryan," I whisper. "I'm sorry. I love you."

I grab hold of another handful of silky petals

and release them onto the surface of the water. They look so crisp and innocent, breathtaking as they float away. Too beautiful to be used as a sign of death.

Right now, as I stand here facing the empty sea, my body feels cold. For the first time since Ryan disappeared, I feel as though he really is dead. The pain of loss is almost physical. It hurts that I never got the chance to say goodbye in person. It hurts not to be able to touch his hand and to hug him for the last time.

But he left behind a clear message. He wanted to punish me.

After I've said my goodbyes to Ryan, Thalia appears next to me and also says goodbye to him. Dylan says goodbye, too, even though he didn't know Ryan.

With the empty basket, I collapse onto a padded bench. I'm not crying, but my cheeks are burning as though fire has been lit beneath my skin.

Thalia and Dylan stand nearby, still giving me a moment to digest everything that's happened, to gather myself before stepping back into my life, a life without Ryan in it, a life I don't know how to live. Where do I even go from here? Where do I start?

Finally, I find the strength to let Dylan and Thalia back in.

"Why don't you both come with me?" Dylan

says, when we leave the boat and approach our cars. "Let me take you to lunch."

"I don't know," I whisper. "I won't be able to keep anything down."

"What do you feel like doing?" Thalia squeezes my hand.

"I feel like going home ... Being alone."

"I don't think that's a good idea, my love." Dylan slides an arm around my waist. "What happened today was heartbreaking for you. Let's help you get through the next couple of hours."

"There's nothing you can do for me."

How can I explain to them how it feels to wake up each day feeling like I'm holding a flame inside my chest?

Right now, I'm a burden to both of them. For the past few weeks, after work, Thalia came straight to my apartment to see how I'm doing. On most days she found Dylan there, doing his best to make me feel better. It's selfish of me to put their lives on hold.

Thalia will always be my friend, and if the tables were turned, I'd do the same for her. But when it comes to Dylan, I don't know if it's fair for me to keep him in my life when I don't even know how to breathe. He lost his own father not too long ago, but my pain is overshadowing his.

Every time I ask him when he will return to

New York, he changes the subject. His businesses need him there. I know he's only in Corlake because of me. That's not fair, and I intend on telling him that tonight.

Even though I'm going through a hard time, my feelings for Dylan have increased. I sense that he feels the same way. If he leaves for New York, I don't doubt for a second that he'll be back. And if he doesn't come back, we were never meant to be, after all.

Dylan's phone rings before he has the chance to talk me out of going home alone. He raises his hand to excuse himself and walks away from us toward his car. His face is toward us as he speaks, his eyebrows drawn, his free hand curled into a fist.

"He sounds like he's involved in an argument." Thalia wraps her arms around her. "What do you think it's about?"

"Apparently his father's businesses are causing him more trouble than he anticipated." Every time I've been with him this past week, endless calls came in, each of them leaving his face flushed with color.

I tried asking what's going on, but he kept saying it's nothing he can't handle and that we should focus on me instead of him.

But now that I've said goodbye to Ryan, it's time for Dylan to make time for his own problems. He's been focused on me for long enough. Maybe with him gone for a while, I can have a chance to try and fix myself up.

"Are you sure you're okay?" Thalia pulls me close.

"No, I'm not. But I'll learn to be." I rest my head on her shoulder. "I have to."

CHAPTER 21

~∞~

"Oh, boy, I've forgotten how much energy it takes to move." I tape shut a box filled with books, all of them belonging to Ryan.

I was surprised to find them in the back of his van. I don't remember the last time I saw him reading a book. But what hurts the most is that many are focused on how to overcome depression. In the end, no amount of information in the world could save him. I couldn't save him, either.

He's been gone for six weeks now, and I'm still not at the place where I can say he's dead. I don't know if that will ever change.

There are times I wonder if he's really gone because I'd be walking down the street and get the same overwhelming feeling that I'm being watched. But when I look over my shoulder, he's never there. So, I tell myself my mind is playing tricks on me and take the next step.

I still have the money he left behind. I've

thought of handing it over to the police, in case it was stolen, but I can't get myself to do that.

Last week, I went as far as driving to the police station only to turn back. I've kept the money well hidden in a kitchen cabinet ever since. I'll deal with it later, after I move.

"Moving definitely sucks, but I think a new start is what you need right now." Thalia folds up Ryan's sheets and lowers the bundle into another box. Like his books, I'll be donating his sheets and most of his other belongings to charity.

Hanging on to them only brings pain, and pain keeps me stuck.

"I still feel a bit guilty, though." I slide the elastic band from around my hair and redo the ponytail.

"Why is that?" Thalia sinks to the floor and pulls her legs under her. "Because of Ryan?"

"Yes." I shrug. "What if he comes back to find his home ...?" I wave a dismissive hand. "You know what? Let's not talk about that."

"Are you sure?" She frowns.

"Positive. Today, I choose happiness. Now, let's get back to work, woman." Being happy is a decision I get to consciously choose each and every day. But it's been hard to feel anything but sadness when I'm surrounded by memories of Ryan and his wasted life. That's one of the reasons I've decided to move. I've found a small studio apartment by the beach.

I still have a lot of debts to pay, but with only myself to think of, my expenses have reduced quite a bit.

"Aye-aye, captain." Thalia salutes and lifts herself from the floor. She heaves one of the boxes from the bed and leaves the room with it.

My mind is back to the money Ryan left behind, wondering what I should do with it.

When Thalia returns, I'm still wrapped up in my thoughts.

"I'm exhausted." She presses her hands to her lower back. "We should take a break. We've been working for three hours straight."

"I think you're right. My stomach is starting to complain. Should we go out for lunch?"

"Let's celebrate first." She disappears again and comes back with a bottle of apple cider and two champagne flutes. She must have brought the bottle with her when she arrived this morning.

My knees creak as I get up off the floor. "What's there to celebrate, though?"

"A lot. You're moving on." She opens the bottle and fills a glass with the sparkling drink. "You're taking a major step into your new life."

With a tiny smile, I curl my hand around the cool glass she hands me and go to sit on Ryan's bare mattress.

Thalia places the bottle at the foot of the

bed and sits next to me.

"Yes, I guess that's true." I take a sip of the cool, sweet liquid. It lingers on my tongue for a moment before sliding down my throat.

I give myself a moment to observe the room. It's the last time I'll see it in this state. Tomorrow, someone will come to repaint it to a white color. In a way that also feels like a loss.

Thalia nudges me with an elbow. "How are things with Mr. Billionaire going? We haven't had time to catch up."

"You really have to stop calling him that." I take another sip. "You know very well he's much more than that."

"Can you blame me? The guy is loaded. I need time to get used to thinking of him as a normal man."

"Well, he *is* a normal man. Deal with it." I allow myself to laugh. "We do normal things."

She raises an eyebrow. "Being flown in a private jet to Mexico for dinner is normal? I don't think so. Not to me, at least."

"You know the private jet and the gifts don't really mean much to me. But I like him for him. He's good for me."

"That makes me very happy. Don't let him go. He's a keeper." She drains her glass. "And I'm not talking about the money. I was just joking."

"I'll definitely try." I place both hands

around my glass. "Want to know something, though?"

"Sure."

I inhale the fruit-scented air. "It terrifies me a little that I like him so much."

"Funny how good things and bad things both have the power to terrify a person, right?"

"Yep." Butterflies explode inside my stomach just thinking about Dylan. "We haven't been together very long, but it feels like it." Now that I have the time to focus on my relationship with him, I find myself wanting to be around him all the time. He travels to New York at least once a week, and even when he's gone only for two or three days, it feels like we've been apart for longer.

"When we spoke last night, I almost told him I love him."

"Whoa!" Thalia's glass hits her knee and the liquid sloshes a little. "You didn't, I hope."

"Don't worry. The words just formed in my mind and wanted to be heard. But I caught them in time." I finish my drink.

"It's that serious, huh?"

"It feels like it." I shrug. "But it's too soon. I don't want to scare him away."

"Wow! That's so romantic, though."

"It is, but what if we don't work? The pain of loss has bonded us, but what if this ... what we have doesn't last? I don't want it to end." I want to continue the candlelight dinners on the beach at midnight and the sharing of fluffy cotton candy high up on a carousel at the local amusement park. I want him in my life.

"Paige, from where I'm standing, I see that you've got a great thing going. Don't overcomplicate things. Take it one step at a time and get to know each other. See where it takes you."

I lower the glass to the floor and flop back onto the pillows, my hands behind my head. "It's hard not to be serious, though. I don't know if we've taken it slow. The moment we entered into each other's lives, everything was already serious. Our shared pain of losing someone we love bonded us. We dealt with serious things from the start."

"I guess that makes a lot of sense." Thalia refills her glass. I shake my head when she offers me more. "You're so lucky to have a good relationship. Kevin and I, on the other hand ... I feel like we're doomed to fail. I can't believe I was put off by him being nice. And now that he's changed, I don't seem to like that, either."

I prop myself onto an elbow. "I thought things were okay. What happened?"

"We fight all the time. Two days ago, we went out for dinner and we fought over which restaurant to go to. He wanted Italian, and I wanted Chinese. The guy just flipped and turned into someone I couldn't recognize. He has quite a heated temper."

"You think at the beginning of your relationship he was just pretending to be a nice guy?"

"Of course, he was. Now I wish I could get Mr. Nice Guy back. To be honest, this side of him kind of scares me." Thalia feigns a shudder.

My mind drifts back to Ryan. I sit up. "I'm going to be honest with you. If you think he terrifies you, you might want to give your relationship some serious thought. If he's acting that way when you haven't even been together for that long, how would things be in a few more months or years?"

"You think he could turn out to be dangerous?"

"No." I sigh. "That's not what I'm saying. I'm just saying that you should be careful and keep your eyes open." I'd love to meet Kevin again to read him for myself, but Thalia's last attempts to get us all to meet up failed. He always found some excuse or other to cancel at the last minute. "What exactly about him annoys you, anyway?"

"Little things, you know. For one, he calls me all the damn time."

"Dylan calls me a lot, too." And often we spend hours on the phone, even when we have nothing much to talk about.

"It's different with Kevin. He …" She purses her lips. "He wants to know where I am throughout the day. It's starting to get on my nerves."

I place a hand on her arm. "What's your heart saying to you? When you think about his behavior, what's your heart telling you?"

"It's telling me to run." She twirls a braid around her finger. "I feel a knot inside my stomach every time he wants to come over, and I feel drained when he leaves. Sometimes I think I should leave him, but I'm a little scared that he might take it badly. What if he hurts me? He almost got physical with me once—"

"Then you call the cops on him." I grab her hand and squeeze. "If he's dangerous, it might be riskier to stay with him than to leave."

Thalia laughs nervously. "This is ridiculous. Look how I'm talking as if Kevin is some kind of monster. I guess he just likes me more than I like him right now."

"And you're okay with that?"

"I don't know. But who cares, really? We have fun together, when we're not fighting. It's not as though I'm going to marry him, anyway. I love my independence too much to get married."

I raise an eyebrow. "You never want to get married? That's new."

"It's a realization I came to only lately. What if I end up being married to someone like …" She bites her lip and stops talking.

"Like Ryan?" She doesn't respond, so I take it as a yes. "Hey, even after what I've gone through with Ryan, I still want to get married. Marriage doesn't have to be a prison."

Thalia stifles a grin. "I bet Dylan will make a good husband."

"Do not get ahead of yourself. We've just been dating for a couple of weeks. I can't allow myself to think about marriage." But the truth is, sometimes I lie in bed and wonder. I wonder how he would be as a husband, what our kids would look like. But each time, I push the brakes and drag my mind back to reality.

"Hello, ladies." We both jump when Dylan appears in the doorway, dressed in denim jeans and a crisp white shirt. "I didn't mean to startle you." He bends to kiss me. "The door was open. What are you talking about?"

A tingle of embarrassment sweeps up the back of my neck as I stand to wrap my arms around him. "I thought you'd be in New York until tomorrow night." I can't help wondering whether he heard our conversation. But I doubt it. If he did, he'd be running for the hills right now.

"I wanted to be back in time to help you move." He steps back, rolls up his sleeves, then lifts the box I just taped shut.

"Don't you dare let him go. He's amazing," Thalia whispers to me before following him out the door.

He's definitely a keeper, which makes it quite hard not to think of a future together.

At noon, the three of us enjoy a family-size pepperoni pizza, and Thalia leaves soon after to meet up with Kevin.

Dylan and I continue working side by side, kissing and holding each other in between finishing up the packing.

§

Before I know it, the sun has dimmed in the sky and the moving truck has moved most of my belongings to my new place.

Just as we settle into my new home, Dylan tells me to stay where I am in the tiny hallway, that he'll be back soon. He returns carrying a glossy white box with a powder blue bow. "Your moving-in present."

"Housewarming, you mean? You didn't need to get me anything." I giggle when he places the box in my hands. "You're my present."

"You can never have enough gifts. Go on, open it." He sits down on one of the boxes and watches me.

I lift the cover to reveal a beautiful, blush lace evening gown with tiny crystals on the bust, and a flowing chiffon skirt. I lift the dress out of the box. "Wow, Dylan. This is gorgeous!"

"It's a perfect match, then." He pulls me close. "I'm sure it will look stunning on you."

"But this is too fancy. Where would I wear it? I don't go to fancy events."

"Not yet. Maybe it's time you start doing that. I have one fun party you might want to wear it to."

"Is that so?" I lift an eyebrow.

"Yes, but first I'd like an answer to something."

"Sure." I allow the dress to fall over my arms like a waterfall. "Are you asking me to the ball?"

"Maybe." He smiles and takes the dress from me, lowers it back into the box. Then he takes my hand and leads me to my bedroom, where we weave our way through the boxes to stand by the window. We don't speak as we gaze out at the ocean.

"This is a nice place," he says finally. "But would you consider moving out again? It might be less stressful to do so immediately before you've settled in."

"What are you talking about?"

He inhales deeply. "Paige, I know we've only known each other for a short time, but it feels so right to be with you."

My eyes widen. "Dylan—"

"My life changed the very moment I met you. I never expected to feel this strongly and so soon, but I do. I'm deeply in love with you." A grin sweeps across his face. His dimples deepen. "What I'm trying to say is, I'd love it if you could move in with me. Come to New York."

"Dylan, no. I ... I can't do that. It's too soon."

"But I'm crazy about you, Paige. That's why I'd like to try and change your mind."

"How do you intend on doing that?" My entire body locks as I wait for his answer.

"Like this." Air whooshes out of my lungs when he lowers himself down, one knee meeting the floor. He pulls a small, leather box from his back pocket. "I want you to marry me, Paige Wilson. Please say you're just as crazy as I am."

My hands fly to my mouth to stifle a gasp. "I ... Dylan. You ... Oh my God."

"I want only you for the rest of my life. Please say yes." He opens the box and a huge cushion-cut diamond blinks at me from its bed of velvet.

I drop to my knees opposite him, tears in my eyes. Asking me to be his wife is crazy, but it also feels so right.

It really doesn't matter how long you know

a person. It's how deeply you feel about them that counts. Dylan makes me want to live again. As much as he wants me to be a part of his life, I want to be a part of his. That's why I don't hesitate before giving him the answer he wants to hear.

"I'd love to be crazy with you, Dylan Baxter."

CHAPTER 22

❧

Whenever I thought of getting married, I'd always imagined having a beach wedding. It's not surprising given that I love water.

Now it's happening. But there's another reason why getting married surrounded by water is important to me. In a weird kind of way, I feel closer to Ryan, as though he can also participate in my happiness.

The sun is just about to set, but the air is still warm against my skin.

After today, everything will be different. I'm not only taking steps toward the man of my dreams, but also the life of my dreams.

Butterflies flutter in the pit of my stomach the closer I get to the dock, where Dylan's boat is waiting.

From the joy radiating through my chest as I tighten my hands around my baby's breath and roses bouquet, one would never think I'd called off the engagement only a week after Dylan proposed.

When he'd asked me to be his wife, I had no doubt in my mind that I wanted to spend the rest of my life with him, which confirms my deep feelings for him. But it also scared me to think we had only known each other for a short time, and I don't exactly have the best track record of making the right decisions. It didn't help that the days after he proposed, I sleepwalked almost every night. I took it as a sign that something wasn't right.

Dylan tried to talk me out of calling off the engagement at first, but then gave up when I told him that maybe I just needed more time to get used to the idea of being someone's wife. To my relief, he didn't break up with me, but gave me my space.

It took three days for me to realize that not marrying him could be an even greater mistake. The idea of not having him in my life made me feel hollow inside.

Now, after a month of being engaged for real, here we are about to tie the knot.

Dylan is standing on the dock, hands in the pockets of his pants. His smile grows brighter as I take the wooden steps leading up to the dock.

The moment I'm close enough to feel his breath on my face, he sweeps me off my feet and carries me onto the boat.

"Hello, gorgeous." He lowers me onto the deck, where I'm surrounded by beautiful flowers and candles in glass vases. "Ready to take the plunge?"

"I can't wait." I lean my head into his neck, unable to wipe the grin off my face. "You bet I am." His lips brush my cheek.

Thalia, who is carrying a miniature version of my bouquet, engulfs me in a hug. "You look so beautiful, honey," she says, admiring my ivory satin and lace knee-length dress with pearly cap sleeves. "I'm so happy for you."

"I'm happy for me, too." I give her a wink and move away to stand next to my future husband.

When Dylan suggested we have a small wedding, I quickly jumped on the idea because being the center of attention is not something I'm good at. And besides, having too many people at the wedding would remind me that I have no family left. We both agreed that in a couple of weeks, after our honeymoon, we'll host a fancy dinner for our friends and colleagues.

Standing by Dylan's side as best man is his friend, Shaun Reamon, who I only got to meet five days ago when he flew in from New York. Dylan said they'd been best friends since college and went on to become business partners.

We all take our places in front of the priest

from St. Peter's Catholic Church, the church in which I'd found peace a few weeks ago.

"I'm going to make you so happy, Paige Wilson," Dylan whispers into my ear, his breath brushing my earlobe.

"And I'll do the same for you." As I gaze into his eyes, I'm unable to believe that in a few moments I will be Mrs. Paige Baxter. Hopefully, with a new name, I can leave behind the old Paige, the one who hurt all the time.

Father William clears his throat. "Everyone ready? Can we get started?"

"Absolutely." Dylan clasps his hands in front of him. He looks so happy.

The priest greets us all again, talks about the importance of marriage, reads some verses from the Bible, then asks us to repeat the important words. Gazing into each other's eyes, Dylan and I promise ourselves to each other. We promise not to hurt the other. We promise to be there in sickness and in health, to love and to cherish *till death do us part.*

"I do," Dylan says the two words that seal the deal.

"I do," I also say after the priest.

We exchange rings, and Father William pronounces us husband and wife and turns to Dylan with a bright smile. "In that case, you may kiss your bride." Thalia takes my bouquet from me so I can be free to wrap my arms around my husband's neck. I tip my head back and Dylan pulls me close and lowers his lips on mine. The moment our lips touch, any shred of guilt or doubt melts from the edges of my heart and I start to breathe. I start to live.

It takes a while for us to pull apart, but once we do, we're both breathless and happy.

After the exchange of vows, the priest and both our witnesses wish us well, then Shaun brings out the champagne to toast to our future together. There are two bottles, one with alcohol and one without. Dylan now knows that I don't drink because of what alcohol had done to my family.

The waiting staff emerge from below deck with an elegant cupcake wedding cake from The Cake Palace and platters of mouthwatering canapés. We enjoy the food in a relaxed and happy atmosphere.

Our wedding may seem simple from the outside, but it's everything I could ever wish for.

After the short celebration, our guests leave us on the boat, allowing us to enjoy our time together as husband and wife.

"You made the right decision," Thalia whispers to me before she steps off the boat. "You two are perfect for each other. And he adores you. Enjoy your honeymoon in Africa. Do send me a postcard, if you remember."

"Of course, I'll do that." I kiss her cheek. "Expect lots of them."

As I watch my friend walk off the boat, I wish for her that she finds a man that makes her as happy as Dylan makes me. She had finally gathered up the courage to break things off with Kevin, and to both our relief, all she got were a few insults and a slamming of the door.

"Pass on my greetings to everyone at BJHS."

"Will do, sweetie."

After our dream honeymoon under the African sun, I'll be moving with Dylan to New York. Margaret and the other staff members were sad when I said I'll no longer be a part of the team, but they all wished me well.

Being away from Corlake will give me the chance to start over with a blank slate, to hopefully distance myself from the toxic memories. I've already applied to several schools in New York. Dylan says I don't need to work because we don't need the money, but I value my independence too much, and teaching math is my passion.

But tonight, we're staying the night in Corlake. As much as it brought me pain, this town is where I've spent my entire life. I need to say goodbye properly.

After everyone leaves, Dylan and I remain on the boat for another hour, kissing and laughing, planning our future, eating imported French truffles, and drinking the rest of the champagne, while listening to the waves rolling.

Once darkness falls, Dylan drives us to the Brookside Hotel, a luxury five-star hotel that had also belonged to his father.

As soon as we step into the lobby, cheers ring out as both guests and staff shout out words of congratulations.

Some local reporters approach us, shoving microphones in our faces, tossing questions at us.

Dylan does his best to shield me from the reporters, holding me close to his side in a protective gesture as we disappear into the elevator.

"I can't believe word of our wedding has already spread." He hits the button to the top floor and gathers me into his arms.

"Nothing stays hidden for long here." I lean my head against his warm chest.

"At least the reporters out here are not as aggressive as the ones in New York." He plants a kiss on the top of my head. "Hopefully, no one will follow us to Africa."

"I hope so, too," I say, exhaustion washing over me. I look forward to a hot shower before slipping into bed with my husband. After weeks and months of trying to keep my head above water, I'm finally out of the storm. I can rest and learn to enjoy life.

Every table in the presidential suite is covered with roses, candles flickering between them. The glinting chandeliers add to the sparkle. Although I appreciate the luxury, I only have eyes for Dylan.

I turn my head to the side as he kisses my neck. My skin tingles when he moves his lips from my neck to my lips.

"Babe, would you mind if I take a shower?" I whisper against his lips. "I want to get rid of all the makeup and hairspray."

"Sure. Go ahead. I need to make a call first, then I might join you. Should I order up room service for later?"

"That'll be nice. You make the choice." I fold my arms in front of my chest. "I do have one request, Mr. Baxter."

"Anything for my beautiful wife." He pulls his phone from his pocket.

"After the shower, no more phone calls."

"That's a promise."

Twenty minutes later, I'm still under the hot shower and Dylan still hasn't shown up. His call must be taking longer than he had planned.

After another five minutes, I turn off the water and walk out, steam rising from my skin.

Stepping out of the bathroom, one towel is wrapped around my body while I'm drying my hair with another.

Dylan is out on the spacious balcony, phone pressed to his ear, shoulders shaking as though he's having an argument with the person he's talking to. Not again.

Poor guy. He doesn't seem to get a break.

I'm about to join him outside, but his words make their way through the slit in the balcony sliding doors and barrel into me.

"Wrong. I didn't just marry her for the money." His words are a furious whisper, drenched in annoyance. "Of course, the inheritance is important to me. But she's important to me, as well." He loosens his tie. "I'm sorry. It's too late. It's done."

I stumble back as though someone has punched me in the face, his words ringing in my ears.

He didn't just marry me for the money? What's he talking about? Who is he talking to?

I'm shaking as I perch on the edge of the bed, my hands clutching the sheets.

My mind is still reeling when he finally ends his call and joins me in one of the two bedrooms.

"I thought you'd be in the shower. I'm sorry I took so long." He places his phone on a dresser. "Come here, Mrs. Baxter." He opens his arms, but I don't move from the bed. My eyes are fixed on his face.

"Before anything happens here, I need an

answer to something." My voice is trembling as it carries the words from my mouth.

"Are you okay?" He comes to the bed and sits down next to me, wrapping an arm around my waist. I pull away, but he doesn't let me go. "What's going on?"

"*You* tell me." I rise from the bed. "What did you mean when you said you didn't just marry me for the money?"

A frown forms between his eyes. "What ... What are you talking about?"

"Were you married before?"

"No, of course not. You know that."

"I'm the only woman you've ever exchanged marriage vows with?"

"Of course." He stands up and approaches me, but I step away. "Where are you going with this? Why all these questions?"

"I overhead your phone conversation. You said you didn't just marry me for the money."

A shadow crosses his features but it disappears just as quickly. "You heard wrong." There's something in his eyes, something resembling guilt.

I can smell guilt from miles away. It's the one emotion that has followed me around for years.

I move to stand in front of him, arms folded. "Tell me the truth. Why did you marry me, really?"

"Because I love you." His words are firm and

they sound honest, but my heart reads between the lines.

"I know there's something you're keeping from me. Tell me now, or I'll walk out of this room."

"All right." He moves away from me and collapses onto the bed, drops his head into his hands with a sigh. "When my father died, the conditions of me receiving his inheritance were that I get married within six months after his death."

"So you found the first willing woman to fall in love with you?" A bubble of laughter forms inside my throat and explodes from my lips. "This was all just a game?" Weakened by his revelation, I collapse against a wall for support. "You played me?"

"No." His head snaps up. "That's not true. It's not like that at all." He buries his fingers into his hair. "At first, yes, I was on the lookout for someone to marry. And then—"

"You didn't expect to fall in love with me; is that it?"

"Yes," he says in a croak. "You have to believe me. Every single word I said to you … about how much you mean to me is the truth. I married you for love."

"No, you married me for money." My voice rises. "That's why you wanted to get married as soon as possible. It wasn't because you couldn't wait to spend the rest of your life with me."

"Please." He gets to his feet and crosses the room toward me, lays his hands on my shoulders. "I love you so much, Paige. That's not a lie. I *did* marry you for the right reasons." He tucks a strand of damp hair behind my ear. "Say you believe me."

"No. No, I don't." Tears well up in my throat. "I don't even know what other lies you've told me. It was cruel of you to pretend you cared about me ... about my brother." I back away from him, raise my hands to stop him from approaching me. "Oh my God. You chose me because I was weak and desperate. My loneliness made me an easy target, didn't it?"

He doesn't respond. After a moment of silence, he nods. "At the beginning my intentions may not have been pure, but you mean the world to me."

"I don't know what to believe right now." I bite my trembling lip. "I can't do this. I can't." My voice fades to a whisper. "I'll sleep in the other room."

As I turn my back on him, the doorbell rings. Without thinking, I yank the door open.

A butler pushes in a tray of food and a bottle of champagne. "The champagne is a wedding gift from the staff, Sir," he says.

"We're no longer hungry," I say, not

bothering to check with Dylan.

The butler glances past me at Dylan.

"Thank you," Dylan says to the butler. "You can leave it there." He points to one side of the room. The butler's eyes keep moving between Dylan and me as he does what he's told. Then he nods at both of us and disappears from the suite.

I'm too angry to care that he must have sensed the tension between us, that he must have seen the tears on my cheeks. I don't care what gossip he'll share with his colleagues once he gets downstairs, or about the news spreading across town like wildfire. All I care about right now is being alone to think.

With Dylan still begging me to believe him, I grab the silver bucket with the bottle of champagne and disappear into the other room.

Devastated that my future is ending before it even starts, I pop open the champagne bottle. For the first time in my life, I have my first taste of alcohol—straight from the bottle.

CHAPTER 23

～∞～

My eyelids are heavy and sore as I pull them apart. For someone who was very upset, I slept deep. Maybe it was the alcohol.

I draw in a breath, but instead of oxygen filling my body with life and strength, the air settles heavy in the center of my chest, making it hard to breathe.

My stomach roils at the remnant taste of alcohol still coating my tongue. I'd had only two gulps of the champagne before coming to my senses and climbing under the sheets, covered in guilt and regret.

As I cover my face with both hands, my intuition tells me something's wrong, but I know that already. Staring up at the glinting chandelier, memories of yesterday drip into my mind.

How I wish it were just a dream and not a nightmare that will soon be erased by the truth. How I wish my marriage wasn't a sham, that

Dylan is the man I thought he was when I fell in love with him.

The way he looked at me last night, the emotions in his eyes had told me that he wasn't lying when he said he loves me. But that doesn't wipe away the hurt clawing through my veins. It doesn't erase the truth that he started out with the intention to use me.

Now what?

My head advises me to get out of the bed and walk out of Dylan's life. But my heart, even in its broken state, is finding it hard to let go of this love I've found, to walk away from the first man who's ever made me feel alive.

One thing I do know for sure is that I've made enough impulsive decisions in my life, and I'm not ready to make another I could end up regretting. That's why I stayed last night.

I turn my head to the windows and focus on the sliver of light piercing through the place where the jacquard drapes meet in the middle. I wrap my arms around myself. The room is warm but my skin feels cold.

In need of a few more minutes to collect myself and gather up the courage to face Dylan, I bury myself deeper into the comforter, pulling it up to my chin as I turn to face the other side. I feel body heat next to me and freeze.

I'm not alone in the bed.

Dylan is fast asleep next to me, facing the

other side. How dare he disregard my request to be alone after what he did?

Teeth clenched, I shove back the covers and swing my legs out of bed, ignoring the comfort offered by the shaggy carpeting that welcomes my feet.

I cross the room and yank the drapes apart. The morning light floods in.

My head swims when I spin around, expecting to have woken him. But he's still asleep, the comforter hugging the length of his body, the soft curls of his hair spilling onto the ivory pillows.

The champagne bottle I started is on his nightstand, now empty.

My throat is tight with anger as I march to his side of the bed and yank the covers from his upper body.

When my eyes land on his face, I jump back, a scream trapped in my throat.

He's not sleeping. His eyes are wide, too wide ... blank. His skin is pale, his mouth parted as though he wants to say something.

As I watch him lying there, unmoving, my world starts to spin. I don't need to touch him to know he will never blink again, to know that his rich, honey voice will never be heard again. I've encountered a dead body before, my mother's.

He's dead, the little voice in my head taunts.

"Shut up," I snap, drops of my saliva following the words out of my mouth, hitting Dylan's face.

This is Dylan, my husband, the man I love, not a corpse.

A sudden wave of panic knocks the wind from my lungs and pushes me to the carpeted floor.

"Dylan, baby, talk to me." I shake him, the same way I shook Ryan when he'd swallowed the pills, and when I thought he had drowned. The same way I shook my mother.

My body numb with shock, I shove the rest of the comforter from his body.

My breath solidifies inside my lungs when I catch sight of the blood on his shirt, smack in the middle of his chest. The same shirt he wore to our wedding yesterday, the shirt he had been unbuttoning when I walked out on him last night.

The stain of red seems to be growing larger as I watch.

My fingers flutter to my throat.

No, this can't be happening. It has to be a dream. I have to be stuck inside a nightmare.

Desperate to wake up, I pinch my arm but it hurts. Although nowhere near as much as my heart is hurting.

"It's not funny. Wake up, Dylan. Please wake up. Honey, I believe you. I need you." Hot tears pour from my eyes as I search for his pulse, knowing deep down I won't find one. I don't.

I slap his cheeks, pummel his chest with my fists, but he remains still. His dead eyes continue to stare up at me but his body is like that of a statue.

Angry sobs break through me as I bury my face into the carpet, my hands pulling at my hair.

As the truth of the moment sinks deeper into my mind, a wave of nausea overcomes me.

I scramble to my trembling legs and race to the bathroom, but I don't make it in time.

Warm, bitter bile gushes from my mouth onto the cream carpet, staining it yellow and green. My knees hit the floor and I retch until my stomach has nothing more left to give, until I'm heaving empty, alcohol-tainted air.

I sit in front of my vomit for a long time, afraid to look behind me at the horror scene.

I can't sit here doing nothing. I should find out what happened, call someone for help.

But what would I say? How can I even start to explain what happened?

I peel myself off the floor and sway to the phone on the side of my bed. I'm about to dial, when I spot the sharp tip of a knife sticking out from underneath my pillow. It's smeared with blood.

I shrink away from the bed, one step after

the other until my back hits the cool window. My trembling hands come to my mouth, my head shaking from side to side.

Questions flood my mind, questions I'm afraid to have answers to.

This has to be a joke, some kind of prank. I couldn't have ... I couldn't have killed him.

My hands leave my face. I hold them in the air, looking at the blood on them. His blood transferred to me when I was shaking him awake. My hands were clean when I pulled open the drapes earlier. Or were they?

I slide to the floor and draw my knees up to my chin. I was furious with Dylan last night, but not enough to kill him.

Before I fell asleep, I hated myself for loving him, for wanting desperately to give him another chance, to forgive him. Now it's too late for anything.

I glance at the phone, cold fingers of dread closing my throat. What if I call someone and they walk in here and think I did it?

The butler who brought us food last night would quickly be able to confirm that there was tension between us. What if the cops find evidence to prove I did it? What if the knife has my fingerprints on it?

For the first time, I notice small stains of blood on the fabric of my wedding dress. How did I not see them before?

You did it.

"No." I spring up from the floor and run past my vomit into the bathroom, shove my hands under hot running water. Red liquid stains the tempered glass basin before disappearing down the drain.

I use a lot of soap, scrubbing my hands until they feel raw. But even after my hands are visibly clean, they feel dirty. In my mind's eye, I still see the smears of red.

I know I didn't kill him, but the police might not believe me. No one else was in the suite with us last night. I was the last person to see him alive.

A nagging thought claws its way to the forefront of my mind. My entire body stiffens.

What if I sleepwalked last night? What if I killed my husband without knowing I was doing it? What if my sleepwalking history is all the evidence the cops need to arrest me?

Right now, everything points to me being the murderer. The knife under my pillow, the stains on my dress, the argument we had last night, my sleepwalking episodes.

Dylan was a wealthy man and I'm buried in debt. All it would take is for one person to believe I killed him for his money and the whole country would believe it.

I can't stay here. It's only a matter of time before someone comes to our suite. Shaun is staying in the hotel, as well. He might decide to come up and find his best friend dead. I can't be found in here with blood on my clothes.

Nothing but escape on my mind, I pull off my bloody dress and change into a pair of jeans and a big, white T-shirt. Then I reach for a wide brim hat I'd planned on wearing on our safaris in Africa.

I grab a small bag and stuff my wedding dress into it, only to yank it out again.

Giving myself no time to think about my actions, I pull the murder weapon from underneath my pillow and clean the handle as I often saw criminals do in movies. Am I a criminal? I don't plan to stay long enough to find out.

I'm about to leave the suite, when I stop with my hand on the doorknob. I can't leave him without anyone knowing. But I also can't make a call from here.

Every second I spend in the suite is a second closer to my arrest. The idea of being thrown into jail paralyzes me.

The justice system is not perfect. Many innocent people are found guilty and thrown behind bars all the time. Due to my unlucky streak, the chances of me being added to the list are super high.

I pull my hat low on my forehead, bow my head, and run.

I take the emergency exit staircase instead of the elevator.

It's only once my feet touch the cool tiles of the steps when I notice I'm not wearing shoes. Too late now. There's no way I'll go back there.

Barefoot and terrified, I make my way through the lobby, expecting someone to stop me, to call out my name. I must look crazy walking around with no shoes, but I don't look up to see who's watching. I don't stop walking until I'm through the rotating doors and out onto the street.

Fighting the urge to glance over my shoulder, I pick up my pace.

A few blocks away from the hotel, I break into a run, ignoring the grains of sand digging into the soles of my feet, jumping over cracks in the sidewalk, ignoring the stares from people around me.

The sounds of a police siren followed by that of a dog barking bring me to a screeching halt. My chest burning with exhaustion and panic, I search my surroundings but don't see the police car.

Relief rushes through me as I continue to run, my feet pounding the ground hard.

When I come across a telephone booth, I slip inside and make the call, I hold my nose to make myself sound different and tell the woman on the other end that someone is dead in the presidential suite of the Brookside Hotel. I hang up before she can ask any questions.

Outside the phone box, I hail the first taxi that approaches me.

The address I give the driver is that of my old apartment. I still have a few things there.

As the taxi pushes through the 6:00 a.m. rush hour, the rational side of me takes over.

Paige, what you're doing is stupid. Running from a crime scene confirms your guilt.

Emotions rage through me as I contemplate what to do. Should I return to the hotel? But I can't do that. For all I know, the place is already swarming with men and women in uniform and paramedics.

The taxi comes to a halt outside the building of my old apartment, which I haven't given up yet in case a miracle happens and Ryan comes home while we're in Africa. I planned on handing over the keys after our return.

I ask the cab driver to wait outside for me and I run into the apartment, grab a pair of shoes, and rush into the kitchen. The shoebox of money is hidden at the back of a cabinet.

Right now, I don't care where the cash came from, who it belongs to. The money Ryan left behind is my only ticket out of this nightmare.

If I'm going to run, I have to do it right. I've already worsened my situation as it is.

CHAPTER 24

❦

I lower myself onto the squeaking motel bed. I have chosen a cheap motel on the outskirts of town, far from where I lived, a good distance from the Brookside Hotel.

As I sit on the lumpy mattress, my hands wedged between my trembling knees, doubts assail my mind. I'm in such a trance I can barely feel my feet on the threadbare carpet.

I should go back, turn myself in. If I killed Dylan, even if I can't remember doing it, I deserve to go to prison.

My mind pleads for my body to move, to do the right thing, but it stays put.

The mere thought of being thrown behind bars makes me feel sick to my stomach. Visiting my father in prison had been one of the worst experiences of my life. I'm not about to end up in the same situation he did. This is no family tradition.

Tears come again at the same time fresh bile

pushes its way up my throat.

This time I make it to the bathroom, but nothing except saliva, tears, and snot plop into the cracked toilet bowl.

I grab a wad of tissue paper and press it to my nose.

The sound of ice cream truck music drifts in through the window. It brings with it memories of childhood. However painful my childhood was, this situation is so much worse.

The ice cream music fades into the distance, and I jump when the sound of my cellphone ringing seeps through the thin wall.

My body is lethargic as I step back into the room and watch an unknown number flashing on the screen. It could be the police, so I don't answer.

I throw myself onto the bed and fold myself into a fetal position, my eyes still on the phone, which has finally gone silent after five missed calls.

An overwhelming feeling of loneliness washes over me. I don't think I can handle this alone. I need to talk to someone even for a few seconds, someone who cares about me, someone who knows I'd never kill anyone.

I dial Thalia's number.

She picks up before I have the chance to change my mind and end the call.

"Paige? Why are you calling me the morning

after your wedding night? Aren't you supposed to be celebrating with your new hubby?" Her words are laced with a touch of humor.

Instead of joining in her humor, I weep, crying harder than I'd ever done in my entire life.

"Oh, no," Thalia says, breathless. "What happened?" A rustling sound comes through the line. She must be sitting up in her bed.

"Something ... Something terrible." I pinch the bridge of my nose, which is now slippery with sweat and tears. "I ... Thalia—"

"I'm here, sweetie. Did Dylan do something?"

I swallow hard. "Yes. No. Dylan ... Oh my God, Thalia, he's dead."

Everything goes quiet. Silence floods the line connecting us. It crackles.

"Paige, what are you talking about?" Thalia asks in a broken whisper.

As excruciating as it is to recall the scene I woke up to this morning, I tell her everything. She's my best friend, and I can trust her completely.

"What if I did it? What if I killed Dylan?" I grapple for air. "I can't remember anything. I can't remember anything that happened after I went to bed."

"Paige, you have to calm down. Try to breathe." She pauses. "Where are you? Are you still at the hotel?"

I shake my head. "I had to get out of there. I can't go to prison," I whisper. "I have to go … away."

"No. Don't do anything you might regret." She inhales sharply. "Come to my place. Let's get through this together. We'll get a lawyer to help you."

"I can't. I'll be found guilty. I know it." I wipe my cheek with the back of my hand.

"No, you don't. You don't know that for sure."

"I do. I feel it." Air whooshes out of my lungs. "Nothing ever works out for me. I'm cursed." Ryan was right when he said happiness is for other people.

Silence stretches between us again, and I hear the sound of the TV blaring on Thalia's side.

"Thalia?" I call and when she doesn't respond, I pick up the remote and flick on the tiny TV in my room. I switch from one channel to the other until I find what I'm looking for.

A bright-eyed local news reporter with a shock of red hair is standing in front of the Brookside Hotel, reporting the tragic story of Dylan Baxter's death, just months after his father died. Scrolling across the bottom of the screen are five words, the final nails on my coffin.

New wife wanted for questioning.

"Could Dylan Baxter's new wife have something to do with his death?" The reporter glances behind her at the hotel. "Keep watching. We'll have more news as events unfold."

My eyes are glued to the screen, gazing past the reporter to the covered corpse being wheeled through the doors of the Brookside Hotel.

I switch off the TV and push a fist into my mouth, rocking back and forth.

"Paige, honey, please listen to me—"

"Bye, Thalia," I say before she tries to talk me into turning myself in. "I love you."

There's only one thing left for me to do, and it has nothing to do with handcuffs snapping around my wrists.

CHAPTER 25

The last traces of copper hair dye first color the rust-stained basin, then disappear down the drain. They remind me of how Dylan's blood had looked in the hotel basin, three days ago.

Three days. Seventy-two hours. Four thousand three hundred and twenty minutes. But it feels to me as though I've been hiding for a year.

I meet my hollow, blue eyes in the foggy mirror above the basin, studying the shadows around them, the pockets of exhaustion underneath.

The past days and nights have taken such a toll on me, I wonder if I'll make it through the next days, weeks, or months?

A lot has changed since I talked to Thalia. As soon as I'd ended our call, I'd gone out and bought a week's supply of food and drinks as well as hair dye and some toiletries. Then I took a bus to Wellice, a sleepy town forty-minutes north of Corlake.

Before heading to Wellice, I had discarded my cell phone in case the police are using it to track me down. I bought a secondhand phone and a cheap laptop from an electronics store close to where I boarded the bus.

As I'd expected, the news of Dylan's murder is now spread across the country and, being the last person who saw him alive, I'm officially the number one suspect.

The photo making rounds all over the news is one taken by one of the reporters we encountered in the lobby of the hotel.

I should have listened to my instincts and not married Dylan. Of course, I would never have imagined that my wedding would end in such a tragedy, but I should have known that happiness is not for me, that every time I try to be happy, something terrible happens.

Many residents of Corlake have been interviewed. Most of them have dubbed me the monster bride. Even if I chose to go back now, to try and prove my innocence, it's too late. Everyone in my hometown hates me. Dylan's death is sure to disrupt their lives and put their livelihoods at risk. Businesses will probably be shut down and jobs will be lost. If I return, I'll be a pariah in my own home.

What's shocking and even more heartbreaking is how the media has uncovered the story of Ryan's disappearance and possible death, and are hinting at the fact that I might not have only killed my new husband, but also my brother, who had been a burden to me.

It would be hard enough to prove I didn't kill Dylan. Proving I didn't kill two men would be almost impossible. I'm bound to end up in prison for one of their deaths.

Tears seep into the corners of my eyes as I watch my crumbling reflection in the mirror. I look different and not only because my hair is now red. Sadness is written all over my face, and it's no surprise. To lose two people I love in the space of just a few weeks is torture. I struggle to keep it together, but every time an image of Ryan or Dylan crosses my mind, tears come. Will I ever get over the pain?

I turn off the faucet—which continues to drip—and place both palms on the cool mirror. I close my eyes.

If only I could share my burden with someone. Thalia is the only person who comes to mind, but I care too much about her to put her in a difficult position. The police have possibly already questioned her. The less she knows about my whereabouts, the better.

I square my shoulders. "You have to be strong, Paige. You're all you've got now." Only I can help myself out of this situation.

In two days, if I'm still free, in order to save

myself, I *will* be responsible for a death. The death of Paige Wilson.

I've spent hours working out a plan of how to disappear. I'd intentionally checked into a motel with free Wi-Fi that enables me to do research online. My searches have yielded information ranging from how to change my appearance to how to get a new identity.

When I wasn't rocking back and forth in a corner of my bed while staring at the door—expecting it to be kicked down—I planned my escape.

I have no idea how far I'll get before the cops catch up, but I'm willing to try. Maybe luck is on my side this one time in my life.

I push a hand through my new hair. No one would be able to recognize me with red, much shorter hair and glasses.

My plan is to cut all ties with my old life and start from scratch. I see no other way out.

When my hair is dry, I exit the bathroom and pick up the disposable camera on my bed. The room no longer makes my stomach churn. Mildew on the peeling walls, old carpet smells, and the slimy shower curtain are a small price to pay for safety.

Half an hour after I leave the bathroom, I upload my photo to a secret website.

Forty-eight hours later, I get a knock on the door.

Beads of sweat pop through the skin of my upper lip as I stand in front of the door, afraid to open it. The person on the other side might not be who I'm expecting. For all I know, it could be a police officer here to arrest me.

"It's me," the man says in a low, smoker's voice. "Should I push the documents under the door?"

My shoulders sag with relief. "Yes."

A thick white, stained envelope slides through the crack under the door and appears at my bare feet.

"The money," the man says, but I ignore him. I have to be sure I'm getting what I'm paying for, that I'm not being scammed.

I rip open the envelope and pull out the social security card, amazed at how real it looks. Everything else looks just as real—the passport and driver's license. I try not to think of the crimes that might have been committed for my freedom.

My breath hitches as I read the name in the passport. "My name is Caitlin Borgen," I whisper to myself.

"The money ... now—" His voice is drowned out by a toilet flushing in the room next door to mine.

"Yes." I stuff the documents back into the envelope. "Please, hang on a second." I take a step toward the bed and pick up a bulging envelope. I slide it through to the other side.

"Thanks," I whisper but I'm not sure he hears me.

I stay by the door until his footfalls become faint down the hall.

Holding on to the envelope filled with the keys to my new life, I slide to the floor.

My stomach is clenched with nerves from fear of what I'm about to do. But this is the only way out, a chance for me to leave my cursed life behind and start afresh.

Of all the decisions I've made over the years, this might finally be the right one.

On the other side of the door is a new life, a new me.

Before fear paralyzes me completely, I grab the backpack with the rest of the money, pull on my baseball cap, and catch the last bus out of town, walking out of Paige Wilson's life forever.

I'm done giving fate another chance. It's time to create my own luck.

The only thing I take with me to remember Paige by are the scars on my heart.

As the bus pulls out of Wellice, an image of Ryan flashes across my mind. Before I can blink away the memories, I remember his threat.

I'll make your life a living hell.

PART TWO

CHAPTER 26

∽

I try not to blink as I stand in the doorway of my bright kitchen, watching my husband, Jared Lester, preparing breakfast, his back turned to me. He's wearing his favorites: camel shorts, a worn-out, ash gray T-shirt, and no shoes.

As a travel photographer, featured in *National Geographic* several times, Jared gets way too many assignments out of town in search of the perfect shot. But whenever he's not on the road, he prides himself on making me breakfast every morning.

Even if he's rarely home for longer than three weeks at a time, I have more than I could have ever wished for. I have a life I don't deserve. I live in constant fear of blinking, afraid if I close my eyes even for a beat, I will find my borrowed life gone.

Inhaling the aromas of baked beans, sausages, and bacon, I gaze through the open window at the distant ocean waves. It's relaxing to watch them roll in and then retreat into the deep sea. There's a road between our front door and the beach sand, but it still feels as though we live right on the beach.

While on the run as Caitlin Borgen, my plan was to dive into a city with a huge population and towering buildings that hid me from sight, but I'm a small-town-by-the-ocean kind of girl. Five years ago, after a year in New York, a bout of depression sent me in search of a place that felt more like the home I'd left behind. My search led me to the quaint, beachside town of Faypine, Maine.

I had only planned to stay for a week in a tiny cottage by the beach, but one morning I decided to go for a swim and met Jared Lester, a handsome man in his late thirties with surfer looks and eyes the same china-blue color as mine. He was taking pictures of seagulls until he saw me and focused his camera on me instead. Afraid he was a private detective, I panicked and bolted. In my rush to get away, I twisted my ankle, and he came to my aid. In the days that followed, he visited my cottage every morning on his way to the beach.

The way he looked after me, the way he looked at me, the way he said my name, healed some of the wounds I used to carry on the surface of my heart. The walls came down, and

I let him in. We fell in love fast and hard. The need to be loved again was so strong that my heart forced me to forget New York and stay in Faypine for good.

Now, here I am, married to Jared and living in a beautiful cottage by the sea. The cottage was a wedding present from him, and it happens to be only a few blocks from the one I'd rented the summer we fell in love.

In my dark moments, I still fear I'll wake up one day to find it all gone. I never stop wondering what he would do if he found out the truth about me. I've tried opening up to him several times over the years, to tell him about Paige Wilson, but the fear of losing him made me pull back every time. As far as he knows, I was born in New York, and my parents, Megan and Dan Borgen, died in a car accident when I was one, leaving me in the care of my maternal grandmother, who later died when I was in college, pursuing an education and mathematics degree.

Maybe it was stupid of me to tell him about my true educational background, but I wanted to keep something from the past—something I loved. Just as much as I could not let go of the ocean, I couldn't let go of mathematics. I'd be completely lost without my passion for numbers. I find comfort in the classroom just as much as I find it in the sea. But I pray every day that no one will find out that my rather convincing college degree is fake and that it was accompanied by a fake resume and references, all paid for with a lot of money.

I tell myself that the past will never catch up, even though the little voice inside my head tells me it's a lie. Every morning I choose to ignore that voice. Today is no different.

"Good morning, Mrs. Lester. I can feel your eyes on my back." Jared turns to me with a smile. He's holding a wooden spoon.

"How do you do that? I didn't make a sound." I lift my hands to my hair to force my red curls into a red velvet hair scrunchy.

"I'd feel your presence in a packed room, my love." He steps away from the stove and gives me a kiss on the lips. In between the breakfast aromas, I catch a whiff of the woody and minty undertone of his cologne. "Let me." He takes the hair scrunchy from my hand and turns me around by the shoulders.

I close my eyes as my husband ties my hair into its everyday ponytail. He thinks I'm a curly-haired redhead, not the blonde I used to be. I work hard to keep it that way, never giving my hair a chance to show its real roots. He once told me it was my hair he fell in love with first, from behind the lens of his camera, before he even heard my voice.

"Thank you," I say when he's done, turning

back to face him.

"Have I told you lately how gorgeous you look pregnant?" He touches my cheek with the tip of a finger. The love in his eyes makes me breathless with happiness.

"You better mean that." I laugh, peeling my gaze from his to my swollen belly. I love being pregnant. I'm willing to pay whatever price it takes to bring our baby into the world. The morning sickness, the heartburn, and all the aches and pains that come with pregnancy are all worth it.

Jared leans in closer, pressing his body against mine, transferring his heat to my body. He puts his arms around me. "You bet I mean it. In fact, I'd like to have a few more after this one."

My stomach twists as I lean back to look into his eyes. We've been married for three years and tried to have a baby from the first day. But we failed over and over again, miscarriage after miscarriage. Just when I gave up on ever being able to have his child, convinced it's my punishment for everything I've done, I got pregnant. But can we really get lucky a second or third time around?

The last months of this pregnancy have been both exhilarating and exhausting. As much as I look forward to seeing my baby, I fear I might lose it. Instead of responding to my husband, I just smile and kiss him.

Jared approaches our kitchen table and pulls out a chair for me. As I lower myself into it, my canary yellow maternity dress drapes onto the sides. Along with a new name and a new life, I've given my clothing style a much needed splash of color. No more blacks for me.

On his way back to the stove, Jared turns on the radio to a country music station. As the music plays, he serves me my breakfast: a full plate filled with toast, bacon, sausages, and poached eggs.

The rumble of the mail van causes me to peer out the window. Troy Wendel hops from the dusty van and opens our gate, a package tucked under his arm. He disappears out of view as he approaches our front door.

"Something else for the baby?" Jared winks.

"Hey, don't look at me like that. Babies need a lot of things." I attempt to stand from the table, but he places a hand on my shoulder.

"Eat. I'll get it." He breezes out of the kitchen to receive yet another package I'd ordered online. I can't even remember what it is.

A few minutes later, Jared reappears in the kitchen and places the package on an empty chair. He bends to kiss me on the forehead. "I'll see you later, my love."

I swallow the bacon I've been chewing and

pout. "You won't eat with me?"

"You're not eating alone." He bends to kiss my stomach.

I ruffle his chestnut, wind-blown hair. "You know I won't be able to finish all this food. You always give me too much."

"I'm sorry, babe. I need to get to the studio. I have a lot to do before my trip to Campeche." He glances out the window. "Why don't you invite Ruby over? She's been trying to get you to meet up."

I raise my shoulders and let them drop again. "I don't know. I don't get why she suddenly likes us. I thought she hated me."

"People change." Jared kisses me again and heads upstairs to get dressed.

Alone in the kitchen, I allow the music to wash over me. I feel safe here, in this town, in my beautiful kitchen. When we'd moved into our new home, the kitchen had lacked life, sucked out of it by mud-brown, broken cabinets, a stained floor and countertops, and mold everywhere. Looking at it now, with its glossy, white cabinets, a tempered glass backsplash, and lots of lighting, it's barely recognizable.

My mind takes me to the time we bought every cabinet and appliance, and how much fun we had choosing each piece.

Our kitchen is far removed from the one in

my childhood, which had been cold and dirty and was never the setting for much laughter or home-cooked meals. The one appliance that worked overtime was the oven, which heated frozen meals.

This kitchen is my second chance, a place I want to fill with love, laughter, and good food.

I feel at home inside this cottage and Faypine as a whole. Except for when I bump into Ruby Whitmore.

Since the day we moved into the cottage, the little old lady with one curly hair on her chin had never once greeted us. She'd pass us on the street pretending she didn't even see us. Apparently, our cottage had once belonged to her best friend, Wilma, who had died a year before Jared bought it. Maybe Ruby has finally come to accept that her friend will not be coming back. Perhaps she's finally ready to welcome us to the neighborhood.

Jared is right, people do change. I make a mental note to make time to accept one of her invitations to tea. She's just a lonely old woman in need of company. What's the harm in me going over? I should be fine as long as I'm careful about what I tell her. Good thing I'm an expert at the lying game.

Jared walks back into the kitchen, wearing the same T-shirt with jeans, smelling of soap and aftershave. "I've got to go. I love you."

"Bye, honey." I get up from the table and sink into his arms. "Don't forget the doctor's appointment at four."

"I wouldn't miss it for the world."

Less than a minute later, I watch him walking out of our gate and stepping into his Honda. After a brief wave, he drives off.

Back in the kitchen, I manage to eat a piece of bread and wash it down with apple juice. My stomach can't handle any more food, but burdened with the guilt of not finishing the meal Jared put so much love and effort into preparing, I pack some of it into a lunchbox to eat at Silver Oak High School, where I'm a math teacher.

It was never my intention to go back to full-time teaching, afraid it would be all too easy to get my cover blown, but after giving private math lessons to many kids around town and helping them improve their grades drastically, word got around about the teacher working behind the scenes.

Just as I had back home in Corlake, Florida, I make math fun for my students. That's a passion that will never go away no matter how far I run from the past.

After a couple of months of tutoring, Georgia Dally, Silver Oak's principal, showed up at my door, asking me if I wanted a job. I resisted taking the job for a month, but the desire to be inside a classroom wouldn't go away until I gave in, terrified that Georgia would discover that my documents are fake. When I handed them to her, she barely even looked at them, more focused on the success I'd had with the students I privately tutored.

Every time she calls me to her office, I fear it's because she knows the truth and wants to fire me, but it's been almost three years, and I still have my job.

At Silver Oak, I park my Volkswagen Beetle in my assigned parking spot and remove several folders from the back seat. Inside the school, several students are hanging out in the hallways. The girls sport navy and burgundy pleated skirts, white shirts, and burgundy ties, while the boys have the same shirts and ties but with navy pants. Each girl with long hair has a ponytail adorned with a navy ribbon.

Every time I walk into Silver Oak, memories of Baxter Junior High flood my mind. The sounds of shoes squeaking on the floor, locker doors slamming, and the smells of sweet perfume, sweat, and hair spray never fail to transport me back to Corlake.

I shove the memories aside before they're followed by the image of Dylan lying dead inside the presidential suite of the Brookside Hotel. My first husband's memory is always accompanied by that of my brother's disappearance, and possible death.

On the way to my class, I greet students, turning a blind eye to those catching up on homework before classes start.

Before I open the door to my classroom, someone calls my name. I turn around with a smile.

Ralph Jenkins, a tall art teacher with hair the color of field oats tied in a ponytail, a tanned, square face, and lips that are always on the edge of a smile, is making his way through the throng of students, hurrying toward me. Although he has adopted the nickname of Mr. Art, I stick to calling him by his real name.

When I started working at Silver Oak, I was determined not to make any friends. I was here for work and nothing else. The more people I let into my life, the higher my chances of being discovered. It was hard at first as I missed having someone to talk to. Every time I saw my colleagues hanging out together, I felt lonely and missed Thalia so much. Over the years, I'd been tempted to give her a call to see how she's doing and tell her that I'm fine, but resisted.

Ralph was so easy to talk to, so kind that it became hard to push him away, and we became friends. And what I loved most about Ralph is that he didn't ask too many questions about my past. Ours is an easy friendship, and I feel comfortable around him.

When Ralph is close enough, he leans toward me for a kiss on the cheek, but I step away. Over his shoulder, I spot a group of teenage boys snickering as they gaze in our direction.

I clear my throat. "I wouldn't do that if I were you."

Ralph follows my gaze. There were a few times where a group of students passed on a rumor that Mr. Art and Mrs. Lester were having an affair. The rumor went on for a couple of weeks, with notes passed around classes at every opportunity. Since we simply ignored it or laughed it off, the lie eventually died down. To me, Ralph is like a brother, and our friendship is completely platonic. It was hard to convince Jared about that fact when the rumors somehow managed to reach his ears. Thankfully after the students stopped making up things, Jared and I never spoke of Ralph again, even though I do notice him visibly tensing every time we run into Ralph or his fiancée, Marissa, in town.

To put my husband at ease, I rarely meet Ralph outside of school anymore. I love my husband and cherish our marriage too much to hurt us that way. I'd never take my life for granted, not for one second.

"Yeah, I forgot." He pauses. "Can you believe Marissa still thinks the rumors about us are true? I keep telling her she has nothing to worry about, that we're only friends. She's not buying it."

"I'm so sorry." I place a hand on my stomach. "I can talk to her if you like."

"I don't think that's a good idea." Ralph runs a hand down one side of his face, over the five o'clock shadow he never lets go of. "Enough about me. How are you and the baby?"

"We're good. We have another doctor's appointment today."

"I'm really happy for you, Caitlin." His deep, baritone voice lowers. "I know how much you wanted to have a baby."

"I'm happy for me, too." I hug my folders to my chest. "I have to go. I need to make some copies for an algebra test I have planned for my class. See you later?"

"Sure."

"Will you stop by the lounge?" I ask.

"Yeah, I need a strong coffee before facing the little monsters."

I reach into my oversized bag and pull out the lunchbox. "Can you put this in the fridge for me?"

"No problem." He takes the lunchbox and walks away. "See you around, Mrs. Lester."

As I watch him walk away, a slight limp in his stride, I take in the scene of students opening and closing their lockers or catching up on gossip, teachers hurrying into classrooms, and parents saying goodbye to their kids. My gaze moves to the artwork on the walls as my baby kicks inside of me.

A warm glow radiates through me. This is my life now. I am so lucky. Paige Wilson is gone with all her bad luck. But how long until I wake up to find it all gone?

I don't give myself a moment to dwell on that. Instead, I resume the walk to my classroom, the heels of my shoes slapping against the hardwood floor. For now, I still have my life. For now, I'm happy.

§

The moment I enter the staff lounge and my eyes meet those of Lilliana Spooner, a chemistry teacher in her early thirties, my stomach knots. She's sitting at the long table in the center of the room, watching me. She doesn't like me. The feeling is mutual.

At every job, there's always someone you can't stand or don't get along with. Lilliana is one of those people for me. She has a way of rubbing me the wrong way every time we meet. I've tried being kind to her, but she never seems to warm up to me, and she never misses the opportunity to point out my mistakes.

As I make my way across the room to get to the fridge, she follows me with her dark, snake-like eyes while twirling a lock of raven hair around her index finger. Ralph is in the room as well, sitting on the opposite end of the table, eating a banana.

Although I don't have a problem with someone disliking me, I can never stop wondering whether she's able to see right through me. Maybe she knows I'm not real, that I'm hiding something. Maybe she sees me right through to my dark core. Or it could be just my imagination.

"Hi, Lilliana." I take my lunchbox from the fridge, where Ralph had put it earlier. Just because she's not nice to meet doesn't mean I have to be the same to her. "How's your day?"

"Not bad." She doesn't cover up the chill in her voice. She continues to watch me, her elfin face pinched, as I take a few steps toward the microwave. It's already occupied, and through the little window, I can see a bowl of soup inside. I wait until the microwave pings before opening it. When I reach inside for the bowl of soup, Lilliana suddenly appears at my side and closes the microwave again. The aroma of chicken drifts into my nostrils.

"It needs longer." She studies her long nails. "I'm sure you can wait, Caitlin."

"It's steaming," I retort.

"It's been in there for a while," Ralph says in a sharp tone of voice.

Lilliana throws him a look. "Maybe I like my food hot."

I don't need Ralph to look out for me. I've had it with her. Determined to put her in her place, I open the microwave again and remove the steaming bowl, placing it on the counter.

"Enjoy." I place my own lunchbox inside the microwave.

Ralph clears his throat. I'm sure he wants to laugh but doesn't want to piss Lilliana off even more.

Lilliana grabs her bowl but quickly puts it down again when it scalds her fingers. Without looking at me, she grips a kitchen towel, wraps it around the bowl and lifts it. Cursing under her breath, she walks through the door, leaving behind traces of her Chanel No. 5.

Ralph and I burst into laughter just as the other staff members trickle in, filling the room with discussions about lesson plans, highlights of the day, gossip, and jokes.

Instead of staying to eat with everyone, I retreat to my classroom to eat alone while preparing for my next lesson. In between bites, I ignore the tightening knot in the pit of my stomach that always precedes a visit to the OB/GYN.

CHAPTER 27

∾

"What did you say your name was?" The secretary moves her head closer to the computer, and I watch her golden-brown eyes move from side to side as she reads whatever is on the screen.

"Caitlin ... Caitlin Lester." I wrap my arms around my body, leaning against the counter for support. I'm still feeling dizzy and unsettled, the way I had felt with each passing hour before we came to the doctor. I still can't get rid of the knot inside my stomach. I'm often nervous before coming for a checkup, afraid Dr. Phyllis Collins would tell me that she doesn't hear a heartbeat. But in a way, how I feel right now is different, the kind of feeling one gets when something bad is about to happen, a feeling that used to accompany me a lot when I lived with Ryan.

"I'm sorry." The young woman looks up from the computer and brushes her blonde hair away from her eyes. I haven't seen her before. She seems to be no older than twenty. "I'm afraid I can't see your name. Are you sure you called for an appointment?"

I glance at Jared, who is standing next to me, his warm breath fanning my cheek. He clears his throat and places both hands on the counter, pushing aside the bowl of M&M's. "I'm sorry, Miss ..."

"Danielle," the secretary says. "You can call me Danielle."

"Danielle," he starts. "My wife called to confirm her appointment four days ago. I was standing right next to her. Are you sure you're not looking at the wrong day on the calendar?"

Danielle's brow creases as she glances back at the computer. "I'm pretty sure. I don't see a Caitlin Lester. I'm sorry. Is it a scheduled prenatal visit or just a routine checkup?"

"Does it matter?" Jared tries hard but fails to keep his voice controlled. He hates it when he feels I'm being treated unfairly, always ready to jump in and rescue me.

Danielle's freckled, cherubic face falls. "I'm sorry. Today's my first day, and I'm not sure if someone forgot to enter your wife's appointment ... or if it was deleted by mistake."

I lay a hand on Jared's arm to stop him from blowing up, then I step in front of him, which is not easy given my huge tummy. "Danielle, it's fine. It's not your fault. Is it possible to make another appointment for a different day this week?" I had my last ultrasound one month ago. Dr. Collins assured me all is well with the baby and there's no need for another scan before the birth. But I made another appointment just to be sure the baby is really developing as it should.

Danielle's face lights up. "Yes, sure. I think we had a cancellation for one of the days. Let me check." She turns back to the computer and starts typing, her blood-red fingernails flying over the keyboard. She finally looks up with a smile. "I can give you Friday at nine. Would that be okay for you?"

"Yes, that would be perfect." Jared won't be able to make it to the appointment since he'll be out of town, but at least he promised to be here for the birth.

"Perfect. See you next Friday." Danielle gives me a small wave.

"Thank you." I reach for Jared's hand, pulling him out of the doctor's office. Outside, we walk to the car in silence. Neither of us say a word. Inside the car, Jared turns to me.

"You okay?"

"Yeah, I'm fine. I'm just disappointed that we didn't get to see the doctor. What if—"

"Don't go there. I'm sure everything is fine with the baby." He takes my hand and lifts it to his lips, kissing my knuckles.

"But I don't want to take any chances. I've had this bad feeling all day, and I just can't help wondering if, you know, something's changed."

"Stop. Don't go down that road." His voice is both gentle and firm. "We won't lose this one."

"Jared, I worry every day. Not a day goes by that I don't think about the babies we've lost. Our two beautiful babies." Tears fill my eyes.

He removes his hand from mine and plants them on the steering wheel. He doesn't look at me. "My love, this time is different," he says. "I just feel it."

"But how do you know?" I retort, even though I don't mean to lash out at him.

"Okay, I don't know. But I choose to believe. Believe with me, okay?"

I nod, and we drive home, where I get into the shower and burst into tears under the spray of water. What if the fact that my appointment was messed up is a sign?

I step out of the shower and dry myself off. At the bathroom sink, I close my eyes, my head tipped forward, my chin on my chest. I squeeze my eyes tight until I feel a burn in my eyeballs, desperate to shut out the dark images in my head. When I open my eyes, I gaze at myself in the mirror.

My tears and the water have caused my

mascara to run. I run a fingertip underneath my eye. In the process, I notice my wedding band. More tears come. I've made so many mistakes, and I deserve to be punished. I probably killed someone and ran instead of doing the right thing. I cheated life. I'm not allowed to be here. I'm not allowed to have what I have. But I don't want to let it go. I want Jared. I want our baby. I want to own this life I'm living.

I pull myself together, get dressed, and go to the kitchen to have dinner with my husband. The aroma of melted cheese and freshly baked bread from the homemade pizza makes my mouth water.

I make a sad face "I wish you didn't have to go tomorrow."

"You and me both." He removes the silicone oven mitts. "But it won't be for long this time. I'll be back in five short days. I'll be here for the birth, I promise. I'm sorry I won't be there on Friday. Make sure to get a picture for me this time."

"I promise."

Up to this point in my pregnancy, I haven't once looked at the ultrasound screen. Dr. Collins tells me everything I need to know while I keep my eyes closed. It's not because I don't have an interest in seeing my baby, but because I'm afraid to. I'm afraid to see the baby only to lose it.

"Ready to eat?" Jared opens a drawer and pulls out the pizza cutter.

"Starving."

We enjoy our meal in front of the TV, watching a romance movie in black and white.

Outside the window, the sun is setting, the ball of fire sinking like a vitamin tablet into the sea. The only light in the living room is coming from a small lamp next to the couch. The atmosphere around us is so calm, romantic, and relaxing. It's rare that we have these moments alone together. Jared is often busy at his studio until late into the night.

As soon as the movie ends and the credits roll, my phone pings with a text message. Jared picks it up from the coffee table and hands it to me. It's a number I don't recognize.

The words freeze my spine.

Enjoy it while it lasts. It won't be like this for long. Xoxo

Fear snakes through me at the same time my pulse starts to slam into my neck.

I'm tempted to tell Jared about the suspicious message, but something inside me warns me it would be a mistake. Thank God he didn't read it before handing me the phone.

"Who is it?"

"Nothing," I pant. "No one, I mean. Just ... a

colleague."

"Ralph?" He shifts to look into my face.

I shake my head. "No, Lilliana." It's the first name that comes to mind.

"Oh." Jared stretches out his legs and pulls me closer, his eyes closed.

"I'll ... I need the bathroom." I struggle to my feet and rush to the bathroom as fast as my feet and weight will allow. Inside, I close the door and lean against it. I bite my fist to keep from screaming out with fear, my other hand still holding the phone way too tight.

Breathe. Breathe, Caitlin. It could be nothing.

I look at the message again. It's still there. It's real.

My mind tells me this moment is what I've been dreading all day. But this is my life. I can't let anything spoil this evening with my husband.

Before I can think about what I'm doing, I hold my breath, delete the text, and splash my face with cold water.

I return to the living room, pretending my world has not just been shaken.

Jared's clean-shaven face is worried as he narrows his eyes. "You all right? Why did you rush out like that?"

I sit on the couch, placing the phone next to me facedown in case another message comes in. "I just ... I felt suddenly nauseous." How many lies will I have to tell him to keep our life intact?

He places a hand on my stomach. "I'm sorry, baby. Can I get you anything?"

"Water." I twist my wedding band around my finger. "I'm fine now. But water would be nice." So would a moment alone to pull myself together.

While he's gone, I lie to myself. The text was not meant for me. It was sent to a wrong number. The past is still in the past. But what if … what if it's him?

Jared gets back before I can answer my own questions. He presses a cool frosted glass in my hands.

I take a sip and lean against him for support.

Later in our bed, warm inside Jared's arms, he touches my cheek. "In answer to your earlier question, the reason I know this time is different is because we couldn't have come this far for nothing."

I press my lips together and blink away hot tears.

Please, let him be right. I don't think I can handle another loss. I need this baby more than he can imagine; now, more than ever. It's not only because I love him so much I want to have his child, but because a baby would be the seal of approval my new life requires, the key to me living freely and completely.

After all the ugly, I long to create something

beautiful. I can't allow anything or anyone to stand in the way of that.

Before falling asleep, I tell myself that dead men don't speak. Ryan is dead.

CHAPTER 28

I stare into the darkness, searching for sleep that won't come. My body is heavy with exhaustion, and my mind is thick with questions with no answers. Much as I want to forget the text I got earlier, I refuse to let go. My mind keeps going over the words, turning them over inside my head until I'm on the verge of going crazy.

Finally, I give up on sleep. I'm tired of tossing and turning. Jared has to get up at 5:00 a.m. for his trip to Mexico. I wouldn't want to disturb him.

I lift his arm from my body and slide out of bed, my feet meeting the cool, wooden floor. Unable to breathe, I stumble through the darkness and disappear into the bathroom, where I flick on the light.

I gulp down mouthfuls of air, but no amount of oxygen is enough to calm my nerves.

I lean over the sink and splash my face with

water to wash away the sweat. My hands are trembling as I press a towel to my face. There's a rumble in my belly. It has nothing to do with hunger.

With sleep out of reach, there's no point in returning to bed. So, I grab a bathrobe from behind the door and throw it over my nightgown. Tiptoeing out of the bathroom, I don't stop in the bedroom but walk through the door and continue on down the stairs. I'm careful to avoid the creaking step at the bottom.

The faint smell of the pizza we ate earlier, before my world cracked, still hangs in the air.

My mind is a roller coaster by the time I burst through the front door. When I reach the middle of the path that travels from the gate to our front door, I stop.

What am I doing? Where am I going? I'm not sure I'm doing the right thing. All I know is that I need to distance myself from my home before the toxicity from my past invades it. I need to be alone to think.

All the lights in the cottages on our street are off except for the one in Ruby's bedroom. What in the world is she doing up at 1:00 a.m.? Or did she forget to switch off the light? I shrug. It's none of my business.

My stroll to the beach is only a five-minute walk down a sandy path lined with wildflowers.

Jared will be beside himself with worry if he

discovers that his pregnant wife has gone to the beach alone this late, even though—like Corlake had been—Faypine is known to be one of the safest towns in the United States. For other residents, at least. Besides, if anyone is really after me, I'd prefer for them to catch me alone instead of with Jared. Hopefully, he won't wake up before I get back home.

The moonlight allows my gaze to sweep the stretch of glowing, white sand, but I don't spot a soul.

"Ryan is dead. He's not after me," I repeat to myself as the cool wind swings my hair from side to side and into my face.

I pick up my pace, walking faster. My bare feet sink into the cool sand.

When my heart starts to race, I stop walking to catch my breath for the sake of the baby. My hands are wrapped around my stomach as I pull air into my lungs.

Tears stinging the backs of my eyes, I gaze out at the inky, black water and listen to the rush of the waves crashing onto the shore. Some of my teardrops drip onto my lips, salty like sea water.

Drained of energy, I lower myself onto the sand and cover my face with my hands.

God, please tell me that the text was meant for someone else.

After all these years, Ryan can't just show up

alive.

The baby kicks me in the ribs and fresh tears flood my eyes.

"It's okay, baby. Mommy's fine. Everything is fine."

We don't know the sex of the baby yet. Jared wanted to know, but I didn't for the same reason I avoided looking at the ultrasound screen. I told him he could ask the doctor if he wants, that he didn't have to tell me. He refused, saying he wouldn't want any secrets between us, however harmless. He had no idea how uncomfortable his words had made me.

What would he do if he knew I've been lying to him from the day we met, that he married a woman he doesn't even know, a stranger, a murderer maybe? He would most certainly leave me. I can't let that happen.

I run my hands over my swollen belly, following the baby's movements. "I don't deserve you, little one, but I know you'll make me a better person."

Sobs break inside my chest and shake my shoulders before they leave my body. It's a good thing I left the house. If Jared saw me weeping, he'd demand to know why I'm upset. Out here, I can cry in private. When I return home, I'll wipe away the tears and continue pretending everything is fine.

I cry for what feels like an hour, but it could

be just a few minutes.

My eyes sore and my body exhausted, I push myself up from the ground and shake the sand from my clothes. It whispers as it falls to the ground, sprinkling onto my feet.

My gaze sweeps the beach again. I'm still alone with the water, the sand, and my pain and fears. I take a step. A candy wrapper crinkles under my foot. It's half buried in the sand next to a forgotten child's shoe.

The beach is busy during the day with children running with their buckets and shovels while their parents follow with wagging fingers, warning them to stay away from the deep water.

Happy people come here to enjoy their lives as they have nothing to hide from themselves or their loved ones. How does it feel to live without secrets, to live life with no cracks on the heart? I envy those people. I can't even remember the feeling of being completely free, with no secrets. I miss it, but I don't think I'll ever get it back.

I push my hands into the pockets of my robe and turn to walk away. Then I remember that I'm still crying. Using the collar of the robe, I wipe the tears from my eyes as best I can, letting them soak into the thick fabric.

The baby has stopped kicking, and I feel somewhat better. I take tiny steps toward the path that leads to our cottage, my gaze straight ahead at my dream home, my dream life. I walk slowly toward the place I want to belong to, never taking my eyes off it.

The light is on downstairs. I never switched it on. The door opens, and Jared fills its doorway. He doesn't see me on the other side of the road as he bends to put on his shoes.

My knees wobble as I cross the road, open the gate, and walk up to the house.

He straightens up, his eyebrows slanted in a frown. Our eyes lock.

"Caitlin, where were you at this time of night? You worried the hell out of me."

"I went for a walk on the beach." I suck in a breath and blow it out slowly. "I ... couldn't sleep."

He pinches the bridge of his nose. "Why didn't you wake me? I would have gone with you. It's not safe out there."

"It's perfectly safe." I peel my gaze from his. "When was the last time you heard of a crime happening in Faypine?" I walk past him into the house, and he follows me inside.

He closes the door behind us, then takes a step toward me, and I feel the heat of his body before he touches me. He turns me around to face him, searching my eyes. I know what his next words will be before he speaks.

"You were crying." It's not a question, but a slice of truth that pushes me into a corner.

"Why?"

I glance down to hide my shame and try to move away from his touch. He tightens his grip on my shoulders, keeping me in place.

"Tell me what's wrong, sweetheart. Don't think I didn't notice that you were also upset before bed. What's going on?"

I search my mind for answers, for a lie I can give him without arousing more suspicions. In the end, I give him the only one he might believe. "I ... I was worried about the baby, after what happened at the doctor's."

He lets my shoulders go and wraps an arm around me, ushering me toward the stairs.

"You know you don't have to worry about that. Being upset isn't good for either you or the baby. You have to try and calm down, my love." He moves his hand up and down the side of my body.

"It's just so hard to let go of the fears," I whisper.

"I know it is. But it'll happen for us this time. You don't have to be afraid."

At the bottom of the stairs, he draws me into his arms and holds me for a long time, his chin on the top of my head. I've always loved how tall he is. I wish I felt safe in his arms. I wish he could protect me from my demons. I want to tell him everything before things come out in the open, before he discovers that I've deceived him. But he can never know who and what I am.

He kisses the top of my head and leads me upstairs and into our bedroom, where he lifts the covers. I slide under them. He lies down next to me, his arms tight around my body.

"Do you want me to call off my trip? Should I stay?" His deep voice is a rumbled whisper in the night.

"No, no." There's a hint of desperation in my tone.

For the first time in our marriage, I'm desperate for him to get out of town. When the sun comes up, I'll still remember the text, the exact words. Even if I want to deny it, even if it turns out the text was meant for someone else, to me it feels like the sign I've been waiting years for. The sign that reminds me that the life I'm living has an expiration date.

It doesn't matter how many days, weeks, months, or years go by. It doesn't matter how many breaths I take. It doesn't matter how fast I keep running. As long as I keep running from the past, I will never be rid of the truth buried deep within me. Wherever I go, I will take myself with me.

I've never been this scared, not since the morning I woke up to find Dylan's dead body. I don't know if I'm even strong enough to fight the past should it show up on my doorstep. In spite of my fears of being alone and vulnerable, I need to make sure Jared goes to Mexico. When he comes back, I'll return to being the wife he thinks I am.

CHAPTER 29

∽

I'm still in bed as Jared stands on the other side of the room, zipping up his suitcase while eyeing me at the same time, a worried look clouding his handsome features.

"Why don't you just stay home today? You didn't get much sleep, and you need it."

"You know I can't sit home all day doing nothing." The truth is, work has always been my escape, even in the days when Ryan tormented me. It won't do me any good to sit around thinking about what can go wrong and when the next shoe will drop. My body is tired from lack of sleep, and my mind is tired from ruminating, but the classroom is still the best place for me. Being on the school grounds, surrounded by people, even Lilliana, would do me good.

I've decided to forget the text from yesterday. Today I will make it through one breath at a time. It's not the first time I've had to struggle with negative emotions. I've done it all my life, and I can do it again. It's just another day in my life—another day to pretend.

A honking sound drifts through the open window.

"That's my cab." Jared crosses the room and kisses me. "I'll see you in a few days. Please promise that you won't go walking on the beach alone in the middle of the night."

"I promise." Since he won't be here to witness my fears, I wouldn't need to find a place to hide. "I love you." I swing my legs out of bed to see him off.

"I love you more." He kisses me again at the front door and leaves me standing there.

After a quick wave in my direction, he gets into the car.

With a sigh, I lean against the doorframe, wondering how much time I have before I lose him. As soon as he disappears into the distance, I close the door and make a round through the house, making sure all doors and windows are locked. Then I jump into the shower.

Most of the time under the jet of warm water, I spend slathering foam around my stomach, talking to my baby. I wish the water could wash away the past before it taints my present. But I can't think about that now. It could turn out that I'm worried for no reason at all.

After a long breakfast of eggs on toast, I leave the house. Nothing eventful happens until I pass Joe's Kitchen, one of the most popular diners in town. Maybe I'm imagining it, considering the amount of sleep I got last night, but it looks as if a black Nissan is trailing me.

Come to think of it, I saw the same car a few minutes ago. I take the first corner to my left that takes me from my normal route, but before I can take a breath, the Nissan appears again behind me. It looks like a man with a dark beard, a black cap, and sunglasses is behind the wheel, but the car is not close enough for me to see who it is.

"You're imagining things, Caitlin." I wet my trembling lips. "It's nothing. We're just headed in the same direction." Except, the car is still there, ten minutes later.

After half an hour of trying to get away from the Nissan, I have no choice but to go to work. We have a staff meeting before class starts. To my surprise, the moment I turn into the street where Silver Oak is located, I glance into the rearview mirror to find the car gone.

I'm sweating and out of breath as I walk into the staff lounge. Everyone is already there, including Lilliana, who's watching me suspiciously as if she knows what's going on. Is that a smile I see on her face? To make matters worse, the only free chair is the one next to her.

I greet everyone in turn and sink into my chair.

Ralph is watching me as well, tipping his pen on a notepad. I move my gaze away from him and draw in a breath. I cough as my lungs reject Lilliana's perfume.

"Glad you could join us, Caitlin." Georgia, wearing the pearl necklace she wears to every staff meeting, stands up from her seat at the head of the table. She gives Lilliana a printed sheet of paper which Lilliana tosses in front of me. "Let's continue."

During the entire meeting, my body is present in the room, but my mind isn't there at all. I'm still thinking about the black Nissan. All kinds of questions are going through my mind. Each one of them causes me to panic even more.

After the meeting, Georgia pulls me aside to ask me the same question Ralph had asked before leaving the room. I feed her the same lie. "I'm fine."

Georgia lifts one of her thin eyebrows. "Are you sure? You look rather pale, Caitlin. Maybe you should take the day off? Go and get some rest. Carrying a baby is hard work on its own. You hardly take a day off anyway."

I wave a dismissive hand. "Not necessary. I'm fine, really." I push a hand through my hair. It's hanging down my shoulders today, still a bit damp from my shower earlier. I'm not a fan of hair dryers.

"If you're sure." Georgia dips her head to the side, her sharp bob brushing her right shoulder. "Don't push yourself too hard. If it gets to be too much, let me know."

"I will." I walk out of the room.

My students are already in their seats as I enter the classroom, but most are on their phones. When they see me, some of the phones disappear into backpacks and purses, but not all.

It takes me ten minutes to get everyone to settle down and focus on the lesson, even though I, myself, am far from focused. With everything going on inside my mind, it's a wonder I'm able to teach at all. After going through a chapter in an algebra textbook, I glance out the window and the hairs at the nape of my neck rise and bristle. My hands grip the edge of the desk so tight, my knuckles turn white.

From my window, I have a perfect view of the street in front of the school. There are a few cars parked along the curb, but my eyes are only interested in one. The black Nissan.

"Do exercise 5A ... with a partner." It's a struggle to keep my voice from trembling. "We'll discuss the answers after the lunch break." I sit before my knees give way. No point in denying the truth anymore. Someone is out to get me. The text was meant for me.

The driver of the Nissan is still in the car. I wish I could make out his face, but I'm too far away now to see him clearly.

I look away, count to ten and look again. He's still there, waiting for something or someone. My breaths burst in and out of me, and my hand clutches my throat. The room starts to turn. I should get up and leave before I faint.

Without saying anything to the students, I rush out of the classroom. To my surprise, I manage to make it to the principal's office. I find Georgia studying one of her many souvenir snow globes. She's a collector.

"Georgia." I wipe the sweat from my face. "I changed my mind. I—I want to go home. I do feel sick."

"Of course." Georgia puts down the snow globe and rises from her desk chair. "Jesus, Caitlin, you look like hell. Can I get you anything?"

"No. I ... I should go." I don't stay long enough to give her the chance to probe deeper into my condition.

I find Ralph in the hallway at the lockers. I'm about to walk past him, but he catches my hand.

"Caitlin, wait a moment. You don't look so

well."

"It's been a long night, and I didn't get much sleep. Nothing to worry about."

His emerald eyes darken. He parts his lips to speak, but I stumble away before I hear his words.

Without looking for the Nissan again, I simply get behind the wheel of my car and drive off the school grounds, desperate to get home.

If I were any other normal person with nothing to hide, I'd go to the cops. But I can't do that. My last internet search a few weeks ago, alerted me that the cops are still after me. I'm still believed to be a murderer on the run.

I only look for the Nissan when I arrive home and park my car. I don't see it, but that doesn't mean my stalker isn't watching.

Inside the house, I close all doors and windows and lock myself inside the nursery. We've decorated it in neutral colors since we don't know the sex yet. I grab a panda bear from a box and sink with it into the vintage rocking chair that had been in Jared's nursery as a baby. I hold the toy to my body and rock back and forth.

The only way I can release the pressure is by crying. I give in to the tears until my sobs turn to sniffles and hiccups. Then I wait for something to happen—for my worst nightmare to step out of the shadows and destroy my life.

I want to know who's after me, but at the same time, I don't. It's much safer to bury my head in the sand and pretend it's not happening.

I look around the room. The baby will be here soon, but the nursery isn't quite ready yet. Jared had promised he'd build the crib—two days ago—but never got to it. In an attempt to hold on to my sanity, I rise from the chair and approach the box carrying the parts of the crib.

Both my body and mind are numb as I open the box and start to put the crib together myself. Instead of thinking about my troubles, I focus on my baby. I force my mind to pretend, maybe for the last time, that my life is not in pieces. The instruction manual is so good that I finish the job in less than forty minutes.

Done, I take my time covering the mattress and folding the little cream blanket, praying this is not the last thing I get to do for my baby.

CHAPTER 30

∞

I wake up in the middle of the night drenched in sweat and disorientated, the sheets damp against my skin.

With the back of my hand, I wipe away the beads of sweat on my upper lip.

It was only a dream, I tell myself. I have nothing to be afraid of.

Like most of the nightmares I've had before, Ryan was present in this one as well. This time we were both on the beach, and he was pushing his wheelchair with me inside it. We had switched places. I was paralyzed, unable to feel my legs, and he was laughing at my predicament.

Waking from the bad dream only offers me momentary relief. When my heart starts to settle, I remember that something had woken me, a scratching sound from somewhere in my room.

I blink a few times to allow my eyes to

awaken fully. With the comforter pulled up to my neck, I search the darkness.

My chest tingles with dread when my gaze lands on the window. It's open. I'm pretty sure I had closed it before going to bed.

I jam my hands into my armpits to stop them from shaking.

"Who's there?" I whisper into the darkness. No one answers. The only thing I hear is my beating heart and the distant rush of the waves.

I have two choices: to remain in my bed helpless and terrified, or to take action. A shot of adrenaline rushes through my veins, and I jump out of bed without thinking and slam the window shut. It's only when the window is closed that it hits me that the intruder could be in the house.

A movement on the other side of the window catches my eye. In the light of the moonlight, I catch sight of a dark figure hurrying down our path toward the gate, pushing it open and running out without closing it. As soon as the person is off our property, he or she starts to run down the street, disappearing into the darkness. As I watch the intruder becoming nothing but a dot in the distance, bitter bile touches the back of my throat.

I lay a hand on my chest. It's vibrating with each beat of my heart. A scream is bubbling up in my throat but refuses to pour out of me. What's the point of screaming, anyway? It's not as if I can call someone to help me.

My hands around my stomach, I sink to the floor and lean my head against the wall. There's no more pretending the past has not caught up with me. What would I do if I find out that Ryan is alive? He's my brother, and I should be happy, but instead, I'm terrified.

I keep thinking about all the threats he'd made to me in the past. What if it was him who killed Dylan in the hope I would be the one to pay for the crime? What if he wants to kill me now? I don't want it to be true. I don't want to believe my brother is a murderer. I'm not even sure it wasn't me that committed the murder during a sleepwalking episode.

Since that day I had been terrified of sleepwalking, but the weird thing is, the episodes stopped sometime while I lived in New York.

But deep down in my gut, I know I didn't kill Dylan. I don't think I have it in me to kill anyone—definitely not the man I loved—asleep or awake. If it wasn't me, it has to be someone who was trying to set me up, and they succeeded. Perhaps that person has been angered that I disappeared instead of rotting in prison. What if he or she is now back to finish the job?

Unsure of what else to do, I bury my trembling body back under the covers, but another wave of fear causes me to jump out again. Praying no one will pounce on me, I hurry to the kitchen and grab the largest butcher knife I can find. I head back to the stairs, glancing over my shoulder with each step, my sweaty hand tight around the knife. I won't return to my bedroom.

For some reason, I feel I'll be safer inside the nursery. Maybe it's because the room is smaller. I push the door open and freeze in the doorway. The knife slides from my grip and falls to the floor only a few inches from my feet.

The crib I built a few hours earlier has been dismantled, the pieces scattered across the room. The scene is enough to knock the wind from my lungs, but what causes my breath to harden inside my throat are the red words scrolled on the beautiful, butterfly wallpaper.

You're over! xoxo

The bile I'd been swallowing down when I saw the stranger on our property returns with a vengeance and pours from my mouth. I try to stop it with my hands, but it seeps through my fingers and spills onto my feet.

I vomit uncontrollably just like the day I

found Dylan dead. It all rushes back to paralyze me—the shock, the hurt, the fear.

No. No. No. I can't go back there. This is my life now. I worked hard to get here, dammit. I paid the price for whatever sins I committed.

I wipe the vomit from my mouth, shaking with both fear and anger.

I walk away from the nursery without bothering to clean up my mess. My legs are still shaky when I switch on all the lights in the house and move from room to room, checking every window.

Done, I stand in the middle of the living room, wondering how the intruder got into the house. The door was still locked, as I had left it before bed. The only two people with a key are Jared and me. We have a spare key, but it's at school in my desk drawer.

A disturbing thought crawls into my mind. What if the person after me isn't from the past at all? What if it's someone from Faypine, someone who knows my secret and wants to taunt me before exposing me? What if it's someone from Silver Oak, someone with access to my classroom? But who?

My mind instantly goes to Lilliana. I couldn't tell whether the person in black was a male or female, but the person following me in the Nissan had been a man with a dark beard. It doesn't add up.

Groaning, I lower myself onto the couch and press the heel of my hand against my forehead. The baby kicks. I rub my stomach.

"It's okay, baby," I whisper. "Mommy will protect you." How will I be able to protect my baby when I can't even protect myself?

I don't feel safe anywhere, not inside my house and not outside.

The sound of my cell phone ringing cuts through my thoughts. I drag myself upstairs to see who is calling. At my bedroom door, watching the phone ringing and vibrating on the nightstand, next to my book of Sudoku puzzles, I wonder if it could be my tormentor.

The phone continues to ring, and I remain in the doorway, staring at it. Beads of sweat trickle down my temples as I take one and then another step forward.

Maybe the only way out of this horror is to face my worst nightmare. A burst of white hot rage spurts through me, and I grab the phone, ready to confront the person who is so desperate to hurt me.

I sink onto the bed with relief when I see Jared's name on the screen. Thank God. I wipe the sweat off my forehead, but I don't pick up. I can't talk to him, not in this state, when my voice is drowning in tears. He'll read between the lines and know I'm not fine.

I didn't get to speak to him before bed

because I couldn't get ahold of him. He doesn't like to sleep without hearing my voice. But I have to let him down today.

The call dies, and I lean back against the covers, breathing slowly through my mouth. The baby kicks again. My heart squeezes.

I don't deserve this baby. I'm selfish for wanting a child. It's for the wrong reasons. I'm only desperate for the baby because I want to create a better version of me, to prove to myself that there's a part of me that's good and pure. I want to feel that I'm more than a liar and a coward.

I find relief from my pain the only way I can. I turn to the healing power of water.

As I stand under the shower spray, washing the vomit from my legs and feet, I wish the water could wash it all away. I wish I could stay longer under the jet of water, but I want to stay on guard in case the intruder returns.

After my shower, I don't find any more surprises, but as I sink to my knees and clean up my vomit in the nursery doorway, I know this is only the beginning, and I better brace myself for whatever comes next..

CHAPTER 31

"You can go in now, Mrs. Lester."

"Thank you," I say to the receptionist, who had been unable to find my appointment when I came with Jared.

When I walked in, she smiled at me kindly and apologized again for last time, then she informed me that Dr. Collins is sick and Dr. Loraine Fern, a new doctor who has recently moved to Faypine from New York, will be filling in for her.

Even though I'm disappointed that there's yet another change to adjust to before the baby comes, I *do* hope Dr. Collins is okay. I already knew about Dr. Collins' sickness before coming to the private practice. After school today, I'd dropped by Dreamy Pies and heard the gossip queen, Doris Charleston, telling some other women from around town that Dr. Collins had a stroke.

I open the door and find a woman in her

mid-thirties with long, straight hair and the longest eyelashes I've ever seen sitting on the other side of the glass desk. Some of her blonde hair hangs down the front of her chocolate blouse that matches her eyes. Her long legs that extend from a black, knee-length, flared skirt, are crossed under the table, fragile-looking feet pressed into velvet pumps the same color as her silk blouse.

Even though Dr. Collins isn't here, everything in her office looks the same: the silver safe under the table, the bouquet of white roses on the windowsill, next to a silver potpourri bowl that releases the scents of lemon and lavender, and the black radio on one of the shelves.

A large painting hangs on the wall behind the desk. It's of a woman sitting on a promenade, looking out at the ocean with black birds flying around her as though protecting her from something. The lonely woman in the painting reminds me of myself.

Through the window, I catch sight of the grocery store parking lot, with people getting in and out of cars, or loading their shopping bags into trunks.

Dr. Fern clears her throat, and I return my attention to her. Her smile is wide enough to reveal the small gap between her two front teeth.

"Nice to meet you, Mrs. Lester." She stands up from the desk and extends her hand to me. She has the smallest, most fragile hands I'd ever seen on anyone, but a surprisingly firm handshake.

"Nice to meet you, too. I was sorry to hear about Dr. Collins. I hope she's okay."

"Yes, me too. She's my godmother." Dr. Fern's lips curl into a bittersweet smile. "Everything was just too much for her. We've been trying to convince her to retire for over two years. Hopefully, what happened will force her to slow down."

"Is she in the hospital right now? Is she allowed to have visitors?" Dr. Collins has been my doctor for as long as I've been in Faypine, and a witness to my earlier failed pregnancies. I'd like to drop by and wish her well.

Dr. Fern shakes her head. "She's no longer in the hospital. She's back home. But, unfortunately, she's not taking visitors. She needs to rest. I'm sure you understand."

"I do." I really do. If they dare open Dr. Collins' doors to the public, her house will flood with pies, flowers, and too many questions.

Dr. Fern flips open my file and glances down. "You're due in four weeks?" She glances up, smiling. "Looks like I'll accompany you to the end of your pregnancy."

"You don't think Dr. Collins will be back by then?" I twist my ring on my finger.

"The stroke took a major toll on her. Her family managed to talk her into taking a few months off to recover. She'll be out of town during that time."

"Oh, okay." I swallow my disappointment. "Please wish her well from me."

"I'll do that."

"Has everything been going well so far with your pregnancy? Any issues you'd like to discuss?" She runs a finger down a page in my folder. "It says here you requested an additional ultrasound. Is there a reason why?" She raises her gaze to mine. Her eyebrows furrow, then release.

"I had two miscarriages before this pregnancy. I just want to make sure the baby is fine."

"I see." She leans back in her chair. "Has Dr. Collins made you aware that your insurance might not cover it?"

"She has. It's fine. I'm ready to pay out of pocket."

"Good." She looks at me for a long time, then blinks and leans back. "Have there been any issues since your last appointment? Do you feel fine?"

"Yes." I avert my gaze, focusing on the red scarf hanging from the handle of a closet. It looks familiar. I must have seen Dr. Collins wearing it. "No, no issues ... not really. Everything is fine." I wish that were true.

"That's wonderful. Nothing like peace of mind for a smooth pregnancy."

I nod and force a smile. If only she knew. Peace of mind is a luxury I can't afford right now. "Do you have any children?" I don't know why, but I glance at her ring finger. It's empty. There's a pale mark that suggests she used to wear a ring.

Her sharp intake of breath makes me look up. Our eyes meet, and I regret asking.

"No." Her tone turns suddenly cool. "No kids." The smile returns to her lips. "But since this time is about you and your baby, let's have a look to see how the little one is doing, shall we? Let's have you lie down and free up your stomach area."

I nod and rise, feeling embarrassed for asking her something that's none of my business. Looks like the culture of Faypine has rubbed off on me. No topic in this town is off limits. How in the world did I come this far without anyone, especially Doris Charleston, peeling away my layers?

I unbutton my teal shirt—that belongs to Jared—and lie on my back on the reclining examination table.

"As you probably already know, the gel will

be a little cool," Dr. Fern says, squirting too much of it onto my belly, then picking up the transducer to glide it on my abdomen. She turns the screen so I can see the baby, but instead, I turn my gaze to the painting of the woman on the promenade.

"Do you want to know the sex? Or do you already?" Her voice sounds far away.

"No, we want it to be a surprise."

"That's lovely." She continues to glide the device over my skin while studying the screen in a silence broken only by my baby's heartbeat.

"Do you hear that? Nice and strong."

I bite back tears of joy. Maybe this is really going to happen. Four weeks and I might actually be a mother. I've vowed to myself that I'll do a much better job than my mother did with me.

I'm relieved when she finally hands me some tissue to wipe myself off and assures me that everything looks great. The baby is nice and healthy.

"You have absolutely nothing to worry about." She returns to the desk while I remain on the examination table, cleaning up and still blinking away tears.

"That's a relief." I'm relieved the stress of the past few days didn't impact the baby. I close my eyes for a brief second and say a prayer of thanks. I haven't gone to church since leaving

Corlake because I felt too guilty to walk into the house of God. But I *do* sometimes pray in the hope that He will listen. I hope He is. I need Him so much right now.

"I bet." Dr. Fern types something on her computer. "Do you have any questions for me?"

"Not at this point, no."

"Good. Don't hesitate to call or drop by in case of any issues. Take care of yourself and our little one." She hands me a photo from the ultrasound. I stuff it into my purse without looking at it..

CHAPTER 32

⚭

I drink a glass of water as Bruce Frary changes the locks on our front door. I'd planned on having them changed the morning after the break-in two nights ago, but Bruce owns the only locksmith company in town, and it was closed. He'd been the one serving this town since his father died six years ago, when Bruce was twenty-four.

I'm so glad he could make it today. I'm tired of sleeping with one eye open. As I had suspected, someone had stolen the spare key I keep in my office drawer, which has made me suspicious of everyone I work with, even Ralph. I have no idea who to trust anymore.

This morning, I considered moving into a hotel for the rest of the time that Jared is away. I soon realized it was a bad idea. It would only take one person to make up a story that my marriage is in trouble and the whole town would believe it.

Bruce glances at me with narrowed eyes from time to time. I'm sure he's curious to know why I'm changing the locks. But I don't owe him or anyone else an explanation. Except for Jared, of course. My chest tightens at the thought of telling him. He'll definitely ask questions, and I still haven't figured out the perfect lie.

"Great evening, isn't it? Not too hot or anything." Bruce dabs his large forehead with a dirty rag he pulled out of his back pocket. "Nice to have a cool breeze again after the heat of the last days."

"It is." He's right. This is the hottest July I've ever experienced in Faypine. "Thanks for doing this, Bruce." I drain my glass.

"It's my job." He throws me a crooked smile. "It's good you're changing the locks. Can't be too safe these days."

I swallow hard. He's clearly digging for information, but he'll get nothing from me. Word travels too fast around here. "I just … I lost a key, that's all." I glance down at my glass. "Can I get you something to drink, Bruce? I have apple juice, lemonade, and water. Or would you like a coffee instead?"

Bruce's grin lights up his face. "Do you happen to have a beer?"

I shake my head. "Jared and I don't drink."

"Then apple juice would be fantastic." He

roots inside his hard-plastic box for a tool.

"I'll be right back." I go to the kitchen with the intention of getting him the drink I promised, but my thoughts distract me and carry me away from the present.

"Mrs. Lester?" Bruce taps me on the shoulder.

I jump and spin around. My wild eyes meet his. How long have I been standing by the window staring out at the ocean? How long has he been standing there?

He raises his hands. "I just came to tell you I'm done. I apologize if I startled you."

"Sorry, I was far away." I rub the back of my neck. "Your drink. I promised you a drink." I open the fridge and pull out a pitcher of water.

"Very far away indeed." He chuckles, wiping his hands with the same handkerchief he had used to mop his brow earlier. I'm grateful when he takes a few steps away from me. The smells of motor oil and sweat coming from him are making me nauseous.

It's only when I hand him a glass of water that I remember he had asked for apple juice, but he drinks it without a word, eyeing me over the rim of the glass. When he hands me the glass back, his callused fingers brush mine, and I jump away as if scalded. I should stop being so jumpy.

"I apologize." He clears his throat. "I didn't

303

mean to—"

"That's fine." I smile. "Thanks for your help with the locks. I'll go get your money."

I move past him and go upstairs to get my purse, which I bring down with me. I open it in front of him and frown. It's empty. Not a single bill or coin inside. I don't understand. I had withdrawn quite a bit of money this morning before work. Where has it all gone?

My stomach twists as I close it again and give Bruce an apologetics look. "Bruce, I'm so sorry. I thought … I must have forgotten to withdraw money for you. Would you mind if I bring it to your shop tomorrow?"

"Sure thing, Mrs. Lester. I trust you. Drop by any time." He pulls out a piece of paper and pen from his back pocket and jots something down before handing it to me. "This is the amount."

"Thanks. I'm really sorry."

"Hey, don't worry about it. I did jobs for you before, and I know you pay—unlike some people in this town."

Bruce walks out of my house, and I lock the doors with the new key, still feeling unsafe in my own home. I still feel ruffled, especially after discovering that the money in my purse had disappeared. I know someone took it. My privacy is being invaded. My life is going up in smoke and there's absolutely nothing I can do about it.

Standing in the hallway shifting through suspects inside my mind is driving me nuts. So, I go upstairs to call Jared.

"How are you doing, babe?" His voice doesn't soothe me as it often does. "You sound—"

"I'm okay. Just tired."

"You shouldn't push yourself too hard. Take a day off if you need it."

"I will." I bury a hand in my hair. "By the way, I changed the locks today."

"Really? Why did you do that?"

"I lost my spare key, the one I keep at the school. I feel safer with the locks changed." I pause. "I heard some days ago, someone's house was broken into."

"Jesus, on our street? Whose house?"

"I'm not sure. I just overhead a conversation at the grocery store. I didn't want to take any chances." I chew the inside of my lip as I wait for his response. I don't get an immediate one. Does he know I'm lying?

"I agree. I'm glad you acted fast. I wish I didn't have to travel so much. Leaving you alone for days on end is torture, especially now that you're pregnant."

"You'll be back home soon, honey." I squeeze my eyes shut. "I just wanted to hear your voice. Get back to work. I didn't want to disturb you." I'm sure Jared will spend his days taking photos and his nights editing them to perfection.

"You can never disturb me. I'll try to call you again before you go to bed. I'll be heading to bed soon as well. I love you both."

I place a hand on my stomach and give a bittersweet smile. "We love you more."

I hang up the phone and go in search of something to eat. Every step I take in my house, every room I walk into, my skin prickles. Even with the doors and windows locked, I still feel as though I'm being watched, as if somebody is keeping track of my every movement, my every breath.

Several times I glance out the window and see nothing out of the ordinary, but just because I can't see the danger doesn't mean it's not there. I wish I could open the windows to let cool air in, but that would be too risky.

Terrified of being alone, I consider inviting Ruby over to eat dinner with me.

Yesterday, I finally visited her, and it wasn't too bad. It was nice, actually. I was surprised that she has a nice side to her. She offered me a piece of chocolate cake and lemonade. When I left, she gave me the leftover lemonade, which I had offered Bruce earlier. It's nice to know she's finally accepted us as neighbors, but I can't just show up at her door when I please, even if she had invited me to go over again today.

I can't invite Ruby over. What if my tormenter shows up and hurts us both? I wouldn't want to put an innocent person in danger. Instead of cooking, I eat a sandwich and a bowl of tomato soup.

For the rest of the evening, I flick through TV channels, but I don't find anything worth watching. As promised, Jared calls to say goodnight. After we hang up, I go to bed. Like the past few nights, I know I won't be able to get much sleep.

I push my hand under my pillow and sigh with relief when it comes into contact with the knife I keep there. I make a mental note to get rid of it before Jared comes home.

I hate sleeping with a knife, especially since it reminds me of the way Dylan had died—stabbed to death. But I need to protect myself.

On the one hand, I want my tormenter to show up. I want to know who hates me so much. I want to know if it's my brother, but my gut warns me that if I meet that person, I could lose everything, including my life.

But how long will it be until the devil comes out of the shadows?

CHAPTER 33

The doorbell rings. Jared is finally home. But what if it's not him? The question pops in my mind when I'm almost at the bottom of the stairs on my way to open the door for my husband. I stop, the sound of my heartbeat thrashing in my ears.

The doorbell rings again, but I don't move.

My cell phone also starts to ring from the bedroom. I'm about to go back to answer it when I hear Jared's voice come through the front door. My shoulders collapse with relief.

I hurry to the door and peer into the peephole just to be sure.

I draw in a breath and put on a smile. Hopefully, he won't read the tension of the last days from my face.

I open the door to find him standing there, his brow knitted, but it smooths immediately, and he gives me a smile I know is reserved only for me.

"Did I wake you?"

"No. You know I can't sleep before ten."

He steps into the house, drops his suitcase to the floor, and closes the door. Then he gathers me into his arms. When he pulls back again, he gazes into my face. "It took you a while to come to the door, that's all. I thought you weren't home."

Avoiding his gaze, I lock the door. "First of all, I was in the bathroom. Secondly, I'm pregnant and not as fast as I used to be."

"Sorry, baby. I should be more patient."

He glances at the door. Reading his mind, I reach into the pocket of my bathrobe and pull out a key. "This is for you." I've been carrying the spare key everywhere with me, paranoid someone would get their hands on it.

"Perfect." He pulls out his keys and removes the old key from the key ring. He replaces it with the new one. "Can I suggest something crazy?"

"Sure."

"I'm exhausted, but I'd love to take you out to dinner." He pauses. "You haven't already eaten, have you?"

"It's nine. You need to rest after your busy trip."

"I'll never be so tired I can't take my wife to dinner." He pulls me close. "Unless you're tired, of course."

I shake my head. "Not that tired. Dinner would be nice. What do you feel like?"

"Dan's Grill?"

"Yeah, sounds good. I'll go get dressed." I walk away, expecting him to follow me. But he remains downstairs.

My chest tightens when I glance in the direction of the nursery. I've only been inside the nursery once after the break-in. I'd planned on putting the crib together again, but I couldn't go through with it. The memories of that night kept rushing back in to taunt me. Yesterday, someone came over to replace the wallpaper with a new one, and I didn't even go in to see how it looks. The baby is coming soon, and I have to pull myself together and pretend to be excited about preparing the room, otherwise Jared will know something is going on.

As I slip into a loose chiffon blouse and my pregnancy jeans, I listen to the sounds coming from downstairs. The water running in the kitchen, the sound of the fridge beeping because Jared forgot to close it, the squeak of a drawer opening and then clapping shut. The sounds of the home I never thought I would have.

A beautiful cottage by the sea, a husband who loves me, a baby on the way. I appreciate the sounds of my life that much more because I don't know how long it will be until everything is taken away. I miss it all already—before it's even gone.

Even though I'm ready to go, I remain upstairs longer than necessary, gathering up the courage to lie to my husband, yet again.

The last two days had been quiet, with nothing out of the ordinary happening in my life, no threatening text messages, no break-ins, no stalker following me around. I'm almost fooled into believing that my life is back to normal, that everything will be fine after all.

To make myself feel better, I've come up with all kinds of lies to feed myself. I tell myself the text was a prank, sent by a bored teenager. The money was stolen by a pickpocket, and I happened to be in the wrong place at the wrong time, or maybe I forgot it in the ATM machine. The break-in was random, and I wasn't the target at all. I bury my head in the sand because I'm afraid to look the truth in the eye. But in a dark corner of my mind, I know I'm lying to myself.

It's all a game. My tormentor wants me to feel safe before dropping the next bomb on my life.

Now, as I stand in my bedroom, I wonder when that next bomb will hit and what it will destroy this time. Is today the day the truth comes to light, and I'm thrown into complete darkness? Can I even lose something that wasn't mine to start with?

Finally, Jared calls for me.

"Coming, honey." I do my best to keep my voice from breaking. After three deep breaths, I grab my handbag, determined to push my fears aside so I can enjoy the evening with my husband—in case it's our last.

Jared is already in the car, talking on his phone. When I walk out the door, the ocean breeze meets me with open arms. It brings me the sweet scent it stole from Ruth's roses. I allow it to embrace me, to try and offer me comfort.

The water calls for me, begging me to go and hide underneath it. I was tempted to go for a swim yesterday, but like every place I step into, the ocean holds too many hidden dangers.

When I get into the car beside Jared, he hangs up and turns to me with a smile. "You look beautiful."

"I made an effort for my husband."

"You never need to make an effort. You're beautiful without even trying."

"And you are one hell of a charmer, Mr. Lester."

How would I ever be able to live without this man I love so much? I thought I loved Dylan, my first love, but I now realize that was only a taste of what true love feels like. This is the real thing, and it would kill me to let it go.

"I'm glad you're home." I watch Jared starting the car.

"So am I."

"Did you get some nice shots?"

"Loads of them. Campeche is one photogenic city. Next time I go there, I'll take you and the baby with me." His eyes light up. "There's nothing not to like—the limestone hills, pastel buildings, the beaches—you would have loved it all."

"I'm sure I would have. It sounds lovely." I look out the window at the passing cars, praying there will be a next time. I'm not even sure we'll have one more day together.

We arrive at Dan's Grill in less than fifteen minutes. The restaurant holds special memories for us. It was the setting of our first date many years ago, and we celebrate all our anniversaries here. The chef knows us by name and all our favorite foods. Since we enjoy most of the foods on the menu, many times, we ask him to surprise us.

Tonight, I order broccoli soup, sautéed vegetables with rice, and grilled sea bass. Jared goes for a plate of pesto and garlic spaghetti with the same grilled sea bass. We share a big green salad between us and a bottle of apple cider. I didn't realize just how hungry I was until the food appeared at the table.

Jared barely says a word as we eat our food. His eyes are on me the entire time. For a moment, I wonder whether he's searching for something on my face. Does he know what's going on? Did he bring me out tonight because he wants to discuss something important?

Since we arrived, I've been studying the faces of the other diners and glancing at the door each time someone walks in.

"Are you okay, sweetheart?" He peers at me through the flickering candle flame.

"Sure, why?" My stomach twists with anxiety.

"I mean, have you been okay health-wise?"

"Yes, yes." The tension melts from my shoulders. I was being ridiculous. He doesn't suspect anything at all.

I pick up a piece of fish with my fork and push it into my mouth, chewing on it before I respond. "The visit to the doctor went well. You were right. I have nothing to worry about. The baby's healthy. But Dr. Collins is sick, and there's a new doctor stepping in for her. Apparently, she's her godchild. She's quite nice." Talking about Dr. Collins' health is a great way to remove the focus from me.

Jared frowns and leans in. "Do you know what's wrong with her? I saw her at the grocery store two weeks ago, and she seemed fine."

"She had a stroke. I don't know the details."

"Goodness, is she okay?" Jared wipes his lips with the napkin.

"Last I heard she's fine now, but she left town to recover at a health spa."

"That's really terrible news." Jared shakes his head and starts to eat again. "Is the godchild at least as good as Dr. Collins or should we look for someone else?"

"I wouldn't want to do that this close to the birth." I lift my glass of apple cider to my lips and take a sip. "From what I could tell, the new doctor is just as competent."

Jared narrows his eyes. "I have to say I'm surprised you're not freaking out."

I put my glass down and gaze past his shoulder at a man in a three-piece suit, who is laughing and chatting with his companion, with not a care in the world.

"I'm trying not to freak out about everything. Some things we just can't control." If only he knew.

"And everything is going to be just fine." He places his warm hand over mine and squeezes. "I'm so happy the baby is okay. I can't wait to change diapers."

"Diapers." I pull out my phone. "I need to buy more diapers." I put a reminder on my phone and drop it back into my handbag, then I pick up my knife and fork to eat the last piece of fish.

"Did you ever find out whose house had been broken into?"

I swallow hard, the food hurting my throat. I lower my gaze to my plate. "I didn't get a chance to ask around. But I feel better now that the locks are changed."

"I'm just glad you're safe. I don't know what I'd do if anything happened to you."

I paste a smile on my face and look into his eyes. "Tell me more about your trip."

"It was exhausting but really worth it. I got what I wanted. I'll show you the shots tomorrow." He folds his arms in front of him on the table. "The only picture I'm interested in right now is the one in front of me."

Undiluted joy spreads through my entire body, but it comes hand in hand with a deep ache. "I look forward to spending more time with you now that you're home."

"I promise you many walks on the beach and late night dinners like this one. I might throw in a few foot massages as well."

"You're making this pregnant woman incredibly happy."

We spend the rest of dinner talking more about the things we'll be doing before the baby arrives. Then I give him the ultrasound picture with barely a glance at it. I still don't have the courage to look. After the events of the past few days, my fears of losing the baby have become magnified.

"She looks like me." He holds it to the light, a tender smile tipping the corners of his mouth.

"How do you know it's a she?"

"I'm hoping for a girl just as beautiful and perfect as you."

"I'm far from perfect." I fold and unfold my napkin on my lap.

"Perfection is in the eye of the beholder. You're perfect to me."

CHAPTER 34

∽

Back home, Jared decides it's time for him to build the baby's crib, even though it's close to 11:00 p.m., and he looks about to drop with exhaustion. He insists he's been putting it off for too long.

He is the kind of person who always gets things done without postponing them until tomorrow. It hits me suddenly why he'd put this particular task off so many times. Like me, he was secretly afraid that I wouldn't be able to carry this pregnancy to term. He won't admit it, but he was afraid to make preparations only for the baby not to arrive. The miscarriages had hurt him just as much as they did me. But he was the strong one.

"Get some rest. You can do it tomorrow." I need more time to prepare for the questions I know will come once he enters the nursery.

"Nope, I'm doing it tonight." He stumbles toward the stairs. "The baby will be here any day."

I follow him upstairs, shuddering as he takes each step. An image of the message on the wallpaper flashes across my mind, but I shove it back along with many others from that night.

He halts in the doorway of the nursery. "What happened in here? Were you trying to put the crib together yourself?"

I wring my hands in front of me. "I tried but failed."

"You shouldn't have tried. I said I'd do it."

I place a hand between his shoulder blades. "I know, I'm sorry. I was bored."

"What happened to the other wallpaper?"

"Like I said, I was bored." My hands move to my hips. "But I sort of like this one better. Don't you just like the little teddy bears? I think they're so cute."

"But you were insistent on us choosing all nursery furniture and decorations together." He grins. "I'm offended that you didn't consult me."

"I know. But I didn't want to bother you with something as silly as wallpaper." I take a breath. "If you really don't like it, we can switch it up."

He puts an arm around me and kisses my cheek. "As long as you're happy, so am I."

"I am … I am happy."

He lets go of me and rubs his hands

together. "Let me build the crib to make you even happier."

"You really don't think it can wait one more night?" I was able to hide the things that had happened in this room when he was away, but what if he puts the crib together and we find it dismantled again? How would I be able to explain it?

"No, it's time."

While he works, putting piece by piece back together, I sit in the rocking chair and read him the instructions, even though I know them by heart. He's done within twenty minutes.

He yawns and stretches his arms above his head. "I guess we're ready for the baby to come."

"Yep. We better get as much sleep as possible before we're parents." I pause. "At least, you should." The closer we come to the birth, the harder it is for me to get a full night's sleep. Having a stalker doesn't help.

"How about a walk on the beach before we call it a night?"

"A walk? Are you serious?" I lean against the doorframe and cross my arms. "Look at you. You can barely stand."

"Fresh sea air is like a sleeping pill to me. I'm trying to wean myself off them."

"You don't need to go to the beach for fresh air. Open the window and breathe it in."

"It's not the same thing. Ten minutes and we'll be back home."

Now that I know someone is after me, I'm nervous about walking around on a dark beach. Anything can happen to us out there, but Jared is so determined. He's already grabbed our flashlights and my coat. He looks excited like a boy on Christmas morning. How could I say no to him?

We hit the beach hand in hand like we used to in the earlier months of our marriage when Jared wasn't so busy. Trying not to glance over my shoulder every few seconds, I force myself to enjoy the breeze that's swinging my hair from side to side, and the sand pushing itself between my toes. If life ever gets back to normal, we have to do this more often.

Even though I'd been on edge for most of the time, the walk did me good. We get back to the cottage both sleepy and refreshed. Jared changes into his pajamas and goes back downstairs to fill the jug of water I keep next to the bed as I often get thirsty in the middle of the night.

After being downstairs for far too long, he returns to the room without the water, and a thunderous expression on his face. His hand is clutching his phone, his gaze fixed on it. He looks about to pass out.

I stop fluffing the pillows. "Are you okay?

What's the matter?"

"I received a weird text message."

"What does it say?" I sit on the bed. Please, God, don't let it be the stalker. Let it be some work-related text.

"You tell me." He looks up at me as though he doesn't recognize me, confusion boiling in his eyes. He has the same pained look he had every time I told him we lost a baby, but it's sharpened by anger.

Instead of reading the text message to me, he tosses the cell phone onto the bed. I'm afraid to pick up the phone, afraid to see whatever it is that has the power to cause Jared's mood to plummet.

My breath is a bubble inside my throat as I read the text message. The moment the words sink into the folds of my mind, the bubble pops and air bursts from my lips in a rush. Just like that, our beautiful evening is ruined. The bomb has hit.

Your wife had an affair. You're about to raise another man's baby. xoxo

The phone slips from my hand. My eyes reach for Jared's in desperation. I want to be offended that he believes the text without even asking for an explanation from me, but in his place, I would probably have reacted in the same way.

"Jared, you don't really believe it, do you?" I clutch my hands in my lap. "You know it's a lie, right?"

Jared doesn't respond. When I stand to reach for his hand, he takes a step back.

"Please, honey, you have to ... you have to believe me," I stutter, choking out the words. "You know I love you. I'd never cheat on you, ever."

"Listen, Caitlin, I'm tired. It's been a long day. Let's talk about this in the morning. I'll sleep downstairs." He picks up a pillow and a bedsheet, and walks out the door before I can say anything more—before I can defend myself.

He leaves me sitting on the bed in complete and utter shock. I want to run after him, to beg him to believe me. I want to tell him that it's a lie someone cooked up to destroy my life. But where in the world would I start?

No, I can't tell him the truth. I also can't let this go. I need to talk to him, to try and explain the best way I can without blowing my own cover.

My hands bunched up at my sides, I hurry down the stairs, almost tripping on them.

I find him sitting on the couch, staring at the blank television screen, both hands clutching his knees, a vein throbbing on the side of his jaw.

At a safe distance, I try to speak, but it's hard to find the right words. The text is a lie. I know that. I've never cheated on my husband. But can I explain it away without opening my can of worms?

"What is it?" He doesn't even bother to look at me.

Despair sags through me.

"It's your baby, Jared. It's our baby. I never cheated on you." I sit on the couch next to him. He flinches but doesn't move away. I turn to face him, my knees touching his thigh. "I'm telling you the truth. I'd never hurt you in that way. You're the only man I love."

I know exactly why Jared is acting the way he is, why the message hit him so hard. His previous relationship had ended because his fiancée cheated on him. He'd made it clear to me from the start that he'll be able to handle a lot in a relationship, but not unfaithfulness. I promised I'd never cheat on him and asked him to make the same promise to me. Now, this.

I touch his arm and close my eyes.

"I'm not Sage. I'll never do to you what she did. I promise you that."

"If it's not true," he leans forward, "why have you been acting strange the past few days?"

"Strange? I don't know what you're talking about."

"You know exactly what I'm talking about. Don't make a fool of me. Half the time I'm with you, you're not really here. You also sounded strange when we talked on the phone. For five days I've been trying to ignore it, but this all makes perfect sense to me."

"Don't do this, Jared. There's nothing going on. I don't know who sent you that message, but it's not true."

He rises from the couch and gazes at me for a while. "Tell me it's not Ralph's."

"Ralph? Oh, my God! I told you so many times that he's just a colleague. There's nothing going on between us."

"He's more than that, and you know it." The sharp edge of his voice cuts deep.

I lift then drop my hands into my lap. "I cannot believe you're bringing him up again." My cheeks flame with anger—not at him, but the situation. "How many times have I told you he's nothing more than a friend?"

He shoves his hands into the pockets of his pajama pants. "So, all the gossip around town isn't true, then? Are they all making it up?" He shrugs. "I try not to listen, but sometimes it's hard not to."

"Kids at school made up these rumors and passed them on. There's no truth in them whatsoever. I told you that before."

"I've seen you with him before, you know. I

325

see how he looks at you, how you look at him. There's something there, something you've been trying to hide from me, maybe even from yourself."

I get to my feet and grab his shoulders in desperation. "That's not true, Jared. People love making up things. They thrive on gossip. We can't let a stupid text message destroy our marriage. It's probably just a prank."

He shrugs me off. "You know what? I can't stay here tonight. I'll get a room at a hotel." He storms out of the living room, runs upstairs, and returns wearing jeans and a white t-shirt. He doesn't glance at me when he picks up the suitcase he hadn't yet taken to our bedroom.

Because of a lie, my husband walks out the door, leaving me with tears coursing down my cheeks and words I want to say, but can't.

CHAPTER 35

∽

I drop the phone onto the bed and gaze into space. It's been three days, and Jared is still not picking up his phone.

Last night, I drove like a crazy person around town, walking into every hotel, asking if Jared is staying there. Each "no" was a knife in my gut.

I wonder how long I'll be able to hold up before my heart shatters completely. I'm both worried and furious at him for walking out on me the way he did—walking out of our home, our marriage.

But each time, my anger screeched to a halt when I reminded myself that I started all this. Everything that's happening to me is my fault. I have no right being mad at him. It should be the other way around. If he only knew who he married.

Feeling as though my body is disappearing into thin air, I strip off my clothes and go to the bathroom, where I stand rigid under the shower, allowing cold water to wash over me, to wash away my tears and take them with it down the drain.

I still have an hour left before leaving for work. I spend much of that time in the shower, leaning against the cool, wet tiles, sobbing hard with my arms wrapped around my belly.

I wish I could protect my baby from all this chaos. But how can I do that when I can barely hold myself together? If only it were possible to press an emotional button and switch the pain off.

I finally get out of the shower and get dressed. I have to keep going even when I don't feel like it. This is my life, and I can't let it slip through my fingers.

I head downstairs for breakfast. As I descend the stairs, I'm holding on to the hope that Jared will be in the kitchen, surprising me with a full English breakfast. I hold on to the thought so tight that by the time I reach the last step, I swear I smell the bacon and eggs and hear the sizzle of them frying in our nonstick pan.

I reach the kitchen and freeze in the doorway.

Everything is as I left it last night. The room is empty, cold, and sterile.

My tears threaten to fall as I sink into a chair at the kitchen table and gaze at one of our wedding photos stuck onto the fridge. The magnet holding it in place had been purchased at a souvenir shop in Vienna, Austria. Jared had a job assignment there, so we decided to combine it with our honeymoon. It was my first time leaving the US. I was so excited I forgot who I was and where I was coming from. I pretended I had no skeletons in my closet.

I look away from the fridge and bite back the tears.

I will *not* cry anymore. It's not good for the baby. But, then again, holding it all in is just as detrimental. I take deep breaths until I feel somewhat calm. It'll be fine. I'll make it through the day. By tonight, I'll come up with a plan. I need to do something to fix this situation.

I force muesli and yogurt down my throat and prepare my lunch for work. With one last glance at the memories on the fridge door, I leave the kitchen, get my bag, and head out to the car. Outside, I halt in the small path to the gate and look around me.

The faces I see are familiar—neighbors heading to work or someplace else. I wave at Ruth, who is watching me from her kitchen window.

I keep up the appearance of being happy. None of them would want to harm me, would they?

As I drive through traffic, I glance several times into the rearview mirror, on the lookout for the black Nissan. It's nowhere to be seen. Maybe my tormenter got what he wanted. Maybe the goal was just to destroy my marriage.

"No, I won't let it happen," I say to myself with determination. "I'm keeping my life and my marriage."

I make it to school ten minutes late thanks to the insane traffic due to a roadblock.

With not much time to pull myself together before the Monday morning meeting, I drop my things in my class and head to the staff lounge.

I breathe a sigh of relief when I find that not all the teachers are at the meeting yet. Georgia is early as usual, glancing at her watch. Ralph, who is also present, is reading a newspaper but looks up and smiles when I enter.

I'm not surprised that Lilliana is among the first people to show up. She makes it a point to always be punctual at every meeting, a way to suck up to Georgia. I greet her, but she barely acknowledges my presence.

I shrug and find a seat far away from Ralph, who frowns at me.

During the meeting, I barely hear anything that's said. And when I'm asked questions, I answer like a robot, giving what's expected of me but nothing more. And the whole time, I'm preoccupied with wondering who at this table or in this town is responsible for derailing my life. Who among my colleagues knows my deepest, darkest secrets? Who took my spare key from my desk drawer and broke into my house? My worst enemy could be right here in this room.

I glance at Lilliana, who's listening attentively to what Georgia is saying and twirling a lock of her hair around her finger. Is it her? She definitely has a motive. But if she knows who I really am, why would she wait years before threatening me? Or did she just find out about my past?

What if it's not Lilliana, though? What if it's someone else more dangerous?

After the meeting, Ralph tries to talk to me, but I raise my hand.

"I need the ladies room. I'll see you around." I have to be careful. For all I know, someone is watching and reporting back to Jared.

As I head out, Georgia stops me at the door as the other teachers trickle out.

"Caitlin, are you okay?"

I force a smile and square my shoulders, feigning confidence. "Of course, I am, thanks for asking."

"It's just that I noticed you weren't quite there during the meeting. I hope everything is all right with the baby."

I manage a smile. "The baby is well. No problems at all."

Georgia smiles. "I'm glad to hear that. If you

decide to go on maternity leave earlier than planned, please don't hesitate to come to me. I'm a mother. After three kids, I'm quite familiar with the aches and pains of pregnancy."

"Thank you, Georgia. I'll keep that in mind."

Inside the staff bathroom, I let out a deep sigh and grip the edge of the sink, my head rested on my chest, eyes closed. I try to count the dots behind my eyelids.

"You okay? Pregnancy getting the better of you?"

My eyes fly open at the sound of Lilliana's mocking voice. I thought I was alone. I didn't hear her enter.

Steeling myself, I whirl around to face her. I recover quickly. I don't want to give her the ammunition she needs to weaken me.

"Why shouldn't I be okay, Lilliana?" I tip my head to the side. If I asked her straight out whether she's my stalker, would she admit it?

"Hey, don't dump your pregnancy hormones on me. I'm just asking if you're fine. You look rather pale. The look doesn't suit you." There's a shadow of a smile on her face.

I pull in a deep breath and study her face for a moment, hands bunched at my sides. My whole being tells me it's her. She did all those things to me. Maybe this is the time to finally face up to her. She's always been a thorn in my side. I can't let her win.

"You've never liked me, have you?" I meet her gaze head-on. She reminds me of those mean girls from high school, the ones who form cliques and make fun of other students, so they can feel empowered.

"I don't need to like you to work with you," she shrills.

She has just admitted it. So if I had to make a list of all the suspects, she'd be the first name on my list. She's not even hiding her hate for me.

"Tell me, Lilliana. How far would you go to hurt someone you don't like—someone like me, for example?"

"Hurt you? I have better things to do, Caitlin. As hard as it might be for you to believe, the world doesn't revolve around you."

"What do you mean by that?" I refuse to back away from her poison. I rest my back against the sink for support.

"You waltz into town and expect the world to bend to your every wish." She gets into my personal space. "You barge into our community and take what you want without caring who gets hurt. You expect everything to just fall into your lap ... like your job."

"I don't know what I ever did to you. Everything I have in my life I earned and worked hard for. Yes, it wasn't hard for me to get this job, but that's because I'm qualified, and I'm damn good at what I do."

She scoffs. "If it weren't for Ralph talking you up, you wouldn't be here."

"That's what you think? That I got this job because of Ralph? Sorry to disappoint you, but it was Georgia who came to me. I got this teaching position because I'm damn good at my job. I don't understand your problem."

"You think I'm stupid, don't you?" Her nostrils are flaring now. "You might fool other people, but I can see right through you. I watch you every day. I see you following Ralph like a lovesick puppy even when you have a husband at home. Don't you have any shame at all?"

I feel myself reeling. This is going further than I'd expected. I might have just opened up a can of worms.

"I don't know what you're talking about, Lilliana. There's nothing going on between Ralph and me. We're friends, and that's all. Men and women are capable of being friends."

"Is that what you tell Jared?" She smiles. "Is that what you tell him every day when you go home?"

"You have no right." I grind the words between my teeth. I want to say more, but I hear shuffling outside the door. It won't be a good idea to cause a scene at my workplace. I have to be professional. I cannot allow my private problems to destroy my job.

"Look, Lilliana, you're right. We don't have to like each other to work together. From now on, let's just stay out of each other's way and do our jobs. You deserve your position, and I deserve mine. That's all there is to it."

She takes a few steps closer, her breath hot on my face again. "You know what? Jared made me promise not to tell you this, but I can't help myself."

"Tell me what?" My stomach turns at her words.

"Before you came along, we were a thing, and it was getting serious."

I feel like I've been hit by a truck and I'm flying in midair before hitting the ground hard. "I don't believe you," I whisper. Of course, Jared had a dating history before me. He told me about his fiancée and other women he dated, but none of them in this town. Why didn't he tell me about Lilliana? Is it because he doesn't want me to feel uncomfortable while working with her? I get that, but I'd rather have heard it from him than the snake herself. Unless she's lying.

"If you don't believe me, ask him. If you hadn't come along, I'd probably have been the one carrying his baby right now instead of you." She frowns. "No, you can't do that, can you? You can't ask him. A little bird told me you're not on speaking terms." She pulls her tote bag closer to her body and disappears into one of the stalls.

I stay for a moment in the middle of the room, unable to move, listening to her urinate. She has to be the person I'm looking for. She has multiple motives to hurt me. She wanted Jared; she wanted my baby.

I place a hand on my belly, and the baby kicks against it.

Bile rises up my throat, and I hurry into a free stall. I position myself at the bowl, expecting vomit to rush out of me but I only heave dry air. When I exit, Lilliana is still in her stall, probably laughing and enjoying my pain and humiliation.

If she really dated Jared, she probably has his cell phone number. She must be the one who sent him that text message. After all, she believes that Ralph and I are having an affair, just like everybody else in town. But I can't go around throwing accusations without concrete proof. I have more to lose. Unlike me, Faypine is her home.

I'm still a stranger in this town. There are possibly a lot of people who might not want me here, who hold grudges I may not know about.

She finally walks out of the cubicle, washes her hands, and fixes her makeup without saying another word to me. Then she leaves me alone in the bathroom.

Tears burn my eyes, but I can't humiliate myself even further. I swallow my tears, take a deep breath, and walk out. On my way to the classroom, I spot Ralph standing in front of the door to the gym. He sees me and hurries to walk beside me.

"Caitlin, is something going on?"

"Why is everybody asking me that? Everything is fine, Ralph. I really don't think it's a good idea for us to be seen together." I keep my voice low, so no one hears our conversation.

I'm pretty sure the walls in this school have ears, and they report right back to Lilliana.

"Did I do something to upset you? I'm wondering because the past few days you've been avoiding me. You even leave work without saying goodbye. I tried calling you several times outside work, but you won't pick up my calls."

"Like I said, I don't think it's a good idea for us to be seen together ... or to call each other."

"I don't understand. We're friends. What changed?"

"I don't want to talk about it. I have a busy day ahead. The kids are waiting. I can't deal with this right now, okay?"

Ralph stops walking and grabs my arm, pulling me to a halt. I quickly pull my arm from his grasp before anyone sees. Thank God most kids are already in class.

I shake my head. "Don't do that again."

"I care about you. That's why I need to know if you're fine. I care about you as a friend."

"Is that all, Ralph, really? Do you care for me as only a friend?"

"Where's all this coming from?" He arches his perfectly formed eyebrows. "What changed between us? You're acting all strange."

I sigh. "Ralph, I'm sorry. This isn't your fault. I'm having a bad day."

"You've been having quite a few bad days lately. I'm worried about you."

"I appreciate that, but I'm fine. Yes, there are things going on in my life right now, but I have to work through them on my own."

Telling Ralph about what's going on would only complicate things further, and it would infuriate Jared if he finds out. "I have to go. I'll see you around, okay?" I start to walk away.

"If you need to talk, give me a call. I mean it."

"Okay," I lie and distance myself from him.

CHAPTER 36

ⴲ

I'm a ghost of myself as I step off the school grounds and enter my car. My conversation with Lilliana in the morning spoiled the rest of my day. I kept running her words over and over inside my head.

I rest my head on the steering wheel, careful not to push too hard. This entire time I thought it could be Ryan, that he was still alive and hell-bent on revenge. Even though I know who my tormenter could be, I'm still unable to find relief. There are still so many unanswered questions, things that happened that are hard to pin on Lilliana. The person in the black Nissan, for example, had been a man. Could it be she's not working alone?

I'm still a broken, confused mess when I start my car and drive to the grocery store on our street. I throw a few basic foods into the cart—milk, bread, tea, eggs, fruits, and vegetables.

I'm holding the bag of groceries, twelve minutes later, as I stand in front of Ruth's gate. Riddled with loneliness, I've been coming over quite a lot these last few days. I've gone over for coffee and cake, and I'd invited her to dinner twice. It's hard to believe that only a few weeks ago, we never said more than a hello to one another. Now she has completely warmed to me. She even shared with me stories of her brief time in Hollywood where she chased fame as an actress.

I've come to like her as well, but not enough to open up to her about what I'm hiding. That's my secret to keep.

I step through the gate and ring the bell. No one answers. I wait for a while before ringing again. I shift the bag of groceries to my other hand and wait. Still no answer.

When Ruth still doesn't let me in, my gaze drops to the potted plant next to the door. She told me she keeps a spare key there and that I'm welcome into her home anytime.

I feel uncomfortable about entering her house, but what if something is wrong? I know that she only leaves the house in the morning to run errands and is usually back by noon. And she couldn't have gone anywhere without her car.

She's a lonely old woman with no living relatives. Now that we're friends, I can't just go away without finding out if she's fine. If she's not home, I'll leave the groceries in the kitchen and get out.

Trying not to feel like an intruder, I open the door. I'm immediately welcomed by the smell of fresh flowers.

Ruth loves to garden, and her house is always filled with vases of fresh blooms in every room. Every time I hear her talk about her hobby, I miss Thalia all over again.

"Ruth, are you home?" I call several times but get no response.

Trying not to worry, I enter her bright, yellow kitchen and place the groceries on the counter. Then I go on the search for her.

Her bedroom upstairs is empty and musty. Not at all as bright as the kitchen, even with the windows wide open.

My gaze lands on the bed, covered with a multi-colored quilt. Her friend, the one that lived in our cottage, had apparently made it for her only a month before she died.

I'm about to check the bathroom when I pass the window and decide to see if she's out in her garden.

"Thank God," I whisper. Of course, she'd be in the garden. Why had I not thought to look there first? And why was it that the first thing that came to my mind was that something had happened to her?

She's on her knees in front of a rose bush, wearing a pair of beige shorts, and a white blouse. A white straw hat with a blue ribbon covers her silver hair, and gardening gloves protect her hands.

I return downstairs and open the glass doors leading to the garden.

Startled, Ruth turns to look in my direction.

"Look what the cat dragged in." She lifts herself off the ground with difficulty. She doesn't seem to care that I let myself in.

Walking toward me, she removes her gardening gloves. A single, white feather falls to the ground in front of her. She steps over it. "I'm sorry, I didn't mean to—I rang the bell."

"No need to apologize. We're neighbors. Use that key whenever you need to. I get carried away when I'm with my roses, and my hearing isn't the best these days." She slips her frail, leathery hand into mine and drops the gardening gloves onto a metal garden table. "Let's go inside. I have some apple pie and fresh lemonade. I was going to bring it to … your place later."

She's so thankful for the groceries that she gives me a hug—the first in our short relationship. When she insists on giving me the money back, I refuse.

At the kitchen table, I accept her lemonade and apple pie.

Ruth sits on the other side of the table and watches me. "Are you okay? You've been looking troubled lately. Is everything all right with the baby?"

I haven't had the nerve to tell her about Jared being gone. But she probably knows already.

I place a hand on my stomach and shake my head. "The baby is doing great. It's just a lot of other things going on in my life right now."

"Do you want to talk about it?"

"It's nothing, really." I take a sip of lemonade. "I don't want to burden you with my problems."

"It helps to let it out sometimes. Maybe I can help."

I'm quiet for a long time, prodding my apple pie with my fork. I pick up a piece and bring it to my mouth. Ruth watches me chewing in silence.

It's driving me crazy not to be able to confide in anyone. From what I've seen so far, Ruth doesn't seem to hang out with the gossiping crowd. Maybe I could tell her just enough to make myself feel better, not everything. Nothing about my past.

"I'm having problems in my marriage." I rub my temple. "Jared—he thinks I cheated on him."

"I wasn't going to mention it to you, but I

heard the rumors. Doris has been running her mouth again."

"Of course, she has." I'm sure she has a lot of eyes and ears in this town.

"Word is you had an affair with Father Travis Jenkins's son."

"Those stupid rumors have been going around for a while." I look her straight in the eye. "Ruth, I never cheated on Jared. Ralph and I are just colleagues and friends. There's nothing more between us." I'm desperate for someone to believe me.

"But your husband doesn't believe you?"

Even though I haven't cheated on my husband, I hang my head in shame. "He's gone. He won't answer my calls."

Ruth studies the roses on the table. The fact that she doesn't respond to that tells me she already knew.

"You don't believe the rumors, do you?"

"Should I?" Her gaze returns to me. Something has shifted in her eyes. The smile is gone. "I like you, Caitlin. I didn't think I would, but I was wrong." She pauses. "But the truth is, I don't really know you. You don't say much about yourself."

What's going on? Why is she suddenly suspicious of me? "I … I just don't like talking about myself."

"And I respect that. Unfortunately, I haven't

been friends with you long enough to know if you are the kind of woman who would be unfaithful to her husband."

"I thought we were friends."

"I thought so, too." Ruth pulls my unfinished plate of pie toward her. "But friends don't lie to each other." The strand of beard on the side of her chin trembles.

"What are you saying?" My mind is reeling with all kinds of questions. This doesn't make sense. She was so nice before. She gave me a hug.

"I gave you a chance to tell me the truth. You didn't." She gets up from the table and takes my plate to the kitchen counter. "I'm good at telling when someone is hiding something."

Feeling as if I've been slapped in the face, I push back my chair and rise to my feet. "I have to go."

"I think that's a good idea." She pauses. "Take your groceries with you. I can buy my own food."

Hurt, I grab the bag and leave in a hurry.

In the safety of my home, I collapse against the closed door. Ruth knows something. I have to stay away from her. I have to keep my distance from everyone.

CHAPTER 37

∽∞∽

It's midnight, and I'm in the living room, too tired to go upstairs to bed. I feel as though I've been run over by a truck, but I didn't really do much today.

I took the last two days off as I couldn't deal with all the stares and whispers. And Lilliana's presence in the school suffocates me, even when she's not in the same room.

The only thing I did today was go to Dr. Fern to request a paternity test.

At first, she'd peered at me in an awkward way, as though judging me, but then her face cleared, and she gave me my wish. She took the samples she needed from me and I handed her Jared's hairbrush to remove some strands.

The results will be ready within a week.

After what had happened at Ruth's house, I knew I had to do something. I couldn't just let everyone believe I cheated on my husband. I hope that when Jared finds out that he's the father, he will come back home.

But truthfully, I don't know if we'll be able to get past this. As long as I'm working at Silver Oak, he'll continue to be uncomfortable with me working close to Ralph. There's no way I'll give up my job as it would be too risky to find another.

I don't even know if I'll still have a job after my maternity leave, considering that Lilliana is not even making it a secret that she wants me out. What if she uses my time away to her advantage and finds a way to convince Georgia to let me go? She could use the rumors as ammunition. But I can't think about that now.

Dr. Fern had warned that my blood pressure was slightly high, and I have to take it easy.

Thankfully, days have gone by, and my tormentor hasn't knocked me off my feet again.

With the heavy curtains closed, the darkness around me is so thick I feel as though I could reach out to touch it. I breathe it in and lean my head back, one hand on my stomach. The baby moves at the place where my palm is resting. It dawns on me that even though I feel so alone, I'm really not. My baby is always with me.

My eyes fly open when I hear a sound. I think it's coming from the front door. Someone is out there. Are they trying to get in?

Instead of sitting there waiting for whoever it is on the other side to walk in and harm me, I push myself off the couch and tiptoe upstairs. I lock myself inside my bedroom, then allow myself to freak out, a sour taste in my mouth.

I sit on my bed, holding onto the knife, ready to do whatever I have to in order to protect myself and my baby.

I strain my ears to listen to the sounds from downstairs. Even from upstairs, I can hear the door being unlocked.

It's a struggle to keep calm. The baby kicks me hard in the ribs, and I rub the spot.

As the sounds downstairs get louder, I move to the windows and throw them open. My gaze lands on Ruth's house. I wish I could call her for help, but I can't. She's back to being the woman I've known for years—a bitter old lady. Our brief friendship has completely dissolved since the conversation about my rumored infidelity. Yesterday, I went over to her house to beg her not to believe the rumors. She didn't open the door, even though I knew she was home, having seen her staring out the window only minutes before I went there.

The wind blows my hair in all directions as I lean out to assess the height from my bedroom window to the ground. Even if I weren't pregnant, jumping out the window would have been dangerous.

I whirl around when I hear footfalls pounding up the stairs. From the nightstand, I grab a hammer I'd put there as an additional weapon. I wait with bated breath as the footsteps approach the door and then halt.

Blood rushes to my head, making me dizzy. I don't care if my body lets me down, but I refuse to go down without a fight.

With the knife in one hand and the hammer in the other, I switch off the bedside lamp and move to one side of the door. I push my back against the wall, ready to strike the intruder as soon as they enter the room.

The door handle is pushed down, but when the door doesn't open, it's released again.

I'm breathing so hard now I'm afraid the person on the other side will hear me.

"Caitlin, open the door. It's me."

My body slumps with relief. I flick on the light.

It's Jared. It's my husband.

"I'm coming." Tears of relief well up in my eyes. I place the hammer and knife inside the dresser drawer and yank the door open. Overcome with joy, I throw myself into Jared's arms. "Thank God." My tears soak his shirt. "Thank God it's you." He doesn't push me away, not immediately. When he finally does, his bloodshot eyes search my face. "Who else could it be?" He pushes a hand through his unruly hair. He looks like he hasn't slept or had a shower in days.

"I thought someone broke into the house. I—"

"I heard your message. When do you get the test results?"

I stumble back and wrap my arms around myself. For a moment there, I thought he came back for me. I was wrong. He's still giving me the kind of look he normally gives strangers. Nothing has changed.

"In a week. The samples were sent to a lab out of town." I try to reach for him again, desperate to get him back. "Thank you. Thank you for coming home."

He shrinks away from my touch and steps around me to get to the drawer that holds our bed linen. Then he picks up a pillow from the bed as he'd done a few days ago. "I'll be sleeping downstairs." He walks out, swaying slightly.

I go after him, moving as fast as my legs would let me, which isn't fast at all.

When I get to the living room, I find him covering up the couch with the sheets.

He doesn't even turn to look at me. Have I lost him completely? My body remembers the feel of his arms around me only a few minutes ago. He had held me for a moment before letting go. It can't be over. He wouldn't be here if it were.

"Why are you here if you don't want to be?"

Anger boils in the pit of my stomach. "It's clear to me that you've given up on our marriage. What are your plans, huh? If the baby is yours, which it is, are you going to take her away from me, is that it?" I never planned on referring to the baby as a girl. It just came out.

Jared glances at me for a second. His face doesn't give his thoughts away, though. I can only guess what he's thinking. Maybe he thinks I found out the sex of the baby, that we're getting a daughter. Maybe he's happy but doesn't want it to show.

He pulls his wrinkled shirt over his head and drops onto the couch, acting as if I'm not even in the room.

A sob rises to my throat as I walk away. My face burns with tears with each step up the stairs.

In the bedroom, I climb into bed, switch off the light, and place my hands on my baby for comfort.

I'm just about to drift off to sleep when I hear a creaking noise, followed by the door being opened. I pull myself up in bed.

From the slice of moonlight coming in through the window, I see that it's Jared, and he's approaching our bed. Maybe he's ready to talk.

I switch on the light and wait for him to start the conversation. When he doesn't speak, I lie myself down again and pull the sheets up to my neck.

To my surprise, he lies down next to me, but doesn't pull me close as he used to. Unable to handle any more rejection, I don't reach out, either. I'm afraid to have him only to lose him again.

My heart almost bursts with pent-up emotions when, after what feels like an eternity, he slings an arm around my stomach and shifts closer. "You really didn't have an affair?"

"No," I whisper. "I didn't have an affair. I swear. The results will prove that."

In a week, it will all be over. We'll get back to the place we were before everything went to hell. Or will we? What if my worst nightmare isn't over yet? The truth remains that someone in this town knows I'm not who I claim to be. If I don't tell Jared the truth, he might hear it from someone else. If I open up to him, maybe, just maybe, he'll be on my side. Or tonight will be the last night I'll be in his arms.

"Jared, I need to tell you something." As soon as the words leave my lips, I wish I could swallow them down again.

What can I tell him? That I left a man—the first husband I never told him about—dead in a hotel room? That I'm a fugitive? That I might be a murderer? I'll be fooling myself if I think he'll ever look at me the same way again.

"What?" he croaks. "What do you want to tell me?"

"Just that I love you so much. And I never want to lose us."

CHAPTER 38

I look across the waiting room. Pregnant women are everywhere, all in their own private thoughts. Some are with partners, and others are alone. Most are reading glossy magazines with faces of smiling babies splashed across their covers. One woman is on the phone even though a small sign on the wall forbids phone calls in the waiting room.

The room smells of baby powder, or I could be imagining it. I don't trust my mind much these days.

I glance at Jared, and nervous butterflies erupt in my belly. I have no reason to be nervous since the baby is his, but I am.

Jared tosses the magazine he was flipping through into a basket and leans back in his seat, eyes closed.

I reach for his hand. The moment my skin touches his, he moves away. I force myself to sympathize with him. In his shoes, I would probably be a wreck, as well. The truth will come out soon enough, and everything will be all right again.

I clasp my hands in my lap and occupy myself with studying the faces in the room. Are these people happy? What kinds of secrets are *they* hiding? I can't imagine any of them going through what I'm going through.

"I need the bathroom," I whisper to Jared and rise. Hopefully, a short walk will get rid of some of my nervous energy.

Instead of responding, Jared reaches into the basket for a cooking magazine.

I carry the ache in my heart all the way to a bathroom cubicle, where I lock the door and rest my forehead on it. I beg each breath I take to bring me relief. The ache refuses to be ignored.

The results of the paternity test don't worry me. I'm worried about what will happen once we get the results and return to our lives. Will everything return to normal? What if my tormenter attacks me from another angle?

After this hurdle, how many more will we have to overcome? How much more torture can I go through before I break? It's so exhausting running from the past.

A sound from outside the door yanks me from my thoughts. Someone is calling my name.

"Caitlin, we're called in." Jared's muffled voice is stiff with tension.

"I'll be right out." I push away from the door.

I don't find Jared outside. He's already in the doctor's office when I arrive.

Dr. Fern steps around her desk and comes to shake my hand. Her handshake is brief and not as firm and warm as the first time I shook her hand. "Caitlin, nice to see you again. I hope you and the baby are doing well." She's all business. No smile in sight; no glint in her eyes.

The residents of Faypine have pulled her to their side. She's judging me just like everyone else.

"Baby is fine ... I think." I drop my lashes to hide the hurt reflected in my eyes and place a hand protectively over my belly.

She waves at the empty chair next to Jared. "Please, take a seat."

As I lower myself into the chair, Jared doesn't turn to look at me. His focus is on Dr. Fern, who has returned to the other side of the desk.

"I have the results. Ready to hear them?"

"We are." I raise my chin to show my confidence.

"Would you like to read them yourself?" Dr. Fern looks from me to Jared.

"No, do it for us, doctor," Jared answers for

both of us.

"Caitlin?" The doctor raises an eyebrow at me.

"Yes." I shrug. "Please open it."

Dr. Fern sighs and opens the envelope. She flattens it out on the desk.

A shadow flits across her features. Her mouth falls open.

"What's going on, doctor?" I can feel my mouth going dry.

"I'm sorry, Caitlin." A line appears between her eyebrows. "I—"

"Am I the father or not?" Jared asks when Dr. Fern hesitates for too long.

She clears her throat. "It says here that ninety-nine—"

"Skip the numbers. Give me a yes or no answer."

Dr. Fern draws in a sharp breath. "I'm sorry. You are not the father of the baby."

Shock slaps me hard in the face. I yank the piece of paper from Dr. Fern's hands. "It can't be." My frantic gaze sweeps across the page. "There has to be some kind of mistake."

"It's unlikely." Dr. Fern leans back in her desk chair. "It's all there in black and white."

I choke back a cry. The page drops onto my lap. I turn to look at Jared. I can feel the heat of his rage without even seeing his eyes. He looks like a volcano about to erupt.

"It's not … Jared, it's not true. You have to believe me."

"You promised the results will prove everything. I guess they just did." He shoves his hair back with his hands, holds it in place, then releases.

"The lab clearly made a mistake. It happens." My gaze snaps back to the doctor. "Please, tell him, doctor. It does happen, right?"

"Well, mistakes do occur, but the lab we used—"

"You see, Jared? You heard her." I reach for his arm, but he yanks it away. "The results are wrong. I promise you that."

"I'm not the father," Jared mumbles under his breath. "I'm not the father." He repeats the words a few more times, then he throws his head back and starts to laugh. "I was such a fool."

"No, you're not. I love you, and you love me. This baby is ours." My voice is deflated. If the paternity test can't prove the truth to him, what power do my words hold? "I'm telling you the truth. I don't know what's going on here, but I didn't sleep with any other man. I've never cheated on you."

"Stop working so hard to cover up your lies," he barks. "It's all out in the open."

"Let me leave you two alone for a bit." The doctor stands up and disappears through the door.

The moment she's gone, our conversation dies. Brittle silence hovers between us like a heavy mist. We sit side by side, staring into space, buried in our tortured thoughts. I have no idea what more I can say to him.

How could this happen? I was so positive the results would set the record straight.

I pick up the piece of paper, running my gaze over every single word and number, searching for a mistake. I find none. It clearly states that my husband is not the father of my baby. There's only one explanation. Someone is behind this. The person who sent the text has something to do with these results.

"I think someone manipulated the results." The words come out in a whisper. "I didn't sleep with another man." I know I sound like a broken record, but I have to keep trying.

"I'm tired, Caitlin. I'm tired of being lied to."

"So what does this mean for us, Jared?" I ask, breathless with rage. "You're ready to give up on our marriage just like that?" My anger subsides as soon as it started. "Come on. What if we do another test?"

"I don't need any more tests done. I have faith in those results. No one manipulated them as you claim. The only person manipulating anything right now is you."

"I'm not—"

"You're trying to manipulate the situation so it leans in your favor. You're working so hard to prove to me that you are the woman I loved, the woman I married."

Sorrow closes up my throat. "You don't love me anymore?" My words are barely audible in my whisper.

He shoves his hands into his hair and closes his eyes. "I can't deal with this right now." His shoulders slump forward, dragged down by hurt. "I'm out of here."

I'm waiting for him to get up and leave, but he just sits there, his hands still in his hair, breathing hard.

"No." I bite my bottom lip to stop it from trembling. "Don't do this to us, Jared. Give me another chance to prove it to you."

"I've got all the proof that I need, right there." He jabs a finger at the test results.

"It's not the right proof." I curl my hands into fists. "Something happened here, and I don't know how to explain it."

"Don't try. I'm out of here." This time he shoots out of his chair and walks out the door, slamming it shut behind him.

A few seconds later, Dr. Fern enters the room. "Are you okay?" Her words are not in harmony with her expression. She's judging me again. Given the results, I don't blame her. "Would you like a glass of water?"

"I don't need water. I need another test done."

"I'm pretty sure the results will be the same." She pulls a folder from a shelf. "I've seen it happen with many patients before."

"But you said yourself that errors can occur."

"In rare cases."

"This could be one of those rare cases." I struggle to keep my voice from rising.

The doctor sits down and pins me with a gaze. "I'm sorry, Mrs. Lester, but I have to ask you to leave. I have other patients waiting. Unless there's something else you want to talk about."

"Fine." I grab my bag and the results and scramble to my feet. "I'm sorry for keeping you."

I step out of the room without saying goodbye. It's not fair for me to be angry at the doctor. But I can't help it. I can't keep my anger from scorching anyone I come into contact with.

As I stumble through the waiting room, tears explode from my eyes. I don't care about the stares or the whispers. All I care about is getting to the car, where Jared is waiting for me. I have to save what's left of my marriage. I don't give a damn what anyone says. I'll do another test at a different lab.

CHAPTER 39

It's raining outside—huge, fat drops plopping onto my head and shoulders like small marbles. Since rain is my friend, I don't bother to cover myself like the pedestrians rushing past me with umbrellas, handbags, or newspapers over their heads.

I stand on the sidewalk with my eyes raised to the sky. My tears burst from my eyes and mix with the rainwater.

My blue, cotton dress is getting drenched by the second, my hair flattening at the top of my head and hanging around my face in wet ropes.

A huge ball of laughter pushes its way up my chest. It spills from my lips and rings in my ears. My life is a freaking joke. It would make for such a great comedy. No wonder Jared cracked up earlier.

I'm shaking with mirth and crying at the same time as people step around me. A toddler stops to stare until her mother grabs her hand

and drags her away from the crazy woman on the sidewalk. They will have one hell of a story to tell at their dinner table.

I'm still laughing when I finally find the courage to go to the car, holding my handbag close to my body to prevent rainwater from getting inside.

What I feel most like doing is throwing myself to the ground and curling up into a ball, but I'm pregnant. It's no longer just about me. My body is no longer just my own.

I push myself forward, one shaky step after the other, barely able to see much through the curtain of rain. When I get to the car, I come to a halt. No one is inside.

I thought Jared would be waiting in the car, but he must have gone home without me.

I stare at my car for a long time as though he would magically appear. He doesn't, so I pull out my spare car key and yank the door open, throwing my dripping bag onto the passenger's seat. I get out again to get the towel I keep in the trunk.

Back inside the car, I dry my hair, face, and hands. Before I drive off, I give Jared's cell a call. It could be he's inside one of the shops.

The call goes to voicemail, and I don't bother to leave a message. I wrap my hand tight around the phone, swallow the lump lingering in my throat, and dial again. This time, I leave a message.

"Honey, I'm on my way home. We need to talk. I can explain everything." When I hang up, my throat is thick with fresh tears.

I'm barely able to breathe as I start the car, afraid of what is waiting for me at home. What if I find him gone and never have a chance to explain? What if he never believes me? What if the second test results come back still saying Jared is not the father?

I can't let that happen. I'll ask a different doctor to administer the test, and I'll insist on a different lab from the one Dr. Fern used. I'll even ask for the results to be sent to me by mail straight from the external lab. Hopefully, it won't be too late by then.

By the time I turn into our street, the heavy rain has turned to a drizzle.

I stop the car in front of the house and count to ten before getting out. My cold, damp dress sticks to my legs when I walk through the gate. Goose pimples scatter across my skin. The chill I feel is not only from the cold. I'm getting the kind of feeling I get when I'm being watched.

I turn my head toward Ruth's cottage. She's at her kitchen window. She raises a hand to wave at me. Since I no longer understand her mixed signals, I don't wave back.

I step over a puddle of water and continue down the path to my house.

At the front door, I stop and lean my head against the wood. After gathering up the courage to face my husband, I stand back, lift my chin, and open the door.

Jared's luggage is in the entrance hall, his laptop and one of his cameras on top of his favorite, battered suitcase.

He's not gone. That's a slice of relief in itself, but he has one foot out the door.

I still have a chance to talk to him. I hear a cough coming from upstairs, followed by a string of curses.

On my way up the stairs, I call his name, but he doesn't answer.

He's not in our bedroom or the bathroom, where I expected to find him. There's only one other place he could be.

Sadness tears at my chest when I approach the nursery.

He's facing away from the door, removing a painting of a rain forest from the wall. Jared's other passion is painting, and he'd painted it himself for the baby.

A weight drops onto my shoulders and pushes down. I wrap my arms around myself to keep warm. It doesn't help.

He spins around and pins me with his gaze, his nostrils flared. Heartbeats pass between us as our eyes lock.

I can't believe he's the man I love more than

I've ever loved anyone before. His face is so completely distorted by anger that it's hard to recognize him. I'm pretty sure when he looks at me, he doesn't recognize me, either. All he sees is a cheater and a liar. He's partly right. Even though I'm not a cheater, I am a liar.

Driven by the desire to get him back, I take a few steps toward him, but he steps away. He drops the painting on the floor. Without a word, he pushes past me and barges out of the room, slamming the door behind him.

I stand in the middle of the room, taking in the baby's belongings. The nursery is ready now. The packages have all been opened, and everything is in its place.

But the baby needs more than the things inside this room—her or his father.

I turn on my heel and follow Jared. At the top of the stairs, I stop to catch my breath. He's watching me from the bottom.

"Don't go." My words are so low I almost can't hear them as they push past the sobs inside my throat.

Jared blinks once, then turns away. He steps into the tiny entrance hall and picks up his suitcase, slinging his camera over his shoulder.

If I let him step out of the door, I might lose him for good. I have to make things right. I don't care what I have to do to keep him with the baby and me.

Finding the strength to fight, I descend the stairs, careful not to trip.

There's only one way out of this mess. I need to come clean. Once he knows the truth, he can decide whether to go or stay. I'll respect whatever decision he makes on the other side of the truth.

When I come close, he doesn't move away this time. I place one of my cold hands on his arm. "Jared, please, you have to listen to me. The results today were really manipulated. And I think I know who did it." I purse my lips. "There's something you should know ... about me."

"What can you possibly say to me that I don't already know?" He takes a step back. "Do you want to come clean? Are you ready to admit that the baby is Ralph's?"

"What are you talking about? Jared, the baby is not Ralph's. I told you there's nothing going on between us. I never slept with him or any other man."

"I'm finding that rather hard to believe. I suspected it all along."

"If you don't believe me, why don't you go and ask him yourself?"

"And get lied to again? I don't trust either one of you."

"Ralph is a pawn in this game just like you." I blow out a slow breath. "There's something much more going on."

"I have all the information I need." His voice cracks. "He's the father of your baby. No point in denying it any longer."

"You don't really believe that."

"Actually, I do." He drops his suitcase and pulls his cell phone from his pocket. He turns the small screen to me.

Your wife is pregnant with Ralph Jenkins's baby. Xoxo

I reel back as if slapped. "Have you ever stopped to wonder who's sending you those messages? I know who it is. But it's a long story. Stay, and I'll tell you the truth."

"Your version of the truth doesn't interest me. It's over, Caitlin. You've destroyed our marriage, and there's no going back."

"Hear me out, please," I plead. "I'm not who you think I am."

"I already know that." He picks up the suitcase again. "I'm not coming back. Don't call me." My heart empties with each step he takes out the door.

I stand in the doorway, still shivering, watching him close his car door and drive away from the life we built.

In a daze, I stumble back into the house and sit on the steps, my head in my hands. My life is in tatters, and I can't even find the strength to weep anymore.

In the morning, when I show up at work, the first person I meet is Georgia, and she sends me right back home, saying I look like a mess and I should use up some of my leave days until the baby comes. I'm too broken to argue with her, so I walk out of Silver Oak. For some weird reason, it feels like goodbye.

CHAPTER 40

I have no idea how I get from my house to the school. Since Jared moved out yesterday, I've been feeling completely lost. I've resisted leaving the house this morning because it's just so hard for me to go out there and pretend I'm fine. But I need to take responsibility. I need to face uncomfortable situations in order to resolve them.

It's lunch break at Silver Oak. Some of the students are outside, hanging out in groups on the school grounds, while others are still in the cafeteria.

Inside the building, all eyes are on me. I get the feeling everyone knows my deepest, darkest secrets. From the looks I'm getting as I make my way down the school halls, and the whispers, I know I've been the topic of discussion. I wonder what they're saying about me.

Ignoring the stares, I put one foot in front of

the other, my head held high. Relief pours out of me when I come to the door of the staff lounge. I draw in a breath and push it open.

Two teachers—one of them a substitute—and Georgia are present in the room. Georgia gets up from the table before I step farther into the room. She looks surprised at seeing me.

"Caitlin, you're on leave. What are you doing here?" Her breath is tainted with the smell of onions.

I avert my gaze. "I … I'm not here to work. I need to speak to Ralph. Is he here?" I've tried to call him several times, but he didn't pick up the phone.

"I'm afraid Ralph is also on leave."

"Why?" I close my eyes when the answer comes to me. I open my eyes again and meet Georgia's. "I'm the reason, right?"

She shifts from one foot to the other. "Caitlin, I'm sure you know that there are several rumors spreading around town about the two of you. It's become a distraction to the students."

I tilt my head to the side. "What are you saying, Georgia?"

Georgia folds her arms in front of her ample chest as though she wants to keep a distance. "I think it's best for you both to stay away from the school for a while until things calm down."

My head hits my chest. "Will I still have my

job after my maternity leave?"

Georgia doesn't speak for a long time. In her silence, I get my answer.

"Oh." I paste on a smile. "I understand."

"I'm sorry. But the parents are complaining. You're an amazing teacher, and you've helped a lot of students get good grades in math, but—"

"Whatever you're hearing is not true. It's all lies."

"I'm sorry, Caitlin. My hands are tied here. I tried to ignore the rumors because I valued your contribution to Silver Oak, but—"

I raise a hand to stop her. "You don't have to explain or apologize." I give her a sad smile. "You were kind to give me this job. I really enjoyed working here."

"I wish you and the baby luck." I don't miss the fact that she didn't mention Jared's name, which tells me everything I need to know. She knows he walked out on me. Someone must have seen him leave and spread the news. But how would they know? What if he was leaving for one of his trips?

"Thanks." With nothing left to say, I respect her wish and leave.

I keep my head bowed, avoiding any eye contact with anyone until I'm outside the school gates and safely inside my car. I lean my head on my steering wheel. The tears threaten to spill. I hold them back. I'm tired of crying.

They all think I'm an unfaithful wife. The results couldn't prove it, but there's someone who could.

§

On my way to Ralph's place, I drop by a different gynecologist in Faypine's city center. He takes the samples he needs and tells me the results will be mailed straight to me within a week.

Before being called in, I'd tried to reach Ralph again, but he still wouldn't pick up. People will have a field day if I go to his house, but what's a little more gossip? I'm done caring at this point.

I park a safe distance from his brick-stone house and wait inside the car, trying not to lose my nerve. What if I ring the bell and Marissa answers the door? The last thing I want is for his relationship to hit the rocks as well. On the other hand, I might get the chance to tell her the truth.

I get out of the car and stroll down the street. About two minutes after I start walking, the door to Ralph's house opens. He steps out, followed by Marissa. He leans in to kiss her, but she pulls away.

My heart goes out to Ralph. He's such a great guy. He deserves to be happy. It's all my fault that his relationship is in pieces.

I'm starting to wish I never came to Faypine

at all. I hate that people are getting hurt because they've come into contact with me.

I spin around and start heading back in the direction of my car. I don't want her to see me. I can't talk to her after all.

A minute or two later, her car blazes past me. Guilt gnaws at my insides. I wish I didn't have to talk to Ralph behind her back, but I need to get to him without anyone standing in the way.

As soon as Marissa's car disappears into the distance, I change direction again.

It's only a short walk to Ralph's house, but I'm drained by the time I reach it.

Every step I take toward the front door, my mind tries to convince me to leave him alone, but I've come too far to turn back.

Since it will take a few days for the paternity results to arrive, I'm hoping I can convince him to tell Jared the truth before he gets used to living without me. It's worth a try. Maybe he can also help me find out who's trying to destroy both our lives.

He swings the door open before I have a chance to ring it. "Caitlin, what are you doing here?"

"I'm here to talk. Can I come in?"

"I don't think that's a good idea." He threads a hand through his hair, which is loose today instead of in a ponytail. "I don't even know why you suddenly want to talk now. I've been trying to talk to you for a while now, and you kept shutting me down, remember?"

"I'm sorry." I pause. "Please, Ralph. I need your help."

"Look, we have to stay away from each other. The rumors about us are messing with my life. My fiancée threatened to call off the wedding if I don't stay away from you."

"My life is a mess, too. We're the only people who can kill the rumors. Jared doesn't want to believe that there's nothing between us. I came to ask—beg—you to talk to him."

Ralph chuckles. "If he doesn't believe his wife, why would he believe me?"

"I don't know. I also don't know what else to do." I glance behind me. "Can I come in or do you want the whole neighborhood to see me at your front door?"

He steps aside to let me enter.

I've never been in his home. It's decorated in shades of gray and black. I hope when he gets married, and Marissa moves in, she'll bring in a splash of color. The interior feels so cold. He asks me to take a seat in the sitting room, but I refuse. I don't plan on staying long.

"Can I get you something to drink?"

I shake my head. "I'm good. Ralph, I need to tell you something." I've realized that hiding from the truth is a dangerous game to play.

"What's going on?" He narrows his eyes.

"I'm not the person you think I am."

"I don't understand." He takes a seat on the couch.

"I think the recent rumors were started by someone who's trying to hurt me."

"Why would anyone want to do that?"

I close my eyes. "Because whoever is behind all this knows my secret ... I think." Even though I didn't want to sit, I change my mind and lower myself into a leather armchair. I keep my eyes away from him as I prepare to tell him my story. "My name is not Caitlin. I became Caitlin because I wanted to hide."

"To hide from what? From who?" Ralph's brow wrinkles. His eyes hold so many questions. I'm ready to answer them all.

Before I lose my courage and crawl back into my hiding place, I launch into my story. I tell him everything.

By the time I'm done, he's no longer on the couch, but at the window, his back to me. The room grows silent for a long time after my confession.

When he turns to face me, his eyes are bulging out with shock, and his hand is covering his mouth. "Wow," he breathes. "I didn't see that coming. Let me get this straight. You murdered your husband and ran away? You—"

"Like I said, I don't remember doing it. I

don't remember anything after the fight we had that night."

"But you had an argument before going to bed."

"Yeah. I was upset that he married me to get his inheritance." I raise my eyes to his. "Wouldn't you be?"

"I don't get it. Why didn't you just go to the cops? Why did you run?"

"I was afraid, Ralph." I clutch my hands in my lap. "Too much evidence pointed to me being the murderer. I didn't want to go to prison."

"Why would you be afraid if you didn't do it?"

"I don't know if I did or didn't do it. I was a sleepwalker. There were times I did things in my sleep that I didn't remember the next day."

"And you think someone in this town discovered your true identity and wants to expose you?"

"Yes. After torturing me first." I clasp my hands together to keep them from shaking. "I know this sounds crazy, but sometimes I think it's my brother."

"You said he's dead."

"Sometimes I get the feeling he really isn't. His body was never found." I swallow hard. "He *did* promise to make my life hell. What if—"

"He's the one who killed your first husband and tried to pin it on you? You really believe that?"

"I don't know what to think. I'm confused. Too much is happening, and I don't know what to believe anymore or who to trust."

Ralph is quiet again, pinching the bridge of his nose. "If it's your brother, why would he wait years to torture you? It doesn't make sense."

"It doesn't make sense to me, either. All I know is that my life is falling apart, and Ryan loved to see me in pain."

Ralph sweeps a hand across his brow. "Caitlin, I don't know what the hell to say to you. This is a lot to take in."

"You hate me, right?"

"No, I don't hate you. But I don't know how to help you. Did you talk to Jared about this? I think he's the one you should talk to."

"I wanted to, but he's gone. And I want him back. I thought maybe you could try to reach out to him, as well. He needs to know that I didn't cheat on him." I pull out a piece of paper from my bag and scribble Jared's number on it. I hand it to Ralph, but he doesn't take it. I put the paper on his mahogany coffee table. "Please try. I don't have anyone else on my side."

"The cheating rumors are the least of your problems, Caitlin. You kept your husband in the dark about your true identity."

"I know I did. I was afraid to lose him."

"I think you should find a way to tell him. He deserves to know." He blows out a breath. "I also think you should go to the cops. You're being stalked by a person who could be dangerous. You need to come clean, or you and the baby could end up hurt."

"What if I did kill him?" My voice cracks. "I could end up going to jail." I lay a hand on my stomach. "I don't want my baby to be born behind bars."

"But you have to do something. You could be in danger. I wish I could help you, but I don't know how to without going to the cops."

"I'm sorry I messed up your life. If you want me to talk to Marissa, I will. It's the least I could do."

"No, I'll handle it."

"Will you tell her ... about my past?" If Ralph breathes one word to the wrong person, all hell will break lose, and I could end up getting arrested.

"I can't do that. That's your story to tell." He pauses. "I'm sorry about what you went through with your brother."

"Thanks." I stifle a sob. "I'm sorry about your job."

"Don't worry about it."

"I better go." I push myself to my feet with

difficulty. "Thanks for listening." Even though there's nothing he can really do, it helped to pour it all out.

Before I walk out the door, he calls for me. "Take care of yourself. I'll keep my eyes open. If I hear anything, I'll let you know. If you decide to run again, give me a call to say goodbye."

"I'm tired of running."

"So, you'll just wait?" His eyes bore into mine.

"I don't think I have much choice."

"At least find a safe place to stay until the baby comes."

I let out a dry chuckle. "The person after me is everywhere."

"Then think about what I said. I really think you should go to the cops."

"Goodbye, Ralph." I'm unwilling to go that route again. Going to the cops isn't an option, not when I'm pregnant.

Back home, I find more of Jared's clothes gone. He couldn't even bear to look at me. I spend a whole hour sitting on the bed, wrapped in a cocoon of sorrow. I try to do a Sudoku puzzle as a way to distract myself, but I can't focus.

Thirst makes me get up and go to the kitchen for a drink.

An old prescription for my prenatal vitamins

that I'd misplaced a while back is on the counter, held down by an empty glass. I'm sure I didn't leave it there.

I pick it up and notice that someone wrote on the back. At first, I think Jared has left me a message. I'm wrong.

I read the words and drop the prescription to the floor.

Looks like someone's life has expired. xoxo

CHAPTER 41

The moment I hear the familiar rumble of a van in the distance, I push away my bowl of oatmeal and walnuts and lift myself from the chair.

I'm waiting in the doorway when Troy Wendel drives his van past my house. In the past, when distributing mail and packages in the neighborhood, he often parked close to our house. Not anymore. He glances in my direction and keeps going. No wave. No smile.

He parks the van close to Ruth's house. Determined not to let him get away this time, I hurry down the path and out the gate, my morning robe flapping behind me. The belt had unraveled when I ran out of the kitchen and fallen to the ground. I don't care that underneath the gown I'm only wearing a t-shirt that's too small for my belly and leaves the bottom half exposed. I don't care that people are staring at me through their windows.

I get to the van—breathless and dizzy—

before Troy has a chance to exit. He's jotting something into a notepad. When he looks out the window, his eyes widen. I move away just enough for him to open the door and get out.

"Morning, Troy, any mail for me?"

No answer. He steps around me to get to the back of the truck, where he takes out some mail and a package to distribute to the individual houses.

"I'm expecting an important letter."

Still ignoring me, Troy starts walking toward Ruth's house, a package under his arm.

"Troy, wait." I grip his arm.

I used to be Troy's favorite house to deliver to. I always go the extra mile to be especially kind to him. His mother has cancer, and he dropped out of college to care for her. At twenty-three, he has a lot on his shoulders. I sympathized with him because he reminds me of myself—the person I used to be. It's not easy taking care of a sick family member all on your own while struggling to make ends meet.

He always stayed a few minutes longer on my doorstep than he needed to. I know when his birthday is. I always had a small present waiting for him in order to make him feel special. I liked to think we were friends.

Now everything has changed. The rest of Faypine have infected him with the "hate Caitlin virus."

Everywhere I go, people stare at me with disgust on their faces. They point and snicker when I walk by.

"Troy, my letter … I was told it should have arrived three days ago. Are you sure—?"

He pulls his arm from my grasp. "I don't have any mail for you, Mrs. Lester." He comes to a halt in front of Ruth's mailbox and slips two envelops into the slit. He continues his walk down the street, not bothering to even look at me.

"I ordered other things, as well … things for the baby," I croak. "Where's my stuff?"

I tag along as he stops at three more houses, delivering a package to one.

On his way back to the truck, I'm exhausted and finding it hard to keep up. I stop for only a moment to catch my breath before running after him.

I wish I didn't have to humiliate myself this way, but the paternity test results are out, and the lab refused to give them to me over the phone.

"Please leave me to do my job, Mrs. Lester." Troy picks up his pace, making it even harder for me to keep up, but I refuse to quit. I follow him back to his van.

"What happened to my mail, Troy?" I ask, out of breath. "Please don't lie to me."

"Maybe it got lost." He climbs into his van

and slams the door shut. Then he drives off.

Ice spreads through my stomach. What am I doing? What am I doing in Faypine when no one wants me here? I can't do this anymore.

As I stand on the sidewalk, hurt and alone, I make a heart-wrenching decision. Once the baby is born, I'll give them what they want. I'll run again. I wouldn't want my baby to grow up in such a toxic environment, surrounded by people who refuse to give others the benefit of the doubt. The last week has certainly left a bitter taste in my mouth.

"Are you happy now?" I shout at no one in particular, turning in a half circle, watching curtains twitch and fall back into place.

The only answer I get is that of someone coughing and a dog barking. I let out a bitter chuckle.

"You must be so pleased now that you took everything away from me."

I must look like a crazy woman, standing out here talking to myself, but I don't give a damn. No point in trying to hide anymore when all my problems are hung out in the open for everybody to gawk at. I don't care if they laugh at me or run their mouths, but I'm still a resident of this town.

The past few days, I've been hiding out in my house, leaving only when I really had to. I felt ashamed and dirty. But that's about to change. I've been good to this town. I helped educate their children. As long as I'm still here, I deserve some respect. I deserve to have my mail delivered.

As I walk back into the house, I can't ignore the irony. I ran away from Corlake to avoid being a pariah among my own people. Look where that got me. The very thing I ran from has caught up with me.

I slam the door shut and go upstairs to change into black pregnancy leggings and an oversized t-shirt. Done, I grab my handbag and head out to the car.

Ten minutes later, I step through the doors of the local post office. Only one teller is working. Thank God for the short line. It's getting too hard to be on my feet for long stretches of time.

I position myself behind an old man in a flannel shirt. In total, four people stand in line before me.

My skin crawls from all the stares. It's hard to ignore the rage pushing up my throat. To occupy myself, I pull out my phone to see if Jared has called or left a message.

A twinge of disappointment ripples through me.

Why do I even bother to look? He's been gone for over a week and hasn't bothered to check up on me.

The line moves too slow for my liking. The postal worker is on the phone. From the way she's smiling, it's a personal call. She ends it when one of her colleagues taps her on the shoulder and points to the line.

When my turn finally comes, I approach the counter and lay my hands flat on its cool surface.

The name on the postal worker's tag is Elsa McAlister. From what I can see, she has to be somewhere in her twenties, no older than twenty-five. I've seen her before at the pharmacy across from Dr. Collins' private practice. I guess she's juggling both jobs. It's not unusual for people in Faypine to have several jobs under their belts.

Elsa peers at me through her long, greasy bangs. "We're closing for lunch."

"But it's only ten o'clock."

"We have an early lunch today." She turns her back to me, placing a box on the counter behind her.

"But I've been waiting in line like everybody else. It won't take long for you to help me out."

She glowers at me. "I'm afraid I don't have the time. You're too late."

When she starts to walk away, I slam a hand on the counter. "Why don't you just tell me to go away, huh?" I don't care who's listening. "Why don't you go ahead and tell me the truth

… that you don't want to serve me?"

"I …" Elsa scratches the top of her head. "I have to go." With that, she disappears through a door at the back.

"Unbelievable," I breathe out. I spin around to face the many faces gawking at me. My anger boils over. "What are you all staring at?"

Someone laughs and several others join in.

"Go on, laugh all you want." I shake my head. "What makes you think you're all so perfect? What gives you the right to judge others when you probably have your own secrets?" I pause for a moment. "I don't care what you say about me. I'm a part of this town, whether you like it or not. I'm not going anywhere. Deal with it." They don't need to know I'm planning to leave town.

I'm seething with both anger and humiliation as I burst out of the doors. When I get to my car, I screech to a halt.

Someone has left a message for me.

Adulterer is written in bold, red marker on my windshield.

"Is this all you've got?" I turn around, watching the passersby watching me. Some look away, and others don't bother to. In the sea of faces, I spot that of Dr. Fern. She looks as disgusted by me as everyone else.

Instead of giving in to the shame, I square my shoulders. "Whoever did this can go to hell."

I try to wipe away the word on my windshield with the towel I keep in the trunk, but it doesn't come off. I can't remove the stain from my life.

Anger roars through me as I get behind the wheel and drive off in a screech of tires.

Another surprise awaits me at home. The nursery is trashed again, and the same words that are written on the windshield of my car are also scrolled across one wall of the room.

That's it. I can't take it anymore. They win. I'm leaving.

CHAPTER 42

The doorbell rings as I pack. I ignore it. I'm not expecting anyone. I'm pretty sure it's not Jared. I left him a message to tell him I'm leaving town. It's been an hour, and he hasn't called back.

I toss a few T-shirts and leggings into a bag. I have no idea where I'm going yet. All I know is that I want to get as far away from this place as possible. I'll stay in a motel in another town until I come up with a plan. I'll get through this. I'm a survivor.

I will do things differently this time around. Instead of looking for a teaching job, I'll start my own business tutoring students online. Until then, I have some money saved up and a little left over from the money Ryan had left behind. It'll keep me afloat for a while.

The doorbell rings again, the sound bouncing off the walls. I continue to ignore it. My phone beeps next. Thinking it could be

Jared, I grab it. It's Dr. Collins' office number. I don't pick up until the caller gives up and leaves a message.

"Mrs. Lester, this is Danielle from Dr. Collins' office. You were scheduled to have an appointment with us yesterday, but you didn't show up. Please, give me a call if you want to reschedule."

I drop the phone and continue to pack. Was that why Dr. Fern looked so disgusted with me earlier, because I missed an appointment? Am I the first person to do that? I'm not going back there. I'll find a doctor who treats me with respect.

I zip the bag shut and pick it up from the bed. I've packed several smaller bags instead of a big one to make it easier for me to handle the weight.

After waiting a while to make sure the person who rang the bell is gone, I take one bag to the car and return for the next. As soon as I get back upstairs, I hear a movement downstairs. Someone is inside my house.

Oh, no. I forgot to lock the door. How could I have been so stupid?

I lock the bedroom door and grab a baseball bat, another weapon I keep in my room. I position myself next to the door and raise the bat as the sounds get louder.

"Caitlin, it's me," Ruth calls from downstairs.

"Can I come up?"

Air whooshes out of my lungs. I lower the bat. First, I feel relief, but it's soon followed by anger.

What is she doing here? We haven't spoken in days. She'd made it clear she wanted nothing to do with me.

I storm out of the room, ready to give her a piece of my mind. I get to the top of the stairs and look down at her.

"The door was open, so I let myself in." She starts to climb the stairs, groaning with each step until she reaches me.

"What are you doing here, Ruth? I thought you don't want to be friends anymore." I walk back into my bedroom and close the diaper bag.

"I came to apologize. I shouldn't have treated you so callously." She clears her throat. "My late husband cheated on me … several times up until his death. I guess it's a sore point."

"I'm sorry to hear that." I pause. "But you believed I cheated on my husband without proof of any kind."

"That was wrong of me to do. I'm sorry, Caitlin." A frown touches her brow. "You're packing. Are you going somewhere?"

"Why not?" I scoff. "Why shouldn't I leave? I'm not wanted in this town."

"But where will you go? Your baby will come

any day. It's not safe for you to—"

"It's not safe for me to stay here. I can't stand the rumors anymore. Don't pretend you're not happy to see me go. You're just like everyone else in this town. You chose to judge before you knew the whole truth."

Ruth peels her gaze from mine. "I saw the results."

"The results of what?" I perch on the edge of the bed, my knees too weak to hold me up. The baby rolls inside me.

"The paternity results." She raises her head again. "Someone must've got hold of them and distributed them around town."

"That has to be a joke!" I grit my teeth, the color draining from my face. "Who would do such a thing? What's wrong with you people?" I get to my feet, but a wave of dizziness makes me sit again. I stood up too fast. "I guess I'm making the right decision getting out of here." Before I can go on, a stab of pain hits my belly so hard I grip the sheets. "No," I croak.

"You need to calm down, sweetheart, for the baby." Ruth comes to place a hand on my shoulder, but I shrug her off. "Stay here. I'll get you some tea. Keep breathing."

When she returns with a cup of mint tea, the pain has subsided, but I'm too much in shock to move. I haven't had that kind of pain before. I'm afraid that one wrong move will bring on labor. I'll wait to feel completely better before leaving.

"Do you feel all right?" Ruth sits down next to me. This time when she rubs my back, I don't pull away.

I take a sip of the tea. "Why are people so cruel?"

Ruth doesn't answer. I don't ask any more questions as we sit side by side. Even after I finish the tea, we don't speak for a long time.

"Do you still want to leave town? Can I talk you out of it?"

She's the most confusing person I've ever met. First, she didn't like me, then she liked me a lot, then she hated me, only to change her mind about me again.

I place the empty cup on the nightstand and rise. The pain stays away. "There's nothing here for me."

Ruth gets to her feet and stands in front of me. "You should stay. It's not safe out there for a pregnant woman about to give birth."

I give her a weak smile. "I can't stay here. It's not safe for my baby or me."

"Where will you go?"

"Somewhere safer than this place."

"What if your husband comes back?"

"I'll let him know where I am once I know where that is."

I bend a little to pick up the diaper bag from

the bed. As soon as my hands connect with the handle, a sharp pain drives through my stomach again. It feels like the worst kind of menstrual cramps multiplied by a thousand or even a million. "Ouch," I cry out. Another bolt of lightning strikes again. This time it knocks me over. I fall onto the bed, on my side, my arms around my stomach. Black dots appear before my eyes.

Ruth lays a hand on my sweaty, glowing forehead.

"The baby is coming." I breathe in and out through my mouth. "Call an ambulance ... please."

"Don't worry, sweetheart. Dr. Fern will be here any minute." Ruth straightens up.

"How ...?" My words are killed by another round of labor pains.

I don't know how long I'm lying on my bed, writhing in agony, but suddenly, through the rush in my ears, I hear a door slam and the sound of footfalls. Then two people are talking. Their voices sound as though they're coming from far away.

Someone with a red scarf hovers over me, but the face is blurred.

Before I can make her out, another labor pain sweeps through me, and my world goes black.

CHAPTER 43

I wake up to find myself surrounded by darkness. My foggy mind is aware something is wrong, but not exactly what.

I try to pull myself to a sitting position, but my body screams. My lower body feels as though it's filled with glowing coals of fire determined to burn through my raw flesh. But at the same time, there's also a weird numbness accompanying the pain.

What happened? It's hard to think clearly when images are mixed up inside my head. Failing to keep my breathing steady, I force myself to find just one thing—an image perhaps—that would help me remember. An image of Ruth's face pops into my mind instantly. The missing pieces fall into place. I remember our conversation. I remember the labor pains.

Alarm bells go off in my ears, the sound so loud it makes my head ache.

On instinct, my hands move to my belly. My breath catches in my throat.

My naked belly feels like a deflated balloon. Something that feels like a huge Band-Aid is stretched out across my lower stomach.

"My baby," I whisper, my hands continue to search the curve of my tender stomach, searching for signs that my child is still inside my womb, safe and sound. I need to keep her safe from the world.

Ignoring the pain pulsing through my body with each desperate movement, with every breath, I search around me on the bed but only feel the crisp, cool sheets.

Instead of my whole body, I turn my head to the side, sure I'm in the hospital, and my little baby is fast asleep in a bassinet close by. I stretch out my arm, feeling the empty air around me. I don't find what I'm looking for.

I didn't lose her. I didn't lose my baby. I let out a tortured groan that scrapes through my tight throat. "Please, God," I choke. "No."

"Hush ..." someone says in the darkness. Ruth? "The baby is perfectly fine."

My sobs die inside my throat. I hold my breath to listen. Have I imagined the sound?

The nightlight is suddenly flicked on. In the soft light, I can see her face. She's sitting in the armchair not too far from the bed.

The smile on her lips doesn't reach her eyes.

She was the woman with the red scarf, the woman who had been towering over me before I passed out.

"Dr. Fern ... what?" My gaze flicks across the room. "My baby." It's hard to speak with such a dry mouth.

"She's a gorgeous, healthy baby." Dr. Fern shifts the armchair closer and reaches out to sweep my damp hair from my forehead. "I'm glad I made it here in time."

My face breaks into a smile. "A baby girl." Tears block my throat. "Thank God. Thank God she's all right." I attempt to sit up again, but Dr. Fern places a hand on my shoulder to press me back into the pillows. She didn't need to. The pain is enough to keep me from moving. It's just that I want to see my baby so badly. She must be in her nursery.

"You should take it easy. You need to heal after the emergency Cesarean section."

"A C-section?" Why am I in the house after a C-section? Shouldn't I be recovering in the hospital?

"The baby almost died. I had to act fast. There wasn't enough time to get you to the hospital." She pauses. "It's a good thing I'm skilled at using a scalpel."

"Thank you so much. Thank you for saving our lives." My smile returns. "Can I see her ... my baby?"

"I'm afraid that's not possible." Dr. Fern rises. The red scarf slides from around her neck to the floor. She doesn't pick it up.

"Is she okay?" Panic riots through me. Just because my baby is alive doesn't mean there are no complications. "Did you take her to the hospital?"

"She's safe and well cared for. That's all you need to know for now." She picks up a white bottle of pills from the nightstand and removes two. "Ruth told me you planned to leave town." She doesn't look at me until she has closed the bottle. "That wasn't smart at all."

A chill hangs over her last two words. "I needed to get away due to personal reasons."

"You could have given birth to my baby in some crappy motel, in the middle of nowhere."

"What?" I blink away the confusion. "I don't—"

"Stop talking and take these." She lifts my hand from the bedsheet and drops the two pills into the palm of my hand. "They will take the edge off the pain."

"No." I drop the pills onto the nightstand. "I don't need painkillers. I'm fine." My mind tells me that something weird is going on here, and I need to find out what it is.

"Suit yourself." Dr. Fern bends to lift her scarf off the floor.

The moment I see it again, something inside

me shifts. I don't understand the feeling it stirs up, but it's right there, attached to an explanation that's out of my reach.

"Where is my baby, Doctor? I want to see her." I pull the covers up to my neck, and shiver as if a chill has settled into the room.

Dr. Fern lowers herself onto the edge of the bed and looks down at me with a cold smile. "Sweetheart, she's not yours. You were just the surrogate. Pearl is mine."

"Pearl?" I whisper.

"Yes." She gazes into the distance with a quiet smile. "My mother's name."

"Excuse me?" I give her a blank look. "What the hell is going on here?"

"Oh, yes. I like the sound of hell. How does it feel to be in hell?"

I don't answer as my mind tries to understand this situation. The woman who delivered my baby is transforming into a stranger with each word.

"Who are you?" The words roll off my tongue before I can register them inside my mind.

"Thought you'd never ask." She gets to her feet and drapes her scarf over her shoulders.

A sudden memory flashes across my mind. I've seen that scarf before, in another life. But where?

"Oh, well, I guess the truth is long overdue."

She dips her head to the side, her hair spilling over her shoulders. "My name is not Loraine Fern as everyone believes. Before I came to Faypine, I used to be called by another name ... Tracey Pikes. Dr. Tracey Pikes, actually."

I tighten my grip on the sheets. "Should I know that name?"

"You should. I'm sure Dylan mentioned me."

"Dylan?" Panic crawls up my spine.

"Yes, darling, the man you killed in cold blood. He was my fiancé." She waits to allow her words to sink in.

I can feel the blood draining from my face. "You?"

"I was the love of his life, the only love of his life." She drops back into the armchair and crosses her legs. Her eyes don't leave mine. "We had our ups and downs, but we always found our way back to each other. Until you butted into our lives."

"Oh my God ... I—"

"You stole him away from me. You killed my baby."

I'm too shocked to do anything but listen to this revelation.

"I talked to him the night of your wedding."

"My God." I force the words from my mouth. She was the one on the phone with Dylan on our wedding night. She's my stalker?

"It was you? I thought—"

"Yes, it's me, your worst nightmare. You thought it was your brother, Ryan, didn't you? You thought he's still alive? That's good. I wanted you to think he was." A peal of laughter breaks through her lips. "No, darling. Your brother was too much of a coward to be able to do something like this. See, back then, I wanted you dead, and we agreed that he would carry out my plan. I paid him well to do the job, but he chickened out." She shrugs. "I had no choice but to get him out of the way."

"You killed my brother?" My hands tremble to my throat. I'm finding it hard to breathe. The money I found in Ryan's room, the money that helped me escape, must have been the payment she's talking about.

"Well, not with my own hands. His life was so messed up that it wasn't hard for me to convince him to commit suicide."

CHAPTER 44

She stands and leans down to whisper in my ear. "We had a plan, Ryan and I. We bonded over our hate for you. He wanted to punish you for what you did to him, and I wanted to do the same. And then he betrayed me. No one betrays me."

Her red scarf gathers onto my chest like a pool of blood, heavy with memories from the past. It finally hits me where I had seen it. It was the same red, Pashmina scarf I'd seen on Ryan's bed. She is the woman I thought he was seeing.

"I want my baby."

"Silly me." She smacks her forehead. "I should have explained myself better." She returns to her seat. "After you stole my man, I discovered I was pregnant. When I told Dylan about our baby, he told me it was too late. Apparently, he loved you." She drags the palm of her hand down one cheek, leaving behind a smear of mascara. She's crying. "He was lying to himself as much as he was lying to me. He only wanted to marry you in order to inherit his father's money."

My throat closes up. Her words are like bricks, hitting me hard, shattering my heart into smaller pieces. "You are—"

"Let me finish. I tried to stop him from marrying you." She grabs her scarf and starts to twist it around her hand. "He gave me this scarf. It was his grandmother's." A quiet smile plays on her lips while the scarf tightens on her hand like a rope dipped in blood. "I was his true love."

"I want my baby." The words push through my gritted teeth. I want to hear everything she has to say. I want her to fill in the pieces of the puzzle that have been missing from my memory. But she's dangerous, and she has my child. I need to know where my baby is.

"Shut up." She shoots me a fiery gaze. "Shut up and let me finish."

"No, you shut up." My rage gives me the strength to fight back. "If Dylan loved you, he would have married you. He left you."

"That's what he told you?" She scoffs. "Well, honey, he lied." She clears her throat. "Dylan proposed to me the week his father died. He wanted to get married immediately, but I wasn't ready. I wanted to focus on my career. I was a top surgeon in New York. But he was impatient to get the money. So, he found the next available woman." She pauses to place a hand on her flat stomach. The scarf she had wrapped around her hand had left an ugly mark. "My plans changed when I found out about our baby. My career took the back seat. I wanted him back. He turned his back on us." Glistening tears slide down her cheeks. "My baby couldn't handle my pain."

"You lost your baby?" I wince as cramps twist my stomach. It's not only my body that's hurting now. Everything hurts, including my heart. I have no idea where the pain starts and where it ends. The last thing I want is to hold a conversation with her, but her tears have weakened her for a moment. Maybe if I sympathize with her, she'll spare my baby and me.

"I was at the hotel that night." She ignores my remark. "I was ready to give him one last chance, to forgive him for hurting me. But he was too stupid to see his chance. So, he had to pay. Both of you had to." The tears have dried from her voice, which has now hardened.

"You murdered Dylan. You said I did it."

"You might as well have. Yes, it's true, I killed him, but it was your fault he died. I wanted to kill you, as well, like I'd planned, but I thought it would hurt you more if I took away what you stole from me. I wanted to see your pain." Her voice turns low and dangerous. "I didn't think it would be so easy. That night, I sent someone to bring up the champagne—"

"It was spiked." My throat closes up.

"You're smarter than I thought you are. I wanted to put you both to sleep before I came up to the suite to end it all. I wanted to do the main job myself."

"Give me my baby, and I swear I won't tell a soul." That's a promise I don't intend on keeping. I've been running from a crime I didn't commit, buried in guilt that doesn't belong to me. She has to face justice.

"You think I'm some kind of fool?" Lightning flashes in her eyes.

"No, I don't. I meant what I said." A question pushes itself to the forefront of my mind. "Why didn't you just kill me years ago? Why wait this long?"

"I wanted you to build a life you love so I could blow it apart, piece by piece. I followed you from the hotel that morning, all the way to that crappy motel, and then out of town. And I had my eyes on you the entire time over the years. I've been waiting a long time for this moment. My job was made so much easier by the people who don't like you in this town. There's nothing money can't buy."

It hits me like a bullet that the people I

suspected, including Lilliana, could all be involved. They were her puppets. Lilliana was probably the one who stole my key from my desk drawer and gave it to this monster.

"It was so much fun to destroy your marriage; now I'm going to take your child, and there's nothing you can do about it."

"You're sick," I roar. "You're crazy to think you can steal my child. My brother and Dylan are dead because of you. You deserve to rot in prison."

"That's how you want to play this little game?" A corner of her mouth twists into a smile. "In case it hasn't hit you yet, you are in a rather fragile state." She places a hand on my stomach and presses down.

A scream splits the air in the room. It takes a moment for me to recognize it as my own. When she releases the pressure and lifts her hand, I spit in her face, my eyes never leaving hers.

"Maybe I shouldn't have closed you up. I should have left you to bleed out." She swipes the back of her hand across her mouth, smearing lipstick over her mascara-smeared cheek. "You're useless to me now, anyway. But I wanted you to know the truth. I wanted my face to be the last one you see."

Maybe it's my imagination, but I think I hear a baby crying from somewhere in the house.

My baby is alive. Tears of both joy and fear well up in my eyes. My body goes slack with relief.

Dr. Fern … no, Tracey Pikes heard the cry, as well. She rises from the chair. "My baby needs me. I'll be back."

"Don't you dare touch my child." I reach out to grab her hand, to claw into her flesh if I have to, but she steps back before my fingers touch hers.

"Don't hurt … don't hurt her." I bite back tears. "Don't you dare!"

She throws me a disgusted look and storms out of the room. The door slams behind her. I hear a click as she locks it.

I want to scream for her to open the door, to bring back my baby, but I force myself to remain calm. She's too sick to reason with. I need to come up with a plan that will get her away from my baby and me without us getting hurt in the process. I have to find a way to alert the cops.

CHAPTER 45

I grit my teeth to contain the pain that's rendering me immobile. I've been drifting in and out of sleep, so weak I could barely lift an arm.

Physical pain is much more bearable than the pain of knowing she's out there with my baby. It's been two hours since she locked me up in the room. I can't find my cell phone anywhere nearby, but I know the time from the traditional alarm clock Jared always insisted on having at his bedside table.

For some reason, he never trusted the alarm on his phone to wake him up at the right time. I'm glad he didn't ditch the clock when I made fun of him. At least I can keep track of time.

I can't just lie here, waiting for something terrible to happen … for Tracey, the monster, to hurt my baby girl.

Every time I hear my daughter crying, my heart weeps with her, and my stomach clenches as though it wants to protect her, releasing cramps that make me twist with agony. An hour ago, it got so bad I was tempted to take the painkillers. I didn't cave, though. How can I trust she's not trying to poison me?

Another desperate cry from my baby slices through the air again, seeping through the cracks in the door. A surge of anger and desperation triggers the flow of adrenaline in my veins. My baby is all alone and helpless. I need to get to her. I'm the only one who can get her out of this dangerous situation.

Biting back a tortured scream, I push myself to the edge of the bed. It's excruciating trying to sit up, but I manage it, sweat trickling down my temples, tears sliding down my cheeks. To hell with the pain. I need to be strong for both my baby and me. She's all that matters to me right now.

I need to find a phone and reach out to someone—hopefully, the cops. I can't let Tracey get away with this. She needs to be punished for all the crimes she's committed, including that of robbing me of my life and freedom. The thought that she killed my brother still burns like a raging wound inside me. But Ryan is dead and gone. He's not coming back. Unlike him, I still have my life. I still have a chance to start again, to live a life of complete freedom. I just need to survive this night—my baby and me.

Once I get to my feet, my knees threaten to give way. My stomach feels like an empty sack. I wrap my hands around it, holding it in place even though my skin hurts to the touch. I'm only dressed in a bra and foreign, mesh panties. My gaze travels to the bathrobe draped over the back of the armchair, but I don't think I'm in the condition to dress myself right now. Being half-naked is the least of my problems.

I blink away the rush of dizziness and take small steps forward, following each with a ragged breath and a clenching of the teeth. I can do this. It's not over yet.

My bags have been thrown into a corner, including the diaper bag that had fallen to the floor when labor pains hit. It takes forever for me to get to them, but I do. I take a moment before bending down to pick up my handbag with one hand while the other still holds on to my stomach. Looking down, I notice a drop of blood at my feet. I'm terrified the stitches have opened. What if the wound becomes infected? Shifting my thoughts from my body to my baby keeps me focused on what has to be done. This is my chance to do the right thing.

If I end up dying while trying to save my baby, it'll all be worth it. Sacrificing my life so she can live is a price I'm willing to pay. I force myself to believe that Jared will find out that he's the father and take great care of her. The thought of my child growing up without me brings tears to my eyes.

My fingers connect with the leather handle of the handbag. I clench my jaw tighter as I lift it. Returning to the bed is even harder than when I left it. Determination gets me there, though. I spill the contents of the bag onto the bed. My phone is not among them. I can feel the blood drain from my face.

My God, what am I going to do now? How can I reach out to the outside world without a phone?

I return the bag to where I found it. She can't know that I'm trying to escape. She probably thinks I'm too weak and in pain to do anything but stay in bed.

Hopefully, she doesn't come back to the room before I'm back under the covers.

Still holding my stomach and myself together, I shuffle to the door, checking to see if she really locked it. I stagger back, disappointed.

My next stop is one of the windows. By the time I reach it, I'm on the verge of passing out. My heart is thudding so loudly in my ears the sound drowns out my baby's cries. I draw in several shallow breaths. Breathing deeply would cause my stomach to move too much.

I pull open the window, the one overlooking

Ruth's cottage. Sea air wafts into the room. It dries the tears on my cheeks.

All the lights in Ruth's house have been turned off, which is not surprising since it's late at night. She must be asleep. I consider screaming in case someone out there hears me, but that could be a mistake. For all I know, Tracey could be standing on the other side of the door. If she bursts into the room, I won't be able to physically fight her off. The knife I used to keep underneath my pillow is gone, so is the baseball bat, and the hammer. The only weapon I can use right now is my head.

The sound of Tracey yelling breaks through the walls, shaking me to the core. I need to go back to the bed, pretend I never left it. I pray she doesn't notice the drops of blood on the floor. I quickly close the window again and shuffle back to the bed.

My heart breaks when the shouting is followed by more heart-wrenching screams of my baby. Back under the sheets, which are now stained with blood, I clutch my chest and force myself to breathe. I want to shout for Tracey to stay away from her, to scream at the top of my lungs. But I saw Tracey's monster eyes. She wouldn't think twice before killing my daughter if she feels betrayed. I hate to hear my daughter crying, but at least that way I know she's alive.

The cries only get louder and more

desperate. My decision to stay quiet falls apart.

Sobbing as well, I return to the window. Since the baby is crying, maybe Tracey won't hear me. I can't leave any stone unturned. I have to try. It's complete torture to raise my voice above a whisper, but I don't give up.

"Help me, please … somebody. She'll kill us."

The lights in Ruth's house stay off. My voice dies to mere whispers. I failed. I need to try something else. Every second counts. An image of the spiked champagne bottle from the past brings an idea to my mind.

I shuffle to the bathroom, stepping over beads of my blood and teardrops.

My baby is still crying, but the sound is no longer as desperate.

I breathe out a sigh of relief as I sink against the bathroom wall.

After catching my breath, I push away from the wall and move to the medicine cabinet.

The first thing I see is a bottle of painkillers. I remove one pearly white pill, push it between my parched lips. I'm about to fill a glass with water to wash the pill down, but I stop. On the other side of the bathroom wall is the nursery. She might hear the faucet running. Knowing I can't have a drink reminds me just how thirsty and hungry I am. I haven't had anything to eat or drink for hours.

Ignoring my body's need for nourishment, I reach into the medicine cabinet again. All the way at the back I find the blue bottle with Jared's sleeping pills. Thank God he didn't take them with him.

I have no idea how many pills I pour into the palm of my bloody hand. I don't have time to count. It doesn't matter, anyway. I need to act fast. She could decide to return anytime. Although, she seems to always be a step ahead. Maybe she already knows I'm out of bed and trying to get out of here. I don't get why she's stayed away so long.

Focus, Caitlin. Don't think about her. Do what you have to do.

I use the bottom of the glass that holds our toothbrushes to crush the pills to a powder, which I pour into a small plastic bag I found inside the cabinet. I push the bag into my bra, between my breasts. I leave the bathroom with a few more painkillers in my hands, which I hide under my pillow for when the pain worsens.

Back in my bed, I think of what to do next. Given that I'm in a vulnerable position physically, I'm hoping I might be able to disarm her with the pills. My plan is to get her to drink them. The only problem is that I have no idea how to get the powder into her drink. I could end up failing big time.

The baby starts to cry again—much louder this time. She sounds like she's in pain. My hands moved to my throat, clawing into my skin. Sobs rake my body as I call for Tracey to let my baby go. Only whimpers come out. My message doesn't reach her.

I cover my face with my hands and pray that God will save my baby.

Five minutes later, in addition to the baby's cries, I hear footsteps. She's coming back. Thank God. Her face is the last thing I want to see, but I'd rather she's in the room torturing me than with my daughter. But the sounds of the baby crying are pushed up another notch, getting louder by the second. Could it be Tracey is carrying her?

Before I can figure it out, the door is unlocked and swung open. My question is answered. Tracey is standing there, my daughter in her arms.

My little girl is wrapped in a fluffy, white blanket I bought her online.

Tracey's hair is just as wild as her evil eyes.

"Make it stop," she growls. "It won't shut up."

"Okay, okay." My words come out in a rush before she can change her mind or worse, drop my baby to shut her up. "Bring her to me." I raise my arms, desperate to hold my little girl for the first time.

Tracey stumbles across the room and drops the baby onto my stomach. I wince in pain, but it's immediately erased by the joy surging through me as I pick up my baby and look into her small, flushed face.

As soon as our eyes meet, she stops crying. My own tears flood my eyes as I pull her close. She's here, she lived. And Tracey was right; she's gorgeous.

"Give her the breast," Tracey barks. "She's starting to get on my nerves. She won't take the damn bottle."

"What ... what do you plan to do to us?" I ask. I make sure to hold her gaze as I position my baby at my breast, careful to keep the little plastic pouch with powder from falling out. The baby is confused for only a second before latching onto my breast. She knows where she belongs.

"Don't you listen?" Tracey tugs at her hair as though I'm getting on her nerves. From what I can see, she has pulled at it quite a few times in the past hours. "The baby is coming with me."

"How about me?"

She reaches behind her and comes back holding a handgun. She must have had it in the back pocket of her jeans. I tense up inside. "For three days, you'll feed my baby. I want her to be strong enough to travel to New York with me. After that, I no longer have a need for you. So,

I'll send you where you should have gone years ago, to the place your brother is now, deep in the ocean." She surveys the handgun. "By the way, this baby is the same one he used to end it all. It was a gift from me to him."

CHAPTER 46

I wake up from a disturbing dream, drenched in sweat and in more pain than I can bear. I don't remember the exact dream, but it was about Ryan. And there were gunshots. Maybe I was reliving the day he was shot, the day that changed everything.

I reach under the pillow for the last painkiller. It's hard to swallow it down with not enough saliva in my mouth.

Two days have come and gone, and I'm freaking out because I didn't get the chance to knock Tracey out with the sleeping pills. She only comes into my room every three hours to bring the baby for feeding. Sometimes she treats my wound and changes the dressing on my belly. I don't understand why she bothers. She plans on killing me anyway. Once a day she also brings me a few slices of bread with watery soup.

My body is weak, and I'm desperate for more

food, but when I asked for more, she took away the last piece of bread I had left. At least I have water to drink. Though still painful, it's getting somewhat easier to move around the room now, to go to the bathroom for a drink or to use the toilet.

I hang on to the hope that my chance to get Tracey out of our lives will come soon. The mere sight of her makes me sick. She won't even let me look into my daughter's face while breastfeeding. Last night, I tried to kiss my baby's head, but a hard slap across the face made me regret it.

"Don't you ever kiss my baby," she shouted. "You are nothing but the surrogate."

My only comfort is that at least I get to see my baby. That's enough for now.

I glance at the clock. It's 9:00 a.m. Four hours have gone by since she brought the baby to me.

I hate not being able to keep her with me, to protect her. I miss gazing at her big, blue eyes, which remind me so much of Jared's.

Finally, my little girl's cry reaches me before the door opens. I ache to hold her in my arms again. It's comforting to hold her, to know that I'm not alone in this. Having her close reminds me that I have to come up with a plan. I have to succeed at whatever I decide to do so as not to endanger her life. I haven't named her. Her name just hasn't come to me yet. I'll choose a name when my heart is free from darkness. Or am I afraid to name her only to lose her?

The door opens, and Tracey walks in with her in her arms. This time she doesn't bring her to me. Instead, she sits in the armchair. Her eyes are on me as she unbuttons her shirt—my shirt, actually.

My breath catches in my throat. She can't possibly be doing what I think she is.

"Let me feed her," I beg her.

"I'll take care of it." Her eyes cloud with more evil than I've seen in anyone's eyes before.

"But you can't—"

"I can. I'm her mother." She's rocking back and forth, her eyes on my child.

I shake my head, disgusted. I guess her actions shouldn't surprise me. She clearly has some mental problems. Why would she think she can feed my baby when she hasn't given birth to her?

"Come on, let me do it." I bring my hands together in a begging gesture.

"I said I'll take care of it." Her voice is a loud whisper. The baby struggles at her breast first, then settles down. But since there's no milk there, she becomes fussy and starts to scream, rejecting the breast.

Thunderclouds flash across Tracey's face.

421

She moves the baby to her other breast as if that would change anything. The same thing happens. She only makes the baby more upset.

"Bring her to me, please." I hold up my arms. "She's hungry."

Tracey doesn't say anything as she stands up, buttoning the shirt with one hand. Her face puce, she drops the baby into my lap, then turns to look away from me.

I quickly open the buttons of my cream pajama top. Last night, after she changed my dressing, I begged her for a pair of pajamas. I was surprised when she gave them to me.

My baby latches on immediately and starts to suck, her chubby little hands holding on to me.

Tracey turns again, hands on hips, her glare hot against my skin.

"I'll try to give her the bottle again tomorrow."

We both freeze as we hear a sound coming from downstairs.

"Is someone else in my house?" I ask without thinking. "Who's helping you?"

"It's none of your business." She crosses her arms in front of her chest.

Disappointment stirs inside me. If someone is helping Tracey keep us hostage, it would be harder to escape. How would I be able to get past two people? Could it be Ruth? She was the one who had called her.

My gaze involuntarily moves to my baby's head. By the time I realize my mistake, Tracey's palm has connected with the side of my cheek. My head snaps up immediately. I don't repeat the same mistake twice. It's too late.

Tracey grabs the baby from my arms and stomps toward the door. "I'll be back in three hours," she throws the words over her shoulder.

"Wait," I call after her. "I need food, please. I won't have enough milk for the baby if I don't eat ... properly."

"I'll bring you bread later," she shouts over the baby's crying.

"Let me eat downstairs, please." I hang my head.

"Who do you think you are to make demands?"

"You're going to kill me." I swallow hard. "Please, let me see my house for the last time, my kitchen." I'm well aware that my request is stupid, and it might backfire, but I'm surprised when she doesn't say anything for a moment.

Her response blows me away. "Fine. I'll let you say goodbye to your pathetic little kitchen. It would make your death that much more painful."

I nod, both relieved and scared that she would suspect I'm up to something. "Thank you." I push one leg out of bed and then the other.

Trying not to groan with pain, I follow her out, wishing I had the strength to grab my child and run.

As soon as we step out of the room, Tracey gets behind me. She must be afraid I'll attack her when she can't see me.

Before we head downstairs, she orders me to go to the nursery, where she roughly puts my whimpering baby in the crib. I hold back the urge to attack her.

Thanks to my condition, it takes a long time for us to reach the bottom of the stairs, and she yells at me at every step.

I'm relieved to find no second person downstairs. The sound I'd heard earlier must have come from outside the house.

We don't speak as I sit at the kitchen table, and she places a bowl of muesli with milk in front of me. It disgusts me that she's in my home, acting as though she owns it, pretending to be the mother of my baby.

When she turns her back to get orange juice from the fridge and pours herself a glass, I survey the kitchen. The knives aren't in the block next to the stove. She must have removed them.

I eat my breakfast with her watching me from behind her long lashes. She takes a deep drink of orange juice and slams the glass on the kitchen table next to the half-empty bottle. She must love orange juice as the bottle that I bought the day I had planned to leave town is almost empty. I try not to look at her as I spoon muesli into my mouth.

She leans against the counter, arms crossed in front of her chest.

"You're pathetic, you know that?" She stretches her arms above her head. "And you stink."

"You won't let me shower."

"No need. It's only a matter of time before you die, anyway."

"You really think you can get away with it?" I ask and just as quickly, bite my tongue. I should be careful what I say to her before she sends me back upstairs.

She eyes me with pure hatred. "I got away with murder once before. I can do it again." She comes to join me at the table, pours herself another glass of juice, but doesn't drink it. "I'm an expert at hiding in plain sight. Actually, maybe the baby and I won't even go to New York. Maybe we'll go to another country. I've always wanted to live in Italy."

I swipe a hand across my damp cheek. "Promise me something."

She takes a sip from her glass, ignoring me.

"Be good to her." I bite back the urge to spit into her face again. "Take care of my baby."

"Stop calling her that. She's not your damn child."

I swallow hard. "I'm sorry. All right, your baby. Please take good care of her."

"What do you think I am, a monster? She's my baby," she shouts. "Of course, I'll take good care of her."

As soon as the words are out of her mouth, I detect a movement outside the window. Through the light kitchen curtain, we both watch a van come to a stop in front of my house, where Jared used to park his car. It's Troy, the postman. Has he forgiven me? Could he be the one who saves me?

Adrenaline surges through my body as it gets ready for flight.

Tracey ducks her head as Troy opens the gate and makes his way to the house. We're unable to see him from the front door.

The sound of the doorbell ringing takes us both by surprise. Tracey is pretending to still be in control, but her eyes are panic-stricken. I can almost hear the wheels inside her head turning.

"Stay here," she warns. In a crouching position, she hurries out of the kitchen, her hand pulling the gun from her back pocket. My first instinct is to shout for help, but that would be stupid. She won't hesitate to shut me up with a bullet. She could also shoot Troy.

This is my chance to carry out my earlier

plan. As soon as she's out of sight, I pull out the sleeping pill powder. The little bag is now slick with my sweat. Holding my breath, I spill it into the bottle of orange juice and her unfinished glass. Terrified of getting caught, I give the bottle a quick shake to dilute the powder, and use my spoon to stir the juice in her glass.

She returns just as I've finished wiping the spoon with the hem of my pajama top, which I notice is bloody. I must have angered the wound while descending the stairs earlier.

It's hard for me not to stare at the juice, to make sure the powder has completely merged with it.

"It's the postman." She sighs with irritation. "Go and tell him to go away."

I gawk at her, unable to believe my ears. Did she just ask me to come into contact with another person, someone who could help me?

"What are you waiting for?" she asks impatiently.

I get to my feet. I'm all too glad to obey her. Except when she follows me out the door, her gun pressing against my spine. "Do anything stupid, and you'll be dead earlier than planned," she whispers.

I swallow through my tight throat. I don't doubt her threats for a second.

I give her a brief glance as I reach for the

door handle.

She moves the gun from behind my back and positions herself behind the door. She's now aiming at my head.

"Good morning, Mrs. Lester." Troy is looking everywhere but at my face as he holds out an envelope. "I have a letter for you today. I'm sorry. I'm sorry about last time. I wasn't kind to you. You have always been kind to me."

I don't answer him for a moment as I try to find some kind of sign to give him that alerts him I'm in danger. I wish he would look me in the eye. Maybe he would see my fear in them, but his gaze drops to his feet.

I reach for the envelope. "It's fine, Troy." I look down at the envelope. It has the stamp of the testing lab I'd been waiting to hear from. "Thank you."

"Really? You forgive me?" He finally meets my eyes.

"I do." As we stand there, a smell drifts up to my nostrils, the metallic tang of blood.

Tracey's eyes are piercing through me. She wants me to end the conversation. I don't look at her. I have an idea. I hope it will work. I blink once at Troy then lower my eyes deliberately. His gaze follows mine. My plan is that he will take a glance down my body. And he does.

"The baby has arrived? Congratulations, Mrs.

Lester." He pauses, and his eyes widen. He has seen what I wanted to show him, my blood. He looks up again, his eyes holding questions.

I blink once more. "Thanks, Troy." I wave the envelope between us. "And thank you for the letter."

He looks at my stained pajamas again, clears his throat. "I should go." He hurries back down the path, glancing once over his shoulder. Good. I have aroused suspicion in him. For the first time in my life, I wish for someone to pass on gossip about me. All he needs to say is that my baby has been born and I'm at my home bleeding. He must have also seen my red, swollen eyes.

I'm sure as soon as he passes on the news, people will start taking strolls past my house, driven by curiosity. The chances of me being heard when I scream will be higher, and if Tracey sees too many people walking by, she might think twice about shooting me in fear someone might hear the gunshot.

Although it seems unlikely, among all the hateful people there might be a kind person who breaks out of the crowd of haters and comes to check on a new mother who gave birth at home and is possibly alone.

Since Ruth didn't bother to come and check up on me for two whole days, I'm now convinced she's not one of the good ones. She has to be one of Tracey's puppets. Was that why she pretended to be nice to me all of a sudden? Was it so she could be a spy for Tracey? Does she hate me that much?

In the corner of my eye, Tracey gestures for me to shut the door.

As soon as the door closes, Tracey grabs the envelope from me. "What's this?" she asks. "Oh, I know what this is." She pushes the gun into her back pocket and orders me to return to the kitchen to finish my breakfast.

While I eat, hoping she would take a drink of her juice, she opens the envelope. A smile plays on her lips. "Smart woman. You decided to get a second opinion. Such a shame your husband won't be able to find out he's the father. You must have been freaked out to get those fake results I shared with you. He was devastated." She tosses the page onto the table. "I have to say, I'll miss messing with your head. It was so much fun watching you running from your shadow. I guess I'll have to give back the rented Nissan and get rid of the fake beard. Oh, in case you didn't figure it out, I stole the money from your purse the day you came to see me for the first time." She now has this faraway look as if she's no longer here with me. "There you were, wiping the gel from your belly and you had no idea what I was up to. I had put enough gel on you to keep you busy for a while."

My stomach roils with anger. I want to reach out and strangle her for everything she's done to me. If I were alone in this without my baby upstairs, I probably would have.

Done eating, I remain in the chair. I dread to be locked up.

She picks up the glass of juice and brings it to her lips.

I hold my breath. *Drink it!* I scream inside my head.

My disappointment is crushing when she lowers the glass again without drinking.

Does she suspect something? Can she read my mind? "What are you waiting for? You've stayed down here long enough. Time to go back upstairs. You won't be coming back down here again. Don't even bother asking."

CHAPTER 47

⌒∞⌒

Each step up the stairs is absolute torture. My stomach feels as though it's being ripped apart at the seams, and sweat is dripping down my temples. I don't even want to know what's happening to my incision. How can I trust that Tracey even carried out the surgical procedure correctly? She lied about being a gynecologist. What if she lied about being a surgeon as well?

Tracey urges me to keep moving by pressing the barrel of the gun harder into the small of my back. I'm tempted to dig my heels in, not because I want to disobey her, but because my body is slowly losing strength to move on. I know it's only a few steps before we reach the top, but I could use a rest.

My mind is begging me to give up, which is not an option. I don't have a death wish. If I die, I don't even want to think about what she would do to my baby. What if she takes it out on her?

My sweaty hand tightens around the railing, and I push through my resistance.

"What's taking you so long?" I cannot believe she has the nerve to ask me that, knowing full well what kind of pain I must be in. I grit my teeth to stop myself from lashing out at her.

By the time we reach the top of the stairs, my breath is coming in quick, shallow gasps and my entire face is covered with sweat, which is now dripping from my forehead into my eyes. I collapse against the nearest wall, panting.

"I don't have time for this." With each word, Tracey waves the handgun in the space between us. "Get moving. I've got packing to do."

Tears and sweat make my eyes sting. I brush them away with the back of my hand. "You can't take my baby. Please don't."

"Is your head so thick you can't grasp information?" She pinches the bridge of her nose. "She's not yours. Get that? You have no one. The sooner you grasp that, the better."

"Please, let me go and feed her. She didn't get enough milk last time. She's crying."

Tracey hesitates for a moment, then pushes a hand into her hair. "Fine. Be quick." She grabs my arm and yanks me away from the wall.

I scream at the same time my baby does. Tracey ignores my pain. She shoves me in the direction of the nursery.

The moment I see my baby's eyes through the slats of the crib, the pain distances itself from me.

I limp toward the crib and stand there, unable to lift her out. Tracey pushes me aside and does it for me.

I clench my teeth as I lower myself into the rocking chair next to a small, round table that has the baby monitor. A small, green light blinks from the baby unit. The parent unit is missing. I'm guessing Tracey has been using it. The monitor had been inside its box the last time I saw it. The only thing I had taken out of the box had been the instruction manual, which I read through a few times.

I lift my hands from my abdomen. They come away smeared with blood. What if no one comes to save me before I bleed out? Tracey doesn't even acknowledge my bloodstained pajamas as she hands me the baby—my baby.

The urge to plant a kiss on the top of the baby's head is so intense it takes my breath away, but one glance in Tracey's direction and I dismiss the thought and focus on the wall instead.

My baby curls into my arms, searching for my breast. I give it to her and close my eyes to relish this moment of comfort before it's snatched away.

In the darkness of my mind, I try to come up with a way to save her. As the seconds tick by, I make a decision. I won't let Tracey lock me up again. She's planning on leaving with my baby tomorrow. I have to do something today.

Tracey sinks to the floor on one side of the door, her eyes and the gun trained on me and the baby. Her face looks crumpled. Dark bags have appeared underneath her eyes.

Neither of us speak. The only sound in the room is that of the baby's sucking.

Use the time to think, Caitlin. Do something. Anything.

What if I survive this ordeal? What if by some sheer miracle the baby and I make it out of this house alive? How would I convince anyone that Tracey had committed the crimes in Corlake, that I'm innocent after all? I have absolutely no evidence to clear my name with. There's still a chance I might end up behind bars and leave my baby without a mother to raise her.

My heart turns over at the sounds of a police car siren breaking the silence. My gaze locks with Tracey's. A small frown appears between her eyes, but it disappears almost immediately. She doesn't seem concerned.

I hold my breath as the sounds get louder. Troy must have gone to the cops. He must have understood my message better than I thought

435

he would.

My stomach drops when the sounds that had given me so much hope disappear into the distance. The silence returns to the room, thicker than before.

I guess no one's coming to my rescue after all. If I'm going to get out of this mess, I have to do it alone. I return my gaze to the wall.

"You thought they were coming for you, didn't you?" Tracey stretches out her legs and crosses them at the ankles. "I'm sorry to disappoint you, but no one cares about you, darling. You're completely at my mercy."

She continues to talk, telling me how someone had given her the key to my house and she had broken into the nursery to dismantle the crib.

"I wish I was there to see your face when you found my little surprise."

Since I already know she was the one behind the past weeks' sequence of events, I don't bother listening to her. I have better things to do with my time. I cannot allow her to distract me.

Bored with the wall, my gaze moves back to the table with the baby monitor. My eyes focus on the tiny, round lens.

My mind takes me back to the day I ordered it online. Jared and I were in bed, discussing the best one to buy. While I didn't mind a simple one that did the job, he wanted a high-tech version with fancy things like a night vision camera, an audio recorder, and a temperature and movement sensor. After almost an hour of going back and forth, I ignored the price tag and allowed my husband to make the final choice. It took me days to read through the manual after it dawned on me he wouldn't be here to set it up.

I guess things happen for a reason.

With an idea tucked inside my heart, I look away from the monitor before Tracey reads through my thoughts.

To kill even more time and get clear on my plan, I strike up a conversation. The baby has fallen asleep, but Tracey doesn't need to know that.

"I don't understand how you could kill a man you claim to love."

"Some people don't take betrayal well. I'm one of them." She pauses. "I'm not the kind of woman who allows a man to walk on her heart and get away with it. I'm not her."

"Who's her?" I ask cautiously.

"My mother." She rests the handgun on her leg. Her face looks tortured. "Why all the questions?"

"Just curious, that's all."

She throws her head back. It connects with the wall hard. She doesn't even flinch. "Dylan wanted a way out of my life. I gave him one."

"What will you do with my baby?"

"Shut up." She smacks a side of her face with the hand holding the gun. "You're really pissing me off. She's mine. I delivered her."

"From my body," I can't help adding.

"Give her back." She gets to her feet and crosses the room so fast it takes me by complete surprise. She yanks the sleeping baby from my arms. It's hard to breathe when I see the gun so close to my child. What if it goes off by mistake?

I do my best to hold it together until she turns her back to me. As soon as she bends to put the baby back in the crib, I press a small, red button on the baby monitor, then bring my hands to the armrests, pushing myself to my feet. "Tracey, how do you sleep at night knowing you murdered Dylan Baxter?"

She spins around, her mouth twisted in a way that makes my skin crawl. "He deserved to die. And I sleep just fine; thank you for asking. Now, move."

That's all I needed from her. Now it's time for the next stage of my plan.

The gun is pressed against my temple as we leave the room. I want to glance back, to take a look at my baby in case it's for the last time. I'm about to do something that could lead to my death or my freedom.

Outside the door, Tracey moves back behind me. I keep walking. As soon as we reach the stairs, I stop and lean against the wall, facing the opening of the staircase.

"What the hell do you think you're doing? I said move."

"I need a break. I'm tired ... in pain." I allow my head to loll to the side.

"Do you think I care? Start walking."

"No." I plant both hands on her chest, shut my eyes, and use every ounce of energy I have to shove her away from me, in the direction of the stairs. A loud gunshot rings as she stumbles backward, eyes wide with shock.

To my horror, she catches her fall by grabbing onto the railings just in time, letting go of the gun which slides across the floor.

Everything happens fast after that. One moment I'm watching her trying to regain her balance, and the next, she lunges for me so fast I don't get time to shield myself from her attack. Her body slams into mine with such force the wind is knocked from my lungs and pain like I've never known before explodes in my entire body.

Groaning, I slide down the wall to the floor and fall to my side. My lungs scream for more oxygen, my vision blurs. I can't move. Through my swimming vision, I notice the gun only a few inches away from me.

Tracey is towering over me now, her face red and sweaty.

"That was a big mistake," she drawls. "I told you I don't handle betrayal well. Since you betrayed me, there will be a change of plans. It's over." She swings back her leg. Before I can protect my middle, her foot comes crashing into me.

I don't even scream this time, too numb with pain. I feel myself slipping away, falling into oblivion, but an image of my daughter flashes across my mind.

I open my mouth to speak, but no words come out.

"What? Is there something you want to tell me before you die?" She lowers her gaze to the floor. I know what she's searching for.

No, I'm not ready to die. I won't let her get away with this. I can't let her take my life. I can't let her steal my baby. It has to end here.

I have no idea where I get the energy, but the next thing I know, my arm swings away from my body and my hands clamp around the handgun before she retrieves it.

I don't waste time. I don't give in to my fears or the pain. The last thought on my mind before I close my eyes and pull the trigger is that of my baby sleeping in her crib, waiting for me to rescue her. I hear rather than see Tracey stumble back.

I try to open my eyes again, but my eyelids are too heavy.

Then the light inside my head switches itself off.

CHAPTER 48

❧

I open my eyes only to shut them again immediately. I give it another try, taking my time so they can adjust to the bright lighting.

Gazing up at a white ceiling, I wait for the pain to attack me. It doesn't come. The only sensation I feel from the waist down is total numbness.

I turn my head to one side. My eyes fill with tears when I notice an empty bed on the other side of the room. I'm in the hospital. I'm alive. It's really over. Relief sweeps through me, but panic follows at its heels.

"My ... baby." The words are hard to push through my tight throat.

"Thank God you're awake," a male voice comes from the other side of me. "The baby is fine. She's perfect."

I turn my head to see Jared, his face as crumpled as his shirt, sitting in the chair next to my bed.

More tears come when he leans in to brush my hair back from my face. He kisses away my tears before they trickle down the side of my face. Then he moves his lips to mine. As I sink into the comfort of his love, I pray I'm not dreaming. This feels way too real to be a dream. "Our daughter is beautiful." He plants more kisses on my forehead, my chin, and my cheeks.

"She's really okay?" My lips tremble with a smile.

"More than okay." He brings his face closer to mine. His mint-tinted breath is warm against my skin. "You're both safe now."

"Where is she?" I turn to look at the other side again in case I missed the bassinet.

"She's at the nursery. You don't have to worry. She's in great hands."

I chew a corner of my lip. "She's yours, Jared. You are the father."

"I know." He slides his gaze from mine, then leans back in the chair. "I saw the test results back at the house."

"You—" My stomach clenches. "What happened to your arm?" A sling is supporting his left arm. I had been so focused on the baby's safety I didn't notice it at first.

"She shot me." He exhales sharply.

I blanch. "Who shot you?"

"That Tracey something woman. But I don't want to talk about her now."

"Tracey shot you? How? When?"

"I came back home, Caitlin. I returned to you and the baby."

"Why?" I cringe inwardly as I remember his rejection, the way he had walked out on me. "Why did you come back?"

"Ralph ... He called me. He told me everything you told him." He lifts my hand from the top of the covers. "He told me that someone was trying to hurt you. That's why I came back. I wanted to protect you. And I listened to your message that you were leaving town. I couldn't let you go. Leaving you was a mistake."

"But ..." I cough, choking on my tears.

"When I arrived at the house, the door was opened by the doctor who was filling in for Dr. Collins." His Adam's apple lifts then drops as he swallows hard. "At first I was relieved someone was there with you. She congratulated me on being a father, then out of the blue she shot me in the arm."

How did I not hear anything? Actually, I *did* hear a gunshot. I thought it was from my nightmare.

"I'm so sorry, baby." I push down the lump stuck in my throat. "I'm sorry you got hurt."

"Not as much as you got hurt, baby." His voice is thick with worry.

I press my lips together. "She wasn't a real

gynecologist. She pretended to be one in order to get to me. She manipulated the paternity test results. I'm so sorry, Jared, for everything."

"No, I'm sorry. I was a complete jerk." He drags a palm down his cheek. "If I had believed you, you wouldn't have been hurt by that monster. I would have been there to protect you. I don't know what I would've done if I'd lost you."

"What happened after she shot you?"

"She hit me over the head with something to knock me out. When I came to, I was locked in the basement."

"You were there, the entire time … inside the house?"

He nods. "Good thing we keep the first aid kit down there. It saved my life. But it drove me nuts knowing that monster was around you."

"Did she say anything else to you?"

"Before she knocked me out, she said she was going to kill you and take our baby. I tried to get out of the basement, but that door is tough. No matter what I threw at it, it wouldn't budge. And I didn't have my phone."

It all makes sense now. The sounds I heard when I was upstairs with Tracey must have come from him trying to get out of the basement. And there I thought it was Tracey's accomplice.

"Jared, I should have told you everything

from the start. I wasn't honest with you for years."

"You know what? I'm just glad you're alive. That's the most important thing to me right now." He tightens his fingers around my hand. "We can deal with everything else later. We're in this together."

"There's so much you don't know, Jared." I take a breath. "I didn't know how to tell you. I really thought I killed—"

"Your first husband? I know."

"I should have told you I was married before."

"I get why you didn't. But now that Ralph told me everything, let's focus on your recovery, okay?"

"I didn't kill Dylan ... That was his name. All these years I worried that I did, but I was set up."

"I know that, sweetheart. If you had told me, I would never have believed you killed someone. You're the most loving person I know." He pauses, shaking his head slowly. "And the way you cared for your brother after everything he did to you is unbelievable."

"I couldn't turn my back on him. He was my blood." Jared and Ralph must have talked for a long time for Jared to already know everything I didn't have the guts to tell him. In a way, it's a relief that I don't have to.

"What you did for your brother makes me love you even more." He lets go of my hand and rubs his temple. "It drives me crazy to think she could have killed you."

"I shot her, Jared. I had to, or she would have killed me." I suppress a shudder. "I ran away from a murder I didn't commit only to end up being a real killer, even if it was in self-defense."

"Sweetheart, she's not dead."

I stare at Jared, baffled. "That can't be. I shot her, then she fell down the stairs. She must be—"

"You must have missed. The cops found her at the bottom of the stairs, unconscious. She must have fallen and hit her head."

My fingers touch my parted lips. "But I shot her before I fell unconscious."

I close my eyes, thinking back to what had happened. I see myself pull the trigger, but my eyes were closed. I didn't get a chance to see if I actually hit Tracey. Maybe in her attempt to dodge the bullet, she went tumbling down the stairs.

"You didn't kill her."

I open my eyes. "Who called the cops?"

"Ruth. Apparently, she heard a gunshot." Jared's face tightens. "I did, too. I thought ... I thought she shot you." He shifts in his chair. "Look, babe, you went through hell. Get some rest. We can talk about it later."

"No. I want to know everything."

Jared's shoulders rise and fall. "Ruth called the cops, but it turns out that she was actually involved in helping Tracey torture you. So were a few other people. They're all in police custody as we speak." He runs a hand across his mouth. "You should have told me someone was stalking you. That's why you changed the locks, am I right? I had a feeling something wasn't right."

I nod. "I couldn't tell you without revealing who I really was." I pause. "Was Lilliana one of the people who helped her?"

He nods. I'm tempted to ask why he never told me they dated, but after going through hell, Lilliana no longer bothers me. "Yes. She gave Tracey our spare key. I think Tracey paid them all. The press is saying she comes from a very wealthy family."

"I still find it hard to believe Ruth was involved. I don't want to. When I was about to leave town, she came over. She was nice again. She made me tea."

"I think she was paid to keep an eye on you. So, she pretended to like you. She confessed to the cops that she came over to our house to stop you from leaving town."

"Why did she hate me so much? I don't get it. I understand why Lilliana didn't like me, but not Ruth."

Jared scratches his beard. "Apparently, before we moved to Faypine, she was desperately trying to buy the cottage ... our cottage. We outbid her."

I'm quiet for a long time. "Wow. I guess she didn't want to accept that her friend wasn't coming back."

"I guess not. But that doesn't excuse what she did to you. That Tracey woman is dangerous."

"She's demented. She said our baby was hers. She tried to breastfeed our child."

"That's sick." Jared frowns. "Why would she think that?"

In a few words, I fill in the holes for Jared, telling him everything Tracey had told me during our time together. "She blames me for the loss of her baby."

"I'm so sorry, sweetheart. I'm so sorry I wasn't there."

Before we can continue the conversation, a nurse with a braid around her head walks into the room. Her smile brightens when she sees me. "Look who's awake. Let's see how you're doing." She moves to my other side to check my vitals. "How are you feeling?"

"Tired." It's the truth. I feel as if I ran a marathon.

"You just need a lot of rest. You should be

fine. You are lucky to be alive after the amount of blood you lost."

"Why can't I feel my legs?"

"Don't worry, you will. It takes a while for the anesthesia to wear off." She plumps my pillow. "Your incision had opened up quite a bit. You needed surgery."

"Am I fine now? It won't open again?"

"You're fine. You just need to take it easy for the next couple of weeks. Take all the time you need to heal. Get as much rest as possible."

I place my hand on my belly. "I will."

"How long will she be here?" Jared asks.

"As long as it takes for her to heal and get her strength back."

Once the nurse walks out of the room, after telling Jared to leave soon so I can rest, I return to the topic of Tracey.

"I can't believe she's still alive?"

"Yeah," Jared says. "Unfortunately she survived the fall down the stairs with only a minor head injury. She's being treated here."

"In this hospital? You're kidding." My hands grab the sheets. My shock yields to fury. "How could they? How could they bring her here? What if she steals or harms the baby?"

"There's a guard at both the door of the nursery and in front of Tracey's room. As soon as she's released, she will be placed under arrest."

"Please, Jared, don't let her come near our baby."

"I'll never let that happen. I promise. I won't let you down again."

"You don't understand. She's dangerous, and she's very sick. You should take the baby home immediately."

"They want to keep the baby here overnight for observation. As soon as they release her, hopefully tomorrow, I'll take her home. Since I only have one arm at my disposal, I've arranged to have someone help me out for a while." He pauses. "You keep calling her baby. Didn't you give her a name?"

"Too much was going on for me to come up with the right name. I wanted to be clear and happy when I chose one."

"How about now? Should we come up with one? I'd like to call her something."

I think for only a moment before deciding. "If you don't mind, I'd like to call her Hope." She was the reason I didn't give in until the end. She was the reason I didn't let the pain destroy me. She gave me the strength to fight Tracey. And she's giving me a reason to start a new life. Hope would be perfect for her.

"I love it." Jared kisses me on the lips. "Hope Lester. It has a nice ring to it."

"I'm sorry to disturb you," a deep, dusty voice comes from the door.

A uniformed police officer with a full, well-trimmed beard is standing in the doorway. "I'm Officer Ted Nash. Glad to see you're awake, Mrs. Lester. May I ask you a few questions?"

"I don't think that's a good idea, officer." Jared gets to his feet. "My wife needs to rest."

"I fully understand, but I won't be long." He steps closer to the room.

My gaze meets Jared's. "It's okay, honey. Go and check up on Hope."

"Okay," Jared says and approaches the door. He turns to look back at me. "I'll be right back."

After Jared leaves, Officer Nash takes the seat Jared had occupied. "How are you feeling?"

"Fine." Sudden panic grips me. What if he's here for me? What if they don't know that Tracey killed Dylan? What if I'm still a suspect? But Jared hadn't given me the impression that I was in trouble.

"Why are you here, officer?" I ask.

The officer removes his cap and scratches the bald patch on his head. "What name do you want me to call you?" he asks, and my blood runs cold.

"You know who I am?" Why did I even ask that question? I'm pretty sure the whole town knows everything about me by now.

"Yes. But I need to know what name to call

you during our conversation." A corner of his mouth quirks up. "I prefer first names."

"Caitlin. Call me Caitlin." I square my shoulders. "If you're here to arrest me, you should know that I'm innocent. I did not kill my first husband."

"Caitlin, you have absolutely nothing to worry about. Tracey Pikes confessed to everything."

My mouth drops open. "She did?"

"Yes. And your baby monitor helped as well. Smart move." He pulls his cap back on his head.

I feel my body sag into the mattress from relief. "So, what is it you want to talk to me about?"

He pulls out a notebook from the front pocket of his shirt. "Tell me everything that happened since Tracey showed up in your life."

"Okay." Determined to do whatever it takes for them to lock her up for good, I close my eyes and launch into one of the most painful times of my life.

When I'm done, his beefy hand pats mine. "That will be all for now. Get your rest. You deserve it. If I come up with more questions, I'll be back."

"What will happen to her?"

"I'm pretty certain she'll be locked away for a long time. You never have to fear for your life or that of your family again. I'll keep you updated."

"Thank you, officer."

He raises a hand when his phone rings. His eyes are on me as he listens to the caller, eyes narrowed. "I'm on my way."

"Is everything all right, officer? What happened?" I ask when he hangs up. The way he's looking at me, I know the call had something to do with what had happened.

"They found Dr. Collins locked inside the basement of the cottage Tracey has been renting."

Shock smacks me in the face. "Oh my God, is she okay?" This entire time we were all fooled into believing she was out of town. I'm guessing even the stroke she'd supposedly had was a lie.

Officer Nash rubs his forehead. "I'm afraid she's not. She's dead."

My body stiffens in shock. I want to speak, but I can no longer say a word as I remember Dr. Collins' lined face, the shock of white, curly hair. If I hadn't come to Faypine, she would still be alive. She died because of me.

Officer Nash tells me he has to go, but I'm unable to respond as my eyes follow him to the door.

My words are still stuck in my throat when more people show up to visit me. Ralph and Marissa, Georgia, and several other teachers—

minus Lilliana—from Silver Oak, bring flowers to my room. The people who once shunned me now treat me like an overnight hero. Even though I still feel the bruises of their rejection, I forgive them and accept their kindness with a bittersweet smile.

"I'm glad you're all right," Ralph says to me.

"Thank you, Ralph," I finally croak. "Thank you for talking to Jared."

"I just did what any good friend would have done. Now, get some rest."

"Yes, you should," Georgia chips in. "Your kids wish you well. They can't wait for you to return."

"My kids?" Warmth spreads through my chest.

Georgia's face breaks into a smile. "Your job isn't going anywhere."

"Neither is your life," Ralph adds, pushing his hands into his pockets. "You belong in this town."

CHAPTER 49

❦

"Caitlin," a familiar voice whispers into my ear.

I open my eyes with a low groan. The feeling has returned to my body along with some of the pain, but it can't compare to the kind I had experienced at home, both physically and emotionally.

If it weren't for the faint light coming from the hospital machines, the room would be completely dark. It's way past midnight.

After a day of visits from way too many people, all I want to do is sleep.

"What?" I ask as I focus my eyes on the face in front of me. It's hard to make it out as the person is too close.

"It's me, Tracey." She leans back for me to get a better look.

I become instantly awake. Even in the semi-darkness, I see her well now. She's wearing a hospital gown, and her long hair is disheveled around her face.

Before I can say anything, she places a hand on my mouth. Her small hand is surprisingly strong. "Hush, we don't want to wake up the other patients."

I lift my hand from the bed and push her hand away. I open my mouth to scream for help, but I don't get a chance.

To shut me up, she shoves the barrel of a gun between my lips.

"Shut up and go quietly. This won't take long." My heart freezes at the sound of a click. "We have some unfinished business, you and I. How could you be so stupid to think I'll let you go that easily?" She gives a low, dry chuckle. "Say goodbye to your useless life."

Having no other option but to surrender, I close my eyes and wait for her to pull the trigger. What are the chances of me surviving her twice? My only comfort is that Hope is safe, and Jared is back to care for her.

Sudden light floods the room, making my eyelids glow. I open my eyes to see Tracey looking behind her, her gun still pressed into my mouth, my lips around the cool metal. I'm afraid to lift my head to see who's at the door.

"It's over, Tracey," a male voice booms. "Step away from her and drop the weapon."

"Go to hell. I call the shots around here."

"Don't make me shoot you, Tracey. Step away now."

I'm trembling inside now as I prepare for my death. But to my shock, Tracey withdraws the gun from my mouth and moves away. Air floods out of my lungs.

She points the gun at the person at the door. "What do you plan on doing to me, officer? Are you going to kill me?"

"If I have to. I need you to drop the weapon."

"I don't take orders from anyone. Ever." She turns back to glance at me with a smile. Then before I can take the next breath, she puts the gun to her head and pulls the trigger.

The scream I'd been holding inside me shoots out of my body as drops of blood hit my face moments before Tracey Pikes hits the floor.

Everything happens fast after the gun goes off.

The room is suddenly filled with cops, nurses, and doctors. I hear a doctor announce that Tracey is dead.

I close my eyes as a nurse wheels my bed out of the room while urging me to keep breathing.

When Jared comes to me fifteen minutes later, shock tainting his handsome face, I break down. "She ... she ... oh, Jared."

"She's dead." He holds me tighter. "It's fine now, my love."

"Hope?" I whisper.

"Hope is safe."

For the second time in a few hours, Officer Nash comes to see me again for more questioning. He tells me the officer who'd been guarding Tracey's room had fallen asleep on the job and Tracey had hit him hard over the head with an intravenous drip stand. While he was out, she took his gun and went looking for me. Luckily, there was another guard in the hospital who had come to check on his colleague and found him on the floor, and Tracey was gone.

"How could that happen?" Jared shoots from his chair, shaking with rage. "How could he sleep on the job? And why wasn't she handcuffed to the bed? My wife could have been killed. How could you people underestimate how dangerous that woman was?"

"I have no words to tell you how sorry I am, Mr. Lester. I'm just glad my colleague got to your wife in time."

"I'm glad it's over," I whisper, still shaken. "I want to see my baby."

"I'll get her," Jared says and leaves together with the officer.

Five minutes later, Jared steps into the room carrying a bundle of pink. As he places Hope into my arms, my tears hit her face. "Mommy is so happy you're all right." I kiss her warm face.

Hope doesn't wake up the entire time I talk

to her, and it's okay. She's safe now.

"Is there anything I can do to make you feel better?" Jared asks, perching on the edge of my bed.

"I want to leave this town. I want a fresh start somewhere with no sad memories. All I need is you and Hope."

"Whatever you want, my love. I'll follow you to the ends of the earth if I have to." He lowers his lips to mine and keeps them there. Our baby starts to squirm awake between us.

"Which name do you want to take with you?" he asks, wiping a tear from my cheek.

"Caitlin Lester, the woman you fell in love with."

"Good," he says, his voice tainted with tears. "I happen to be crazy about her."

THE END

Thank you for reading *Don't Blink*. If you enjoyed this book, please leave a review.
To be notified when L.G. Davis releases a new book, visit www.author-lgdavis.com to sign up for her newsletter.

To get in touch with L.G. Davis visit:
www.author-lgdavis.com
Email: Liz@lizgdavis.com

Printed in Great Britain
by Amazon